In Times Wanting

Randy & Beth

Hope my music & pictures
come close to your work.
Enjoy
all the best
& Thanks
[signature] /2013

Don Quixote,
the original painting by Angèle Gagnon, which inspired the cover design.

In Times Wanting

A Novel

Kevin Morris

GSPH

GENERAL STORE PUBLISHING HOUSE INC.
499 O'Brien Road, Renfrew, Ontario, Canada K7V 3Z3
Telephone 1.613.432.7697 or 1.800.465.6072

http://www.gsph.com

ISBN 978-1-77123-028-5

Cover art: Magdalene Carson, after a painting by Angèle Gagnon.

Printed by Image Digital Printing Ltd.
dba The IDP Group, Renfrew, Ontario
Printed and bound in Canada

Library and Archives Canada Cataloguing in Publication
Morris, Kevin, 1945-, author In times wanting / Kevin Morris.
Issued in print and electronic formats.
ISBN 978-1-77123-028-5 (pbk.).--ISBN 978-1-77123-806-9 (epub).--
ISBN 978-1-77123-807-6 (mobi).--ISBN 978-1-77123-808-3 (pdf)
I. Title.
PS8626.O75755I5   2013   C813'.6   C2013-903623-7   C2013-903624-5

DISCLAIMER
In Times Wanting is a work of fiction. Names, characters, places, and incidents
are products of the author's imagination, or have been used fictitiously.
Any resemblance to actual events, locales, or persons, living or dead,
is entirely coincidental.

For Angèle

Acknowledgements

This novel has evolved with the help of a number of people. Sue Stewart's initial review, and an early copy-edit by Sylvia Pollard, gave me the confidence to continue with the story. Both Sue's and Ann Ireland's book edit convinced me to undertake a comprehensive rewrite. A special thanks to GSPH for their belief in the novel, especially to publisher Tim Gordon for keeping me sane and on track, to Magdalene Carson for design, and to Jane Karchmar for editing — it would not have happened without them. Phil Caron has been terrifically dogged with his unsparing and incisive comments. Thank you as well to Frans Schryer for his gracious help on my miniscule Nahuatl. Finally, many thanks to my life's companion, Angèle Gagnon, for her ongoing support and forbearance, as well as for her editorial eye and her perceptive and subtle suggestions.

Poem from *From the Bellybutton of the Moon* by Francisco X. Alarcón (New York: Lee & Low Books, 2012).

CHAPTER 1

A moment to eternity

FEAR OF EXECUTION had to be far more real than the execution itself. It helped that Porfirio was there at his side, a teenager. Berrin grasped at the sliver of hope this youth brought him; his only hope, given their situation, in the back of a pickup bouncing through cornfields under a scorching noonday sun, kneeling side by side on the floor with their hands tied behind their backs and surrounded by private militiamen. A quick glance at them didn't help allay his fears. The two older men, in trousers and sport shirts, sat on the floor, their backs against the tailgate, gripping rifles that lay across their legs. The younger two, in jeans and T-shirts, crouched and leaned back against the cab, rifles across their knees, more casual than the older men. The one sporting a baseball cap stared at Porfirio and smirked, almost inviting him to jump clear and make a run for it.

Porfirio grunted, then glanced at Berrin to share his disdain. The rifleman took this as sufficient bait.

"*Eh, cabron. No se preocupe. Yo me encargaré de su novia.*"

Berrin understood more than he wanted: This punk would soon be homing in on Porfirio's girlfriend. He knocked his elbow into Porfirio's side to silence any response. Porfirio stared straight ahead, the rifleman's snicker that followed choked out by the billowing dust and the absence of other responses, no one else wanting to be drawn in, either.

The rifleman couldn't have been much older than Porfirio, and the same dark complexion, Nahua, while the others were clearly mestizo. Not a simple case of class struggle, Berrin realized; you can't overlook petty motives, like a teenage love triangle. He felt even more naïve and stupid.

An old *campesino* in a nearby field bowed his head as the pickup drove past. He could not have missed the fact that Berrin was clearly a foreigner, a northerner, how his sunburn had turned his arms and face a bright red. And the farmer was not moving, not running to alert anyone. *Shame on you*, but no sooner thought than dismissed, because the indictment best fit himself.

The shame was his own. It was he who had failed, not making it back to their rancho, not warning Eileen, not getting her out. He who never had a doubt about their mission, about their project in Cochitlahuantla, likely the hamlet highest in this region of the Sierra Alta, a thrill in itself, shared equally by all ten of his fellow students scattered through these mountains, all fuelled by a Paulo Freire commitment to community development, all dedicated, and all too unaware that the ranchos were helpless, that the real power lay in the lowlands, around Tepepantiango, the central town in the region, the pueblo, where he and Porfirio had been arrested. *No, abducted,* Berrin corrected his thoughts, for these militiamen had to be *pistoleros,* armed retainers for any one of the regional *caciques,* the strongman, landholder, politican . . . he had only just begun to understand the intrigues at work here.

Beyond the *campesino,* at the back of the field, a few thatched huts huddled within a stretch of sparse bushes, absolutely no one else in sight. It was then that Berrin's last bit of hope died.

He looked out onto fields of corn that sped past them, voracious rows of stalks eating up the nutrients, the green revolution in the lowlands with its feed of fertilizers and pesticides, in the mountains the seasonal sweep of the slopes as the Nahua slashed and burned into more sparse bush. Corn, centuries of corn, centuries of soldiers, consuming the land, nourishing its people, everything inextricably connected, as unalterable as the fact that he, too, would soon be left to bake and shrivel in the sun like another hacked-off husk of corn.

Porfirio would die, too; labelled an agitator, but if anything the outsider, a survivor, his baby face still full of youth's innocent determination ... was it his ancestors' call that haunted his gaze now? A ghost even before he'd had a chance to inseminate the earth with his own sweat and tears.

They stopped across from another pickup. More *pistoleros* jumped out of it and approached them. Berrin recognized one of them, the man in the red-striped shirt, the one who hadn't hesitated to give him and Porfirio the once-over as they were marched out of the barracks in Tepepantiango.

Porfirio stared back at Berrin again, his eyes now furious. In a moment, one of the *pistoleros* would yank the tailgate open to pull them down. Ahead, just steps away, the land dropped, plastic bags scattered around the rim — a dump. Two of the militiamen approached, one with a handgun and one with a machete, young, with nervous, numb faces, but all identical in their determination to get it over with. Porfirio's elbow jabbed his side, insistent, and as soon as his feet struck the dirt, Porfirio started to run, a senseless lunge through mayhem. Berrin ran after Porfirio, to at least die beside him, but at his fourth step, he heard the burst of rifle fire, and, as he jumped to launch himself into space, a sharp pain sliced through the side of his head. He was rolling down the embankment, still conscious, instantly realizing how lucky he might be if he were to relax and roll, like in childhood dreams when he'd always be able to land safely after high, soaring flights over his homeland fields.

Then the abrupt stop, winding him, the extreme effort to lie motionless in the curl against the end of a fallen coconut tree he had spotted like a snapshot a moment before the butt end of the thick trunk came crashing into his stomach, a moment that should have opened up to eternity.

CHAPTER 2

A tell-an-image age

NOT LONG AFTER ALL, only back in town since the summer, and already Eileen's returned . . . flat out on her back a few feet away, spread-eagled familiar, sleeping.

And no husband in sight, the double surprise. Though the upshot for him, a bit on edge all evening from keeping to the utmost restraint.

The anticipation, a good sensation this time, and a better universe unfolding.

He remembered their first evening in their rancho, Cochit-lahuantla. They had arrived dead-tired after a full day's journey by donkey over two mountain ranges, and surprised to find that their only available lodging was the cement basement of the school, but built above ground. "Good enough," was their spontaneous response, exhaling it almost in unison with a shrug and a laugh to make light of any complications this might create. The light-heartedness carried them to the conclusion that the only bedding for their first night together was a simple cot of rope mesh strung between a set of crossed sticks: a sawhorse-like string bed. Simple, Eileen had said, throw your sleeping bag on top for a mattress; my sheet can do for a blanket. As for their fears, she spoke of taran-tulas, he of scorpions, though she was certain no scorpions lived that high up in the mountains. And so they climbed in and found themselves pressed together side by side in the slope of the string. But too afraid of making a wrong move, he never did reach around to hug her, and after a few minutes, she crawled out and unrolled her own sleeping bag on the cement floor below him. Then she strung a rope around the bedding, her line of defence, it seemed. And so they both had survived the night. The next day, she found a cot for herself and moved to the opposite side of the room under the window.

He should have lain down beside her, a bit of consoling, a bit of laughter, not so innocent now, either of them.

He felt a blunt pain at the base of his sternum; it was returning, as the muscles around his diaphragm contracted. It was an annoying reflex that had occurred more than once lately, independent of his will, and no amount of introspection alleviated it. Perhaps the coconut tree had done its damage.

The evening's events raced through his mind. Eileen's appearance had been sudden, but he shouldn't have been surprised. Even though he had written her, a chance encounter was inevitable, as Ottawa was still little more than a village of small huts. Earlier in the evening, the knocking and simultaneous shoving against the door had snapped him up from his notepad to her greeting him in a tight-lipped grin with a "Hello, Berrin," and "Don't-bother-to-get-up," while shedding her shoes and unbuttoning her trench coat. "I have to put my feet up for a sec. Jeff is in Toronto with the children visiting his parents — at least that's what he says — and I'm here looking for a job. And dead tired." Then her descending trajectory across the room as she threw her suitcase like a curling stone toward his bed before collapsing onto it.

He had been working on a new universal language, in the middle of comparing his new alphabet to the knot-work images in a large coffee-table size book, *Celtic Art*; so obsessed was he in this that it took a few seconds to pull his mind away.

He did get out a "Well, hello," when she sat up and pulled off her coat.

"The better half of life is always out of sight," she joked, a nervous edge in her voice carrying her apologies for dropping in so late. Since he had missed the beat of her opening salvos, she had obviously picked up on his defective television — only the left half lit — to break the ice between them.

Too lost to the world — a matching epigram might as well have belonged in that alternative universe that quantum physics postulated. No time even to get out of his chair. Apart from being on the obese side, like everything else in this tell-an-image age, his reactions were half what they used to be.

He looked back at his pad of key-shaped letters, with the thought to explain his project, though in truth he was wanting as much to distract her from the obvious destitution of his room, little more than an add-on to the main house, almost a lean-to, slanting slightly into the back of the house, a co-op full of students with their conversations drifting in like an afterthought through his open door, which connected to the kitchen.

She was holding her coat in her lap. He moved to stand up, but she insisted: "That's okay. Stay where you are. That's how I remember you, seated and reading." She threw her coat at her suitcase and fell back onto the bed. "When did you shave?"

The moment when their conversation finally took on their long-ago familiarity, with its echo of an Irish lilt neither of their families had lost entirely since landing on the shores of the New World a century or more before. He closed his book, and, leaving his writing pad inside as a bookmark, placed it on top of the pile of books on his desk.

"My beard was beginning to turn white."

"You look younger without a beard."

He had kept his beard since Mexico, where the month-long jaunt through the mountains outlasted his supply of razor blades, and he discovered the delight of razor-free mornings.

"I had a dream about it. Right after quitting the oil rig off Newfoundland . . ."

"Oil rig! I thought you were up north, lost in some gold mine."

"They're all abandoned. I had to move on."

"Well, an oil rig. Not bad."

"It was a measly job, working in the kitchen."

"So how come you're bunkered down here?"

"I needed to get back to writing." Not entirely true. It was his language program that was pulling him out of a long stretch of unease, in fact, out of an almost permanent state of paralysis, so much so that at times he couldn't think or speak in complete sentences, reality appearing only in fragments, missing important clues, and so his writings were lately little more than the tailings of a spent mind. To say *writing was still his hope* would be the truth, but a desperate truth, and he'd not impress with that kind of talk.

"And here we are, both back in Ottawa. Things are picking up again."

"We'll see. So, getting to do what you want must feel good."

"The first night back, I dreamed I was bicycling into the city, like it was the end of a long journey. I was nude and clean-shaven. In the dream, the first thing I did was buy a suit. When I woke up, the first thing I did was shave."

"In the nude, eh?"

"It's dressed to descend, and naked to ascend. Yeats once put it something like that — a favourite of yours, if I remember."

She might have caught his real allusion, because she stared at him as if at a scholar's footnote. She never talked about her breakdown in Cochitlahuantla. She had resolved to get on with her life — in this life. He had learned a bit from their project officer, Arturo Durán, after Arturo had returned from retrieving her from the Sierra. Her problems had begun shortly after he had left their rancho for Tepepantiango to treat his foot infection, then ending up being knocked totally out of the game. She had disappeared unnoticed around the same time. Some *campesinos* found her wandering lost on a mountaintop outside Cochitlahuantla, dehydrated and delusional — and completely naked, one of the *campesinos* had reported, and mumbling something about Christ and redemption. She should have been at least wearing a *sombrero*, they laughed . . . those loco gringos. They covered her with flour sacks, tied her to a mule, the rope running under the mule's belly from one foot to the other, and brought her back to the rancho.

"No evidence of her being molested," Arturo had added, "but with your near miss as well, Berrin, it's better we shut down this project area before there's a strike three." While the assault on himself was definitely political, her trauma was more likely a carry-over from earlier in the summer when they had visited Guadalajara to hear Ivan Illich, who had been invited to speak to their organization, the Co-ordination of Inter-American Student Programs. A Catholic bishop and social activist, working out of the acclaimed CEDOC, his research and policy institute in Cuernavaca, Illich was sure to solidify their commitment, as CIASP was an invention of the Maryknoll order of priests, who, on a summer's stay in Mexico City, had their epiphany when facing a row of corrugated tin shacks that stretched down the street across from their posh Americana Inn.

Illich thought little of good deeds as an answer to the north-south divide, and he had aimed to shake the Canadian students out of their middle-class perspectives. Toothbrush missionaries, he had called them. Some of the Canadians were working with students of architecture from the local Instituto Politecnico in Guadalajara, building housing for the poor in a barrio outside the city limits. When Eileen heard of a planned *manifestation* protesting the slow extension of basic city services into their barrio, she thought it was time for the travelling salesmen to hit the tarmac. And then the army attacking the marchers, well, the street people, their front.

Too many memories, Eileen still silent, as if contemplating the floor, washed-out green linoleum. "Maybe I'm the prodigal daughter moving back to your neck of the woods." She looked up, eyeing him directly. "Still feeling you've missed out on something?"

"I think I have, and I've been punishing myself for it ever since."

"Perhaps. Love is the best garment, isn't it? And suffering makes garments irrelevant."

"I thought it was love that made garments irrelevant."

"The same old Berrin. I get serious and you get flippant."

"Sorry, Eileen. I didn't mean it to sound like that."

Eileen shrugged and smiled, but kept to a moment of silence.

She looked around the room, as if taking inventory, then asked about his new life. He ran through the names of his housemates and the dynamics at play as best as he could divine them, given the characters in play. "In short, a co-op, with too many students around for my own good."

"So, maybe you don't need another one around? I was thinking to pick up my own life again."

"Great, you should have finished your degree before taking off to the country. But the times are better, now, and the entertainment scene has improved. There's a local artist-run centre down the street. Performance artists are the fashion now. Someone strips every time, back to the Garden of Eden." The note of incredulity in his voice conveyed his more honest assessment.

"It could be about being true to yourself."

"Be true to yourself, bare yourself."

"I thought that was what you wanted."

"I guess so."

"And as exasperating as ever," she added.

He *was* sticking to an old habit, but in the manner of being too careful, too worried about not being attuned to her moves. He lifted one leg across a knee, but it felt more like a pose for watching a chess match, and let it fall back to the floor with a thud.

"But who wants to suffer? Maybe that's what you're saying, Berrin. We do get tired of suffering, I know that much. And now it's me limping back to the city, with barely a shirt on my back."

She looked away, at the Tiffany lamp.

"Berrin, I think my rural quarters," patting herself on her hip, "are in tatters as well. And it's this ass that's now taking a licking."

He nodded. She had followed Jeff up the Ottawa valley, an impetuous move, given how short a time they had known each other, and into the country, another surprise, given Eileen's natural need for people. The only other house nearby was abandoned and fell down a few months after they arrived, the general store had burned down a decade before that, and the Catholic church was torn down some time afterwards. He never knew why they had chosen such a desolate spot. Likely, she had needed to stop before they had driven too far out of the city, the roadside sign still standing, directing them off the highway to the one-house village. Jeff didn't mind how far out he got, he had plans to sell insurance to the country folk.

Circuits Man, his nickname for Jeff from his very first impressions of him.

"Mister Circuits Man has come full circle, hasn't he?"

A probable slur, meant to arrest any talk of Jeff. She nodded slightly.

Jeff, a dog, cur, the curse on his efforts to get something working with Eileen upon their return to Ottawa after their Mexico trials, publishing their ill-fated politics and entertainment magazine, a misdirected effort from the outset, *The Left Bank*, a misnomer for a culture rag, anachronistic as well, its time in the city's cultural scene would have had to await the nineties when the full emergence of gay culture became the trendsetter for the national capital, if not for the country itself. "Down to earth" was how Eileen had described Jeff to him that last night on the job together.

The slight had stung. And then came his reasoned protests. They had been so close in Mexico. Had he not stood by her in the hospital afterwards? But a crisis will definitely open your eyes. That was the plain truth of it, he had realized; his feelings were much clearer with Jeff's arrival on the scene.

But Eileen had already moved on. "A little too late for that," she had retorted. "You aren't really angry enough. Always so dispassionate, so earnest, as if that's what glamour means for you."

Never his view of himself, actually. He could have persisted with what he knew was true, their friendship through college, their training program for CIASP, with their many late-night romps through the city that invariably led to heated debates about politics, she invariably pushing the conversation away to a novel she'd read or a film she'd seen. And then their troubles in Mexico. His love for her had emerged slowly, but it seemed almost preordained in retrospect; it shouldn't have been a surprise to her.

However defined, his glamour had obviously evaporated after Mexico. *The Left Bank*, only a stepping stone on her road to recovery. She never did see the irony in her attitude toward his strong work ethic, given Jeff's own business plans, which had cast a spell over her from the outset. Stock markets, nothing could be more mature. No one else in their circle would have even glanced at a *Globe & Mail* or an *Economist*. *Mother Jones* and the *Canadian Dimension* had been his stock-in-trade.

He had asked her instead what could be glamorous about an electronics repairman, with his get-rich-quick schemes, like the one who had left his parents' basement full of unopened boxes of television sets? "You're wrong. He's a businessman who doesn't accept defeat. He knows how to deal with the world."

Jeff's schemes would continue to be endless circuits that led nowhere.

She crossed her arms on her chest.

"I think he's got a lover, and I know who it is. I met her in the local bar. He thought I didn't notice the little eye exchanges between them. But she was right up front and centre that night. The lead singer. She must be playing a gig in Toronto, so he's visiting his parents all of a sudden. Bringing the kids to see the grandparents. I don't think they retired to babysit."

She pushed herself up against the wall at the head of the bed.

"I'm sorry to hear that," Berrin replied.

"Maybe he's like most men, has a lot of difficulty distinguishing between love and duty."

"Perhaps."

"I should have seen this coming. Everything became so tense and complicated, so damn heavy. He doesn't say what's on his mind. He drifts away."

Berrin bit down on his temptation to allude to the clichéd "unbearable lightness of being," though it would bring a definite stop to this talk of Jeff. Difficult to avoid, though, think it and it exists. Like Bertrand Russell's theory on the excluded middle, think of a white mountain and the white mountain exists. Jeff existed as her lover the moment she considered the idea, and Jeff existed because he believed women had thoughts only about him. As for himself, the logic dictated that he remained the excluded middle.

So, she still wanted to live with Jeff.

"Are you sure about the lover?"

Eileen laughed.

"Tell me more about her. Big breasts, I bet."

"Something petty like that, as you would say."

Chastised.

"Since we moved to the country, all he does is work, or rather travels around building his network of contacts, and according to him I don't do anything."

"Guys get bushed and women go nuts when they move to the country. You grew up there — like most women, the most sensible move is to the city as soon as possible."

"My mistake was not learning to drive soon enough. Oh, my gosh." She moved to get up. "I forgot. I parked on the street."

"It's fine; there's no snow yet. Maybe I could get you a drink?"

She shook her head and leaned back against the wall again. No headboard; he'd need to get a proper bed. She looked down at her legs and pressed one nylon toe against the other.

"It was a few months ago. I suggested we take a break. I wanted to go canoeing back to that log cabin at Lac Lapeche. Do you know that Jeff first seduced me there?"

"I don't need to be reminded, Eileen. Lac Lapeche, appropriate."

"Meaning?"

"The first time he dropped by our magazine office, he sported a tie that looked like a fish pasted to the front of his shirt. How could you have forgotten that?"

"I might as well have brought along my fishing rod. But I was picturing something more romantic."

"It all did call for that." She hadn't caught the allusion . . . that he was the first to have made that canoe trip with her, out to the abandoned trapper's cabin at the far end of the lake, the romance of it commanding their silence, hidden as it was in the middle of a tiny, tree-capped island, its isolation probably the only reason it had survived when the government decades before turned the region into a park and demolished the few other buildings on the shore. To escape beaches full of city vacationers, they had canoed across the lake and taken the left branch that stretched farther off into the wilderness, where they eventually came upon the island. She must have told Jeff about this, their one romantic outing, and he had jumped at the opportunity to up her pleasure. His sense of humour.

Memories held for far too long. An island, it could be reduced to nothing more than the lake bottom sitting high and dry, atop other timeless layers of sediment. Sentiment. *Sedere*, to sit and sit and sit.

Nevertheless, the love nest had been in remarkably good condition. A rustic table with blocks of wood for chairs, an oil barrel tilted on its side for a stove, and rusted pipes rising up through the slab-wood roof . . . even tins of beans were left on a shelf under the window, the panes of which were remarkably all intact. And the bedsprings — they were covered with boards, awaiting the carefree picnickers.

"I suppose many romances came to a head in that cabin." Berrin said.

"He was so tender, that first trip."

Like how he'd stroke his tie, his fingertips moving up and down the fish scales.

"You know something, we never did return to the lake after we moved to the country. He always had the same excuse: the water would be too cold or he had to rush off for a meeting. But you know how warm it's been this summer. I had to be a pure bitch to drag him from his work, but we were going canoeing at last. The beach was full of people. Then I lost my sandal. It fell off my foot when I pushed away from shore. I looked back for it. People were splashing all around us. I thought it had sunk. I dove for it, he dove for it. We must have looked so ridiculous, because the water was only a few feet deep, even at the front of the canoe. We couldn't find it anywhere. Such a little thing, but he got more and more angry. A five-dollar pair of sandals. I wanted to forget about it and head out to our island. But we never did leave. The kids got tired sitting in the bottom of the canoe and started crying. He was still ducking underwater, he yelled at them to be quiet, then he began walking up and down the beach. I took the kids to play in the sand. An hour later, an old woman found my sandal floating to shore in front of her, about thirty feet down the beach. I'd forgotten the sole was made of cork. And he clammed up. Ridiculous. I imagined him burying himself in the sand and the kids digging him up and we would all be laughing again. But he was angry about something. I had ruined his day. But of course he had this thing going."

"Maybe an early mid-life crisis."

"I even told myself that I should try accommodating it — I mean, her. How naïve can you get, *eh?*"

Eh. Understood. Another valley girl, an easy catch.

Eileen lowered herself down on the bed, pulled the pillow from under the blanket, and propped up her head.

"Maybe we both didn't love each other. And love will always have its revenge."

"Yes — kids."

"Oh, Berrin, you can be a real shithead." She pushed her head back, more in frustration it seemed than in anger, and looked up at the ceiling, exhaling a lengthy sigh.

"I know. Just ki —"

Puns, couldn't avoid them, less cruel than irony, and they showed up the nonsense in life. Another habit to break with. Her infatuation with Jeff might have been a necessary part of her recovery back then. Now she had to get on with her life, while still trying to protect her nest.

"I couldn't imagine quitting Jeff, especially after Jessie came along."

"I was thinking about that."

She closed her eyes.

"The apple of your eye, as my mother would have said."

"Yes, Berrin, our Garden of Eden."

They laughed, lightly. The familiar banter was returning. And with a family. Children would change this exchange, he could learn; it's not that he didn't enjoy kids. But with the ex always there up front in this change? More than a question mark.

"Berrin, where's the washroom?"

"Oh, out the door, here, through the kitchen, and down the hall. It's at the head of the stairs. Someone may be sleeping upstairs, though."

"I'll be up and back lickety-split." And she was up and through the door — in a jiffy.

The banter was a relief. Just had to keep it going.

He touched his temple and felt for the scar, his one permanent Mexican memento. He couldn't still be so damaged. Just the misgivings lingering. The past was past, if not long gone.

CHAPTER 3

It's all obscene

TEPEPANTIANGO, MEXICO. Berrin stood at the doors of the sacristy, facing a middle-aged Nahua woman, the padre's servant. He had greeted her with a *Buenos dias*. But she only smiled in response, as if sizing him up anew, while pulling on the tassels of her bright orange *rebozo*, a long shawl that often doubled as a baby-carrier, its shimmering silk fringe, though, speaking more of her social standing as the padre's employee. He switched to *"Teotlaquiltih,"* one of the few Nahual greetings he knew, and started to explain himself. More of her smiles, but she didn't seem to want to step aside and let him pass, which was puzzling, for she would have seen him enough over the previous week. But with no acknowledgment even of the impatience in his hand gestures, he bowed and slid past the woman and headed down the short hallway to the kitchen, pursued by her, now protesting in Spanish, "The padre is having his breakfast; he doesn't want to be disturbed."

Padre Nómez was silhouetted against the rear doorway of the kitchen, looking very much the humble parish servant, his soutane a subdued blackness against the sun-filled garden outside and a lemon tree that hugged the red brick wall to the right. He was stooping over an adobe stove about to drop an egg into a saucepan of water that was set to boil on the open flame.

The servant passed on through the kitchen, keeping her silence, walking past the padre and disappearing through the door into the back garden. Padre Nómez raised his arms in surprise, "*Buenos dias*," and pointed to the table.

"So, Berrin, you didn't leave on the bus as I told you to."

"Padre, something came up."

"Something always comes up, and you are always digging something up. That's the problem. What I hear is that some of the leading citizens of our pueblo are a bit concerned about you." A touch of anger darkened his already weathered features. "Your safety is very important; your projects can wait another day. And that beard makes you look too much like a *bandito*, more than enough for the army to give you problems." He started to smile as if to mask his concern, but frowned instead.

Tepepantiango was a quiet town, a regular stopover for tourists, a picturesque pueblo high in the mountains, a day's third-class bus ride out of Mexico City, suddenly appearing past one of the many bends in the highway that wound its way up through the Sierra Alta. More recently it was an army barracks that greeted you at the edge of town. The sacristy, manned by its prematurely aging Padre Nómez, provided a haven for anyone seeking help, medical or other. It was in his residency that Berrin had recently lain bedridden while recovering from blood poisoning in his foot.

"I need to return to Cochitlahuantla to get Eileen out, and the others."

"I will send someone to lead your friends out as soon as possible," Padre Nómez said.

"I can warn them myself — Eileen especially, she's a very stubborn woman. I can be up and back in two days."

Padre's turned back to his egg without answering, clearly not in accord.

Berrin knew his case was weak, but how to explain he needed to make amends with Eileen. Perhaps quarreling with her was simply a case of getting on each other's nerves, and Eileen needing time by herself. She had returned only partway with him after they decided he needed penicillin. She agreed with him that while he was gone she'd return to the neighbouring rancho where four other CIASPers were staying. If she got lonesome for her rancho, a round trip home to Cochitlahuantla and back was only a two-hour walk, but he couldn't stop thinking that she had immediately returned to Cochitlahuantla.

Initially, he had argued that instead of himself making the long trip down to Tepepantiango, he could stay and rest for a few days with her in the neighbouring rancho, as one of the students there was a nurse, and could confirm the need for the trip down to a doctor, or not.

"You don't cure blood poisoning with Aspirin," Eileen had insisted, irritated.

"Maybe some good humour would help."

Eileen wasn't to be fooled. "Nurse Joan, with the red hair and large mouth." Not attributes that Eileen shared. Nor Joan's sense of humour, posted above the doorway of her hut, "Don't sweat the petty things, and don't pet the sweaty things."

Padre Nómez sighed. "It's very late, Berrin. And you are young. It takes many years to understand your own innocence, *mi amigo loco*." He gave his egg a poke with his spoon. The flames from the wood fire flickered at the base of the pan. The water began to boil. He looked at his watch before he spoke.

"I still cannot understand why things are as they are, the quarrels among so many family groups that too often lead to bloodshed. But take some good advice when it comes your way. Berrin, when your Maker is knocking at the front door, you are permitted to try and exit by the back."

Berrin looked away from the good padre to the map on the wall across from their table. A one-way trip up to Cochitlahuantla was a good eight-hour trek at the best of times.

"*Gracias*, Padre. It is late, you are right, so I will leave early in the morning."

He almost regretted having to leave. After the first few days it had taken for the penicillin to kill his fever and see the lump in his groin diminish, he'd begun exploring the pueblo, and his excursions lengthened daily. He had come to see that the problems in the mountain ranchos stemmed from the power brokers in the flatter lowlands.

Padre Nómez looked at his watch again. "*Bueno, para mi*, it's my stomach that will kill me. You know Señora Gomez, the old woman you call the herbal lady that you met down by the River Araña. She told me to boil my egg no more than a minute and have it with that tea there in front of you. Rosa."

She appeared at the door.

"*Por favor.*" He gestured to her to pour a cup for the guest.

The padre removed the blackened aluminum pan from the flame and reached down to the opening in front of the stove, which looked like a large, square rock with patches of bare adobe bricks plastered onto its sides. He jiggled the ends of the sticks that poked out and broke up the fire.

Berrin sipped his tea. "It tastes like cranberry."

"Rosa, *pan dulce.*"

Berrin fingered the roll of sugar-sprinkled bread that Rosa dropped on his plate. He was too agitated to eat.

Padre Nómez scooped out the egg with his spoon and crossed the room to sit opposite Berrin. He broke off the top of the shell, and the albumen ran down the sides over his fingers; only a thin layer of white coated the inside. He quickly raised the decapitated egg to his mouth and gulped down the contents. Rosa poured some tea for him, her face mirroring the slight grimace that his made.

Berrin hunched over; his hands encircled his cup. His mind was on a photograph in his vest pocket, evidence enough that the padre's words were right about the danger he faced. But he lacked the courage to take it out right away. The padre was twirling his eggshell in his hand. No one spoke for a moment.

The padre glanced up at Berrin, worry lines now running

across his brow. "Well, then, Berrin, about tomorrow, it may be safer in the mountains."

"Not much, Padre." Berrin decided to lead up to the photograph. "Last week, Eileen heard of a *peón* at the edge of our rancho who wanted to kill us. She says even the women don't like the fencing project we're working on."

"You know that the *ejidos* are communal lands? This goes as far back as the Mexican revolution."

"I know, but the teacher owns the cattle, and so we are helping him fence off the *ejido land*. It means more protein for the rancho. He seems sincere about that."

Padre Nómez smiled. "Berrin, who will really benefit is the question." He began spooning out the thin layer of cooked egg that lined the shell. "That new highway they pushed up from Mexico to Tampico, it passes very close to our region, and everything has changed. Everyone sees redemption in cattle, even a few of the land-holding Nahua *campesinos*, like your friend the teacher. But most of the cattle are shipped out, and too much bad stuff is coming in."

Berrin had already come to realize that the politics were mind-boggling. And he also hadn't paid much attention to Eileen's views — much like the padre's — that the *ejido* was not the teacher's to do with as he pleased. He had acknowledged that, but he had held to a basic view, that their project still could improve the nutrition in the rancho. Even in the neighbouring rancho, where CIASP was working on a water project, the people in the centre of the rancho would benefit. Projects, Eileen had exclaimed, always projects — what about listening to the people?

"Well, Padre, that might explain why someone is ripping up the fence at night."

"I see the cattle and the fences and the tractors growing in numbers. But the people never have the basics, and now never enough jobs, and then the young people will be leaving, too."

A rattling from the corner of the room turned both their heads. Rosa was pouring water into a large black enamel pan. A pile of men's socks lay on the table beside her. Padre looked down at the floor where some water had spilt on the red ochre tiles. He seemed about to say something, but turned back to Berrin.

"Who is the *juez* now? I don't remember."

"You know all about it, then, Padre. The *juez*. Eileen said it's a joke to be the elected head of the rancho, when the teacher will take over the land no matter what the *juez* or the people say. She might be right. But, it's Jesús Gomez. Do you know him?"

"*Si*, if I remember correctly, Jesús lives next to the *ejido*. That communal land is really communal there; it feeds many of the poorer souls in and around the rancho. As for the teacher, his father was able to get him some education in Mexico City from some coffee he grew. They were better times, a couple of youth actually made it to Mexico City to study. But by the time he returned as the teacher and took over his father's land, coffee prices had dropped. So he's turning to cattle and wants to fence in everything. The cattle used to roam free. Now it's reversing, large areas now fenced for these new breeds . . . and then the tractors . . . this change isn't employing many people."

"Jesús did take me through their *ejido*. He showed me the beans and potatoes. I had never noticed them. And the bananas, mini-sized ones — they are so much sweeter than the kind we get back home."

"*Si*, I think we're out of them, actually. Rosa, you will remember the bananas?"

"*Si*," Rosa whispered, and kept to her washing. The water wasn't splashing much now, as if she didn't want to miss a word.

"Jesús is old but he's enterprising, Padre. It is confusing. I can't see cattle surviving on *zacate*. The teacher plans to plant that stuff, little more than scrawny clumps of grass."

"*Si*, he could keep only a few cows, and he'd have the stubble from all the crops to feed them, like we always did. But it's more than a matter of a fence. This battle goes back before the revolution. Our own church is as deeply divided."

Berrin stopped a moment to reflect, taking a bite out of his roll of bread. "Yes. Padre Sanchez was riding away as I entered. He didn't wave back to me."

"*El Padre.*" Padre Nómez tapped his spoon on the table. "Padre Sanchez arrived a few months ago from a seminary in Mexico City. I was happy at first to have him. The evenings can be long, and he helped me in the beginning with my sermons. He finds references in the Bible that are good. But he spends more time now outside the sacristy, and I fear that the good padre is becoming a stranger to his church."

"And to this town?"

"He moves in the higher circles." He spooned out the last of the cooked egg that lined the shell. "*Si*, where every man is his own boss." He reached for the salt shaker and shook it vigorously over the slice of egg, as if in defiance of all doctor's orders. Then he rolled it in a tortilla and bit an end off. He sighed heavily, the crow's feet around his eyes deepening.

"Tell me, *Berrin*: Did he follow the main road out of town?"

"Yes," Berrin said, for an instant not catching the implications. Then he remembered the army barracks. "I hear that your young padre also carries a pistol in his belt under his soutane. *El Pistolero de Dios.*"

The padre smiled, or rather, his eyes did. "I'm afraid he's not inspired by the theology of liberation. I didn't think this agrarian conflict would become so violent. I should never have invited you students here. *Pero, es claro*, you must leave immediately."

"*Si, es claro*, Padre, the violence is bad." He reached into his jacket pocket and pulled out a photo, but held it face down without immediately looking at it.

"Porfirio came by my door this morning and handed me this and then ran off."

"Porfirio? Ah, *si*. He was my altar boy until last month. He wanted me to call him Sr. Hernandez, but he's still a boy."

Berrin first met Profirio when all the Canadian students were preparing to leave the pueblo for their ranchos. Porfirio appeared as one of the porters assigned to carry their supplies up the precarious mountain trails. Eileen had been one with Berrin in her surprise, a cruel rite of passage for a Nahua boy.

Porfirio next appeared as the son of the catechist when Berrin met him with his father, days later, in their rancho, Cochitlahuantla, both armed with machetes and heading off for a day's work in the fields. Confirmed: Porfirio, an itinerant worker, a *peón*, but still appearing to Berrin as much too young; an injustice in it, somehow. And now, he was about to reveal to the good padre Porfirio's new status, that of an agitator.

"I recently lent his father some money out of our small credit union for a sugar mill. It meant a lot to Porfirio. But some don't like this. Foreign money, even if it comes through the church. What is your expression? . . . it upsets the apple cart."

"His father is the catechist in Cochitlahuantla, I see." Berrin hesitated, and nodded. The catechist, a surrogate priest who could perform basic Catholic rites, and the padre's right-hand man in the rancho; the teacher would be getting a bit of competition.

Berrin flipped the photo to look at it, but could only focus on the black bar across the bottom. He handed it across the table.

Padre Nómez looked at the photo, then sank back against his chair. He dropped his head as if in prayer.

A *campesino* held a machete with both hands raised above his head. He stood in front of a naked woman strung upside down. She was tied by each of her ankles to an overhanging limb of a tree. She hung facing the camera. Beside her, a man was seated on the ground, tied to the trunk. He appeared to be dead, his torso crisscrossed with cuts and his face blackened with what must have been cigarette burns.

"They were our best teachers."

"Padre, is that Señor Fonseca with the machete?" The man was in profile, his face partially shaded by the rim of his straw hat. The incriminating detail, in the foreground, the partial view of an arm in army uniform to the rear of Señor Fonseca and the hand holding a gun; the photo was taken a second too soon, not leaving the soldier time to step fully out of the shot.

"Señor Fonseca attended my Spanish classes. You can see he wouldn't do such a thing. He's a good man."

"I heard that the army suspects any Indian who can write."

"*Alfabetizacion* makes trouble, *por cierto*. But none of my students are political." He looked again down at the photo, staring for what seemed an eternity, then blinked, his face darkening further.

"Padre?"

He looked up. "*Jóvenes*. They were so young."

"Do you think Porfirio is dead now as well?"

"*Posiblemente.*" He raised his voice. "Porfirio was a good boy." He dropped the photo beside his cup.

"I feel we're all implicated."

"*Posiblemente*, Berrin. It is all very obscene. Sometimes I think the best I can do is pray for my people."

Berrin stared at the photo lying on the table between them. Rosa crossed behind the Padre and sneaked a peek over his shoulder. She shrieked and covered her eyes with her *rebozo*. Padre Nómez flipped the photo over, rose from his chair, and put his arms around her. He whispered some instructions. She left without looking at Berrin.

The padre sat down again. "I told her to help Señora Fonseca look for her husband and the teachers, to go to the usual places first. I will look for Porfirio myself."

He flicked the corner of the photo a few times, then gently placed his mug on top of it. "Porfirio is dead because he gave you this photo. It is clear now that you must leave *pronto*. I will find you a guide who knows the trails well at night."

A dog barked outside, close enough to be near the stone fence that surrounded the front courtyard of the church. There was a commotion at the front entrance, and Rosa came stumbling back into the room. Three soldiers followed, shoving her aside.

The taller and older of them spoke. "Padre, we need to talk with your friend. He is a troublemaker." The two others grabbed Berrin by the arms and hustled him toward the hallway without another word of explanation.

Berrin had only time to glance back at the padre standing behind the table, his face stoic. From the back of the jeep, he saw Rosa leaving by the side gate.

Berrin was sitting alone in his cell when Padre Nómez visited later in the evening. Berrin tried to reassure him, he had not been tortured, only questioned, roughed up, and very intimidated, but nothing more.

"I even began feeling relaxed a bit. It was kind of funny. The image of Christ hanging on the wall behind the captain's head, you know, the one with the heart wrapped in thorns, but his wreath looked more like razor wire. I had to smile. The captain didn't appreciate that."

The padre did not smile.

From the captain's front office, the tinny sound of a TV Soap drifted in.

"There it is, Padre. Civilization prevails." *Keep up a brave front, however transparent*, Berrin thought.

A moment's silence, then the padre spoke in a sombre voice. He had grabbed the photo when he heard the dog again, but from the door, he could see that the barking hadn't alerted them to Rosa's mission. He would pray for him, he told Berrin; inquiring minds were to be treasured. He would also pray for his parishioner, Señor Fonseca, for his teachers, for Porfirio, whom he still could not yet address as Señor Hernandez. He would pray for them all, but later. Their souls were secure in their salvation, he was certain of that, he said, they were good souls. But first he had to pray for Padre Zacate. He lowered his head. Yes, and then he would have to pray for himself, for his moment of mortal sin in that second glance at the photo. "*Es verdad*, Berrin. We are all implicated."

CHAPTER 4

Standing at the brink

WHEN EILEEN HAD RETURNED from the washroom, she leapt back into bed, crossed her legs, and leaned back against the wall. Her smile spread into a long yawn.

"You need to sleep," Berrin said.

"You're right, but it's been so long, hasn't it?"

"I want you to meet the co-op gang here. You'll like them — there's three of them." She should be interested, he thought. Well, perhaps not so much in Jill and her partner, Barry, a couple who seemed to define the health of their relationship by the amount of time they quarreled. But Stephanie, a possible friend, the resident professional student, trying to live a normal life as an artist, and the only one in the co-op with whom he could carry on a trivial conversation; she might rekindle Eileen's interest in the arts.

"Great. A get-together at breakfast. That would be fun." She yawned again, and slid lower down onto the bed.

He didn't want her to sleep, not right away. "I can get us a drink." She closed her eyes and smiled. Consent.

He had slipped into the kitchen, but there were only a few cans of cola in the fridge. A bit too chilly for that. And too late for coffee. He checked the cupboard above the counter. A can of Inka, the standard coffee substitute, warm, and it made one virtuous. The supply belonged to Jill, the resident activist in the co-op, though it was Stephanie who worked at El Sol, the health food store in the Market, getting her hands dirty with it. Jill preferred being the health food advocate when she wasn't cultivating relationships whose chief ingredients had to be rigour and commitment. Rigour or commitment? He had confused the two, perhaps weighing in on the rigour too much. He tossed the Inka from hand to hand. Hopefully, Eileen would like it.

He decided to check with her and stuck his head through the door to ask.

Flat on her back and fallen asleep.

And so he had grabbed a cola, turned back to his armchair, and waited.

Best to wait and walk with her to the corner store for some beer. Or better yet, a bottle of wine to celebrate in style. Anything to brighten her spirits, keep the conversation going, now that the old magic had returned, and toast a future together. Not such a daunting task.

Eileen had entered by the side door, a Bytown original, a thin wood panel with peeling yellow paint. Apart from his bounty of books covering the walls, his possessions amounted to a few essentials: his armchair, the bed, with the television beside it set on a chair, and a Tiffany lamp on his desk — the only object in his room that suggested any kind of luxury.

Let's face it, down and out and now living in a shanty, a muffled existence apart from the world, his attempt, it was clear, to become un-implicated, uncomplicated — another escape. And being older than the others in the co-op had left him separate as well. It was taking a toll. He was eager for Eileen to wake up. Continue the talk, fill in the gaps, get a fuller picture — meaning, where did he fit in?

And then to the larger question, the children, made more present by their absence — how would he fit into their lives? A definite shortcoming, how he had failed to consider children all his life.

Doctors might label his present condition as post-traumatic syndrome. But accepting any PTS-like prognosis would make it too easy for him to escape again . . . to avoid what should have mattered all along.

Or would his overweight body be the deciding factor for her?

He shifted in his armchair; both their situations were weighty in equal measures.

He did feel sorry for her, though he had warned her years before about Jeff: a charlatan, a fraud artist — or a hoodwinker, as his mother would have branded the guy.

He'd let too many years pass since Mexico, since her flight into a pastoral paradise. His own flight had been to get as far away as possible. His initial impulse had been to return to Mexico, where their story had taken root, where he might pick up more clues for what went wrong, but he had headed in the opposite direction, into Canada's Nordic wastelands. And never once had he questioned himself on that move, another probable mistake. His retreat had landed him decades back, at least in terms of life development; the outcast in the outback, disappearing into the hinterlands of jack pine solitudes. Just remembering that time made him nauseous, his stay away, astray in a land of bewilderness, a harshscape of rocky outcrops, outgropings, fixed as one of so many meaningless markings in a barren land. There was no way he could exaggerate the stupidity of that move. Pining away and disappeared in the hinderlands, nothing more than flatlands of hard rock, hard earth, too thin-skinned and wasted, good only for cutting or digging — or self-exile.

Likely not an easy run into a new millennium for them this time, either. But surely a bit of happiness was possible, however unbelievable, with them standing at the very brink of it.

Yes, and teetering; and as liable to stumble yet again.

A chill; he shook off the shiver and stood up. A bit of faith, he chided himself, otherwise, it's back to a downward spiral. Like this house, turn-of-the-century construction, good only for student housing. Two narrow storeys with white clapboard on the outside, badly in need of a paint job, plaster buckling on the inside walls, likely two-by-three-inch studs, too thin a skin against the winter. And no storm door, the cold already sniffing you out like a wolf snapping at your heels. He picked the overcoat off her suitcase and draped it over her. She stirred, an arm reached out and clutched the coat, but she only turned on her side and continued sleeping.

Eileen's head was off the pillow and twisted in the direction of the television, as if transfixed by the semi-demon tube.

As divided as he was. Even with the sound turned down, the background buzz remained, a kind of torture, but a presence he needed. At one time, Eileen had cautioned him on how his workaholic drive would atrophy the few social skills he did have. "God preserve me from people," he had quipped back, quoting some writer to explain his need for solitude. Then, more to the point, "Work makes me a decent human being." Certainly another appropriated and idiotic axiom. The truth took another moment to surface, though he felt he had adequately camouflaged any personal reference by giving it a universal slant, "In truth, Eileen, standing eye-to-eye with an eternity of solitude will drive anyone to work." His touch of sarcasm hadn't gone unnoticed.

Eileen had teased back, "Sure, as my father would put it, if you're not living on the edge, you're taking up too much room."

Apt. But now he had his own reply, because, becoming a single mother, she'd be enough on edge with the work cut out for her.

Her clothes were surely an exercise to foil that fate: A tight-fitting red and orange striped sweater and an equally tight plaid skirt, Quite plump as well, her body heavier than he had antici-pated, moving into middle age, however unwillingly. Her face in sleep betrayed strain and disappointment and revived his worry for her mental state. A shadow seemed to dull the lustre on her brow and cheeks. Perhaps a play of the light, lying as she was between the desk lamp and television. Unnerving nevertheless, how her face had that waxen patina as if under a wrap of celluloid. Her formerly frizzy and ginger hair changed as well, dyed a dark reddish-brown, a mismatch to her attire, perhaps a cut readying her for the corporate world, how it fell in a uniform wave to her shoulders. But he'd not be commenting. She still had flare, a passion that even her breakdown in the rancho hadn't quenched entirely.

Her black rayon overcoat didn't fit, either; almost a throwback to their former times, the expensive, full-length style that newsmen and politicians preferred, wide collar, shoulder cape, an overly long belt, an extravagance of buttons and lapels, but a layering of meanings that signified something he no longer . . . he no longer gave a hoot for.

She seemed to be pulled in as many directions. But this was not the time for analysis. Relax, each to their own. He let himself sink back. Being swallowed in the folds of an old armchair felt good. Or, perhaps too safe. Almost so deep as to disappear. That old, deep-seated inclination of his, to disappear.

Still, the armchair was something solid under him, with its high, square arms that easily took his weight when he first had tried it at the Sally Ann's: chunky but solid, exactly how he wanted to be; solid, that is.

But then, there was the corduroy, its brown-ness. He had bought the armchair despite disliking the colour. And too narrow — he hadn't noticed this, either — too shut in, even the idea of it, arms up, straight out; *a sleep-slumming ragamuffin* would be his mother's ribbing now nailing him down.

He looked up from Eileen toward the rows of books that covered almost all the wall space in his room. Board-and-brick shelves, except for the space between the window and door where he had fitted a narrow bookshelf he'd purchased at the same time. A ragtag setup, cheap, reams of words — and words are cheap; one of his father's favourite sayings.

He ran his fingers down the arms over the ribs of the corduroy. Surely a word to mull over, corduroy. A childhood delight that had come with its own double-edged blessing: a dark brown corduroy suit with short pants. At first prancing about proudly before his mother, how it would make him stand out at school; then the teasing during recess, as he was the only one in shorts. Another memory, the suit being homemade.

Corduroy, cords. Cordwood, a more deep-rooted memory. The only stovewood his father could afford, its bark also a dark brown, the castoff from a local sawmill, and the inevitable chimney fires in the dead of winter.

Poverty cripples. No desire for cords since childhood, denying himself, no doubt, ignoring the fun and the frivolous. No choice, it seemed. But then he'd never felt the choice was his, that he had a choice to choose.

He had made money at times — what single man hasn't? And never once on pogey. But to be the head of a family, to be the catch that Eileen would now be after? The thought would once have frozen him in his tracks; and, no doubting it, a sliver of fear remained.

A post-Mexico paralysis? More likely, it was a sort of ancestral fear that always stopped him: the fear of being without, being the outcast, the tinker of the family. How well he had hid his fears and donned a new mask when finally he did shed his home trappings — off to university and diving into projects that promised the world, or at least a changed world; he and Eileen were one in wanting that.

Perhaps their downfall was as simple as giving advice that no one wants, one of his father's favourites that had remained his only comment on his mission to Mexico, advice always earns you a grand pat-on-the-back thanks.

His own life? Definitely lived in limbo for too long, and rendered trivial when weighed on the public scales. But he could report he was turning it around. His life of late was more on the up, carefree, and — why not — primal, if not bending toward the creative . . . well, the inventive, at least, considering his language program, *One World Language and Peace*, a surprisingly positive element in his life, which probably more than anything had brought him to thinking of her. And so to surprise her, he had written, penning the letter in a light-hearted tone, to come across a bit of the rascal, a persona shift that any trickster might recommend to regain attention, though the plans about his stay in Ottawa admittedly became somewhat vague the longer his letter got. But he had written to her in the postmodern vein, where you don't ruin a good story with all the facts.

Trust that your time has come this time and not go scurrying off into the shelter of other Precambrian shields.

She moved slightly, leaving one arm bare and limp across her chest, its muscle clinging to the bone. Breasts as ample, still. But wrists too thin, and hands equally narrow, long, and delicate, as if inviting an embrace, something he didn't remember about her.

He sat upright. Bellow out the good news, obliterate the silence of the night like a town crier.

But of course, she had to sleep.

Not even the sound of a clock in the room. She would like that.

But it wasn't the antidote he needed, for his impatience now to act. He needed to break the silence.

He remembered how once as a kid he had cracked the ice on the lake on his uncle's farm. His uncle Alex would have been furious to learn he had ventured up to the lake alone. And newly frozen over. No snow yet fallen to render the ice its forbidding blackness. So thin and clear, he was walking on glass. Though the floor of the lake lay no more than a foot or so below him, he was looking down at a distant sepia valley. The fish, there had to be fish, such was his conscious concern, when in retrospect, it had to have been the frigid silence. He crouched and jumped, and then jumped higher. His third attempt rent the air as the sickle-shaped crack sprang across the ice like a pack of howling wolves racing to the hunt, the sound ricocheting off one mountain slope back across the silver icescape to the other cedar-lined ridge. He was a god in the heavens.

He reached between his thighs and grabbed his empty soft drink can. The dark bud of a last drop of cola grew on the rim of the can, holding onto its plastic-coated shell of aluminum. He licked at it, touching the sharp tab opening.

He leaned forward, bending into another memory, of a game Eileen had once thrust at him.

"Shove your tongue deeper into the slot, Berrin. You have to feel the pain immediately if you're going to understand me."

"That's sadistic."

"De Sade and God have that much going for them."

"You scare me sometimes, Eileen."

"When I was a kid I once chased my brother around my bedroom trying to stick him with a pin."

To ram it totally inside, the anticipation of lacerating pain, metal ripping flesh.

He stuck his tongue in, got a sting, and withdrew it slowly.

De Sade delicious. Were he so bent. And never much the postmodernist, with their bent on deconstruction, dismembering, much the same. Fundamentally, wasn't he still that kid standing on the frozen lake, needing to leap again with the same desperate and confused desire? He needed only to move the conversation forward, past their mutual straits, into more open landscapes.

If only it were as simple as metaphors. His eyes started to water.

He tried relaxing again. He inhaled deeply, and the dry, autumnal air spread through his body and flushed his arms, lessening his anxiety. Twisted once too often, the tab broke off and fell to the bottom of the can with a tinny rattle. She didn't move, the sound startling only himself, sharp like the edge of the slot where he rubbed his fingertip in circles.

Feel the pain; she had responded with that touch of irony any modernist needed to remain sane.

The pain — and the promise, the plans. Perhaps therein lay the real story, how it all flowed. And so, whatever had been his plans, he'd have to see life more from her side of things. Which includes the kids. Logic at least dictates it. But, he had to admit it, he had to move past the logic.

CHAPTER 5

Above the Araña

THE GREATEST JOY in the ranchos were the children, their smiles and hugs bringing out Eileen's brightest smiles. But too many had died, which hit her hard. A summer-long drought had dried up most streams, and the shallow wells became breeding pools for mosquitoes and bacteria. The drought was more severe in the mountains, the afternoon showers too brief. Routine had maintained their spirits, for Berrin, his daily trips with the *peóns* into the *milpas*, sloping fields of sugar cane and corn, and for Eileen, the morning literacy classes in the church with the children and the daily rounds through the rancho to teach hygiene. Word spread to the surrounding ranchos that the Canadians had medicine, so it wasn't a surprise when one morning a lanky stranger, his machete hanging loosely in a leather sling from his shoulder, came by their basement lodgings. His tall frame and sparse beard distinguished him immediately.

Eileen rose from the table where she was updating her diary. "*Tonaltih,*" the man said, then adjusted his greeting, "*Buenos dias. Notoka* Augustino Ramirez," and Eileen replied with her, "*Buenos dias. Me llamo* Eileen." Berrin answered in kind, while grabbing his *morral,* a binder-sized straw bag that contained the essentials any *peón* needed for a day's work in the Sierra. He slung it over his shoulder as he advanced to greet the stranger. Eileen glanced over at Berrin and touched her chin to draw attention to the stranger's beard, sparse and patchy though it was. "Likely French genes," Berrin remarked in a lowered voice. The stranger bowed gracefully and lowered his spotlessly white straw hat to his chest. The handshakes followed, always gracious and delicate, no more than fingertips brushing each other's palms.

The man proceeded in a mixture of Spanish and Nahuatl, Eileen carrying most of the conversation, Berrin holding back; her French had given her an edge in picking up another language. The visitor spoke of how hard the drought had hit the ranchos, finishing by coming to the point of his visit; his sister-in-law had a very sick baby. "*Necessitamos pastillas, por favor.*" Pills again, she said to Berrin, in English; she had frequently lamented how Aspirin was tragically all the medicine they had. Magicians with their North American medicines, Berrin's conclusion, how else could these *campesinos* see them?

It took them the rest of the morning to walk to the man's rancho, sticking to the paths that followed the upper ridges of the mountain range. As they approached the first hut, they met a young girl seated astride a toy dog with wooden wheels carved out of a dark wood so smooth and rounded that it might have been an Inuit sculpture. The girl's cinnamon complexion was as smooth as the toy, her corneas like black licorice, features delicate. Eileen looked at Berrin, who was now walking beside her: "Beautiful, isn't she?" His eyes were glued to the child as well: "I remember the chunky and square-faced children in those Rivera murals in Mexico City. Makes you wonder what he was seeing." The girl looked up at them as they passed, her silence curious and friendly.

Their destination was four thatched huts farther on, larger than expected, but with the familiar dim and cramped interior, the oval space divided in part by a half-wall of roughly hewn boards that supported a shelf with a few books. A touch wealthier than the average *campesino*, perhaps a teacher, but likely earning a meagre salary nevertheless.

A red rash covered most of the infant's tiny body. The mother squatted beside her baby, who lay on a bundle of rags on a straw mat set directly on the ground. She was as tall as her brother and as spindly, but more weary, her eyes watering from the smoke that rose from the sticks smouldering inside the circle of rocks in the centre of the hut. She kept washing the infant down with the moist end of her faded blue *rebozo* that she'd dip in a gourd of water beside her.

Another woman, they guessed her to be the mother's sister, stood off in the dark perimeter, bent over her *metate*, a curved slab of square stone carved out of grey volcanic rock, her rounded back rocking back and forth as she ground corn with a matching rolling pin. She eyed Berrin momentarily, then caught Eileen's roving eyes and smiled. She turned to a bench behind her and pulled a cloth off a plate stacked high with tortillas.

"*No, gracias, señora.*"

"*Agua pues,*" and she immediately dipped a small, spoon-shaped gourd into one of the larger water-filled gourds set against the wall beneath the bench.

Water could easily mean malaria, dysentery, or any number of other possibilities. Eileen offered the out: "*Café caliente, por favor, señora.*"

The mother half-smiled and handed them stools to sit on. Hospitable, but she had to expect medicine and they never wanted to pretend to be doctors. Eileen tried to press upon her the urgency of taking her baby down to the doctor in town.

The mother looked down to again clear flies away from the infant with a sweep of her hand.

This rancho was no different from most others, where the Nahua had retreated over the centuries to survive in the mountains. A hamlet of thatched huts, scattered around a church and a school, spread like a bald orange spot on the mountain's summit. A few hundred *peóns* and a couple of slightly educated *campesinos* who might serve as part-time teachers and catechists; never a pharmacist, let alone a doctor. There was no evidence even of the work of a herbal lady, such as their porter once displayed when showing them a machete cut on his leg, bandaged with rags in a cake of mud and leaves. Proper medicine was a long day's journey away, across a mountain range, down through the valley, across the Araña — now passable given the extended drought — then across a second mountain range before the final descent into Tepep-antiango. Eileen was not surprised that her exhortations for the mother to make this trip were met with a silent stare.

The sister stopped her grinding to speak. She held up four fingers, and said in broken Spanish that four other children had died in the area in one month.

The mother wiped sweat off the baby's brow. If the cool damp-ness of the cloth brought relief, it didn't show; its limbs limp, noth-ing moving but its tiny chest quietly rising and falling with each breath.

Eileen was putting questions about the child's illness, search-ing for answers. Berrin remained seated on his stool slightly behind her, sipping coffee; a pause allowed him to ask the sister: "When does her husband return?"

"Her husband was shot by soldiers."

Eileen looked down into her coffee, a black pool. She could not imagine what being a widow meant for these women, the extended family a necessary insurance. The magnitude of the mother's loss was now all too apparent. There could be no more children.

While they were talking, Augustino reappeared at the doorway, bowed under a load of firewood. He straightened and yanked the rag-like tumpline off his forehead. The load of sticks dropped from his back to the ground. He wiped his brow, turned, and taking out a cigarette, stood at the doorway. The cigarette was nothing more than a tightly rolled tobacco leaf. He smoked and listened, holding his cigarette by his fingertips as if it were a toke. With the mention of the soldiers, and the silence that settled in, he picked up the story. A few weeks before, her husband had been arrested and was being transported to the federal prison close to Mexico City. He was left to sit beside the rear door of the car, a set-up, *es claro*, he said with emphasis. When the car slowed down near the summit over the town, he pushed open the door and bounded down the mountainside through the field of corn, heading for the forest ahead. But the corn came no higher than his waist, and the soldiers in the rear car shot him before he was halfway to the bush.

Augustino stopped, held up his cigarette to look at the ash building on its end, tapped the ashes onto his tongue, and swallowed them. Then he took another drag. A routine action.

"*Niños*," the mother said, "*niños*."

"*Si*," Eileen said softly. "*Los soldados son demasiado jóvenes.*" Yes, basically child-soldiers . . . *Niña*, also the name of one of Columbus's ships . . . there had to be another name for man-child.

Berrin looked over at Eileen and said, "It's the phosphorus they need."

"What?" Her contorted face said it better, an absurd response.

He hadn't sensed the degree of her dread; his own incongruity more apparent, his large, beefy frame squatting on the tiny stool, bowed to the piping hot coffee. He turned his head to the side in a pretense of studying better his cup, a shiny earthenware pinch-pot of orange clay shaped like a gourd. He balanced the cup gingerly between his fingertips and blew at the steam.

She considered telling him about the possibility of lead poisoning, something to crack his easy complacency, but speaking more English at that moment was impolite.

But Berrin read enough into her glance, as if she wanted to say: *See, so much for your structural theories of community development.* But she had heard his reply often enough, *And what can a few Aspirin do?* Their different takes on community development was definitely taking a toll on their friendship.

A fly had landed on the infant's eye, and Eileen watched the mother as she again flicked at it with her hand. Her cotton blouse was wet from milk dripping. There'd be no relief for her engorged breasts, from her child's — nor her husband's — mouth.

Augustino walked over to the shelf and took down the books. Her husband had studied in Mexico City, he said. An algebra book, a medical dictionary of tropical diseases, and a history of the Catholic Church in Mexico. Eileen stared at them in his hands. Berrin nodded, but said nothing as well. Augustino turned away as if embarrassed, replaced the books on the shelf, and told them in an insistent voice of a meeting in the school, "*Venga, esto sólo tomará un minuto.*" He nodded to his sisters and exited.

Eileen and Berrin stood up to follow. The tortilla lady handed them a mini-banana apiece, a token offering that came so often with house visits that they'd learned to accept it with gratitude.

Eileen dropped hers into her *morral*, then rummaged through it some more. She handed over two Aspirins.

"It's not that simple," Berrin whispered as they turned to leave.

"Simple? That's it for you?"

"All right. You're right. You're right. Tomorrow morning we'll try to take them down to Tepepantiango ourselves."

His eyes now were insistent as well, no time for more debate.

Again, the gentle brush of fingers on palms, and smiles.

As they emerged from the hut, Augustino bowed slightly, and showed the way with his outstretched hat. They headed out across the central square, blinding hot under the noon sun.

People were milling around on the second-level verandah of the school. In the yard in front of the building, children were playing volleyball, the net nothing more than a string tied between two posts.

"*El inspector escolar?*" Berrin asked, looking at the activity upstairs.

"No, *un funcionario del pueblo.*"

Augustino's scornful "No" reminded them there would seldom be a classroom full of children.

Eileen looked across at the volleyball game, the children probably rounded up to impress the officials. A diminutive man stood on the sidelines watching the game. He must have been returning from the *milpas*, his cotton clothing no longer so white, the strap of his machete sheath criss-crossing his chest over the strap of his *morral*. His *sombrero*, though, was of a spotless, waxy white, as if it were his most precious possession, a style less frequently seen, distinctive in its stiff roundness but appearing like a melon on his head. The volleyball looped toward him, and he jerked into action as he had seen the kids do. But he completely missed the ball with his flailing hands as he lunged at it pell-mell. It bounced off his hat and tumbled down the mountain slope, to the uproarious laughter of the kids.

Even Augustino laughed, as if welcoming a moment of normalcy. He turned and was about to head for the stairs when he stopped, and led them around behind the building to a hut that gave no appearance of being inhabited. Facing them inside was a table piled high with a dozen or more large rolls of cheese, the large, black lettering of the labels as surprising as the cheese, Canadian Black Diamond. Augustino explained this was part of the payment for work being done on a community hall and jail. Berrin recognized the word: "*Carcel?*" he asked, to be certain of it. "*Si*," Augustino said, and pointed to the school's basement: The basement would double as a jail in the new building. But, there was a problem: The people had never had cheese and so were feeding it to the pigs and dogs. He offered them a roll. Eileen shook her head, smiling, and looked back at Berrin, who understood, it might not be good to get implicated here, and made a face of disgust: "*Gracias, Augustino, no me gusta.*"

Augustino smiled for some reason, "*Gracias*," he said, and turned back to the stairs. People were still lingering by the back door on the second-storey verandah. The three of them entered and sat at the back wall on chairs that had been immediately vacated for them.

A *peón* standing before a desk at the front of the room was holding up a document as if to read it. Three officials sat across from him, the one in a light linen suit obviously an important outsider. The *peón* spit on his thumb, pressed it to an ink pad, and then stamped his print onto the paper. The official in white cottons, likely the teacher, motioned for the next man to approach.

Another *peón* stumbled in through the doorway, his trousers and shirt soiled and wet with sweat. His melon-shaped *sombrero* identified him as the man they had seen outside. The smell of *aguardiente*, Berrin had tried it once during a rest period in the *milpa*, the real *fire-water* locally distilled from sugar cane; it explained the *peón's* immediate condition. The man kept to his purpose as he made his way up the centre aisle to the desk and held up his thumb in front of himself, then spit. He missed his thumb, and everyone could see that his spit had landed on the teacher's face. He turned and staggered back out of the room without leaving his thumb-print on the document. He was smiling.

They stayed overnight, billeted as planned in the same school basement. And again at ground level. Eileen had remained looking out the window while Berrin brushed his teeth and sat on his cot. He was happy they at least agreed on the Black Diamond cheese, but now was not the time for further discussion on politics. Obvious enough, though, that a connection with the meeting existed, but Augustino had gotten up and followed the inebriated *peón* out the door and the others who remained after the meeting were strangers — as was he — so it was not a simple matter to come right out and put questions to anyone.

The window was without glass or casement, open to the night air. Eileen remarked upon their luck. She would not have been able to sleep below ground that night.

"Why? Can't you handle a bit of depression?"

He saw his mistake immediately, but habit unconsciously ruined his effort at correcting himself, "Sorry, Eileen. I'm trying to raise your spirits."

"You *what?*" Her spurt of anger surprised even herself. She moved from the window and sat in the chair at the foot of her cot, obviously trying to control herself. She burst out half crying, half laughing, then leaned forward, looking down at her chair, as if her emotions were checked momentarily by its image. It was hand-crafted such that the carver's whittling gave a rich ribbed texture to the rungs and legs, its deep blood-red paint dulled with smoke and crazed with age.

A minute passed, only the physical surroundings made sense to Berrin now. "There's a chair like that in my grandfather's house back home," he said, without reflection.

"Thanks," she said. "It's beautiful, isn't it?"

At midnight, she rose and walked back to the window opening at the foot of her cot. Berrin had sensed her need for quiet, and had lain in his cot for some time without speaking, but finally fell asleep. Her feeling of antipathy toward him had abated.

She rested her arms on the cement ledge. The air was damp and cool, like those late frosts in Canada that nipped the first buds of spring.

She peeled her banana and took a bite of it. The silence of the night was broken by bouts of barking scattered through the rancho. She listened to the clicking and buzzing sounds of different insects, unaccustomed noises that only accentuated the silence. She remembered the silence that shrouded Augustino when he appeared at their door that morning, an almost jesting silence that crouched behind his words as he requested pills for his niece. The same silence that later surrounded the interior of the hut where the sick child lay, a self-contained silence that nestled deep within the heart of the mountains themselves.

Here they were, snuggled at ten thousand feet under a silence of stars and a moon that appeared to glitter with its carbon shadows.

The widow's hut lay across from the children's playground that spread wide before her, but in the darkness her hut felt no more than an arm's reach away. Through the vertical slits in the wall, she could see the small fire inside. It cast a flickering silhouette of the mother's form between the sticks and slabs, her only protection against the night. Eileen watched her as she rocked back and forth, squatting on the ground, her arms crossed above her bent knees, cradling her baby.

Through the balcony floor above, Eileen heard the soft voices and mild laughter of two men talking in Nahuatl. The night muffled their friendly banter. The men would likely be leaning over the railing and looking toward the widow's hut. The mother's sudden cry registered a moment of respect, and the almost inaudible sobs that followed seemed to be carried away by the renewed stream of their words, words that flowed on down into the darkness of the valley beyond.

CHAPTER 6

A failure of nerve

STATIONED TOGETHER in their project site, their first time together and left alone to their own devices, no doubt at the time that they could make it as a pair.

He reran Eileen's entry in his mind; again, left to their own devices, but not so naïve this time.

She was facing the television, her eyelids almost open, as if her dreams were now caught up in the sitcom. Her face held its youth well.

Not ten years earlier, their first year in college . . . no, it might have been fifteen . . . difficult to make sense of time another life-time ago. The Oblates of Mary Immaculate still ran the college then, when religion defined his instincts before politics took over, followed by cynicism, then despair, and finally the numbness. Perhaps Eileen's fate as well, though no one would have forecast such trajectories in their lives.

He clearly remembered their first meeting. She was walking out of the office of the students' newspaper, *The Clarion*; or, rather, she had appeared in front of him. In his dreams sometimes he saw himself trekking down the corridor to submit his first article and again encountering her as an apparition. He blurted out a question in his soft stutter about the whereabouts of the newspaper office, then cursed himself for not asking something more personal. Not that there wasn't the opportunity, because she seemed to linger over his question, while he hovered that one step short of being close enough to her. She nodded toward the office and said she volunteered there in layout, or did. They liked the layout — it increased their circulation — but her own article was of no interest to them. Her rapid-fire delivery left him stupefied, and in the instant when he averted his eyes as if to spot the office she ducked past him and disappeared around a corner.

He couldn't decide how much this memory consisted of fragments of the dreams that had plagued him for weeks afterwards, or the actual event. But he had been struck dumb, left lost in the hallway, frozen in his spot, and still feeling very much like a fish out of water.

A fish. Appropriate. For the size of the fish was the measure of one's manhood.

But when he peered through the ice on his uncle's lake, his concern had been for the fish. How could they survive with the lake frozen over? Punch out a hole and let the air in. But the ice was too thick. Though the line of the crack showed the ice to be no more than an inch thick, he was not heavy enough to break through. The fish must have hibernated — such was the extent of his reasoning then, perhaps like the cedars that leaned out from the banks. Frozen, but remaining green throughout the winter.

Fish, subliminal. That most potent of Christian icons, like the figure on Saint George's shield, the Vesica Piscis, "Vessel of the Fish," full with the smell of the female was how some ancient scholarly text put it. Or the more metaphysical Oriental version, a pointed oval yoni. A universal fundamentalism, how the erotic has always trumped the rational down through history.

And that tightness there in his undercarriage? Hardly the erotic. He laughed. Still a big, fat, fatuous green kid, canting — can't.

That lingering reservation about kids. But he could come around on this, this time. Although it might not matter in the end;

she's had her kids, even with the few childbearing years remaining for her. Her dark nail polish spoke of other ambitions.

She never needed polishing, nor the nylons. Her feet stuck out from under her overcoat, as small and as delicate as ever, like fragile stilts, a mismatch to her otherwise bountiful body. The same legs that had sped her away from their disjointed publishing venture and into the backwaters of Quebec.

Dreams. They invariably begin as desire and die with the arrival of children. A definite faux pas with that idea. Still the shithead.

If he hadn't got up for drinks, he might have made more progress. Then again, a bit selfish of him surely, with her lying there without her kids. And not that hospitable, either; he hadn't even hugged her when she first entered, regardless of the facts of the story.

He needed to regain the potency. Perhaps follow a bit of analysis if need be, surprise her with that. Too content too long with simply enduring. She likely saw his retreat up north for what it was: an escape, a journey through his own wasteland.

He sat up in his armchair and leaned forward. The tingling in his sternum a persistent reminder. A bit of calisthenics, and he stretched his arms straight out and swung them back and forth. Not much relief in that. He clutched his sides.

How to shed his doubts? Passion, *passio,* the Latin root, *suffering,* and then its complement in Greek, *pathetic,* words that didn't promise much promise.

So many people looking to love when it's what one accomplished that gave meaning to life — a thought no sooner articulated than he saw its anachronism. But it was one belief he'd find difficult to jettison.

His patterns through life . . . he'd need to reconsider them. His patterns, his paths. Paternity. Nothing was *pat* any longer.

Even language was failing him. A frightening thought.

If words didn't hang together, split them apart, like lovers sometimes needed to do.

As they had done, split apart, then split.

Flight ran in his family. He thought of his Uncle Alex's trip to Ireland and his aborted love story. He reached across to his desk drawer, pulled it open slowly to avoid making a noise, and drew out two letters, though he had virtually memorized them already, from his many readings of them, hoping to see some lineage behind his own missteps in love. The letters were written on note-size paper yellowed and brittle with age, leftover relics that his mother had found in Alex's bedroom after his death, written by Alex's Colleen. They were the only real evidence of Alex's love of his life, as his mother never cared to talk about it. Alex's first trip had to have been an escape from the farm as much as a visit to his brother Martin, who was studying outside Dublin in a seminary for late voca-tions — Martin's escape route, that later took him to British Colum-bia as an Oblate missionary, a fisher of souls, where it turned out the fishing for fish was hard to beat. But for Alex, the youngest of the family, his break came during his stopover with relatives in Dublin when he met Colleen and remained another three weeks. Neigh-bours looked after the farm while he was away, the only observation his mother had made on the affair, as if that explained enough.

He skipped down to the middle section of the page facing him. Coleen's handwriting reflected the perfect calligraphy of the time, as sure and clean as his mother's, as if written on lined paper.

> . . . work as usual, and kidded myself that you would be waiting at 5:30. But no Alex, and I felt very lonely. I went to bed about 8:30, had a good cry and a stiff "hooker." Got up the next morning at 6 a.m. and met Connie. She was very disappointed that you were not with us, so I explained the position.
>
> Well Alex. I hope you enjoyed your stay. I hope you were not disappointed we did not have a more hectic time, but you did say earlier on that you were not up to it. And that was enough for me. The rest of the gang were a bit

annoyed they did not meet you, but I don't care the time was too short. And I was very selfish I know to keep you all to myself.

Not up to what? The question cried out to be asked, but the back-to-back, two-page fragment explained nothing. Most likely a family gathering for Colleen. And a failure of nerve on Alex's part when it came to committing himself in public.

Then washed up, his story fit for a barb in the pub recounted down through time in a song and a drink. Desire adrift thereafter, from swell times to swill times, the classic tempest and shipwreck, then back to a surreal land of postdiluvian debris, purged and proper for the remainder of his life.

That epic drive to build and settle down, not to be ignored or belittled, his own recent dream evidence enough, with its Noah-sized flood, Yahweh's cleansing act — if only we all could so recklessly start out all over again. In the dream he had survived, but without the redemption. He easily remembered the details upon waking, being washed up on shore, his scramble through a forest, and then coming to a clearing where a woman in a long dress is stepping out of a cabin carrying a pail.

And spots him.

If only. She walks around to the corner of the cabin, heading for the rain barrel, and he wakes up before she can turn and see him.

Berrin automatically raised the pop can again to his lips. Empty. He eyed the sliver of metal, as threatening as before, but with no dark bud. "The dark waters of Imperialism," Eileen's take on Coca-Cola. A time to be done with as well, when agitation was the sole mark of a committed existence, when he and almost everyone else in their circle wore only black, oblivious to the imperialism of time, to the irony in adopting what a few decades earlier had been the fashion of fascism.

He unintentionally squeezed the can, the bent aluminum crackled, but Eileen only turned on her side. Likely to continue sleeping for the next hour at least. Then another tinny noise amplified by the silence as he set the can down on the desk. Leave the letters as well. Time for his own hooker, unshod was best for his exit this time, and the cold linoleum bit through the holes in his socks as he crept out, clutching his boots.

Stephanie stepped through the front door as he opened it. A flushed face, her freckles redder than usual, such a perfect match for her full afro-like head of red. She pulled off her coat and hung it on the wall hook at the bottom of the stairs.

"Going out, Berrin? It's getting cold. You should put on a coat."

"I'm just off to the corner store."

"Can you pick me up a quart of milk? I have to get started on a grant tonight. That *jerkhead* Jerome didn't get a dissemination application ready as he promised, and the deadline's the day after tomorrow."

"Canada Council?" It had to be, but he couldn't think of another response. Finishing her degree was her priority, and trying to get by as an artist, which included making the gravy-train tour through artist-run galleries across the country with a piece of installation art. The Toole Gallery, the local artist-run centre where Jerome worked, had been the first to present her. Found art was her focus now. He couldn't recall the title of her recent piece, though she had already explained to him how she was wrestling with developing a form of fractured sculpture, somewhere between the visions of the Synchronists and the Constructionists, all this beyond him even as she had added in an academic tone of voice, as if ridiculing herself, or more likely Jerome's curatorial essay on the exhibition, "I'm leaping the margins into the unknown." He pictured Stephanie madly racing down a track, jumping over an endless line of hurdles. And he joked, "Like my mother would say, never look before you leap."

Her sculpture consisted of a rising conveyor belt with computer monitors bolted to it, "like bubbles on a curvilinear form," she said, arms sweeping into a circle as if to encompass the universe. He could see that, viewing it from a distance. And rotating to a taped message that he couldn't quite decipher at any distance, but he had remained too irresolute to comment any further.

"Thank heavens there's at least Canada Council. It's slim enough pickings as it is. Maybe Jerome's punishing me for not being that friendly with him. Go figure. His wife just left him."

"Really?"

"Now the guy's falling apart. He should be fired."

An arts grant was a must to tour her installation; but Jerome's salary also depended on helping artists get them. She picked up her backpack that she'd dropped on the stairs and slung it over her shoulder.

"What about his two children?" Berrin asked.

"Francine took them. He gets a visit an afternoon here and there. I'm with her on that."

"Someone should talk with him."

"Good idea, Berrin. Why don't you? A good guy-to-guy talk, you know."

"I'm not that close to him."

"Look at it from our position."

"And that is?"

"Do you think any woman could get through to him?"

"Well, it seems he attracts enough attention."

"Until they get to know him. But he seems to like you. Tell him to go for the divorce first, then he might get lucky again, though it'll never be with me. He actually hates women and doesn't know it."

She was already starting up the stairs, as if she didn't care one way or the other if he talked with Jerome. He pictured her now like one of her computer monitors rising up the stairs, for she surely would be working late into the night in front of her own screen. He answered after her. "All right, Stephanie, perhaps I will. I could drop in on him."

"Good. And thank you for the milk."

But he couldn't immediately move to turn away and exit.

"Berrin, I do mean it. Thanks. I doubt if it will help, but give it a try. Not to reconcile them. Francine has too long ago crossed the Rubicon for that. But it might go easier for her and the kids."

"Maybe, Stephanie. Maybe. We'll see."

He stepped outside, feeling happy. Stephanie was good for him. She surely would be good for Eileen as well.

CHAPTER 7

Spinning its magic

EILEEN HITCHED UP her skirt and took another step forward.

The water wasn't getting much deeper, the one benefit from the meagre rainfall all summer.

She spotted Berrin glancing back.

"Watch out for that hole on your right," he shouted, but not meeting her eyes.

He could at least have shouted, "Watch out, Eileen." But he hadn't spoken her name once all morning.

And she didn't need a protector, he should know that.

These clear, rippling waters would snap anyone out of a foul mood.

His voice was unjustifiably gruff. Perhaps too much sun. Peeking out from under the rim of his straw hat, his sandy curls seemed singed by the extreme heat.

He had awakened irritable and remained preoccupied all morning, a crusty distemper that transformed his dishevelled appearance into that of a scrappy bear bent on getting back to its den. But Cochitlahuantla was a three-hour ascent straight up that mountain that rose volcano-like before them from across the river, and home was another school basement set among thirty or so huts on top of it.

The march under a scorching sun was reason enough for either of them to be on edge. And yesterday's trip, it had been next to useless; even if the child hadn't died right away, they likely wouldn't have got it down to the clinic in time. Berrin was right about that — and there were many other children needing help, the thought she had awakened with, and with that she had somehow bounced back, her mood improved, or at least her resolve had. But Berrin was obviously affected more than he realized. At breakfast, he had denied anything was the matter. He was keeping it bottled up and she was the one about to explode.

She scooped up some water and washed her arms. The pebbles and sand massaged her feet. The rush of cool water grabbed at her ankles.

This was the river Araña, spinning its magic.

Berrin would not see it that way. For him, the river was the boundary that, once crossed, placed them in their target territory for the summer. She felt a renewed determination; she needed only to make friends with the mountains and its many trails, return to their rancho, and learn how to make tortillas and cook tamales.

Such clear waters.

Not fully four weeks since their group of CIASPers were waiting in town, ten of them impatient to move out to their ranchos, excited by the prospect of riding horses through the mountains, then giddily nervous when they saw that their only mode of transport was donkeys and a few hollow-eyed packhorses. Those sleek horses that the padres rode had disappeared. Then came a final review of the terrain while she stood beside Berrin and looked at an old wall map in the church sacristy that had served as their headquarters and lecture room for briefings on the region. They were trying to make out the route and locate the name of their rancho. She spotted a river that cut across their path, but found no name on the map for it. She wondered aloud how deep it was.

"Likely an easy crossing point," Berrin had said. "The drought has lowered all the rivers. Padre Nómez says it's the Araña."

"Which means spider, doesn't it?" she had responded. "I read that the Aztecs thought spiders were the souls of warrior women." He had shrugged, he didn't know that. "Yeah, warrior women from pre-Aztec times, ready to return to earth and devour all the men who had killed their husbands."

"It's the same the world over, isn't it? There's nothing more fearsome than a woman's revenge."

She stood in the middle of the river, not wanting to move, wanting to move him. "Araña, if he isn't going to lighten up soon, you can swallow him whole at his very next step."

The river was transparent like crystal, with sunlight dancing and riding the waves, stretching threads of silver sparkles around her. Araña's web had caught her soul. The shimmering waters were like numberless spiders scurrying past, delighting in the warmth of the sun.

She waded toward the embankment and sat on the rocks, setting her boots to the side. She still needed the feel of the sand under her feet. Berrin had detached one of his *huaraches* and was rubbing his heel, freed temporarily from its wet harness. He had gone native, shedding his running shoes for these local sandals made from cutouts of car tire treads. He had first spotted the pile of *huaraches* in the market in El Fuerte where they had retreated to recuperate from the killings in Guadalajara. He had seized upon them to humour her, though they seemed more like a self-awarded badge of honour. This morning, he had decided to stop wearing socks.

Berrin took some gulps from his canteen. She drank from hers slowly. He rubbed his heel some more and made as if to speak, but didn't. Although they'd been friends back in Ottawa, the continuous daily contact was new to them both; she had to give it the time to adjust.

Jungle vegetation closed in, the valley floor pungent with fresh growth, despite the drought. She hoped to find some bananas, or, given the height of the trees ahead, some mangoes.

"Berrin, I don't want this baby's death to do me in, but it's almost the last straw. Maybe it's because her husband was also killed. Maybe it's how life went on around her as if nothing had happened. Did you see her this morning?"

"No."

"Her hut seemed to be abandoned."

"I think it was."

"So you noticed. I asked around, but no one knew where she'd gone. Some men were working on the hut next to hers, but they didn't know anything."

The men had been having too good a laugh to give her questions much attention. They were handing sheaves of sugar cane leaves to one of two other men working on the roof. He in turn handed them on up to the other man on the top ridge, who bent to stuff them into the holes left where the rotten sheaves had been removed and then hurriedly tied the new ones down. They had to do a deft jig not to be bitten as they constantly disturbed the rats that lived in the old roof.

"Did you see those men dancing along the top of the roof?"

"No."

"There was a bunch of children laughing at them. They told me her name was Señora Martínez. We forgot to even ask her her name."

He looked up at her and then down at his wet *huaraches*.

She wanted more than his glum mood and monosyllabic responses. "Maybe our problem is what was talked about in the training seminars. Propinquity . . ."

"What? I feel like a caged animal."

She stumbled for a response, "I see." She felt foolish. Their training sessions had been designed to fortify them against a number of obtuse cultural phenomena labelled in precise sociological terms: culture shock, colonialism, indigenization. But they weren't much use in their present straits. She tried again.

"I guess we're used to more distance, being more removed,

objective. And being here alone by ourselves, it's not what we expected."

"I don't know why they keep this Indian project open, when we virtually know no Nahuatl at all. They should have shut down these sites and found us a project with everyone else in the Plaza-flores area."

"But there's an epidemic here." She felt a shiver, as if she needed to shake a chill. She stepped from the shade to the water's edge and dipped her toe back into the flowing waters. If he looked up, he'd see her fully before him.

"And I'm studying journalism, and you're an arts student. We're not getting much done around here. They need doctors, better houses. Joan may be doing some good; she's a nurse, at least. Our only accomplishment here so far is starting up the fencing project."

She turned to face him. "All you guys think about is building things, bigger and better projects. I'm not talking about fences. I don't know what I'm talking about, actually, but it's more than fences."

"You have to talk about fences. Take that kid, for instance. Just letting him die like that." He shoved his foot back into his *huarache* and fastened the buckle.

"You can't say that? The army killed her husband. How can they trust any official — doctor or teacher or anyone else? I'd like to spit on them all as well."

She had heard enough from women in their huts while he was off in the *milpas* all day. She returned to her rock to put her boots on.

He looked over at her. "And that'll do a lot of good, won't it? It's the teacher who's heading up the fencing project. We'd get more done if someone weren't going around at night ripping it up."

"It's the *juez* and his men."

"How do you know that?"

"Why don't *you?* is the question. You're obviously not talking it up that much with anyone."

"The men don't talk much out in the fields. It's not as easy as making those house calls."

"The catechist's wife told me how the *juez* hated our so-called community development."

"The catechist has the church. The teacher and his brothers have the cattle."

"My point, exactly. There's a lot we don't really see. Isn't that what Padre Nómez's been telling us?"

"But if more people owned cattle —"

Berrin stood up, not finishing his sentence. She returned to tying her boot laces. He grabbed his *morral* and pulled the strap over his head. "Maybe you're right. Much like people everywhere, how everyone tries to do everyone else in, to be one-up. Maybe it's this fucking heat that castrates you." He started toward the forest.

He had conceded a bit, but his choice of words also surprised her. Castration? The jungle growth, smothered under a seemingly perpetually vertical sun, spoke instead of the mystery of life and death. But they were at least talking again. She followed him up the embankment and past some palm trees. No coconuts. Maybe there were coconut-producing palm trees and non-coconut trees. But there was no fruit under the mango trees, either. Only the bare ground and the heat and the abounding vegetation.

CHAPTER 8

The divine dancing on delicate feet

CHILLY — but Berrin welcomed the cool aerial shower. Into the leaden landscape we dive, a night without stars — but then it never got truly dark in the city.

Needles of cold pierced his cotton shirt. Should have listened to Stephanie. Which way to go? No dithering, diddering, soon the teeth chattering. Plough ahead. Could turn right toward Somerset Street and straight downhill to the pub. Buttoning his shirt up tight, he took a few steps in that direction, then leaped to click his heels in the air, like an Englishman with a derby and cane, happy, but he almost tripped in landing. Stick with the Irish. Only a pub in that direction at any rate, drafty and no true tippler without the wine. And a dim trip, with no street lights up ahead; a dog pisses on a pole between here and Vermont and the power's down. Must be down at all the cross streets as well. The neighbour's house also in black. Usually home now that they're retired, though they were holding onto the bakery in the Byward Market. He had baked bagels there in his college days, shuffling them in and out of the oven on a long wooden spatula, and when he returned this time it was the first place he dropped into, already anticipating the rays of doughy heat washing over his face. No luck, but they did tell him of this room in the building beside their house. Some private joke, it seemed, since this over-the-counter tip was given in a bouncy, tricksy artifice for which he could recall no grounds whatsoever. However, he'd been thanking them ever since whenever he'd spot their daughter outside his window sunbathing on a lawn chair in their common driveway, bronzing her bikini-clad body between flaps of tinfoil she held open in her lap, neither he nor she too worried about UV rays.

He turned back toward the well-lit Lower Town. Can't want for the wine, but did he need to tread so far afield? He stopped again, contemplated returning. Be resolute, for a change. What else would she do if she awoke but wait for him?

And Stephanie's milk, he couldn't forget that. He continued walking. Giorgio's, another two blocks, might still be open. Stephanie, a riveting listener who read you well, likely even that he was a bit attracted — probably as much by her determination as by her art. A painter before switching to installation work, she still kept some of her artwork on her bedroom walls. He had seen them the previous week. He couldn't remember what took him upstairs to her room but he was glad he had gone. Two large paintings dominated the room, each both about four-foot square. A small sketch next to the door elicited his first response. It depicted the silhouette of a woman stepping out of her bathtub.

"Is this an early work?"

"Yep."

"My mother would have called that just so much filth." He turned and smiled.

Stephanie was seated at her desk reading a document with a pen in her hand. "Good for your mother. Sticking to her guns. But I bet not so good for your sexual education."

"It had its downsides, I agree. And she wasn't alone. Her brother was a missionary for the Oblates in British Columbia. He'd come home the odd summer to help on the farm. He caught me once looking at drawings of fancy, semi-nude blondes in an old art magazine, *Art and Life* — I still remember its date, 1924. I found it in the attic. I thought he'd take the magazine away, but all he said was, 'You need to slay the dragon first, then you can get the damsel.' And then he walked away, laughing to himself."

"Sounds like he had slain a dragon or two more than your mother."

"All I could think of was the picture of St. George in my Sunday missal."

"Another knight on his merry way. Well, any dragon so brazen as even wanting to kiss a girl deserves to be slain." He matched her chuckle as she returned to her work.

Her paintings offered a distraction. Their overall effect was a sense of filling out space, at least that of the canvas, perhaps their most optimistic feature, for otherwise they were depressing, veering to the abstract, unlike the silhouette piece.

"So these are your recent work?"

"Not that recent. I'm done with paintings." She returned to scribbling notes on the document.

The more abstract of the two featured indiscriminate brushes of greys and muddy blues that produced a generally dull landscape. In the centre, a snake-like terracotta pattern crossed upward into the sky, a lightning bolt . . . no, more like slanted stairs or a key-shaped form.

"I see a building, and a key-like form, or is it a broken wall climbing upward?"

No answer. She remained bent over her desk, like the serrated circle of red in the lower right-hand corner of the painting, a balance to the window of turquoise hovering in the sky in the opposite corner.

In the second painting, she had moved toward something more defined, yet more pessimistic. A skeletal figure of a defiant but solitary Don Quixote approached the viewer from the centre of the canvas amid structures suggested by dabs of greys and whites, as if lost in a cityscape after a nuclear blast. Two thin broken lines of black streaked like razor wire across the midsection of the devastated city. Depressing, but more captivating; he wished she had pursued this theme more.

Why she had dropped painting and turned to cold, mechanical wizardry, he couldn't imagine. Conceptual art. Perhaps her head-strong Athena persona had won out over her psyche. Or some failed relationship, someone preceding Tshabalala, her current lover. In any case, her installation work remained inscrutable to him. Much like he must have appeared to her, because he had no ready reason to explain his visit.

He had tried pushing the conversation. "I like this cityscape a lot. You fill up the space well, but somehow you leave it open." Except for the smaller sketch, he realized that the paintings actually became more claustrophobic the more he looked at them. Tortured art, how it should be.

She swung around on her chair to reply. "I have always been in too much of a hurry to fill up the blank spaces. Got to be more patient with that." She smiled, holding her document now on her lap. She said nothing more.

He had no other move left. "Well, see you in the morning," and he apologized for interrupting and made his lame exit.

He waited for the traffic lights to change. Hardly the dragon slayer, though the mystery in that myth still captivated him. There was Manuel Pintao's *The Immaculate Conception*, a carved wood bas-relief depicting the virgin rising out of a slain dragon, which he came across while studying Mexican culture. And there remained Saint George's shield, where his research led him to the Vesica Piscis, a figure often found in medieval times carved into a tree trunk at a crossroads to offer a journeyman a moment of contemplation as he stopped to consider his options.

At his own crossroads. Feeling more like the coiled dragon secluded within his cave, looking out over the human landscape, too taken up for too long in protecting the family jewels.

When the lights turned, two women crossed the street at the opposite sidewalks. Their red capes swept along a few inches above the pavement, giving the impression they were floating over the ground. They were huddling together as they walked, a convergence of spheres in an exclusive universe, their arms gesticulating from each side as if they, too, wanted their say in the conversation. He couldn't catch more than a glimpse of red or blonde hair under their hoods — perhaps nothing more than the rouge cast by the satin lining of their capes. Whispers of laughter hung in the air as he reached the far sidewalk and they swung left in an opposite arc through some iron gates and up stone steps to disappear into a church.

He remembered being inside that church a few times himself. The first time was years before, pulled in by a peculiar nostalgic curiosity that can nip at the agnostic heels of any university freshman. The other was the winter he left Ottawa for the north, on his way to a bus stop for a final Christmas visit to his parents, when a bout of a particularly deep sense of abandonment drove him yet again into the church. The priest, young and bearded, suitably chic and obviously somewhat ahead of his times, had incorporated a slide show into his Christmas sermon. It humoured him, but as the sermon dragged on, he found himself yielding to the mystery of the interior space. As he sat in the darkness, the solitude pressed down upon him, an unwanted strain on his soul that at least confirmed its existence, while in a converse movement he felt lifted upward into the vertical space of pillars and vaulting arches, a balance that revived if only for a moment the innocent hope he had as a child whenever he sat within a church.

The two red riding hoods were likely oblivious of how much they moved with this same mystery.

He glanced to his left and saw the university arts building down the street, its stone siding matching the church's, and a revelation came to him about the sense of mystery in that earlier visit. It was not so much the architecture or even that Christmas Eve service that stopped him in his thoughts, but the memory of a card that fell out of a prayer book that in a moment of distraction he had picked off the pew beside him. He remembered viewing the Renaissance painting and resolving at the time to learn more about Venetian art history. The prayer-card version of the painting featured a prized little cottage-like temple beside a mirror-calm lake, a Madonna on a throne to the left of the temple, a ponderous St. Peter leaning on a fence in the background to the right, while an arrow-studded St. Sebastian stepped to the centre of the painting, where a few naked children danced hand-in-hand in a circle.

The artist might have intended to make St. Sebastian's blessed state of resignation the focal point of the painting, but it was the children's delight that was remarkable, and possibly most desired. It poured forth, infectious, their joy fresh, too young yet to know desire — but most desired when there's no echo back. He understood it now, the core mythos, mirth fallen like a bird mutilated, unable to spread its wings, earthbound thereafter, until inevitably your own natural lightness becomes resented, and a leaden compliance mutates into that celebrated angelic acceptance that brands most religious icons.

And then he remembered the fear he had recognized behind St. Sebastian's resignation, the sadness in the Madonna's gaze, the inquisitors foreshadowed in St. Peter's face. The same weariness that brewed within all the prima donnas of the world, including those in his own co-op. The artist himself likely had not survived his own inspiration.

He looked across the margin of lawn to the moss-green patina on the stone foundation of the church. Its Manichean beauty surely was what pulled those two hooded ones inside, sealed by the iron-braced door that clanged behind them, the iron likely forged from the very picks of St. Paul's crusading armies, who so treasured the silence of women. He felt angry again, as they also should have been, were they fully conscious of the gangrene that awaited them within.

The journalist in him rose to the fore. He was not aware of many instances where priests were accused of assaulting mature women, at least not since the Enlightenment overtook the fulsome Middle Ages. Perhaps it was this security in itself that lured the caped ones inside.

Or possibly the very darkness within was their magnet, sidling up to undeniable powers in the underbelly of life. The devil in us, his mother's expression. A thought that turned his mind to Tshabalala, his mystery likely an antidote that Stephanie sought, given the slant of her art. An escape, a resurrection, the man did revive her spirit wherever they were together. And Eileen, from the crackup in Mexico to the crackpot Jeff, now needing to escape herself.

And as for himself? Not that difficult to pin down the diabolic powers at work here, either. There was his stint in the seminary to consider, similar enough to his mother's convent phase. Family pressures? His father was never that insistent. The patriarch would be his grandfather, caught in a photo at the farm during the mandatory Sunday rest day, seated in front of the verandah on a chair under the apple tree, arms crossed on his chest in his black suit and white shirt, his face stoic with its bushy moustache, staring inscrutably into the camera's eye. Likely the nudge behind his mother's vocation, and for her choice of the Dominicans, whose historic mandate was every Catholic's divine mission, "Keepers of the Holy Grail." The Dominicans, more rightly the Dominators, the *Keepers of the Thought Police*, something she wouldn't have known at the outset. Nevertheless, before taking her final vows, a slipped disc in her upper back left her bedridden for weeks. Spinal surgery was the doctor's recommendation, followed by the final orders from the Mother Superior: The church needed healthy troopers.

Was it the unchallengeable rules that drove her away? he had once asked her. Or perhaps in the end, Fall River, Massachusetts, was simply too far away from the farm?

"Oh, I don't know. It was just against my nature. And then seeing myself stuck in a wheelchair for the rest of my life, it didn't strike me as a good idea," she had answered.

They had both escaped in their own ways.

CHAPTER 9

Fighting for his life

THE PREPARATORY SEMINARY had been an exciting change for him, beginning high school and too rural to know the alternatives. And leading to ordination, the inevitable outcome that he never gave much thought to; enough that it was his mother's wish. However incongruous, given her own break with the convent, her faith in the Church itself remained intact. In his eager innocence, he welcomed the prospects, living in the big city of Ottawa, with the traffic and theatres and restaurants, then the unexpected pleasure he found in the symmetry of the multi-storeyed seminary with its crenellated roof and stone walls and its domineering St. Patrick statue in the alcove above the front entrance, all evoking the mysteries of a Medieval quest. Being a resident in the boarding school brought him new clothes, a bed with a side table, pyjamas with bathrobe, and the showers that came with the unfamiliar questions posed by a room full of naked bodies. So unsure was he of the situation that he had asked the dorm priest for permission to enter the shower. Then came the new-found foreign-student friends at the pool tables, who soon had him snookered into beggary by flipping coins that began with one-penny bets and ended with his losing more than his parents could ever begin to forgive.

"Maybe you need to ask the padre next time for permission to play these risky games."

"I never ask permission from no one," he protested, his effort at deflecting the jab clearly without effect, but the Latinos' laughter proved friendly, and the bet was forgiven with a handshake.

He was still seen as the "model seminarian," inbred, given his parentage, but a condition that left him on the outside and without close friends. One early "friend" he dropped the day this self-assigned elder brother entered his room and reprimanded him for lying on his stomach in bed — perhaps because he was reading a magazine and not a book, but this flimsy analysis left him with a quietly simmering anger about the incident. And over time, the general slant of the place unnerved him, the arid routine and the predominance of collars and dark suits — like a vice squeezing the breath out of him. And then a dream — or rather, the nightmare — that finally broke the spell.

His misfit status peaked for him the evening following the nightmare, when he had gone to see his spiritual director about it. He had hesitated before knocking on his door, an inarticulate fear that turned his stomach. But he knocked and entered. Before he could talk, the priest motioned for him to sit on the couch while he took to his office chair; Berrin found himself eyeing the varnished oak of the chair. His spiritual director swivelled around and pulled a photo from the top drawer. "Here is something I want to show you, Berrin. An immaculate thing of beauty, a piece of art." He held up the photo, perhaps to highlight that it was framed, and handed it to him.

Berrin glanced at it but averted his eyes immediately, preferring to study the specific properties of the photo instead of taking in the picture itself. It was a small black and white Polaroid, cheap, unlike his mother's family photos, where the photographic paper was a high-quality bromide that yielded the sepia tint that lasted for years. Moreover, the photo was framed in thin strips of pinewood lacquered with Varathane, a miniature copy of the frames that surrounded a few large, naïve paintings of white-tailed deer that hung in the summer kitchen of his uncle's abandoned homestead house. But these overwrought technical thoughts couldn't hold off the reality of the scene to which his eyes reverted, almost involuntarily. A boy's nude body lay on a gravel road, frontal view from shoulder to mid-thigh showing a small, wooden pole from a fence or some other shrapnel of an accident that had penetrated the boy's hip about six inches above the genitals.

He gagged but suppressed the urge to vomit. The priest talked on about the perspective and lighting the camera caught. The vice again turned in his stomach, and his analytical bent took over. Who would have taken the photo and why? And why was the boy naked? The photo was of course part of the police officer's routine investigation, and he, the priest, called to the scene. But art?

The priest was smiling, very satisfied for some reason.

He glanced back at the photo and the boy's limp penis dangling in death. He recalled his time as a boy when he first experienced the explicit connection between nudity and art, and his uncle had thrown out his dragon and damsel challenge, with a tantalizing amount of intelligence behind it. Perhaps the framing of the shot was meant to be classical, capturing the sex of the boy at the expense of cutting off his head. But what he felt was a hard pit in his stomach; the brutal reality of the accident snipped any possible stirrings of the erotic.

He remembered the stories that circulated the corridors and rec rooms, such as which boy now was the Wednesday night wrestling partner of the dorm priest. Now this. Nightmares spawning nightmares. Instincts told him to exit as quickly and discreetly as possible.

His nightmare the night before . . . he was in the basement chapel with his fellow seminarians, in the lineup leading down the centre aisle to the communion railing. A senior ahead of him walked through the gate in the railing and took an axe from another boy who was standing on the opposite side. A sober routine seemed to be in progress, cross back, kneel, lay your head on the wooden railing, and wait while the new boy stepped up and swung the axe and sliced your head off, the executioner then walking around to lay his own head down.

Berrin in turn had walked through the gate and done his duty. He remembered it took two chops to finish the job. He then swung back around, kneeled, rested his arms on the railing, and laid his own head down. The railing remained shiny and clean — a bloodless railing, a bloodless act. Then suddenly he was up and running down the aisle and out the door, where he crossed the highway to hide in a construction site. From his stakeout under the flooring of an unfinished house, he focused on the highway to make sure no one was following him.

The terror he felt was the same as when, as a child, he had crouched low in his uncle's old hay barn to look out between the logs while some wolves tore into Goldie, his border collie, who was backed up against the fence along the front field and hopelessly fighting for his life.

But the terror that had set him free.

The next morning he packed two suitcases and left at first light, firmly resolved to be free of the seminary. Nevertheless, he felt like a condemned man in his final walk as he descended the dormitory hallway, hoping to avoid the other seminarians before they had gathered for morning meditation in the end room. But they were already kneeling in their pews and could easily see "the model seminarian" marching out the door, carrying his two bulging suitcases. And then the joy of it: the others now knowing as he passed their open door. He was pleased with himself for once.

He remembered his spiritual director's name. Father Pailey, supposedly a distant relative. And his friend's name, the one whose head he had chopped off. Finnbar. The fair-headed lad of promise had also left the seminary shortly before him. The only news afterwards was that Finnbar was married and driving a taxi.

But he stuck to his studies as if they were a life raft. And in the background, his mother.

When he had entered his parents' kitchen at breakfast time, his suitcases tattled it all before he had time to open his mouth. But the only explanation he could give his mother was his nightmare of beheading and his need to get out of there.

To his immense relief, her response was quick and certain: "You did the right thing. It wasn't your head they were chopping off, it was your body, my poor man."

CHAPTER 10

Lower down

GIORGIO'S WAS CLOSED. Berrin considered his next move. He walked on, down the hill, toward Rideau Street, a bit farther than planned, but there were any number of shops along that main drag. He kept a good pace, his mind still dwelling on his seminary days, trying to ignore the cold. He would have fared better had he joined in on the shenanigans of the Saturday night club when his Latino friends skipped out with their bottles of wine they had probably pilfered from the sacristy during the week and gathered below Hogs Back Falls to sing and howl at the stars, like wolves above the roar of the water, for such was the yelp they gave whenever they scored a particularly difficult shot at the pool table. Fitting then to drop in at San Antonio's, order some Corona as a nod to lost times. A friend owned the Tex-Mex restaurant, the kind of friend who never let the length of time between reunions matter, and who still talked mostly of women whenever they met. And the kind of friend who'd bend the liquor rules to hand over some takeout in a bag. Only a half-block farther.

A pizzeria, a grocery store — he could return later; a tattoo parlour — sixty dollars, two piercings, the lettering in blood-red capitals; paying someone to stab you — the bargain, not once, but twice. San Antonio's was next, with the pink neon cactus in the front window and the hacienda-size door made from some exotic wood imported from Mexico. Tough business, penny margins, and the street's almost deserted.

· A large, middle-aged man walked toward him. Al. A shiver of anxiety shook Berrin, as if he had stepped back in time to Bour-lamaque, the small gold-mining town in northern Quebec and his own exile years. Big, lumbering Al crossed through the light, his half-bald cranium fossilized metallic in the chromatic neon signage. And obviously a helpless derelict now, in his wrinkled, light-blue suit and soiled shirt with open collar, no tie . . . a white tie had always been his calling card for all public outings. Broken blood vessels stretched up Al's neck to a face mottled with large patches of red skin as if pasted onto his chalk-white cheeks. And a receding hairline now, like his own high forehead, a resemblance that annoyed Berrin.

Al had been a fellow boarder at the Bourlamaque Hotel, a French teacher in the local Catholic high school down the street behind their hotel. Himself, he had resorted to working at a small newspaper in adjacent Val–d'Or after he discovered that the gold mines were shut down. Prospecting for the fun of it brought them together. He would take Al on weekend outings to get him out of his hotel room, a soul in obvious need of help. When Al wasn't teaching, he slept, mortally afraid of dying from a heart attack by forty as his father had. He would take Al on a stroll around the abandoned gold mines, circling the desert pan of dried, acidic sludge. Al preferred sitting on the high, road-like embankment rather than scrambling with him down the outer side to hike through the forest. The sun-baked miles of mesa-like wasteland stretching out before Al told him what the surface of the moon was like, one of his favourite topics being his theory that Christ was a lunar alien.

Al's very size prohibited any dodging past him, even for Berrin. When he was face to face with Berrin, he started talking in the same soft whisper Berrin knew him for.

"Hi, Berrin. You know, I'll soon be a millionaire. I'm suing the Liberal Party over my engine they stole. The suit is with my lawyers. Joe Clark was kidding me about it yesterday, calling me a millionaire."

Another of Al's topics, his revolutionary automobile engine that got a hundred miles to the gallon; Berrin recalled his own dad telling these stories, how in the early days of the automotive industry these inventions were suppressed by Big Oil. Al had provided good material for Berrin's first stories, such as the morning he arrived early at school and, finding the front door locked, grabbed the large iron handle and yanked the door off its hinges. Alien powers of the abducted, Berrin had joked, but Al's sense of humour had obviously also been abducted.

Al leaned in closer to maintain secrecy. "I have to be careful. The last time I was in Toronto to see my lawyer, the police tried to arrest me."

A car pulled up beside them. A girl alighted, wearing a black leather skirt and frilled bodice, and up-front cleavage in the cool night air, sized up at once as Al glanced at her, her bare limbs half-lit under the street light. Then Al blinked and retreated a step from Berrin; disengagement time, perhaps recalling another time past, fright bright in his eyes as he turned and hurried back down the sidewalk to disappear into the shadows.

The girl disappeared into the grocery store. Stephanie's milk, Berrin reminded himself again, but first, the drinks. Still he lingered. The girl's boyfriend, in suit and tie, was huddled over his steering wheel, staring through the windshield down the sidewalk. Snug and secure inside his carapace of steel and glass. God-like. Berrin remembered his first car and that first ride on his own, the delicious sense of order that rushed through him, how it encapsulated him and pulled together all his frayed energies, effortlessly propelling him into the world, certain that his magazine enterprise with Eileen couldn't but succeed — all that sense of being from an old beat-up Volkswagen.

The owner's son was working the bar. He ignored Berrin as he approached, and continued wiping down the counter.

"Hi. Is Clyde here?"

"Nope."

"I'd like to have four Coronas and a bottle of house wine. Take out, please; Clyde doesn't mind. It's Berrin."

"No problemo," and he stepped around the end of the bar and marched down the aisle that mimicked a cattle run between rough wooden railings that corralled the customers. Off to phone the boss first, Berrin surmised.

He ordered a cola from another waiter.

Jerome. A call to him now was as good a time as any — the least he could do for Stephanie, and probably Francine as well, though she was only an acquaintance. Stephanie was somewhat right about his friendship with Jerome, but it was his quirky art that appealed to him . . . more like stunts than art, for Jerome never pretended he had the same knack as a Picasso with a bicycle seat and handlebars. Even his view of minimalism made sense when he'd rant on about how there's less and less control over one's life.

He asked the waiter for a phone.

"Hi, Jerome. It's Berrin."

"I don't have time to talk. Why are you calling?"

He didn't expect hostility, but it provided a follow-up. "Why so cranky? I was thinking about you. Stephanie came in and she was furious about something. I was wondering."

"Women. If it's not Stephanie, it's the wife."

"I don't follow."

"She's such a fucking cold bitch, only too glad to be out of my life."

"Stephanie told me you guys were separating."

"Yes, and I'm her seven-year curse that's ended."

"But you still get to see the kids, don't you?" He couldn't remember if Stephanie had told him this or not, but the likelihood remained that Francine wouldn't deny him access. "That has to be a partial victory."

"That's about it. She dropped them off today, said the children needed to see me, as if I didn't know that, but not a word about anything else. Very matter of fact about it all. The same old Francine."

"I haven't seen you in a while, either."

"I'm heading over to the gallery. If you want you can meet me there."

"Sorry, can't tonight."

"Whatever."

"No, really Jerome, I'd like to see you. Something came up. I'll drop by your apartment soon enough."

"Suit yourself, Berrin." Then he hung up.

Perhaps best to leave him alone, Berrin's second thought.

He shoved the phone back across the bar, "Thank you. Another cola if you don't mind. Thanks . . . No sound for the baseball game? Never mind, sorry." Miniature television screens played in the rows of liquor and wine glasses hanging by their stems in the overhead rack. A running commentary poured in from the far end of the bar, where a gang of teenagers played spinning on the stools, probably keeping close to the entrance of the pub. Definitely underage. The shortest one spoke up in a squeaky voice. He was obviously the youngest, barely a teen, but with the poise of a leader, still needing to impress.

"He threatened me with the ruler, the old fart. Just let him try. There's a trick to it I heard it from my grandpa once when he was stoned and talking. You put a hair across your palm and when the strap hits it, it cuts your hand. Works like a charm."

The volley of *no-way, sweet, right on* confirmed this as a bit of choice intelligence. Berrin couldn't imagine much squirming in this sector of town at the sight of a little blood shed by those brats. If tough love was making its resurgence anywhere, it would be here in Lowertown.

He recalled a time in elementary school when tough love reigned. The first day back at school in Grade 2, he was excited to be back with friends and sizing up the new teachers, when the new principal appeared before his class and pointed to four students at random. "You and you and you and you," and he was one of them. "To the front, face the class, kneel, hold out your right hand." And from inside his blazer, the principal pulled out a strap, one swing each, down the row . . . his hand was ablaze. The principal turned to the rest of the class and said, "Now, that's what the rest of you will get if you don't behave yourselves this year." Poor Marie Smithe, she was the best-behaved in the class, why was she also strapped? Marie, who lived in the posh house in the village.

His stomach rumbled, followed by a cramp. The cola was doing its work, and he headed for the washroom downstairs. His pants dropped, his wallet dropped, but he decided not to bother bending for it until he'd finished. The outside door opened. The kids had followed him downstairs.

"It wasn't close." The squeaky voice.

"They'll sweep the Cubs and the Mets."

"A great game. You can't get as close a shave, but a win's a win." Tap water began to run.

"The refereeing stinks. I mean, instead of having a man on second and third, the inning was over."

"Every game I see that ref he makes a boner."

A moment of silence. Paper towels pulled from the dispenser.

"Hey, do you think the Jays'll take it?"

The squeaking voice, "Well, as the great Yogi Berra put it, when you come to a fork in the road, take it."

Before Berrin could catch on, a hand had darted under the door and grabbed for his wallet. It missed, and his foot nicked the wrist on its second try. A sharp cry. He tried then to stomp on the hand, which unbelievably was stretching for a third try at his wallet, but his trousers hobbled his aim. He kicked the wallet farther back against the wall.

He shouted and banged his fist on the door.

"You cheap punks, wait till I get a hold of your butts." They were out the door before he could pull up his pants. He barged out into an empty washroom. The sink was almost overflowing, plugged with the paper towels.

Kids. He realized he had little to fear from them. He might be slow, but the mirror reminded him that his 250-odd pounds and six-foot-two frame was still a strong deterrent.

Making it back upstairs was more daunting. The waiter pointed to a paper bag on the counter, and he paid for his booty. A heavy enough load to carry. He would start exercising if only gyms didn't suffocate him, always smelling of sweat and sneakers. The open street was empty with the night and the phosphorescent lighting, his kind of gym.

But first nip into the grocery store. And a plastic bag for the beer and wine. He turned to enter, but the store was dark inside. The only choice now was to head up to the mall. Which was opposite the Toole Gallery. He could only hope that Jerome wouldn't be crossing his path.

CHAPTER 11

The reaches of desire

SOON THEY WERE out of sight of the Araña, and the path swung up through a forest where a group of men on the slope below were sawing lumber by hand on makeshift wooden platforms. The lumberjacks were dressed in loose white cotton shirts and baggy trousers stained with sweat and earth. Two stood astride two parallel logs as they pulled their crosscut saws up and down in sync with their partners underneath. Another, standing on a stump, grinned as he searched out Eileen's eyes, while she marvelled instead at the stump beneath his feet. The saw cuts met near the centre where the wood fibres had pulled apart as the tree fell, leaving the shape of a porcupine nestled between his feet. Berrin hadn't noticed her moment of reverie, and gave the lumberjacks only a courtesy wave as he lifted his attention back to the path where it turned out of sight up ahead. He seemed intent on keeping the pace he had calculated necessary to get them home by lunchtime.

She had to walk faster than she wished to keep up. Nor did he slacken much when they passed some *campesinos* gathered around a large tub at the edge of a hillside of sugar cane. One man bent over the tub and fed stalks of sugar cane through a set of three large wooden wringers that were standing on end in the centre of the tub. The wringers reminded Eileen of her grandmother's old washing machine. These rudimentary ancestors were turned by a haggard donkey harnessed to the end of a pole that was connected to the top of the centre wringer, leaving him to circle in a constant cloud of dust. Off to the side, two other men stood next to a steaming pot, attending to the fire under it. One youth, barely a teenager, reached down into the pot to poke a stick of sugar cane into the syrup that he then began licking. A dozen or so bricks of the dried cane sugar lay stacked in the shade of a small lean-to of sticks, each brick tightly wrapped in banana leaves. She wished Berrin would have stopped; she wanted to talk and suck on a stick with them, and maybe prepare one of those tidy bricks herself for a gift back home.

In a half hour, they had risen above the fields of sugar cane and were threading their way through waist-high corn, small, parched cobs clinging as barely to life as to the steep mountain slope. Up ahead, a lone *peón* moved down the path toward them. He carried a torso-length bag of corn on his back, his machete swinging loosely from its shoulder strap. His clothing was cut from flour sacks, the red lettering faded but legible on his chest, *HARINA DE HIDALGO*. He stepped off the path to let them pass. Next time, she resolved, they would have to step aside sooner themselves, but there was nothing to be done presently but hurry past him. He heaved his heavy burden higher onto his almost horizontal back and adjusted his leather tumpline. They bowed to him in turn and continued on in silence.

The sun was now at their backs, but it bore down as if they were its only prey. Eileen's skin burned even under her blouse. The climb got steeper, the path rockier, and her breathing heavier. The parched air was cleansed of any other sound. Birds were a rarity. Wild animals must have been hunted to extinction ages ago. Her weariness pressed her to the ground. Her thighs ached. It was obvious that she was not as used to these treks as was Berrin. Her distress came out as a deep sigh. Would she ever become acclimatized to these heights? she asked herself, her lips shaping the question but no sound coming out.

Berrin seemed to notice her fatigue and slackened his pace.

The ground ahead was a steady rise; she needed only keep to a steady pace. The land's pungent sweetness replenished her strength. With each flat-footed step she took, she felt she was planting a kiss firmly onto the parched earth. She hadn't been told about this closeness, how the heat of the day could envelop you and the humidity of the night penetrate you, the earth like someone's body beneath you. She looked up at Berrin. Only a slice of his determined face was visible; his straw hat had slipped to a comical angle on his head.

How had she measured closeness? How had he? To sense it, to survive it, you needed to be open, to be opened up.

She found herself submitting, drawn into the depths of the valley below, into the stillness. A new landscape was unveiling itself. There was more to this land than the mothers with their dying children. There were the women bent over their *metates* grinding corn, a child happy with the toy that her father had carved for her, fruit as sensuous as sin, raw images almost too tender to be touched.

The path levelled off and joined another. She recognized it as the one that their donkeys had followed some weeks before while transporting them into their ranchos. And ahead, the path swung upward again. Again, the abrupt rise of rocks. Last time she'd been totally petrified, gripping her donkey with her legs and bending forward with nothing to hold onto but its short and bristly mane as it balanced on the loose rocks, moving ever so slowly and kicking at another rock higher up for a foothold, steadily picking his way behind the donkey higher up, both seemingly oblivious of the near-vertical drop beside them.

She smelled the rubber of Berrin's *huaraches* as she bent forward to grip the rocks, almost kneeling to mount the steepest middle of the ridge. The strap fell down his heel, revealing a blister that would soon break. The muscles of his calves bulged as he pushed up over the top. He turned and offered her his hand, and she gladly took it.

Once over the rise, she brushed at the streaks of yellow earth that stained her skirt. Berrin stared, perhaps in wonder at how the earth blended with the burnt-sienna tones of her dress, but said nothing. She sat against the embankment beside him. The earth breathed its sweetness born from centuries of cultivating corn. A breeze started to blow. Dark clouds were gathering at the far end of the valley.

"Berrin, remember that old folk tale of the man who lost his shadow? Well, I think I have found mine here."

"How's that?"

"You know those bright ideas we started out with? Tooth-brushes and aspirins . . . better hygiene. I think chewing on sugar cane is probably as good for your teeth. Certainly tastier, and it gives some energy for tramping up and down these mountains all day in the sun."

"This hellish heat must be good for something. It's like quick-sand. I feel I'll melt and dissolve into the ground if I stop just to take my breath. You're lucky—you seem to tan so easily. I just burn."

"I'm burning up as well. If my parents knew what it was like here, they'd have a fit. I think they see Mexico the way the Victorians saw India: an exotic retreat. At least my father would." She hesitated, glancing down at the hunter's knife that Berrin had begun wearing in its sheath strapped to his belt. "And you do, too, though in a different way, don't you? I mean, in the way that it's a challenge."

His eyelids fluttered, the only evidence of his surprise at her question. He blinked a number of times as if to regain control.

"Challenges run in the family. My uncle Alex's was how to raise beef cattle on a field of rocks cleared out of the Gatineau hills, certainly as good a challenge as taking on these mountain slopes. 'Hamburgers'—his brother out west put him onto beef cattle, the wave of the future, just like here, it seems. But he was never cut out to be a farmer."

"I see. My mother's French, but my dad's as Irish and as stubborn as you."

He looked directly at her, expressionless, as if deciding something. She was from Masham, a village up the Gatineau River as well, but mostly French and therefore never much a part of his world.

"You're right, I guess I can be stubborn." He looked down the bank they had climbed, not a deliberate posing, lost perhaps in what he was about to say. "My dad once told me a story about my grandfather, actually the only story he's ever told about his dad: one time, before there was a road, he had to carry a sack of flour up the trail from the mill in Wakefield to his farm, a good fifteen miles north, and he met a bear. Which, of course, he killed after it tore open his sack of flour, though I never got any of the details."

Berrin believed the story, she saw it in his face. One of many stories that held the seeds of progress, fragments for the future, needed if you were to fortify yourself and not weaken. Some form of grounding; she needed it herself, so why begrudge him his sentimentality? But it was a different story in this part of the world. She wanted to say this to Berrin, but his looking away now stopped her. She might even have mentioned that she had followed his suggestion and read that book on the Conquistadors, though only the one; she hadn't the stamina for another analysis, pre- or post-Columbian. They only succeeded in dulling your senses, not least one's common sense about these matters. The most generous view she could take of Columbus was that he was a primitive celestial navigator. Sooner or later, someone else would have stumbled onto the new world; he didn't even know how to use the navigation instruments he had taken on board. His millenarian dreams of venturing into the unknown amounted to little more than self-promotion, with no regard for where he went or whom he hurt in the process — and certainly, travelling out to sea so far away from home carried the promise of returning home a wealthier and more mysterious man.

She glanced across at Berrin, who wiped his brow and looked up at the clouds. He wanted to get things done; but *Not so exotic after all, was it? Fighting disease and illiteracy and poor hygiene.*

She then looked away as well, but downward. The Araña was now nothing more than a ribbon of foliage that hemmed the base of the mountain slopes. The cornfields swayed in sweeps of shadows and yellow light.

"Eileen, it'll be raining in a few minutes. I remember there's a growth of pine farther on off to the side of the path."

Moving on again. But she did feel better. He had at least addressed her by her name.

They hurried along. The clouds rolled down the valley, almost at eye level. They would soon be literally dodging the angry thunderbolts of the gods. Berrin stepped off the path and they crossed a stretch of blackened earth where the bush had been burned to prepare another slope for seeding corn. The tall pine trees ahead seemed an aberration. The ground under the trees was bare but for an abundance of yellow needles that converted the grove into a magic hollow of amber.

Berrin flopped down beside a tree against the slope. Eileen sat on an upturned root below him where the ground levelled off. A mist settled, and warm drops of rain fell. Given the heat, the threatening storm was dissipating as quickly as it had formed and the shower would again be brief and gentle.

Berrin took off his straw hat and flipped it onto the stem of a broken branch above his head. He looked up at it and sighed.

For a while, they sat quietly, listening to the drizzle in the trees. She found herself growing slightly perplexed, as you would when you had waited for that moment when happiness might catch up with you and it finally might have.

Berrin broke the silence first. "Wouldn't a highway and a bridge or two really improve this place?"

"You do like your modern conveniences," she quipped back. She remembered their first pit stop inside Mexico, in Monterrey, after three days of McDonalds, Colonel Sanders, Big Boys, and finally the Taco Bells during the last leg of the bus trip through Texas. Their first Mexican meal, and what does Berrin order? A hamburger. He must have been the only one in her group who didn't lunge for an authentic burrito or enchilada. But she detected a new tone in his voice, a note of self-mockery that was both charming and disarming. "And where are those hamburgers? I'm hungry."

"Good idea," he laughed, and reached into his *morral*. Lunch would be the two eggs he had hard-boiled in the morning and a couple of badly tattered tortillas, enough to get them up the remainder of the mountain and along its summit to Cochitlahuantla — and home.

When Eileen had finished eating, Berrin passed her his canteen.

"You won't get much holding your mouth open in this piddly drizzle."

"I could always wring out my blouse."

"Now, that's an idea."

She rolled onto her back and propped herself up on her elbows. Her head dropped back and her hair fell away free. Overhead, the trees disappeared into the slow tumult of clouds.

"It's really such a beautiful country."

As if in answer, Berrin moved lower and leaned against a trunk.

Her blouse stuck to her skin. She looked down at her chest and thought of the mother's wet blouse. She tried to imagine herself larger with milk. No, she wasn't ready. And if reincarnation was real, that child had best return to its own mother. She wondered about that possibility; who could be the father and what would its chances be another time around?

She combed her hand through her hair to wring out the rain and dropped her head back again so that she was looking up at Berrin from an inverted perspective. His mouth was open, like a sunfish hovering in the rain.

Then she saw it. His eyes betrayed the expectancy, with the eyebrows dangling underneath in an incongruous manner, a desire that she should have detected earlier, and that she had misjudged all through the morning.

She sat up and hugged her knees.

"You know, Berrin, last night I couldn't sleep. I remained at the window to wait with Señora Martínez. Afterwards, I returned to my cot and you stirred in your sleep. I shone my flashlight across the room at you. You know you had kicked your sheet off?"

"I see. Well, I can't sleep with any clothes on."

"But you were awake, weren't you?"

His look fell from her chest to the root beside her. "It's not what you think. A dream woke me up. I think I kicked at something in my dream. But I did wake up. I guess it was right before you shone the flashlight at me."

"Tell me about the dream, then."

"I don't often remember them. But last night I was in bed with you."

"I could see that." She laughed, lightly.

"There was no sex. Not yet."

Yes, she knew. And she feared that she might need more time as well. "So I guess we were only talking. And then you kicked me out of bed?"

"No. A crack opened up in the bed and we fell through into the basement."

Her laugh burst out of her.

"Doesn't make sense." He hesitated as he began to blush. "How could we fall? Since we were already sleeping in a school basement? But I guess that's how dreams are. The place felt dangerous, as if full of tarantulas. And then there were these women, naked. One of them started to approach me. I couldn't stay, I told her. I had things to do."

Yes, she thought, the Araña *was* taking her revenge.

"I find you and we head for the stairs. Something is closing in behind us. You are through the door when I look behind and see one of the women transforming into a huge tarantula. The crack of the open door is getting smaller and smaller. I kick at her, or the spider, I don't remember, then I wake up."

She lowered her head. She had wanted to crawl in beside him, right after coming from the window.

He remained frozen in his spot.

She looked up at his hat hanging in a most nonchalant manner above him, as if waiting for him as well.

"Berrin, it's strange, but you probably had your dream around the same time the child died."

He looked at her, a blank.

"Souls can hang around for some time, waiting for a chance to be reborn."

And beseeching us, or acting as mirrors on the reaches of our desire.

"But you see, they never have much time to wait, and when the moment passes, they turn into devils."

His puzzled look remained unchanged. Her mood dropped. If only he had invited her into bed, instead of turning over and away from her.

She wanted to approach him. On all fours.

It was he who shifted his weight onto his knees, then somehow holding a position somewhere between rising and sitting back on his heels. But, she thought, she could move closer, come face to face with him, straddle his thighs, cradle his head between her arms.

At first he would need some direction, she told herself, his hands following her spine upwards and tickling her ears. She could spread her arms out as a bird does when ready for flight. He would touch her upturned chin and follow the trickle of rain with his finger as it ran down her throat and between her breasts.

The light breeze, their skin wet, the anticipation. She knelt as well. He was one of those guarded animals that had long since disappeared from the sierra. She shivered and rose higher on her knees, easy on the spongy earth, the unquenchable earth.

He fingered a button on his shirt as he scanned the treetops.

If we were only less afraid of dreams. The thought clung to her like her wet blouse.

She pictured Señor Ramirez in his mad rush toward the forest, a sharp contrast to Berrin's present immobility. She was about to stand when he reached over to touch her arm. A spark of electricity tingled her skin where his finger touched her. He moved toward her, his body tense. His hand trembled.

They hugged. She could see the ridge of his spine visible under the collar of his shirt as it curved downward. The soles of his feet were white and smooth. He had jettisoned his *huaraches*. His soles curled backward with his toes at an awkward angle against the rise of the ground. One heel bleeding.

CHAPTER 12

The mysteries of the Toole

THERE WAS NO JEROME in sight as Berrin walked past the walkway that led from the street into the arts building, formerly an old Bytown courthouse. As he continued down the sidewalk, staying close to the low stone wall that fronted the building, he looked through the iron fence topping off the wall into the front courtyard, where some youth were smoking up at a picnic table. Next he passed the International Youth Hostel, the former jail, and his last resort had he not lucked out on the student co-op. The tall walls surrounding the prisoners' exercise yard next, the last hangout for the unfortunate Patrick Whelan, the putative killer of Darcy McGee, he must have had this thought while circling around in there, with a hanging awaiting him. Canada's last public hanging, now a parking lot. As he approached the Laurier Bridge, he spotted the bedrolls and scattered plastic storage bags of streeters high up where the embankment levelled off under the overpass. No dogs.

He only needed to cross through to the university parking lot, take a shortcut through the campus, and be home in five minutes.

A familiar giggling echoed from beneath the overpass. Eileen and Stephanie dropped into view from the low embankment on the far side.

He waved in response and pulled the quart of milk out of the bag that he clutched to his chest.

Stephanie shouted, "Thanks, Berrin. I guess I could have gotten it myself, after all. I'm giving your friend a quick tour of the artist centre. I forgot the Canada Council application forms." She glanced over at Eileen. They smiled, old friends already.

"And I thought I woke up to an empty house."

"Sorry, Eileen. I went for some drinks . . . It took longer than planned."

As they turned back, they merged into a line of youth heading through the stone pillars of the entrance to the courtyard, and the Toole Gallery. A spiked bright-orange Mohawk caught his attention. Everything else about the man was black: jackboots, belts, leather trousers, save for the silver studs on his vest and the row of giant safety pins down one sleeve.

"Looks like an event." Berrin said.

Eileen brightened up. "A night out, it's great."

Stephanie pushed through the glass doors into the foyer, and they followed as she bounded down the steps into the semi-basement that housed the gallery. As the warm interior air hit him, Berrin shivered; he hadn't realized how cold he was. Instead of following the crowd through the gallery to the Toole Club in the back, Stephanie turned right down the hallway. Laughter burst from within the first office. Berrin knew most of the crew, Jerome, Barry, and Jill, but not the teenage girl dressed in a loud, flowery blouse and black tights.

Jerome was sitting astride his antique oak desk at the back corner of the office. His loose-fitting black suit and white shirt hid his pudginess. "It was a prop in my video. But you're right, Jill. We have to find a better setup for the poor guy." He was looking at a quart-size fishbowl that sat on the window ledge at shoulder level behind him, filled with water and containing one lone goldfish. He had his hand over the top as if to stop the fish from jumping out.

"I think he needs a mirror." Barry laughed, decked out for the evening in his blue suit.

"He needs a companion," from Jill, with the body of a pug,

short, plump, and solid, though her face had the perfect roundness that luckily would keep its beauty, perpetually young and attractive enough. She leaned against the wall opposite Barry. They usually attended these openings together, but tonight their relationship wasn't much on display.

"He needs a bigger budget," Jerome said, the priority for him. Being an artist turned videomaker, he would barely be making ends meet as administrator of the gallery.

"He's swimming in circles," Berrin said, as he turned to Stephanie and smiled.

"If the fish doesn't starve, it'll die from the heat coming off that rad," Stephanie said, and reached for a pile of papers on the wall rack inside the door. Not finding the forms, she turned to leave.

"Wait up, there." Jerome caught Berrin's eye with a smirk more than a smile, and grabbed some brochures from a desk. "If you guys are visiting the gallery, here's some pamphlets on the exhibition — but we've run out of Stephanie's."

"A peculiar smile, isn't it?" Berrin whispered to Stephanie as he followed her out.

"Quite perceptive, Berrin, and pay attention to the liar embedded in that word."

"Oh, Berrrrin!" Jerome called through the glass partition, and Berrin stepped back through the doorway. "Can you give me a hand later on? I need help hammering some shipping crates together. Stephanie was paid to prepare the paintings for shipping back to Newfoundland, but she used only some cardboard and a bit of Styrofoam. She's so impractical." Then, bowing toward the blousy leotards, while remaining seated on the desk, he beamed, "Berrin, meet Elise, our new student placement."

"My pleasure," and he shook hands with her, catching her heavy French accent in her "Thank you." Jerome's slight blush underscored the unstated point of this introduction; one of the perks of the job, a steady turnover of wide-eyed innocents. And French as well, perhaps to replace Francine.

"Sure, Jerome, but can it wait until the weekend?"

"I can lend a hand," Barry said, freeing Berrin to leave, and Jerome nodded and looked down at a stack of papers on his otherwise bare desk, as if considering some pressing work.

Berrin turned as the sound of running feet came down the hallway, and a young man appeared at the doorway, bent forward in a crouch, a toothy smile and silver goatee pointing to his hand. He had thrust it forward to present a vacuum-pack cellophane bag hanging from his fingertips. It contained a dark, sausage-like object.

"We've got it, Jerome. By courier. Isn't it beautiful!"

Berrin didn't need more than a quick glance to recognize his prize.

"A turd?"

The skeletal ghost of a man turned to disappear back down the hall, his footsteps finally fading into the gallery and headed for the club, obviously very delirious about his procurement for the upcoming exhibition.

By courier? Berrin's expression as he exited the room was one of bemusement, but he kept his tempting offer to himself. He found Stephanie in the video office, leaning over the glass-topped coffee table, flipping through some papers, while talking in rapid fire to Eileen standing beside her.

"The kids are with Francine. He's a jerk and totally losing it. She just left him, and already he was hitting on me this afternoon." A few pamphlets went flying onto the floor. Berrin picked these up and dropped them with Jerome's handouts onto a side desk, then set his bag of milk and wine on the table, glass tapping on glass. Stephanie looked up at him, then back to Eileen. "Screw the wife's best friend."

There was to be no avoiding the fray. "Maybe he doesn't know you have a new boyfriend, Stephanie."

"Oh, he's met Tshabalala." She walked back to the filing cabinet in the corner.

"He asked me to help him build some crates."

"I told you, he's a liar. Those crates are done, but he hasn't bothered to look. He's up to something else."

Another concocted story on the fly. Stephanie had warned him about Jerome's stories, face-saving fabrications that always put someone else in a bad light. But you had to marvel at how well he held his audience, even adding to it.

"I agree, Stephanie. But seeing he's into the separation shenanigans, he has to have his troubles keeping on top of things."

"He's a gossip who takes his smoke breaks every half hour and doesn't give a damn if the place goes belly-up. And no one on the board sees it. Spread some paperwork across your desk now and then, look busy. He's a mess, but it's not because of the divorce."

She lifted a small, black plaster statue from another pile of papers on the windowsill, glanced at them, and raised her hand in triumph, "Got them," then replaced the statue. The fourth monkey with his hands crossed on his belly.

"Stephanie, there's your gargoyle."

"You're right, Berrin. How could I have missed it?"

The monkey was the trophy for the best short documentary screened at the local Spool Festival operated by the Canadian Film Society. Jerome hadn't won it as he had hoped . . . *Do No Evil* . . . fitting. In a recent dream, Stephanie found herself sitting in a professor's office at his desk, editing some material for him. Jerome enters, lifts her up, now transformed into a dark statuette, and places her on the top shelf. She had recounted the dream to Berrin over the breakfast table: "A trophy — that's exactly how he sees every woman."

"Eileen, I'll show you the gallery. There's a few installation pieces still up. Mine won't be turned on — Jerome says he wants the attention on the performers in the club. I wouldn't dream of competing with them in any case. You'll see what I mean."

Though he knew there was a fridge in the club, Berrin decided to leave his bag of drinks on the table; it didn't look like they'd be staying long.

A few of the gallery lights along the entrance wall were left on to make for a safe trek through to the club. A small crowd of patrons had spilled out of the club, sipping their wine and congregating. The gallery walls were bare. In the centre of the rectangular room lay a medium-sized cedar canoe with wings attached to its middle, constructed out of equally beautiful cedar strips.

Eileen looked puzzled by the spectacle, then exclaimed: "Ahha! *La Chasse-galerie, Acabris! Acabras! Acabram!*"

Berrin remembered. "Eileen, this is the English version. With wings you can fly and get high and never fall."

Eileen laughed: "Yeah, show me an Englishman who never falls."

Stephanie listened, but looked undecided. "You know," Berrin explained, "the bewitched canoe in Quebec folklore."

She then laughed as well. "Ahha. Well, Eileen, I don't know what my installation will remind you of, but anyhow, it's over here," and she headed to the far corner of the gallery.

Eileen walked around Stephanie's installation, four bulky, blank-eyed computer monitors attached to a ladder-like conveyor belt, the two underneath hanging as if on meathooks.

"I'm sorry, Eileen. It's a piece of junk unless it's operating. It moves around to a sound track," Stephanie explained as she rotated her arms in the air, then dropped them to her hips.

Her piece looked somewhat sad, Berrin thought, being abandoned in the semi-darkness, but if he had to choose between the canoe and hers, he'd still take hers. He wondered about the source of her inspiration — and how much is often lost in the execution. It could very well have come from his uncle's farm, so like the old hay-bale elevator that stretched up to the top mow through a hole in the side of the barn, now abandoned to time.

He remembered his mother; he was supposed to phone her.

Stephanie spoke up again. "Eileen, I like what you said about the canoe. I wish I had made mine somewhat whimsical as well. And I wish you could have seen it working; the new exhibition is going up right away. Jerome didn't even give me a decent amount of time to tear down. I suppose I should do it now while I'm here."

"I could help," Berrin said, without a moment's reflection.

"I wouldn't hear of it; you're hosting your friend. I'll find someone in the club — there's a good turnout tonight."

Cheering erupted from behind the gallery's wall, and they saw the reanimated patrons across the room crush forward into the club.

Stephanie turned to Eileen:"The new exhibition is called *Scatology*. Jerome sees it as a broadside to art. The full title is: *Scatology, the Crock of Contemporary Art*. He claims it's a critique of the sorry state of popular art in galleries across the bourgeois world. But it's as much a verdict on his curatorial skills."

More applause, and they decided to move as well toward the club's entrance. The crowd had parted to give space to a collection of chocolate cakes aligned in a row on the floor in front of the bar. The stage area up ahead was in darkness. A woman, wearing only a red plastic floral apron, stepped from behind the bar, then marched down the row, stomping on each of the three-layered cakes. She walked straight ahead into the darkness of the club area to renewed applause.

Eileen whispered back to Berrin. "Too bad, eh, you didn't have time to bite into those cakes." Berrin nodded, successfully restraining his laugh.

Stephanie had ignored the frustrated housewife and moved down the bar toward the main club area. The bar lights were dimmed, and overhead spotlights flooded the stage to the right, accompanied by a cacophony of crashing noises and a blaring soundtrack of a city at rush hour. Three virtually nude people had moved into action, one banging open and shut the vertical-facing drawers of a black filing cabinet that was lying flat on the stage floor. A second sat astride another horizontal cabinet, slumped backwards, hips humping to the rhythm of the banging drawers. The third body, he didn't consciously identify which sex here, either, was gripping the sole remaining vertical filing cabinet and rocking it back and forth while also ramming its drawers to add to the bedlam. They wore the helmets and visors of riot-control police, painted in bright rainbow colours. Bar-coded camera batteries were strapped with black duct tape to their arms, and red and yellow cables led to various parts of their bodies, with additional duct tape in exes stuck on their visors, and other strips wrapped around thighs to hold large, vintage cell phones, nipples also crossed out with black electric tape . . . yes, two women, as well as the one bent over the horizontal cabinet, which required some stamina, their skin too glistening to be men, but the sex wasn't the issue, like Lego people, or cartoon characters whose eyes are crossed out when knocked out, knocked up, gyrating in their orgasmic spasms, rocking back and forth, memories from the cradle in our new world order.

Berrin snatched a brochure from the counter.

"We exist in a hyper-kinetic landscape of technology, corporations skewering us in data mediated systems . . . redrawing boundaries . . . control and communication . . ."

The utter aridity of the language . . . Berrin shook his head. But he was prepared to give the performance its due, the kinesics of zealots. An overhead projector sprayed the on-stage performers and audience with images of commuter trains, computers and industrial parks, office towers, parking garages and ramps, jets traversing the skies.

Heads then turned to the floor area, where a few tables had been cleared away from the front of the stage. A tall, sinewy male counterpart had appeared through the back door leading in from the video facility. This performer was virtually nude as well, in army boots and wearing a black welder's helmet over his head with what appeared to be camera lenses in the eye slot . . . a mystery, though, what codex generated this media arts extravaganza. In one hand, he held what appeared to be one end of a vacuum cleaner hose that was strapped to his torso and ran down his abdomen to a narrow spout that was strapped like a parallel penis to his genitals. In his other hand, he carried a clear plastic bottle half-filled with a dark red liquid. He lay reclining on both elbows on a yellow sponge mattress on the floor, raised the bottle to his mouth, then started humping with his cohorts on stage while blowing into the hose, the plasmic liquid squirting upward, smearing his body, mattress, and floor equally, and spraying onlookers who had crowded too close to this Fountain of Youth.

Whistles and applause.

"The baroque before the fall and decay," from a tall man with curly grey hair and a chiselled, aristocratic face, suited in white linen with a video camera and white tripod bag hanging from one shoulder, the professorial comment delivered to seemingly no one in particular. "Agreed," Eileen said, looking back at Berrin, who nodded in turn. Not enough, he thought, that the avant-garde plays the erotic as vulgar, but why the need to shatter all sensibility? Bludgeon the person and the personal, annihilate nature, man's ongoing quest.

He looked around, half-expecting a few epileptic seizures and apocalyptic visions to erupt from the hematic morass of bodies to add to the clattering din. Enough even to let loose the ghost of Patrick Whelan clanging down the back halls of this basement haunt.

Time to drag one's admittedly tight ass out of here. Would Eileen follow? And Stephanie? They had moved to the end of the bar, Stephanie bent to a stranger's ear.

The orange bulging toque identified the stranger, Tshabalala, his trademark headgear. The Rastafarian garb, likely his escape from Islam. More likely a Christian, being from Botswana. And likely surprised to encounter Stephanie here. Cruising when the girlfriend's absent, then running into this dose of culture shock. He wouldn't mind being a fly on the wall, listening in on their conversation after the night's events.

But Stephanie was smiling and motioning to Eileen, wanting to introduce her.

More sobering voices caught his ear as he turned.

"Where's Marge? She always outdoes everyone at openings by stripping and strutting her stuff on the front sidewalk," spoken in a raspy whisper by the gaunt, grey-bearded man in black leather leaning against the front of the bar, his eyes hidden behind fan-like shades clipped to his glasses.

"The inseminators," a teenager next to him said, a trinity of studs in her eyebrows, cheek, and lip. Her friend beside her took a drag on his cigarette; he wore a silver loop in his earlobe that had stretched it into a respectable bit of African mimicry.

Berrin looked again toward Eileen and Stephanie. They were immersed in conversation with Tshabalala. Time enough to call his mother from the video office.

He passed the canoe; it did elicit memories of the farm and the lake — and his recent week-long dreams of bulls and flying cows, the series still puzzling him. The zeitgeist. The young girl with the studs did support this thought. Bacchus was back with a touch of a tauroctony scene, more fun and spectacle than awe . . . the club's bloodletting a more collective commingling in the ordeal pit. *The Mysteries of the Toole* have been inaugurated.

The office was empty. His bag was still sitting on the coffee table. If only he had a corkscrew. He picked up the phone. Where to call? The farm or Old Chelsea? Old Chelsea, he was supposed to be driving them from there up to the farm. Not long distance.

Silence, but his mother had definitely answered the phone. She'd never talk until callers identified themselves, figuring the onus lay with them to answer first, much like people waving at you from across the fields — they shouted first. He strung out the moment of silence for as long as possible.

"Hi, Mother, it's Berrin here."

"Oh, hi, Berrin." Surprise mixed with a touch of fear in her voice, as if forgetting that someone had called.

"How are you doing?"

"Oh, everyone I can."

"Everyone?" His mother and father remained as recluses whether in Old Chelsea, a skier's mecca this time of year, or the farm, where their neighbourliness never extended much beyond the farm's thousand acres, half of fields and the remainder of bush and beaver swamps. His dad's interest in the farm had narrowed down to the bush part, providing a retreat for hunting and prospecting.

"Where are you at now, Berrin? You know Dad's too old to operate the machinery." They always had called each other Mom and Dad. Berrin was her last remaining hope to make the farm work. Too many incidents had dampened Dad's interest, like the one Berrin learned of on his last visit. He had sat with his dad on the front porch while his mother kept indoors out of the autumn chill. His dad's voice soon dropped to a loud whisper. "My neighbour asked me yesterday if we had an old harrow on the farm he might borrow. No problem, it's sitting up there rusting away in the weeds with everything else. But when I mentioned this to Mom, she lit into me — I had no right to give him any plough. And when I tried to make out the neighbour's phone number on the wall, she walked by and tried to rub the numbers clean, but that only blurred them more. When I asked her to quit, she went crazy: 'bullying her,' I was."

"You still there, Berrin?"

"Mother. Dad there with you?"

"He's on the couch, staring out the window, moping."

Likely gazing at the ridge of Sumac that bordered the front lawn; his silence seemed to speak of a stubborn resignation to life's twilight years, without a bright spot anywhere. Impossible to nail down how such a distance had settled between them.

"And you, Berrin, you're forever gallivanting across the country like a tinker. Why don't you settle down?"

He felt her voice become weaker, almost pleading.

"Mother, I've got a job here in the market. I know you actually prefer the city yourself. Didn't you originally leave the farm for Fall River?"

A renewed uproar of applause from the club drowned out her reply.

"Mother, you'd be sure to enjoy the galleries here. Lots of opportunity to speak your mind. I've come full circle here, back to where *your* uncle started out. You remember, the blacksmith . . . he had a shop in the market, but I haven't found hide nor hair of it yet. And there's the Rideau Centre. Shopping centres are the new cathedrals."

"New cathedrals, me arse." She was having none of his teasing. "Did you ever see a copper kettle mended with an old tin can? You were never interested in shopping. If you opened your eyes a bit, you'd see what's important."

"You're my reality check, Mother."

"Berrin, you could do your writing on the farm. It would be so much cheaper than the city. And with a woman. You were right about Alex. I don't want you to be alone like that."

"He didn't have to be alone, did he? I mean, there was Colleen . . . she did come to visit that once. He had a second chance."

Another story left hanging, Colleen's coming after her own mother died, when she stayed a week or so on the farm with Alex. Her leaving a final cut-off.

"I don't know much about that. In any case, it's families a farm needs, young families."

He detected a note of lingering anger, if not regret, in her voice. But he'd not be getting her version of the story this time, either.

"My prospects were never good on that score, either." Tempting to mention Eileen, her breakup, a ready-made family. His mother had always liked Eileen, despite the *bit of French in her*, as she'd phrase it. But it was best to stick to his cardinal rule, never discuss personal matters with your parents.

"Mother, I was calling to let you know I do want to see you, but I can't drive you and Dad up to the farm this weekend; maybe next."

"You should have married Mavis and settled down instead of taking off to the city as you did."

"You're still the romantic."

"I talked with her on the steps of the church last Sunday. I told her how you visited now and then. I said that surely the farm could foster some coming together, so many lives separate when everything seemed shaped to fit so snugly. Then she blushed for some reason and went shy again. Such a sweet woman. I don't want to meddle, but she would make you a good wife still. You two used to talk a lot on the phone, remember, exchanging math notes almost every night."

"Maybe I can look her up some time."

"The brush-off, is it now?"

"I'll drive you guys up next weekend. I have to go now, Mother. 'Bye."

"Yes, do come by, Berrin, you promise?"

"I promise."

He replaced the phone, leaned forward with his elbows on the desk, and dropped his head into his hands. Spectres of the past.

Maybe the ungodly din in the club was all about keeping such things at bay.

CHAPTER 13

Of ghosts and sprites of the Sheerie kind

A FEW WEEKS BEFORE, he had been sitting with his mother at the kitchen table in the bungalow on the farm.

"There's no denying it, Berrin. I was leaving the chicken coop with a few eggs in a bucket when I saw the shimmering down at the barn, by the pole gate at the corner of it. The shaft of light poured down from the sky, and Alex appeared at the gate. I dropped my arm I was so surprised — I almost lost my eggs."

"The pole gate? That's amazing. It's still like new, isn't it Mother? Ironwood — it can last a lifetime."

"I knew I was wasting my time telling you. Just like your dad."

His dad had refused to take the trip up this time, and neither of them had insisted.

"I'm not surprised Alex was appearing at that very spot." She reached for her deck of cards that sat in the middle of the table.

"But, Mother, the light's likely from the phosphorus in those rotting fence posts lying in the manure and mud behind the barn. It can shine like stardust." Dead wood will glow with it . . . a story his father told him, how on a hunting trip at dusk he had seen an old tree trunk giving off a faint blue light in the underbrush.

"Stardust, heifer dust." She shuffled her cards.

"I remember Alex talking about the Sheerie light. It's like a mist — it hugs the ground on a cool morning or sits over swamps. It's so irresistible, he said, if you wandered into it, you'd be lost to the world forever."

She spread out her rows of cards, keeping her eyes trained on the table, her lips compressed, eyebrows arching to create thick, leathery furrows across her forehead. "You don't believe a word I say."

"Well, I guess it's like the farmer who said: I don't believe in fairies, but then again I don't think they believe in me, either." Not a hint of a smile on her lips. "Mother, you have to agree: The ground below the barn is a bog with years of the cattle going to and from the creek. I was almost pulled in myself when I was a kid, one evening, remember, after a heavy rain — you and Alex had to pull me out, and I lost both of my new gum rubbers."

"'Twas at noon, and the sun was shining, and you got too close to the creek."

"Then that shaft of light must have come from sunlight reflecting off the tin roof of the barn."

"It's so rusted it wouldn't reflect the devil's arse. Alex was standing right there in front of the barn, as plain as day, looking at that old door. My, it's been four years, hasn't it? I never thought to see him again this side of me grave."

"Yes, and wondering who would now be shovelling out those years of packed manure in the stalls." And the main support posts in the stalls still rotting away at their bases; he felt almost guilty enough to replace them himself, something mythic about it, after all. It would be a shame to lose another heritage barn.

"I'm telling you Alex was looking at the door. There's barely any of that red paint left, now. He almost died doing that job."

He remembered the story; she had told it before.

"You know how Alex painted that door? He used a formula his dad once told him about, blood mixed with lime and red ochre from the shore of Marl Lake." She was fingering the handle of her teacup, remembering.

He looked past her out the window to the rise of the far hill that hid the lake. For some reason, he had never walked the original homesteader's road that traversed the farm and circled behind the lake on past the pond called Marl Lake that lay a mile or so farther on.

"That's something I could do today, Mother — visit Marl Lake."

She caught his eye. She'd not be distracted by this detour.

"It's no surprise he'd want another look at that door. He painted it the day he butchered the last of the pigs. He caught the blood in a pail and mixed up a batch in the wheelbarrow while the pig lay on the stone boat up behind the ice house . . . more fun it was to paint the door, but then he had a devil of a time dealing with that pig afterwards."

She paused. These were new details.

"He had to rebuild the fire to bring the iron crock to a boil again. It has to be piping hot to scrape the hair off the hide, you know. He practically wore himself out with all that . . . and in the evening he was leading the old mare into the barn when it reared up and struck the wheelbarrow. He had left it beside the door. The handle caught him in the stomach and almost gutted him like the pig."

"It's not hard to see him exploding; he had a temper." Likely the point when the paint started blistering from the curses he'd let loose.

"His temper matched his spunk, Berrin. You could do worse than taking after him that way, though he liked his reading as well. At least you match him in that."

CHAPTER 14

The public fashion

A TAP ON HIS SHOULDER. Eileen. She pointed to the window with her chin.

"Had enough of the club, I see. I had to phone my mother."

"I'm glad you're still around."

"She wants me to drive her up to the farm. It's becoming a routine."

"Let's go. You look dead tired."

"I was daydreaming about the time my uncle killed a pig. The real, down-to-earth kind of bloodletting."

"Makes you wonder what *this* is all about."

"The stud girl called them 'The Inseminators.' You have to wonder, were they banging the drawers, or was it vice versa?"

"Well, Berrin, it's a bit of fun, that's all it amounts to."

"You're right. You can't criticize, in any case. If anything, it gets too personal and you have to backtrack and apologize and you end up feeling guilty and second guessing, then it's time to give flowers, hold hands in public, return to church." Remnants of old arguments with her, he could laugh at them now.

"Time to down some of that blood-red wine. Let's go."

The fresh air invigorated their walk. Eileen looped her arm into his, like lovers do.

"You seem to be doing all right here in town." She squeezed his arm tighter. He let his other arm fall to his side, heavy, but the plastic bag would likely hold.

"I'm not doing much with my time, Eileen. The writing's not amounting to anything. I've been thinking about all this new technology coming at us, the same, I guess, that's plaguing those poor saps back in the club. I surprise myself getting interested at all."

"So, have you finally switched to using those bloody computers?" she giggled. He forced himself to ignore the extra pitch in her voice.

"Can't avoid the temptation. But I have to write all my first versions by hand. Ever see the movie *Brazil?*" Berrin looked across at her.

"Nope."

"That club scene comes right out of it. The New-Age literacy where everyone's a bureaucrat and can't even write their names legibly. Our house is full of computers and everyone's handwriting's also going to the dogs."

"Well, Berrin, the natural rhythm *was* taking a beating tonight."

"Perhaps we should have both stayed in the bush."

"If only. Neither of us could escape the city for long." She yawned and pulled the lapels of her overcoat together.

They were crossing the empty parking lot leading up to the university. He pulled into himself as well, not from the wind so much as from his memories of the campus. What an eternity that period had assumed as it capped his youth . . . the emotions and turmoil it nursed. And he never belonged; he had felt like another anonymous marker in the mesmerizing centuries of warfare and romance that the college curriculum threw at you. He had studied hard and tried to rise to the challenge, like in the CIASP movement; but in retrospect, it was his own emerging consciousness that baffled him the most, that and the immediacy of the opposite sex. Like her arm now snuggling in his.

"You're right, and now I'm living in a student co-op. It's as if

I've never graduated or moved on. So it's very good to see you, Eileen."

"You need to write more letters — it'll improve your handwriting."

"If anything, the one trend I don't regret missing is the slant on languages that's taken over all of academia here. Deconstruction; Barry's been lending me his books on it. Everyone's *deconstructing* language, shaking it up — that's the word that's sure to trip you up."

"I'll hold on tighter."

"Better to pull apart words than blowing up the world, I suppose."

"You always could find a meaning in anything."

They were now passing in front of the Fine Arts building. Ahead of them, three street people huddled together near a mailbox. Not the regulars, faces too young. Eileen spotted them and slowed her pace.

"Probably in from your part of the country, Eileen. Most of these street kids are from rural areas."

"They seem to be hatching something."

"Likely breaking into that mailbox. You can't blame them."

"They look so lost. I shouldn't have got scared."

"The regulars keep healthy by keeping a dog with them."

It was generally the young ones who made him uneasy. He had found that the older and more weathered street folk with their quirky behaviours interested him more.

"Maybe we should invite them along, give them a meal at least?"

"Those kids would probably piss you off soon enough."

As they brushed past them, their voices were murmuring in unison, "Hail Mary, full of grace, blessed art thou among women, lead us not into temptation —"

The few seconds in which he slackened his pace was enough to confirm that they were indeed praying.

"Right, blessed virgins must never do that," he whispered.

Eileen shot a quick glance backwards, toward the one girl in the trio, her skin darker than the others. "The Black Madonna of the group," she whispered back.

"The pancho helps." Otherwise, her attire was indistinguishable from that of the guys. Jeans and jackets, Jesus-length hair, gaunt faces, and vacant eyes. "It's amazing how religion still reigns as much as it does. Look at all the churches around here. Still blaming the victims."

His night's walk was coming full circle with the looming St. Joseph's again up ahead, occupying the entire block across the street.

"Look, Berrin, there's a sign over the basement door. It's a shelter for women. Maybe they're psyching themselves up to go in."

"The Madonna, maybe. The Mission House for men is down the hill back there."

"I'm glad someone is offering beds for them."

"Bastions against the seedy souls from Lower Town. And you can be sure the bulk of the social service grants goes to providing better bedding for the bishop of the parish."

"It's those poor kids you have to think about."

"I think you're shivering more than all of them put together. I'll stir up a hot chocolate or something. The house is around this corner."

"Great. Feels like home. I wish my kids were here with us."

CHAPTER 15

A leapfrog to bliss

HE STOOD AT THE BACK DOOR of the kitchen, holding Eileen's cup of Inka and looking down at her sprawled on his bed, asleep again; unbelievable. But he felt happy. She had wished her kids were with them. He looked around . . . nothing but books, and he now wanted nothing but her. Sentimental? If only. Her presence brought the room into focus, dispelling any confusion he had about their night on the town. It was she who sharpened his sense of place and belonging, hollow words that he wouldn't have used a few months earlier, borrowed buzzwords of the curatorial ilk: mapping and boundaries, intervals and margins; words, though, that did help him locate his feelings, at least help to corral them and focus — he'd admit that much.

Boots off. Tip-toe to the armchair.

No light needed, a match to the darkness outside. No street lighting this far back of the house, but never as dark as those moonless nights in Cochitlahuantla.

Blessed art thou among women. A universal canon. Surely anyone in his position would not but feel that the woman lying before him was anything but an angel.

His Colleen.

The television was off.

He reached for Colleen's letter.

Connie will write you soon and tell you about her trip. I
have the song "Moonlight in Mayo" for you. And you'll get
it soon. Your prayer book you left on the hall chair, so I'll
send it on later, as I think I'll need to get a Customs Declaration to send it.

Well Alex, I have plenty to remember you, every time I
light a cigarette, or powder my nose. That's every day. And
often. I have started to save all my money so [undecipher-
able] two years. And if you can't make it, I will or die in the
attempt.

Don't forget to take things easy, because I am there
watching. And God help you if you overwork — there'll be
a terrible "mark" on [undecipherable]. This is just a note so
you'll get it when you . . .

The end of the page, the rest lost. And nothing more on that trip
in the second letter, either.

He fingered the brittle paper. "Moonlight in Mayo," then the
cigarettes and powder. Perhaps his uncle was scared off by her
grit, burdened by the same lingering canon that those street youth
rattled off, implying that all women but the Blessed Virgin were
sluts. Difficult to escape the conditioning. Lead us not into temptation, lead us not into the depths, down, down toward Lucifer.

Lucis and *ferre*, the ferryman leading you into the light, a belated
insight that would surely halt any pilgrim in his tracks. *Deofol*, the
Nordic term, more his lineage: *to throw across*. Somehow it felt like
a more full-bodied term, a most definite temptation.

Didn't Jesus himself speak of the devil as the spark from
heaven? A difficult truth that churches spent centuries trying to
hide, suppressing mystics, witches, and all dissidents whose visions
were not to be allowed let loose upon the faithful, let alone affect
the official canon. But even Christ had to spend three days in Hell

before he could rise into Heaven. Try that as a corporate logo, Your Holiness: Christ and Lucifer, celestial twins, shaking hands and embracing.

He recalled the children in the Venetian painting. They circled with such buoyant abandon, still oblivious to the inflexible but clinging devoutness closing in upon them. Colleen, like Eileen, obviously someone who had not lost her spark.

The divine dancing on delicate feet.

He tried to remember who had written that about children. Nietzsche or Rilke? Sounded more like Rilke, though anyone in love with the divine spark feels like a superman.

Eileen's hippie flight to the countryside, to Mother Earth, the same simple hop-skip-and-jump that his uncle had hoped for with Colleen — a leapfrog to bliss.

Hard to hold the faith.

His eyes drifted back to the stack of books on his desk. His writing pad, still sticking out of *Celtic Art*. Beneath it lay James Kelman's novel, *How late it was, how late*. True enough. He looked down to the bottom two books, *The Collected Poems of W.B. Yeats* and *Why God Loves the Irish*.

Surely the Second Coming is at hand.
The Second Coming!

The Second Coming for Yeats had to be Maud Gonne. Or was it Maud gone that fed his spark? A kindred outcry there, neverthe-less; despair's rout.

He could be reading the poem to Eileen. She had always loved Yeats.

Why God Loves the Irish. He pulled it from the bottom of the pile. Something light. Not a particularly notable book, but its faded, water-stained, shamrock-green cover was what had caught his attention when he first spotted it in his uncle's aban-doned farmhouse. For years, old books had been left stacked in the hallway shelves, his nostalgia for them equalling his mother's for her albums of snaps. He flipped to the back pages and grunted in recognition of the theme as he read the promo caption for *My Unknown Chum*: "Clean literature and clean womanhood are the keystones of civilization." He must have read this at some point, his instincts somehow telling him now to reach for it.

What he pictured next was the television image of two lovers lying dead a few yards from a bridge in Sarajevo, a Croat-Serbian couple shot as they rushed to freedom. The woman's arm lay limp across her lover's chest.

Ethnic cleansing. The Bosnian tragedy had been broadcast so often that no one could not but know what levels of barbarism remained in the world — and the media's equating them to a Romeo and Juliet, further diminishing the tragedy.

Cleaning up on the women, while we are reduced to mere voyeurs, TV images screening lives, keeping us safe and distant, no matter what the bloodletting should be telling us. From high in the Caucasus Mountains, television images of Croatian women standing outside their remote but soon-to-be-burned-to-a-shell farmhouses, the same hopeful and enduring faces that he found in his mother's albums. And the same inbred anticipation as she pored over her black and white snaps of the farm, naming the many uncles and aunts and grandparents and retelling a story of each in turn, begetting in the telling his own extended family who had somehow survived their cleansing by famine, still bearing up through her very telling of them.

He glanced back at Eileen. The same determination in her high forehead and cheekbones. Country folk alike everywhere.

Why God Loves the Irish. Why he Eileen? His keystone? That alone would be enough.

He flipped to the front page of the book. A 1916 edition, the author had to be writing his book in the times leading up to the Easter rebellion in Dublin. Did it all still come down to politics? He had had his own share of recent political discussions around the co-op kitchen table about "resurgent nationalism in the midst of a new world order," repetitive arguments that grew so cliché they left you numb.

A New York address for the publisher. The author, Humphrey J. Desmond, possibly a refugee himself. Nevertheless, he couldn't have known the numbness of contemporary existence, the sanitized labs of computer chips and processors, the explosion in communication technologies that paralleled drive-by shootings and slaughter in the schools, computer viruses and superbugs, collateral damage, shared risk, serial monogamy.

Serial monogamy: Berrin's mind felt like a slot machine stopping on these words.

A single woman again and moving on. Serial monogamy, the keystone of contemporary life.

Any culture critic worth his grain could point out the obvious fault lines in civilization. Being rutted out of the primordial family was the original sin. The total destruction that high-tech violence wreaks upon a neighbouring nation engendered therein. The office rage he witnessed in the performance tonight, like road rage, but a more pedestrian stimulant. Or virtual sex while typing with one hand — a fallback option.

His mind was racing again. He took a deep breath to refocus. The central question remained, what had she to fall back upon? His berth didn't amount to much. An old woollen blanket for a bedspread, faded orange and worn (proper bedspreads always reminded him of his parents' bed). But tucked in tightly at the corners.

He had to put a stop to his endless debates with the world. He was swimming in circles, a fish out of water, free. He laughed.

But without a doubt, Eileen's minimal goal would be making ends meet.

With a weary shove, he pushed himself from his armchair, walked around the bed, and covered her with her overcoat. Her fingers curled next to her cheek. She looked like a child clutching a perfect pebble.

Best to leave the bedroom door wide open to let in the heat. He retreated through the kitchen down the hall toward the sofa bed in the living room. He hated sofa beds. And it was brown.

CHAPTER 16

Lapping at the underside

BERRIN SET HIS ALARM, eight a.m.

His new alphabet had been inspired by his digital clock, but its genesis lay with one of his limitations in life, his difficulties in learning a second language. His *One World Language and Peace* meant progress, a complete, international-in-scope, literacy program.

The wide range of letters possible from the clock's digital numbers dawned on him one morning while he lay in bed putting off work a few minutes more. He had found himself drifting back to the mural patterns and panels he'd seen in Mayan temples. The digital numbers were uncannily similar to those rectangular key borders and square spirals. He had begun stringing together the frieze and fret patterns as if he were again a child inventing a secret language. His research was quixotic, following as it did his own circuitous path, which now was taking him through *Celtic Art: The Methods of Construction*, its detailed drawings suggesting a design for a codex that would bridge the gap between his alphabet and that of the ancients.

"Somewhat pea-brained," Stephanie had teased when he ran it by her. He did congratulate her on her wit when she flicked her sunglasses with her finger, "Like my rose-coloured glasses — also meant for the new world order."

And then there would be Eileen's take, time to return to earth.

The thought was enough to sink him again. He rolled onto his side to lessen the bumps from the mattress; sofa beds definitely stuck it to you. He rolled again, closer to the edge of the bed.

And on his back once again, regardless of his virtuous inventions — how else to describe them? Or himself? A cloven-self . . . the classical terms did fit better, bisected by his years of witless effort and tortured writing . . . bereft, and cleft.

And to his left, Eileen was sleeping. They lay side by side on a cot in a one-room shack. They were about to make love when he hesitated, afraid of something. A sound . . . as if a dog were drinking at a puddle outside the door. The noise was coming instead from under the trap door on the floor. He lifted it and saw water lapping at the underside of the floorboards. The water had been rising outside, flowing down from the mountainside. Broken twigs and rotting debris floated on the surface. He peered into the liquid blackness, not seeing a reflection, and realized that the water wouldn't be rising any higher; they'd be safe. Something tapped his shoulder, and he turned to head back to bed.

He awakened to Eileen pulling back his blankets. He had been thinking of something important, then she was sleeping beside him. He smiled.

"Can I crawl in? That room of yours is freezing."

The openness of the living room made him look around.

"Don't worry. Stephanie left with her boyfriend. The others returned a good half-hour ago. I haven't been able to sleep since."

No skirt. Eileen's bare knee was propped on the edge of the mattress, her pillow under one arm and the corner of his blankets gripped in her other hand.

"Sure, jump in. You'll freeze out there."

She smiled. "I don't know how you're going to make it through the winter back there." She pushed her legs deeper into the blankets and stretched out alongside him.

"The books along the walls might provide some insulation."

"They only insulate you from the world, you cuckoo bird."

She adjusted her pillow, then relaxed again. They were lying face to face.

"I hope my feet aren't too cold," she said.

"I'm used to cold feet." They laughed together.

She laid one arm across his chest. "It's much better snuggling up than sleeping alone, isn't it? Hey, relax some. I'm not going to gobble you up."

"I'm just not used to this."

"Surely you're not still harbouring fantasies about me."

"Another neurosis, I guess."

"Neurosis and fantasy do not a couple make. Try putting your arm around me." She grabbed his wrist and lifted it onto her side. "How long has it been!"

"If you count my dreams, only a few seconds ago, we were together in our shanty."

"Dreams don't count."

"Well, then, the last time was in a bar in Val–d'Or."

"With a girl of ill-repute?"

"I didn't give it a thought at first. I suppose . . . I was too desperate at the time. Turned out to be much less than even a one-night stand. The experience did confirm one thing, that sex isn't everything."

"So it's only a princess who can claim this Irish prince?"

"You can laugh, but frankly it was all too bland to even rate a telling. Once back in the bar, I timed how long *my princess* took with another customer; turns out I hadn't done all that badly."

"Some bravado, finally. But don't get me wrong, Berrin; this is only snuggle-up time, clear?"

"I'm Irish, never presumptuous."

"Not presumptuous, eh? Then you can wipe that smile off your face."

"What's the worry? Mid-thirties and I'm single still." A touch of disappointment rose in his voice; he couldn't hide it. He tried to relax. His arm remained on the spot where she had placed it. "I'm above average, though. The average age for us Irish to tie the knot is twenty-seven."

"Bravo again."

"Says I'm not your average easy catch." He grinned, silly, but then she laughed again. His arm was now resting on her shoulder. "Did you know that Ireland recently passed a law allowing divorce, but the surprising outcome is that 80 percent of the applicants for divorce are women? You see, it's as hard getting rid of an Irishman as snaring him in the first place. So, watch out."

"You're still harbouring those big ideas." She gently pushed her finger into his chest, next to his heart.

"Sometimes the big ideas just come. You can't control them. Take my dream just now." He moved to touch her chin and then began winding one of her curls around his finger, then tugged on it to break with the cliché.

"You're turning into an imp. So, what was this big idea in your dream?" She moved her hand upward toward his temple, toward his scar.

He leaned into her neck, "I'll whisper it," and began to nibble her earlobe.

She twisted her head aside and giggled. "It tickles too much."

He lay back, but closer now to her. He touched her chin again, then moved to kiss her on her lips. Again she turned aside.

"Sorry, Eileen." He pulled back slightly. He could taste her smell.

Eileen spoke softly, as if she were remembering some forgotten incident. "We make sex out to be much more complicated than it is. That's what men think, isn't it?"

Not the response he hungered after.

She seemed to push herself back into the moment and hugged him. "I do want to make love with you, Berrin." Instinctively he knew that for some reason she had decided now, and only now, but he quickly jettisoned the thought. She moved her hand down under the blankets. "Well, you Irishmen can sure be ready when the time is at hand."

He moved again to kiss her, but again she turned her head aside, "It's too sensitive." Movements on her part, tugging at her underwear, kicking, and then she snuggled closer, crossing her leg over his. She took his hand and guided his fingers to where she needed them, staying with him for a certain delicate time. She walked her fingers up his chest, as if to trace the trunk of a tree, and slowly branched out along his clavicle, moving down his arm to again take his hand back to herself, to further caress her. There, she said, on the ripening fruit. The Garden of Eden, he thought to himself and smiled. She moved to mount him. He felt as if he were a huge boulder on the summit of a hill onto which she'd climbed like a wild animal to sun herself and take in the view. It was easy entering, so cavernous that he now felt too small. She giggled, smiling down at him, and moved in deeper.

And in an instant he came, too fast even for himself, still the balm of total release, the fulfillment she must have thought he wanted.

CHAPTER 17

King of Ashantee

BERRIN SAW A NOTE lying on the kitchen table. Quickly scribbled.

good morning, Berrin
had to see an old friend about a job
will likely return home afterwards
could you come out and visit me on the weekend
eileen

He didn't know how long she had slept with him, and now he'd missed her leaving. Definitely making an ass of himself. He had fallen asleep immediately; well, she wanted him to relax. His dream had already primed his passion, a move and he was at the peak, she had to understand that, but there were no explanations exchanged. He first checked his bedroom upon awakening. The bedcovers were thrown back. Only her sweater remained, lying over the back of his armchair.

The vacant bedroom annoyed him. She had rushed off first thing in the morning. Home to hubby . . . but, of course, there were her kids.

He needed breakfast, but it was a bit early for rattling pans. He filled the kettle at the sink, plugged it in, and sat at the table.

Who knows when she'd return. He'd best travel up the Pontiac as soon as possible, understand more of the terrain there. No more assuming anything.

He grabbed the phone book lying on the counter and reached for the phone. The bus schedule. For English press one. He pressed one. For administration press two. He waited. For schedules press three. Three. A recording droned through the main routes to Toronto and Montreal. For more information, press four. Sorry, we're open only from nine a.m. to nine p.m.

"Fuck." Having to climb *trees* . . . so much for evolution. If not a monkey, those things make an ass out of you.

Jill walked into the kitchen.

"Talking to yourself again, Berrin?"

Her pyjamas rounded out her form, a few sizes too large, both her and the pyjamas. She was carrying a binder, already armed for the day's battle.

If only it had been Stephanie who had entered first. "I was cursing these damn phone trees and call waiting. When Ma Bell gets to charge for local calls, those highway robbers will have a field day. They must think we're all still monkeys."

"Monkeys?" Her dark eyes registered something of a reprimand coming. To avoid her scrutiny, he crossed over to the sink again and grabbed his bag of coffee from the overhead cupboard. No avoiding another *problématique*.

Ridiculous. No need for paranoia. He was unsettled, but face it, it was about Eileen's departure. Her teasing. Indeed, given his shanty quarters, he was the imp, the chimp, the *King of Ashantee*.

Jill continued frowning while she set her binder on the table. Her body had sunk deeper into her pyjamas.

He glanced down at her binder.

"Interested?" She pulled out a few pages of printouts. "I need an editor. I can't be objective anymore. You say you were in Mexico. Tell me what you think."

She hadn't asked about Eileen. Perhaps she hadn't noticed

they were together when visiting the gallery, thinking she was Stephanie's friend. He thought for a moment about correcting that assumption, but that was another blunder to avoid. Political correctness would creep into her first few salacious queries, with a follow-up diatribe against Jeff, then about men in general, ending with a totalling of his own surplus value as a lover. Or some other such script. Anything other than a direct question about Eileen; but don't ever ask her about her personal affairs. And should Barry come down, be prepared for a mini-show trial with her the presiding judge. Not a chance for a favourable outcome of any sort, regardless of the direction the discussion took.

He took her paper, an essay, it seemed, and sat in his chair. "Global Villages in the Nuclear Age." Not what he needed first thing in the morning.

Someone came skipping down the stairs. Barry, an ectomorph with the veneer of a nonchalant intellectual. Not a student, either, though he worked full-time in the university bookstore. He faked a yawn as he entered. The real insider, the reborn flapper with the suitable anachronism, a pencil-thin moustache, his trimmed black hair slightly pillow tossed, and the pale blue polyester suit again, wrinkle free, ready for work.

"Looking for a second opinion, Jill?" Barry asked.

"You betcha."

"Be sure to give her yer best shot, Berrin. And don't laugh, or she'll knock your block off."

"That's about all I get from him, Berrin, a laugh."

The Fibolg Meets the Milesian, a title he could submit to the Zombie Video Festival. Smile, one way to move beyond his usual role, arbitrating their spats, customary for the affably fat, though he wasn't so fat as to adequately play that part.

Distraction was needed, flip through the pages, but he couldn't string the print into thoughts.

"Give me a clue about it, Jill? It's too early to concentrate." He half-succeeded at being lighthearted.

"You've seen the movie about Karen Silkwood a few years back? You know, the one that Meryl Streep played in? An oldie, but now the nuclear trafficking is happening in our backyard. It'll blow up in our faces yet."

"I haven't been actually following that line of politics."

"Then you need more action in your life, Berrin. We're planning a demonstration. Did you know that your old Mexican friend is in town? Arturo Durán. He's coming with us."

Arturo. Definitely a surprise. "That's quite a coincidence, Jill. I was thinking of him last night."

Arturo, still connecting with Canadians; he should have guessed. But meeting up with Jill? Last he heard, Arturo was studying some brand of psychoanalysis. Revolutionaries definitely needed clinical help more than ever. Unexpected, but the prospect of meeting Arturo did brighten his day.

Jill pulled out a full-page poster from her binder. Three lines of a slogan were printed in large block letters, like those stamped on crates:

HONK AND HALT
TRITIUM
TRANSPORT

"Nice."

"It's not my line — Stephanie came up with it."

"So, Arturo is in on this?"

"I only saw him a few minutes last night, a mutual friend introduced us. I think he's meeting with a bunch of NGOs, but he might show up for our demonstration. Next Tuesday we plan to shove one of these posters under each windshield wiper at the lights near the field where they're preparing to construct the new American embassy. It's right after the long weekend. Drivers won't see a thing except this."

He could imagine the bedlam. "A sound strategy, Jill. Too bad

I'll be working."

"We'll be right around the corner from you. You can easily take the time to nail a few windshields."

The kettle started whistling, and it was Stephanie arriving who unplugged it. She patted back her wealth of hair, brushing an unruly strand from her eye, and reached into the cupboard for her mug and stash of instant coffee. Limber and nimble in her tallness, in jeans and yellow cotton shirt, as casual as she could get for her long day ahead, for surely she was behind in her grant writing.

"'Morning, Stephanie. You're up early. What time did you finish packing up last night?" Berrin asked.

"It was late enough. Tshabalala and a friend of his helped."

She sat at the table with her coffee and opened a book she was carrying, a thick coffee-table tome.

Barry and Jill resumed their bantering, which both Berrin and Stephanie ignored.

Berrin leaned over to identify the book. Contemporary art. "You must have gotten a Canada Council grant to buy that book."

"Library." She eyed Berrin with a smile and resumed flipping through the pages. Art and making a living were her concerns, not politics, but the real dollars came from pumping out graphic design contracts from her bedroom and holding down the part-time job at El Sol. She sipped her coffee while giving each picture a quick glance as if she were looking for one in particular. Berrin got up again to refill the kettle and plugged it in.

"What's funny about my writing?" Jill was leaning back against the end of the counter.

Barry stood with arms akimbo between her and the table. With everyone included, a perfect healing circle.

"Why not title it, *Freeze Your Sperm and Seize the Firm.*"

Berrin laughed. Jill's paper must have been a speech for the rally. She rolled her eyes, and Berrin looked down at Stephanie's book to avoid being dragged in further. A photo of a painting caught his eye.

"Who's the artist, Stephanie? That photo on the right?" Berrin asked, and took to his seat again.

She didn't answer, but slid her book around a quarter turn toward him and got up to make herself some toast.

Barry leaned over, "Nice." But he couldn't follow up, being pulled back toward Jill by an insistent hand gesture from her.

Berrin wanted only to study the picture. The painting directly mirrored his dream. The archetypal synchronicity . . . there might be something to that, after all. He checked the reference number in the index. "Quaternity," by Anselm Kiefer. The painting presented the interior of a shack. The identical plank flooring, but Kiefer had added his own symbols, which could have as easily fit into his dream, given Eileen's midnight visit. A snake wriggling across the floorboards and tongues of flame sprouting out of a trap door. Even the trap door. It looked as if Kiefer had placed a ruler directly onto the finished painting and drawn the square with a pencil, as if as an afterthought, as if he had recalled a dream of his own. Keeping escape routes open, both of them.

An angry bark. Jill was pushing Barry away as he tried to kiss her on the neck.

"Stop that. I don't need a sexual pacifier."

Barry pulled away, more frustrated than embarrassed, "Back to the melodramatic — good strategy, good, good, Jill." His face flushed red, and he looked over at Stephanie, who was standing by the counter, awaiting her toast. "Don't you think she's carrying all this a bit too far, my friend?"

It was Barry's sperm that now froze under a Gorgon's glare. And hard to miss the slight sideways shift in Stephanie's head, a Tshabalala move, her half-smile askew, the upper lip kinked mildly to the left.

"That's right, Barry, keep your enemies closer." Stephanie's delivery was again deadpan.

"Now, that's funny," Jill laughed.

Barry pinched at his moustache. A mystery why Jill was attracted to him.

Barry turned on Jill. "Maybe you should try some of that humour instead of resorting to your melodramatic capers." He looked back at Stephanie. "That's why she's angry with me. I won't go along with her so-called facts. For instance, who are these three nuclear scientists who were allegedly knocked off by the CIA?"

"Barry, don't try dragging me into your problems. You both should knock it off." Stephanie flipped open the side doors of the antique toaster and reached into the fridge for butter. "Try having breakfast first."

She wasn't angry, just very matter of fact . . . exhausted, it seemed, even before the day had begun. Berrin, though, took comfort in the fact that, no matter how raw their conversations, no one ever got so angry that the co-op might split up.

Jill reached to retrieve her paper from the table. "This is a waste. Forget it, Berrin."

A slam of his hand on top. "It's okay, Jill. I'll read it at work."

"All right, I'll drop by at noon and pick it up. I'm going upstairs to dress." She left without looking at Barry.

Barry watched her until her steps sounded up the stairs, and then sat at the table, expressionless. Stephanie pulled her book back around.

His moustache twisted with a smile. "Berrin, it seems Stephanie goes for the more sophisticated double entendres."

Berrin shrugged. Stephanie started chewing on her toast.

Barry persisted. "You can't be taking this stuff seriously, Stephanie? Fires and snakes. That guy is more likely interested in shacking up with someone."

Stephanie held her toast above the coffee, soaking up the steam. No reply.

No humouring here, Berrin realized; Stephanie's stance was best, focus on the toast.

Barry's diatribe continued. "They're signs — signifiers — that's the word for it, isn't it, Berrin? But they're only words, leaving you to free associate with them, with the text . . . it's all about the text, isn't it? Whether it's a painting, performance, video, or even the CIA, we have to provide the text and make it up as we see fit." Barry might have for an instant considered adding installations to his roll-out, but he seemed to wilt instead.

Barry then turned to stare at the kettle on the counter and rubbed his nose, as if cursing the contraption responsible for generating another cup of coffee. His nostrils curled inward.

Silence from Stephanie's corner, her head bent over the book, her finger flicking at the corner of the page.

"I'm going to work," Barry said after a few more seconds, and disappeared down the hall.

Stephanie called after him, "Don't forget your lunch box." No sarcasm, more like a scolding. She was mildly angry, but she grinned.

"Must be his time of the month," she said, as the front door slammed.

"I'm surprised he works in a bookstore."

"Maybe he should be switching jobs with you in the market," Stephanie said.

"No, thank you. I prefer the street-smart weirdoes there any day." He blushed, uncertain if he were slighting street people or Barry. "He should have eaten breakfast, seeing it's my turn for cooking supper tonight."

"Berrin, who cares? Do you remember the last time he cooked? It'll be the sunny day before he'll ever do anything as original as actually cooking." Her thrust of criticism startled him.

"Why were they at each other's throats like that?"

She looked at him as if to ask something in turn. Instead, she pulled her long, wiry hair over her head and with an automatic twist of her fingers tied it into a bun. Her red hair stuck up like a ball of fire, held taut by the blue and silver-streaked elastic band.

"He's not happy with anyone around here."

"A carryover from last night?"

"His father's a Liberal cabinet minister. You didn't know that, did you? I think his slumming days have caught up with him. It's amazing he's hung in this long."

"That's a switch, then, the guy trying to change the girl."

"You should have seen them wrestling with that performance last night, philosophically, that is; or, rather, hermeneutically — he was strong on that, a bit like you, there, Berrin, with the theory, but I can have a sane conversation with you. Anyhow, Jill finally came down on him with total approval of the show. She was one with it all, she said — I had a good laugh at that. He was furious with her, and her entire circle, he shouted . . . they were not in their right minds, the performance was pure madness, incomprehensible, he shouted . . . his anger finally drove him away. I don't expect he'll hang around here much longer, either."

She stood up. "Well, I've got to get that grant off. I have only till noon, then off for my El Sol shift." She dumped her dishes into the sink. Washing-up was at mid-morning tea break, her routine, disciplined.

"I guess you'd prefer to stick to your art than work there." He didn't want her to leave right away.

"It's money."

"My first paying job ever, you know, I gave back the money."

"Oh, to be so carefree again." She slapped her cheeks a few times as she looked at herself in the mirror, as if to wake herself up.

"The job was in a movie theatre."

"You've come full circle. Maybe you can link up with Jerome."

"So, what does that mean?"

She turned around and sat back against the countertop. "Nothing, Berrin. Sorry. I tend to link men together when I'm angry. I have no cat to kick. So, why did you return your money?"

"I was working as an usher to help cover my first-year university tuition. Sixteen, a rural sixteen and *from the sticks*, and there I was, working in a theatre, a chance to see as many movies as I liked. The head usher gave me a flashlight and stationed me at the top of the stairs and told me to watch for his signal: He'd shine his flashlight against the stairwell landing and I was first to signal back on the opposite wall, then go down to see him. So, a few minutes later, there's his light."

"And your first real act of rebellion?"

"It was totally illogical. Why light up the theatre for nothing, even if it's only the stairwell? I went straight down, but he didn't want anything, just to see if the new boy kept to procedure. I shrugged and returned to my post, and sure enough, a few minutes later, there's his light again, and I descend again for nothing. I got so angry I burst into tears and quit on the spot. I handed my envelope with my first week's pay advance to the manager at the door to his office and ran out."

"You should see some of the characters in the health food store."

"The staff?"

She hesitated for a second. "And customers."

"Well, you *are* in the market."

"The respectable types can be the most delightful. A man came in last week. I was working the cash. He looked like how I imagine Leopold Bloom to be: white shirt and spotted tie, more Irish than even you could dream of, Berrin, and very happily inebriated. He didn't stagger but stood directly in front of me, leaned over the counter, and placed his order. He slurred his words, but everyone in the store heard him shout out his question." Stephanie turned, leaned over the sink and shouted at her reflection in the cupboard mirror, "Do you have anything to keep my wife offa me?"

"Wha — !" Berrin let out a spewing guffaw, Stephanie following suit.

"And then there was total silence. And then, he repeated the question as loud as before. So, I guess the world is changing for the better."

"Lucky he's not back in Ireland; I hear the Coleens are divorcing their men in droves. So what did you do?"

"Sold him a bottle of de-alcoholized wine."

Her shoulders dropped.

"If only it were as easy with those two." She lifted her eyes towards the ceiling, then turned around. "I'll need my book back, Berrin. I need some references for my grant. And then pile on a bit of postmodern jargon to placate the peers."

"So, Barry is right about that much."

"Agreed — about that much."

He closed the book gently, glancing at the title again to remember it. He could pick it up at the library himself.

"I can lend it to you later," she said with a wide grin.

Her slender legs scissored down the hall, then stopped and returned.

"By the way, Berrin. If you need an extra blanket."

"I was wondering if you had noticed. Thanks."

"Was hoping you'd say you wouldn't need one."

"I wish I knew myself."

CHAPTER 18

La vista d'el tiempo

THESE MORNING ROUND TABLES can't become a habit, not with the twenty minutes it takes to make it to the market. Maybe a bit of jogging. Heart knocking too soon. Heartburn. Or a carryover from the childhood stretch of rheumatic fever. Berrin touched his chest, already out of breath after jogging one block. Soon as loony as Al about the old ticker.

A bus approached the intersection; best go with that this morning. The articulated version, for "The Technically Smart City," the good citizenry casting the slogan aside, but not the bureaucrats, the buses already eroding with the salt, and a toss-up with each snowstorm whether they'd make it to the top of a hill without jackknifing.

Bureau-rats, who can't "c" anything. He could toss that line to his new colleagues at the market.

He showed his bus pass to the driver, no smile back from her. Still, the upside, a good choice of seats. In a few years, his old body will be spilling over into the other seat, the belly already feeling as if a large bag of groceries were hugging him.

His projection screen changed as the bus crossed a wide boulevard, and, for an instant, between the rows of buildings, he thought he caught the crest of the water jet fountain at the Hull Casino in the distance, set in a water-filled quarry, algae green and rimmed with rock.

Perhaps just steam from a rooftop vent.

But the image of water lapping was solid, against the rocks . . . and under the floorboards of his dreams. Water, the dominating symbol, the domineering mother. A wonder how it warranted that rap. The latest update for mythology: water came from comets. Water then spoke as much of the heavens . . . indeed, his head was in the clouds too much.

Something more elemental, focus on the one-room shanty. His body. Seventy, eighty-some percent water — and threatening to submerge him entirely. His stellar size might have suited him for the gold mines up north and the oil rigs offshore, but in the end, those far-afield voyages were nothing but delusions, deluges, like his pretenses at seeking out material for his writing.

His summer walks definitely had improved his skin tone. The diet, though, had to be the better strategy. He-who-leaves-table-with-stomach-half-full-lives-twice-as-long, he could see himself delivering the truisms to Eileen's children. Then bring on the fresh vegetables, swallow the sunlight.

Get in touch with your instincts, as Stephanie would say.

His physique hadn't turned Eileen off, however long into the night she might have stayed. He was beaming inside, though her absence at breakfast had darkened his mood. To have her appear at the breakfast table would have brought some normalcy into his life.

Two women from across the aisle speaking in Spanish caught his attention. One was old enough to be the other's mother, except their chatter was too lively and friendly. "*Y salió . . . Vancouver . . . cafeteria . . . para uno año.*" Singular words that told much of the story. A boyfriend or husband? Likely a boyfriend. And still a provider, given their mood.

He wiped his window with his coat sleeve to clear his view. *Plunk* on the window, a pigeon — and he remembered the water-melon exploding.

The rally had been peaceful up to that point . . . A holiday-like crowd of students from the local *politecnico*, but easily outnumbered by the many residents from the *barrio* outside Guadalajara who had joined in the march. He was walking under a long banner beside Eileen and a handful of architect students from the college. The students had made it their mission to design and build simple and inexpensive housing in the *barrio*; now the residents were demanding some services. The chanting had subsided as singing started up a few rows behind them. Eileen was ecstatic.

"I hear there's about thirty thousand in their *barrio* already. It may not be on the city's official map, but this will catch the mayor's attention."

"You were right — I'm glad we came."

"Finally Berrin's descended from the clouds. I didn't think you would relent and come along."

"I wanted to know more of the facts."

"Lots of telephone poles, but no telephones, them's the facts. It's wonderful so many marchers turned out."

Some pedestrians going about their business stopped momentarily to wave or whistle at them as they turned a corner. As they left their neighbourhood and were moving toward the business sector of the city, the cheering diminished in numbers. The multi-colours of the shoppers and storefronts dazzled the eye in the shimmering morning light. A donkey pulling a cart full of watermelons slowly squeezed past them, trying to keep as far away from the traffic as possible.

"Parades and crowds always overwhelm me; I always cry." Eileen's eyes were teared up.

"The spectators *are* thinning, Eileen. I heard there are killings every evening around here. And the Tlactleloco Square massacre in Mexico City is something nobody will forget. The middle classes don't want trouble."

A flare crossed the sky in front of them and, as if on cue, a watermelon exploded in the cart ahead of them, startling everyone.

It could have been a firecracker, or a car backfiring. Another crack, Berrin recognized it this time, definitely a shot. A voice behind them screamed in alarm, "We're wearing white gloves, don't shoot us!"

But there were no guns in sight. The doors of a rusted white van across the three lanes of traffic slammed open, and men in civilian clothes poured out, shouting and waving sticks, banging them together and smashing at the hoods of passing cars as they hurried across the street.

They were rushing the marchers.

Another scream. *"Tiradores en los techos!"* Berrin looked up and scanned the rooftops across the street. The shooters were well hidden. His next thought: *The army.*

Then he saw that the sticks were shafts of sugar cane sharpened at both ends.

He grabbed Eileen by the wrist to run, and she grabbed the hand beside her, but not in time. A yellow shaft rammed into the stomach of her fellow marcher and Eileen screamed as the hand pulled away to grab at the stick piercing her. He held onto Eileen's wrist and headed toward the clearing behind them, forcing his way through the scattering bodies. They tripped over someone, a girl on her hands and knees, a teenager, with a white glove in her left hand — or was it a handkerchief? The archway ahead led into a large indoor market, where the shots were beginning to turn heads. He continued running with Eileen in hand through aisles of shoppers still fingering the *maize* and tomatoes and a table piled with fresh fish, with their eyes milk-white orbs . . . and that was where he stopped and fell to his knees and vomited.

Oh, poor bird, a child behind him whimpered. A pigeon that so far had escaped the city's new extermination campaign. Little flying rats, carriers of diseases. With luck, the rear wheels of the bus finished it off.

His antipathy toward the bird was illogical, but it was sudden and sharp. The ambiguity of the white gloves had always troubled him, a naïve student's stunt or a repeat of the Tlactleloco Square massacre when *agents provocateurs* in civilian dress opened fire on the surrounding army columns, protected from the return fire by the identifying white gloves they wore on their left hands.

The bus stopped and the driver stood up. A man entered, uniformed as well. Changing shifts. Berrin looked to see if they wore gloves, not logical, but yes, but black. The woman grabbed her back support off the seat, stooped to pick up her lunch box from under the steering wheel, and bounded down the steps. How easily she abandoned the bus, after driving it through the morning. She barely returned a smile from the new driver coming on duty. She then crossed the street and headed for the glass doors of an office tower, her windbreaker still open.

Not like the bus drivers in Mexico.

"Berrin, I love how they take pride in their buses."

Eileen was beaming. The spectacle up front had cheered her up. The bus driver had covered his dash and visor with an array of statues, the ever-present Lady of Guadalupe with an unlit candle at its base, photos of family, rosaries, and other religious and personal icons.

"They do make their buses a home for everyone, don't they?" he answered.

"It beats sitting in a seminar room. I could not take another Marxist critique of how American anthropologists ignore the impact of capitalism on the post-Columbian world. You can bet your bottom dollar those smug academics have their underpaid Indian servants back in their fenced-in houses. You certainly didn't see any academics marching with us."

She didn't need more politics, so he changed the subject.

"The *mercado* must be around here."

The central plaza of El Fuerte had swung into view. They planned to spend a few hours here, then bus on to their lodge to rest for a few days. Arturo was taking a flight into a small airport nearby. From Mexico City, he had heard about the attack on the marchers, the city's police chief decrying the violence a good twenty minutes before the attack had actually happened in Guadalajara. Arturo told him to take the overnight bus to get her away, pronto. Arturo wanted her sent straight back to Canada, but she was vehement in her refusal. A return to Mexico City was too stressful, since they weren't scheduled to leave for the ranchos for another week. Better the *Mesa del Norte* and the open spaces of the *Barrancas del Cobre*, the distraction seemed to be working.

The bus geared down. The loud squawking and flurry of chicken feathers from the roof overhead signalled disembarkation time. Their map indicated the market was close by. A stoic youth with a shaved head and wearing a soldier's uniform stood up and exited at the front of the bus. Glancing out his window, Berrin saw a palatial building with barred windows and camouflage-painted army jeeps parked in front.

"Let's get off here, Berrin," and before he could protest, Eileen was bounding down the aisle of the bus, hopping over the bulging sacs of produce and other baggage that cluttered the floor. She was back to her erratic and impetuous self.

And heading toward the jeep.

"Eileen, where are you going? The market's in the other direction."

"I wanna see something."

Her head turned to follow the young soldier from the bus who had disappeared through a large, arched entrance into an interior plaza that housed a troop of soldiers, apparently relaxing on their mid-morning break, some leaning against the stone posts of the verandah that enclosed the plaza, another sitting against a jeep's fender, enough information for him to hurry her on down the sidewalk before anyone caught them staring inside. A second, smaller archway caught her attention, with stone steps leading upward. He bolted after her.

He emerged on the roof, three stairwells up. He spotted a soldier at the far corner, standing guard but looking away out over the town. Eileen was crouched behind a large, curved vent; he had no idea what she was up to. Her vent was one of many standing like chess pieces on the roof, which luckily afforded a good number of hiding places. She darted across to the next one, a larger one, then looked back at Berrin. He was lost in panic, his mind a blur of fear and an intense urge to race back to the stairwell. He must have signalled her — or she had awakened to the danger on her own — for in the next instant, they were bounding back down the steps to emerge still unnoticed onto the sidewalk outside.

No more than two or three minutes had passed. What was the purpose of it all? She might have been smiling as she stood there in front of him, looking up into the clear sky, or even laughing, but he couldn't sense anything beyond his anger, buried in the numbness that blanked everything but his awareness of themselves still standing, alive. It took another minute for relief to sink in, his senses returning. It was all a purging for her. She was now walking down the cobbled sidewalk toward the bustling market ahead, as if off to shop for her morning groceries.

She stopped beside a pile of *huaraches*, stacked beside a sunbaked and gaunt man dressed in rags and sitting cross-legged on a straw mat. She stared at an equally emaciated man sitting with his dog next to the vendor, who in one hand clutched a bottle of *aguardiente* between his thumb and the two remaining fingers, which were fused into one. With his other still-intact hand, he patted his *morral*, out of which the milk-white dog stuck its head.

Berrin stepped up to the *huarache* man and began to barter, but quickly accepted the overpricing and, turning to face Eileen, he draped his arm around his new-found buddy to make his pun, "*Lo mejor de las almas*, the best of soles," while he held out his pair of *huaraches*. Hamming it up with the machismo, it might lighten her mood.

Eileen responded with a slight smile. "It's like parish picnics back home when I was a kid. I could wander off, free, no parents to watch me." She then turned away, with the air of an orphan, depression obviously hitting her again. Clearly, he still stood outside the perimeter of her space, a stranger looking on.

Arturo had joined up with him and Eileen at the lodge, where they then took a taxi out of town and pulled up to a *tienda*, with its whitewash peeling, and a bus parked in the open yard, double the size of the canteen. Their driver spoke in a rapid fire, as if he were fed up being harried by tourists, but confirming he would wait for them, *Va, va, es cercita*, is not far, *voy quedar aqui*, I wait, *va, va, no es lejos*, go. The trail dropped down behind the *tienda* and wound along a hillside of flowers. As they walked along, Berrin had felt compelled to break the silence that had gripped everyone.

"Arturo, your recommendation about taking a bus was right on. The landscape was great. And we lucked out on a first-class coach, like an airplane with a stewardess who offered us a pillow and a Coke."

"Si, good to relax after so much trouble." Arturo didn't turn, but kept his eyes on Eileen ahead of him and on the narrow path itself. She kept her silence, her attention, too, on the turn ahead. The trail widened, and Arturo hurried up beside her. He spoke casually to her, but not smiling, "I'd love it if we could continue on to Chihuahua, but the caves are too full of tourists this time of year."

The trail stopped at a lookout with the canyon below, the *Barrancas del Cobre*, described in the tourist brochure as larger than the Grand Canyon. Arturo spoke up again, in a louder voice, "Ah, *éste es el major*, the best, *no*, Eileen?"

A river snaked through the chaparral a mile away below them, following the canyon that faded to blue in the distance. Fog like tuffs of cotton candy clung to the bends of the river.

Eileen, still not speaking, ducked under the guard railing. She stooped and started crawling with her feet stretched out before her, down the slight slope toward the canyon dropoff. Arturo dropped under the railing as well, and Berrin followed. They crept as gingerly as she had, to where she sat with her legs dangling over the edge. They sat on opposite sides of her. Arturo dropped a stone over the edge and counted a long ten seconds before they heard it striking anything.

"*Bastante peligroso, non?*" Arturo reached over Eileen's head and gave her a gentle hug. *Dangerous indeed*, Berrin thought, *overwhelming*; the vertical drop brought on impulses he dared not speak of.

"Berrin, we're living on the edge, no?" Eileen shouted, as if over a strong, howling wind, but the air was deadly calm.

"*Exacto, mi bonita*," Arturo answered. Courting oblivion, Berrin realized, the medicine she needed, and Arturo interjected again. "My father was a pilot all his life in a local six-seater that flew tourists all the way up the *barranca*. One day the cloud ceiling was so low that he turned to me and told me to count the seconds off with him. He said he knew from habit when he had to turn away from one canyon wall to the other, and so we continued on our zigzag flight up the canyon. You have to know when to turn, *eh, mi señorita? Pues es siempre una vista magnífica, como muerte, non?*"

Eileen leaned back and smiled at Berrin, "*Es claro, eh, me cabron?*"

Teasing, a good sign, Berrin thought.

Arturo continued, "This was Pancho Villa's country when he had to retreat and hide out, but now the route is a major bottleneck for *contrabandistas* and their drugs."

And then Eileen shouted, "*Claro. No pasaron.*"

Then silence again. Not the faintest echo, as the opposite wall of the mountain range was too far off.

Eileen sighed, then followed with a light laugh, and they all laughed together, perhaps because it was the unreality of their position, and their laughter was definitely putting them in additional danger, Arturo almost losing his balance as Eileen reached over his head to reciprocate his embrace. A moment of consideration, and together they leaned back and on hands and buttocks pushed themselves ever so slowly by their feet away from the edge and back up to the lookout point. Over the next three days, they retraced their route back to Mexico City.

Berrin wiped his window again. A corner grocer's storefront, the only colour on the street, with its shelves of fruit — bananas, watermelons — in the front window. It was nostalgia he felt, which surprised him. Buses transport, in every sense of the word.

He remembered the bus schedule he needed for up the Gatineau. He'd phone first thing at work.

A woman in the seat across the aisle grabbed his attention. A senior, but fighting that fate with orange hair dye. The woman was adjusting her yellow headphones. She then put her pocketbook back into her shopping bag, grey cotton, hemp probably, testament to her commitment to the ecology . . . her tinted hair a close match to the embossed lettering on the cover of her paperback, her earrings wobbling like fishing lures, silver and black metal circles. She patted her hair; her hand bore the beginnings of liver spots. Definitely past her trolling days. Her head tilted to the floor, perhaps in a moment of reflection brought on by the two women chattering in front of her. Then a jolt; the bus had jumped the sidewalk as it turned a corner. Her arm in its pink sweater reached up to adjust the headphones.

But no denying what her horizon beheld, *la vista d'el tiempo*, the nothingness behind it all, and then the panic. Such as his clarity of mind when he spotted the soldier across the rooftop. A bit of Eileen's old-time religion could be the antidote: deliverance, throw yourself into the void.

They came to the rise overlooking Lower Town. The low-rise city spread out below, with the clear blue waters of the L'Outaouais visible in the distance. An arch of white spray cutting an arc toward the far shore told of some hardy water skier in the distance. Why had he never taken to such pleasures? Not even once visiting the casino, though it wasn't in sight right then, hidden behind the ship-shape foreign affairs building straight ahead. Maybe he should have spent his life simply going for the money.

Somewhere to the left, upriver and beyond the horizon, lay Eileen's home. And a bit downstream to the right, also out of sight, the point where the Gatineau River flowed into the Ottawa, ending its long journey down from the Baskatong Reservoir in northern Quebec. Another trip he could have made, by canoe. Follow the Gatineau up some thirty miles and he'd be close to the farm. Out of sight for how long? He was wrong in letting it drop out of his life.

No denying it; the pull of the farm was becoming greater than any memory of Mexico. It could provide a fit for both their lives, for him and Eileen. Yet, there he was, suggesting to his mother, "There's nothing much left of the farm. Just sell the whole kit and caboodle." And, there goes the farm, his childhood, and any future he could have with Eileen. The devil's work, as his mother had once exclaimed.

"Sell to whom? Developers? They are only good for doing the devil's work. You saw what happened to Hendricks' farm, and don't tell me it's because it's closer to the city. There's no greater sin than letting hordes of skiers traipse across good pasture land. Can you see it, a ski lodge planted in our beaver meadow?"

How often he had seen her crossing her fields, smelling the growth and revelling in the excitement of the harvests, and relived through her stories. How as a youngster she made skis from barrel staves. And her bet with Alex about riding Dolly bareback to the far gate and back again, which she promptly did, winning the bet but unable to sit for the remainder of the day. Then her revenge that night, a story she always told as if for the first time, when Alex had sunk his feet into a pile of nettles that she had stuffed into the foot of his bed under his blankets.

Such memories . . . he had his own . . . he had felt the same. He had made his own treks as a kid into the winter's expanse of white, once sliding over a field of crust while lying on his back on a sleigh, surprising himself with the serenity, shrouded in it, keeping so still that he became like a pupa inside its chrysalis.

"If you'd seen what the farmland was like before, Berrin, you'd know that houses don't belong."

His mother's staying power, that he had to admire, however divided the farm left you.

CHAPTER 19

The farm

THE FARM, which both heals and bleeds, only too easy to forget the latter, Berrin thought. Mother's grounding, but for her brother Alex, it meant buried in a boundless wilderness. And how would Eileen take to it? A canoe would definitely help.

Hard to appreciate when staring out of a steamed-up window of a bus loaded with city folk. In 1860, the homestead meant freedom, the last of the lots still available in that Irish enclave, at the end of the Borough Road up against the Gatineau hills, in a valley by itself, unto itself. It had to have been a happy time for them, securing two of the one-hundred acre lots on the three-mile stretch between the village and the mountains, with the ownership for free after the twelfth child was born — which took two wives. By far one of the most beautiful farms in the region — he had to agree with his mother there — once the forest was cleared and the swamps drained. And the circle of ridges and mountains around it providing the needed seclusion from all the neighbouring clans.

His mother's snaps told how inviting it was, when full of family and animals and promise. A St. Bernard sprawling on its belly on the lawn alongside a girl in a jumper, his mother, her arm around the dog's neck, shielding her face from the intruding camera. In another photo, she's in overalls, sprightly and sappy and sitting on the roof of a Model T with her legs down the front of the windshield, one of four black sedans parked side by side in front of the homestead house, with their chrome headlights and grills sparkling in the sun. A gathering of family and friends is interspersed between the cars, obviously an outing for the city folk, the men squinting toward the camera awaiting the signal but looking slightly upward, as if surprised by a hawk's cry overhead, all serious in their black suits and white shirts. Alex's father, certainly a mirror-image of his own father, lean and sinewy, stands off to the side by himself, white hair and a rosy face parading a full walrus moustache. The women, summery in their long white dresses, glance sideways at their men who linger near their cars.

One of these ageless young women and two of the men would be his mother's siblings, still teenagers but dying soon afterwards from the tuberculosis brought into their midst by a relative return-ing from a winter's logging in the lumber camps up north.

A question, that had to be a concern: Could the TB have remained in the old house? Were he to renovate, Berrin thought, how safe could it be?

The troubles with the TB did pass. Sometime later, his mother is back in the saddle, caught in another snapshot, dressed in her own white dress and riding bareback on one of the first of a long line of Dollys on the farm, perhaps the very day that she and Alex had made that bet.

He realized that each of her old photographs could be a short story on its own. Such as when she's carrying a pail of water at high noon to the men in the fields harvesting oats, her brother Alex now atop the Gobbler, the name given to the tractor because its large rear wheels would each turn separately when hitched to a too-heavy load. Perhaps the photo was of the day Alex got stuck in a patch of mud, working each brake alternatively, his temper ratcheting up in sync, and his sister joking to break the tension, "You look like a gobbler scratching at the grass."

Alex, the youngest male of the family, ending up alone on the farm, caring for his mother, scratching out a living — and having to scratch about everything else. And time never on his side, trying to keep up with the times, begrudging every change as not the one he most wanted. "You didn't have enough dairy cattle, anyhow, remember?" Alex's mother would say. "I miss the fresh milk, but your beef cattle are up to forty, and purebred Herefords. You're the pride of the county, Alex." The only encouragement she could give, too old then to help in any other way. Placing her in a home was out of the question. Alex had to begrudge his fate, his turmoil evident in the odd remark: "If it wasn't that the farm backed up against all that crown land, it wouldn't be so grand. The cattle are happy — they're free to roam wherever, as far north as the tree line, for that matter."

And then too late to leave when finally free. Who would hire a vagrant farmer approaching fifty? Nor were there any prospects for marriage. Those long winter months with not another house in sight, the forest around hemming you in . . . enough to drive anyone loony.

On one of his last visits to the farm with his mother, Thanksgiving, when the colours on the surrounding mountains were at their best, Alex had exclaimed. "Visitors always like the silence so much!" He was turned away from them, slouched in his swivel chair looking out the picture window of the bungalow, not moving, simply staring. Not the first time Alex had expressed his exasperation, but his anguish had never before been so clear. "Try a few winters of it. There's loads of company then, like the blistering winds and the banking snow and the freezing stiffs of trees."

He did look tired on that visit. "Alex, is there anything special I can get you before we leave?" his mother had asked as she picked up a basket of laundry sitting on the coffee table.

While she looked toward Alex at the window, his long legs in their green overalls stretched out in front of him and his boots on the floor beside him, her gaze followed his toward the three tallest pine trees above the far ridge that hid the lake. Alex had begun to sell off some timber in the last few years, but he left the three pines alone at her request. The pines had stood together ever since they were children.

"You know," he said without looking back at her, "there's no loons on the lake this year."

This drew his mother back to the couch, and she sat with the basket on her knees. "I haven't heard any whippoorwills yet this year, either. You know something, Alex, I have never seen a whippoorwill."

"It's those new cottages on the other side, they'll soon be three rows deep. I should have bought the other half of the lake when I had the chance."

"Oh dear, that was so long ago."

"You remember how the deed was written, how Grandpa put it? Seventy-eight chains and thirty-two links of Gunter's chain, bearing south twelve degrees and forty minutes West to range 10 of said township of Low at the old original and undisputed post marked on a maple tree about four inches in diameter. It's a mouthful that I memorized long ago, thinking it was important for some reason. And I've seen that tree, it's now a hollow trunk — the natural end of things. Grandpa could have afforded to push the line a few chains more easterly and wiped out all these problems."

"You can't know what his reasons were, Alex. Keeping neighbours friendly is so important, you know that."

Not long afterwards, Alex would be dead, from a heart attack, the blockage of the arteries likely caused more by a buildup of regrets than by his steady meals of meat and potatoes, always followed by his tannic sludge of Salada tea and Carnation milk because he never emptied out the tin teapot during the day, always throwing in another handful of tea, then a light-up as he reddened the end of another roll-your-own Players, the sailor on the tobacco pouch another reminder of a voyage not taken.

But the stories continued: His mother becomes the farmer at seventy years of age. He observed her once standing on the knoll between the car garage and the old ice house where a dozen chickens were pecking at the ground around her. She was scattering grain from a pail that she held in one hand. The lone gander approached and flapped its wings at her and began squawking. Protecting the chickens, no doubt. Likely the last male left on the farm. She swung her feeding arm back and forth to chase it away. When that didn't work she banged it on the head with the pail. Still the gander only backed off a few steps, its head swinging back and forth on its long neck to find a better angle to jab at her again — and as likely as not, therein lay the origin of fencing.

Grouping geese with chickens, the first of his mother's schemes, after having to give up most of the Herefords, keeping two cows to clear the land of burdocks and weeds. And now she had a few Angora goats, with plans to card and spin some wool and sell it to those hippies who'd opened a craft store in nearby Wakefield, the first time he'd heard her speak kindly of hippies. They might trade their handloom for some mohair, his mother explained, wasting away as it was in their front window, Mrs. Gleason in the village having told her already of their window display of antiques.

And the fallow deer. A television news clip convinced her about a farmer south of Kingston who was making a go of selling them for breeding. One couldn't look a gift horse in the mouth . . . ample enough reason, she had said, to purchase a buck and some does.

Scheming, or survival? When she entered the bungalow after feeding the chickens, she remained quiet, deep in thought. From his seat at the kitchen table, he had startled her by speaking up: "Mother, farm work is forever. Too bad life isn't."

"Berrin, you never leap if you always look beforehand," she said. "Alex was a stern man, like his father. I remember him as a hard-driving taskmaster, always having to prove he was as good as his neighbours, I guess because he was illiterate. He'd be pleased now. We're doing exactly what he wanted."

He ignored the confusion in the pronouns. "If I ever did start up here, the deer would have to go." For housing for the deer, she had only the old ice house, not much protection in winter; for the past two winters that she'd kept them, the first deep cold spell mercilessly killed off most of the summer fawns. "Mother, they would be as much a trap for me as the cattle were for Alex."

"Not a trap, Berrin," she had snapped back, as quick as ever. "If anything, the cattle were just not enough for him."

He switched to talking about the goats, a positive note. They did attract him for some reason, an animal with rectangular corneas had to be respected. But still, he told her, they came with the need of a building and repairs.

"You're right. Alex was never good at repairs, especially with machinery, but you couldn't call that a fault. He preferred to read, like you, Berrin."

Books. Alex probably suffered from a kind of Hardy-like neurosis about them. Never the settler, better the native, a story-teller. Friends from the city always bringing him a new book to read and then sitting for hours at the kitchen table, listening to his stories told in his Irish accent. They'd be forgetting that they had come for a swim, and as sunset approached, he'd have to remind them to hurry up to the lake while there was light enough left.

"Mother, I do prefer reading." Not the timber in him as in his ancestors.

She probably had read his mind, for she had turned away and retreated to the sofa, keeping her silence.

He pictured the remaining pieces of farm equipment scattered throughout the farm, rusting away in the weeds: The Gobbler up beside the ice house, the hay baler next to the horse stable, each one enveloped in weeds.

But beauty *was* born in the silence. He had no rebuttal for that thought. He had forgotten true silence. The flutter of a swallow's wings as it dove down from the barn inches from your head, or the whirl of the hummingbird hovering in the buttercups at the corner of the old house. The silence that cities don't allow.

CHAPTER 20

No man's land

BALLS OF ORANGES and blues and yellows marked the clear autumn sky. Sudden flashes of flame from bursts of propane, the sound blocked out by the rattle of the bus and the chattering of the masses as the hot-air balloons floated low across the river toward the city, lifting tourists higher, a bird's-eye view of the capital as it approached Thanksgiving weekend. The balloons floated closer, slowly, in what appeared to Berrin from inside the bus to be perfectly calm air, blanketed in a benumbed wintery serenity, closest to the heavens anyone was going to get.

Stephanie's style came to his mind, likely the best for survival in this urban wasteland. Contain the fire, transform it, rise above it. Don't be snuffed out by the chaos in the streets below.

Berrin stepped out of the bus onto no-man's land. He pulled his windbreaker together against the frosty air. Virtually no one in sight; no need to have rushed to work. A typical weekday in autumn for the market. Across the street, his workplace, the Byward Market building, taking up the entire block, looked equally deserted.

A lone couple, possibly tourists, stood reading a plaque on the side of the building. He'd taken to reading plaques at random when he walked to work, changing his route each day, and discovering how the odd statue could hold forth a surprising story, like that of Sir Galahad in front of Parliament Hill, placed in honour of a Henry Harper, an Irish gentleman who would mingle with the capital's dignitaries by skating on the river below Parliament Hill — until the day he drowned trying to save a damsel who'd swung out too far onto thin ice. "What else can I do?" Harper's supposedly last words, as recorded on the plaque, thrown out to his friends as he rushed to the rescue. Berrin had investigated the story in the library: a youth full of obvious promise, and now amounting to nothing more than a heritage footnote; from mythic deed to tourist curio.

However regressive his attraction to the Sir Galahad statue might have been, it's the story that had held him, that drive that could only spring from the depths of sheer survival, as if he needed now to ingest it anew, that inbred fibre that had carried his own great-grandparents from Ireland, escaping first the Great Famine and next the coffin ships, and then being promptly marched off to the quarantine shacks on Grosse–Île and toward the ordeal of another internment, yet not yielding to that fate, either, their determination set on returning to a farm. Some gumption at least, a mistake to have forfeited it in his flight up north.

He resisted crossing over to work. Instead, he watched a familiar figure crossing ahead of him. This was a particularly ageless man with a hooked nose and puffed cheeks who sported a Caesar's profile in a toga of rags. Berrin anticipated the pattern, the man halting every ten feet or so along the sidewalk and glancing backwards, as if pondering some momentous decision or performing the requisite public gesture of reconsideration, as if that were the true measure of one's existence. This time the man continued up the sidewalk a short distance, then turned back to the corner to reconsider with his ancestral elegance which street to take, then continued on in the original direction, again exercising his will in a public manner.

Berrin's job at the market left him with plenty of time to observe these characters. He did enjoy them, though it was usually the summertime that saw them thriving. Summers were busier, and more fun, holding to a tempo of times past, with its scramble of foraging and dealings. Cars angling along both sides of the streets, packed together like sardines, crowding the vendors' booths . . . farmers displaying their produce along the Market building, where they competed with crafts inside the building. It formerly housed the farmers, another casualty to the image-makers. But the building had been renovated, followed by the rents, the farmers then electing to stick to the streets, finally crafts taking over the empty space inside, all this transpiring under the aegis of a socialist-minded mayor. Such was the history as he saw it behind his job in the Market.

Today, only a few produce vendors had set up along the street, plus a solitary stand on the sidewalk beside the Market building. Most of the tourists, it seemed, were up in balloons. The few stragglers were less likely to be shoppers than listless souls in search of a comradely chat over a cup of coffee in a café. But those shops were almost as vacant, slick concessions that had sprung up over the past decade wherever a staple business went belly-up.

A large sandwich sign blocked his path, the sidewalk otherwise deserted. Steps led up to a local bar. Diversifying their market by hosting a film club, post-underground, probably. Tom Hanks stared out from the poster. *Joe Versus the Volcano.* The everyman Tom, cradled by his star blonde, atop a red suitcase afloat on the ocean, with a volcano exploding in the background. It was difficult to ignore the upside to such slick schlock. The life of stars. He could see himself polishing off a Jamesons with Hanks in the bar, stringing out a good yarn, ignoring the daemons that as surely nipped at his heels as at his own.

But best to stay the taps, at least till after noon hour when the co-op gang was slated to show up. Maybe invite Barry and Jill for a drink, relax a bit. He couldn't recall ever a moment when they had carried on a convivial conversation over a breakfast coffee. Never the urge to drain the dregs, clear their throats, hawk and splatter the sidewalk, or any such purging. It was difficult to believe in yourself these days. You almost had to reinvent your image daily and market it incessantly with all the skills of a practised politician in order to tolerate it.

He liked to arrive early for work, taking in the sights and smells of the smaller shops and outdoor booths. This was his great-uncle's territory a century ago, his blacksmith shop somewhere nearby where he serviced the stagecoaches that ran from the Market across the Ottawa River to the terminal in Aylmer five miles upriver, now an upscale heritage apartment complex built, like all the core build-ings in the region, from blocks of limestone. Compressed histories, centuries of glaciers compacting the silt of previous centuries, and had he been alive in the time of those floods, he would now be standing at the bottom of the Champlain Sea that had flowed in as the glaciers receded, above him bowhead whales and ring seals and belugas. And a time seagulls best belonged, for they were now clearly replacing the pigeons.

He hadn't yet identified the stagecoach terminal at this end of the run, nor the blacksmith shop, likely built with less durable material. Little of his history left. He had checked the many period photographs that lined the walls of the administrative offices in the Market building, viewing with a magnifying glass the signage on each building, but no evidence of a Brown or a blacksmith's shop. Only the flavour of the times shone through.

One photograph in particular caught his eye, presenting an elevated, wide-angle of the street next to the Market building. Horse-pulled buggies still outnumbered the few Model T's that worked their way through the congestion, men in white shirts with braces and open black suit coats, some watching workers unloading wagons of their barrels of nails, kegs of beer, boxes of produce, and haberdasheries. A woman stood in the middle of the street near the front of the Market building with her back to the action, facing the camera. She was dressed in a full-length white dress with a lace collar buttoned tight to her neck, standing as if looking up at a camera in the sky. A Renoir portraiture, ephemeral, like her own lot in life, or rendered such by the expanse of time travelled in his looking back upon her. The magic of photography. Still, he wondered why the photo intrigued him. She had the air of not belonging to the city that encircled her. Perhaps she longed for a voyage away, to the splendour of a Bonaparte's Third Republic, though her sharp figure as likely aimed to cut through time itself, her uplifted gaze reaching for the future, the spread of time the only space that might have pleased her.

As he could live no such past. He had come close to the promise in Mexico . . . such was the pull that it still had on him . . . A prisoner in time, its constraints inextricably defining him — as good an explanation as any for his paralysis.

He could no longer deny his own state of mind when he had sat down beside Eileen overlooking the *Barrancas del Cobre*. The fear that came with sitting at the edge of what had to be one of the highest ridges of the canyon had settled over his body like a hangman's hood. Yet once he was seated beside her, so compelling was the view that his very physicality wanted to reach out over the spread of terrain below him and into the limitlessness of the space; surely, were he to step over the edge, he could have continued to walk out into the very beyond, as if at that moment the sheer quantum exercise of his will at such intensity would have bent time and space themselves and opened up the vital pathway to another dimension.

But he hadn't taken that step. All an inextricable urge, best suited for an analyst's couch. But, to think he might have. Flatulence put a squeak in his step as he turned to cross the street where the woman in the photograph had stood, and he found Al approaching. The encounter somehow fit his mood. It had been a kindred enough time up north, the respite he needed after Mexico, and from Eileen, he couldn't deny that, while residing at the Bourlamaque Hotel, a log building that could as easily have been pictured in the Byward Market showcase. His room had been opposite Al's on the second floor, more than suitable, the hotel sitting on the edge of town that backed upon the original village of log cabins. One of his stories had been set in that village. He had asked Al to translate it into French to divert him from his obsessions, but nothing ever came of it.

Al looked down at him, his face flushed and his frame bent slightly forward as if anticipating the winter winds. Still the whistling whisper in his voice.

"I saw Joe with Turner, you know, the Liberal leader."

"Chrétien is the Liberal leader now, Al." Any kindred feelings were quickly dissipating.

"I was seeing my local parish priest, at St. Mary's. He told me to forget the whole thing. But afterwards, I saw him approach Paul Martin in the front pew. It was after the mass was over. You know how the Conservative Party is six million in debt. Now they're going to sell the rights to my engine to the highest bidder."

Conservative or Liberal? Nothing to be done with this madness.

"How do you know that, Al?"

"Well, I was giving Sheila Copps French lessons, and I must have mentioned my invention in passing."

Hang around too long and become as unhinged. Berrin glanced behind himself, the Fish Market.

"Al, I can't talk now. I need to buy some fish."

As they were talking, a van had backed up against the sidewalk behind them. A woman was stepping down from the back of it. She was carrying a basket full of lobsters. Perhaps it was her appearance more than his dismissal that drove Al away, because he immediately fled, nodding a *See you later*, and scurried off around the corner.

A cigarette drooped from the centre of the woman's lips. Her age? It was hard to tell; slightly older than himself. Her two hands clutched the basket at her waist where claws hung heavy over the side, pinching at the air. Her long white smock was open at the front, giving her the look of a gunslinger. Her gaze took in Berrin, momentarily. A cut ran from her hairline down to her eyebrow — no, only a strand of hair, falling from her bandana into her eye.

For a moment he felt upbeat, with an urge to tuck the lock back under her bandana and kiss each of her freight-strained eyes. With an almost automatic gesture he raised his hand to the side of his head and touched his scar. The militia's rifle shot had sliced his temple from hairline to ear lobe, but luckily hadn't cut through the skull. Only a severe concussion. It was certainly the scar that had grabbed the attention of the fisherwoman.

Public buildings suffocate; he couldn't abide them, though thankfully the Market building was tolerable. Like a cathedral, red brick with a high-arching dark metal ceiling, and virtually without walls because plate glass stretched along both sides, the glass walls doubling as sliding doors for the summer season when goods could be displayed on the sidewalks. Craft booths lined this see-through perimeter, and others stretched down the centre. His booth was located at one side near the middle. To his left, at the end of the centre booths, a diner area: a hut with a thatched roof that housed a Mexican fast-food kiosk, its kitsch killing any sentiment it might otherwise have evoked in him. Tables occupied the spaces on both sides of it where craft booths would otherwise have been, the politics inside the building now focused on the struggle between the crafts and fast food vendors for more space. A row of plants separated the tables from the aisles, the only green in the place.

Many of the booths had yet to open for the day. Stan, a lapidarist, a fair-haired, youthful Pan with a permanent, impish smile, was seated across the floor from him behind rows of brooches and pins. He was reading his morning newspaper. Two booths stood in the middle aisle between them. One was little more than a stand supporting a small cabinet filled with watches and jewellery made by a friend of Stan's, inlaid with his polished, cut stones. To the right of it, a booth of watercolours, closed. The less-expensive prints of the Parliament buildings and stretches of tulips along the Rideau Canal faced the aisle to catch the attention of tourists, who generally preferred Berrin's side of the building, away from the crowded farmer's street. In the summer, the sidewalk outside often turned into a shouting arena as merchants with imported goods tried to drown out the home gang. Berrin looked out onto the deserted walkway, bare except for the usual scattering of discarded wrappings, cigarette butts, and the odd piece of rotting vegetable that had made its way around the building. On the sidewalk across from him, behind Stan, stood the solitary farmer he'd seen before, now placing a few cans of maple syrup on a table already piled high with cartons of eggs, the only vendor who seemed to have maintained a supply of the sap throughout the summer. Plastic sheeting for shelter now stretched around and over his space. Below the table, the orange circle of heating elements spoke of the inclement hours ahead.

To open his own booth, Berrin simply had to count the cash float from the day before and sign his name on the daily sales sheets, a separate sheet for each of the crafts in his booth. He put the sales book under the counter and sat back on his high chair. To dust or not to dust?

He could read Jill's speech; still plenty of time before she arrives. Twelve pages — too long for a speech. He skimmed it. Clearly a university paper. A turgid and somewhat rambling essay, almost a converse rant to Barry's, ranging in concerns from the encroaching totalitarianism of the nuclear state to the counter-insurgency system of fortified villages used by the military in Guatemala.

"The poor will always be with us," his mother's analysis. As apt as her comment on his near-death experience: "I hope at least they knocked some sense into that thick skull of yours."

It wouldn't be him knocking some sense into Jill's.

He took stabs at the essay through the morning, interrupted intermittently by a sale, and eyeing the passersby. Winter weather was earlier than ever, the pedestrians generally dressed as skimpily as himself.

At one point late in the morning, Stephanie appeared from behind him. Her smile frozen, preoccupied.

"Hi. I thought you were holed up, grant writing," Berrin said.

"Eileen phoned. She wanted me to ask you if she could stay a bit longer if she needed to. I told her of course you wouldn't mind."

"That's good news, Stephanie. Thanks." His surprise was only too obvious.

She fingered the Tiffany lampshade on the end of the counter and gave him the eye again. "Nice lamps."

"I lucked into an authentic one at the Sally Ann."

"And what might be your other design ideas to brighten up that room of yours?"

His smile was irrepressible, but she was getting nothing more from him for the moment, except for the dull clanging as he ran his finger through the row of stained-glass earrings hanging on a rack on the countertop.

"Something to buy her, maybe?" And she turned away, as if to take in the rest of the crafts.

She eyed the stoneware; their cobalt blues, celadon greens, and oxblood reds occupied the middle area in front. Sheepskin slippers and vests and children's leather shoes covered the wall across from the pottery and flowed onto the bottom shelving by the window under the raku.

"A bit cramped, you'll have to lose some weight, Berrin, to manoeuvre around here." She walked over to the window that displayed the choice pieces of raku. She picked up a tall vase. "It's so smooth and beautiful."

And very black, he wanted to say, but only smiled.

She still read his mind. "Funny, funny. Have you seen him? He said he'd meet me here for lunch."

"Sorry."

She then spotted Jill's essay lying on the countertop.

"Something kept bugging me all morning, Berrin. Were you agreeing with him?"

"You mean Barry?"

"Who else?"

He winced, and grabbed his shoulder as a sharp pain raced across it.

"Bursitis."

"Like I've said before, Berrin: Dump your red meat and soft drinks. But what about this morning?"

Her visit was turning into a grilling. It caught him off-guard.

"Who knows what Barry meant? I liked the photo of the painting, the one of the shack. I'll have to read up on it. What's the artist's name again? It was like my —"

"You seemed to be agreeing with him."

He wanted to massage *her* shoulders, because his first impression was correct: too, too intense. "I did laugh a bit, but it was nerves, from their bickering."

"I didn't want to think you were agreeing with him."

She replaced the vase. "Husbands. They're a scary lot." At that moment, she caught her image in the stained-glass mirror hanging in the window beside the raku. It seemed to startle her.

Mirrors, stealing a part of your soul. He saw it each time a customer looked into one of them, hoping that if they'd stare long enough they'd identify that incarnate something they so desperately needed beneath the silvered surface.

Stephanie turned away, not a consumer.

"I think Eileen is meeting up with her hubby. She didn't exactly say that — I'm reading between the lines. I imagine she needs a fallback position."

"That might be it."

"If you see Tshabalala, can you tell him to wait here for me? I'll make a quick round of the block. See you later." She headed back down the aisle to the rear exit.

Why would she care what he thought of Barry? Whatever was bothering her, it likely had more to do with Tshabalala; he was certain about that hunch.

He caught his face in the mirror atop the jewellery counter. Stubble, he had forgotten to shave, which would have highlighted his scar.

His image, like his opinions, wasn't one that merited much weight. A nondescript cotton windbreaker, plaid shirt, and tan trousers, which he never did iron, surely another reason why the fisherwoman had dismissed him. Perhaps he would be better off nude. He started picking specks of lint off the knees. She loves me, she loves me not, she loves me. His legs bowed slightly outward as if he had had rickets as a child. His trousers were baggy because he never could afford his proper fit. What of it? His image lacked only the proper curatorial statement. He gave his knee one final brush.

His new shoes were definitely a piece of art. J.F., the leather-worker two booths down, had made them for him, the price almost a gift. "For my hardiest drinking buddy," J.F. had said as he leaned from the barstool to punch into his buddy-buddy shoulder. He had gone to some length to customize the shoes, though given the way they let his feet spread flat and thin, they looked more like beaver tails. Stan had had a great laugh over that. A true Canadian underfoot.

The food vendor at the far end of the building had a more profitable sense of humour: Beaver Tails, cinnamon-flavoured sweetbread sold to tourists year round. See an American tourist and you inevitably saw a Beaver Tail hanging from his mouth.

Though he missed the outdoors, he realized he had come to like this space, its ironies, and the company it offered.

And a new circle of friends who could help Eileen.

He grabbed the phone book from under the counter. A human voice this time. Confirmed, a Saturday trip up the Pontiac, at dusk, which made little difference, since recent hurricane-strength winds had stripped the Gatineau hills of all their autumn colours.

At that moment, a bag lady approached the booth. She set her bags on the floor and reached into the sheepskin booth, stretch-ing for the pink baby slippers. Fingering her memories. Maybe

Stephanie was pregnant. An absurd thought. Drop the intrigue. Or Tshabalala wanted to move in with her. Or vice-versa, she might have put the proposition to Tshabalala and scared the living daylights out of him.

The bag lady caught his vigilant look and patted the baby slippers back into place, then momentarily smiled as she moved them up one level on the sloping shelf and snuggled them between the adult slippers. He'd fix that later. She picked up her fully loaded plastic bags in each hand and turned as if to counterattack his unspoken reprimand, her skin darkened from her years out of doors, weathered a reddish brown, almost indigenous.

"You are full of nice stuff, I see." She spoke in a smoker's voice, a raw timbre to her words, ancestral how it resonated, the wisdom of crones, She stepped forward, obviously wanting to buttonhole him, or corner him on some misdemeanour herself . . . a flash of memory, momentary but sharp, as Eileen once had caught him.

CHAPTER 21

Qui no sabe

INFECTION HAD BEGUN in Berrin's heel and progressed up his leg. Had he paid more attention to it than he had to her over the past few days, Eileen quipped, he would have caught it sooner and avoided a needless trip into Tepepantiango. She had suggested taking an alternative path as far as the Araña, one that the women preferred, not as steep, though slightly longer . . . give his aching foot whatever relief they could, since no donkeys could be found; seemingly they made only one-way trips into the mountains then disappeared — or probably dropped dead, she added. Walking down mountains still proved harder on his legs than going up, he said, but he wasn't complaining, though he was developing a slight limp. They were now in the valley, and she was accompanying him only as far as the river. He had insisted on going on alone from there; he didn't want to trouble her more. But she was as reluctant as he to admit how much duty had replaced their recent moment of intimacy, however tentative it had been.

The path swung along a well-constructed log fence, the first they'd seen in their many journeys between ranchos. An old peasant woman stood on the opposite side of her gate, watching them approach. She was wearing a bright, full-length yellow dress over a blue one, likely to keep her warm, though each layer seemed to add to her dignity. She opened the gate and offered her wrinkled hand. Fingers brushed palms. Her *rebozo*, dyed a solid crimson, fell from her shoulders and revealed an intricate mosaic of bright yellow, blue, and red thread along the neck of a white blouse under her dresses. Eileen was reminded of the Celtic knot-work her grandmother had embroidered on her dresses, as intricate but never the celebration of life that these home dyes yielded, with the warm weave of its knit, lines intertwining, a commingling.

"*Tonaltih. Tikneki atl?*" the old lady asked, looking first up at Berrin, then up at Eileen.

Eileen recognized the greeting, and the last word, *atl*, having heard it so often from the women while washing laundry on the rocks down by the well.

"She's offering us some water."

Berrin's look reminded her of the questionable state of the water.

The old lady seemed to recognize their worry and bowed slightly. "*Ce tlalochtli . . . momentito, momentito,*" she said and hurried with short, deliberate steps back to her hut.

Her hut was a simple, square, one-room with a corrugated tin roof and full boards on the walls. A short piece of log hung under the eave near her window and honeybees buzzed about its shallow end. Three chickens and a pig rooted about the yard.

Berrin turned to Eileen and grinned. "*Momentito*. Probably the only Spanish word she knows. *Tonto.*"

Eileen's neck muscles tightened and she looked to see if the old woman was out of earshot. She was, disappearing through the door.

Berrin caught the flash of anger in Eileen's face. He kicked at the ground, winced, and looked up into the trees.

"I'm sorry."

"It's not that simple"

"I said I'm sorry."

"I know what you meant."

He turned back to face her. "I didn't mean it that way, not really. I was only repeating what the men sometimes say of themselves."

"But it means only one thing."

They both knew that Mexicans, those of Spanish descent, that is, called the Indians *tonto*, meaning stupid, meaning they couldn't speak Spanish. Anyone who wanted to clearly look could see how the indigenous suffered their colonial legacy. In Tepepantiango they had appeared somewhat diminished and crippled, their backs always bent under some phantom burden. Here in the mountains, they went about with determination, bowed only to their heavy loads of wood and corn.

Berrin hesitated and then spoke. "You're right."

He added. "I guess it's part of our Lone Ranger lore." He laughed from nerves. She returned a puzzled look. "My dad loves that old series. All those years, the Lone Ranger was calling his sidekick *Oh Stupid One*. And Tonto in turn was calling the Lone Ranger *Qui no sabe*. Know nothing."

The lady emerged carrying a fruit in each hand. She handed one to each of them and put her fingers to her mouth, nodding all the while. The fruits were the size of oranges but covered with scales like small pineapples in shades of indigo.

"Do you know what they are?" Eileen asked.

"No. Never seen one before." He unsheathed his hunting knife and cut his open. The fruit resembled a kiwi, with black seeds scattered throughout the flesh-coloured body that hosted an orange pulp at the core. He cut a slice off and handed it to Eileen.

The core felt firm. The fruit tasted like a lemon that was also sweet. She slowly took it into her mouth as if it were a sacrament. She smiled and gave Berrin hers to cut, and the lady returned a toothless smile as they finished their fruit. Eileen tried to thank her and again they touched palms.

"*Tlasokamati. Tonaltih, Tonaltih.*" She smiled.

"*Gracias. Buenos dias, buenos dias.*"

Eileen followed Berrin down the path, repeating the old lady's parting phrase over and over in her mind like a mantra. In a few minutes, they would be reaching the Araña. Neither wanted to say much to the other. On arriving at the bank of the river, they hugged, polite. She promised to stay with the other students in the neighbouring rancho. He crossed the Araña, not so cocky about it this time with his limp, and disappeared into the underbrush without stopping to wave back.

CHAPTER 22

Something to hold on to

THE BAG LADY stopped at the counter in front of the Tiffany lamp, but continued to sway from side to side.

"Is it okay I look around? All this stuff you're selling, it's European? No? We aren't that bad, are we? Nice work."

A Slavic accent, Berrin decided. Her treasures, in red net bags clutched in each hand, old clothing stuffing one, and the other, plastic bags possibly containing more bags. A green felt bowler hat touched her ears, but the earrings fit, large, gold-plated full moons swinging beneath the rim of her hat, each like a child's rope swing in a tree. Her polka-dot skirt stuck out below a yellow cotton raincoat. Berrin glanced outside, more likely snow than rain.

"I like to treat myself to somethin' now an' again. My, a bit pricey. I make rice paper lampshades, different from this stain glass stuff. I do Japanese-like paintings on them. I'm going to sell a painting to buy somethin'. Nice painting, a scene from a boat on the canal and you look up and see all the buildings of the city. The frame cost me fifteen bucks."

He hoped she would pull out the painting itself, but her storytelling was clearly her forte. Her eyes doggedly fixed on him as he looked past her to see Jill entering the building, followed by Stephanie and Tshabalala, who were smiling together. Happy

lovers — his fears were groundless — a match in their heights, tall
and sinewy, her hair slightly brighter than Tshabalala's orange knit-
ted toque. Jill must have insisted they join her. And then, to his
surprise, Arturo entered, pushing though the double doors behind
them, each hand on a door, the exact and charming movements
that distinguished him.

The bag lady was unfazed by his abrupt withdrawal around
the end of the counter, looking down at her bags as if she did
have something to show him . . . his twinge of guilt dismissed as
he stepped around her. She turned as a tank does with one tread
not turning, then jerked forward on down the aisle, looking for
another ear.

Arturo was already seated at a table, opposite Jill, Tshabalala
at his side with an arm hooked over the back of his chair, and
Stephanie across the table from him. And Barry? On cue, bursting through the door and pulling up a chair at the end of the
table, everyone greeting each other simultaneously, though Jill was
immediately leaning into the table, likely to tap into Arturo and
the politics of Mexico.

Berrin stepped behind the plant barrier, coming up beside
Arturo to surprise him. "*Hola, mi amigo viejo,*" and tapped him on
his dark, curly head with Jill's rolled-up essay. The greying on his
temples a reminder of the decade plus since their last meeting.

Arturo's face reddened more, eyes always wide open to life's
surprises. He stood to greet Berrin.

"*Cabron, que tal.* Is this where you're hiding out? I thought you
were still wasting away in the bush up north," his long arms and
large hands gripping Berrin in a hug.

No such *ambrazo* since they had parted ways at the hospital in
Mexico City. Arturo had returned to Tepepantiango to shut down
the projects and move the students into Plazaflores, a town farther
north and lower in the valley and more Spanish speaking. Arturo
had been too preoccupied to get back to Mexico City by the time
he and Eileen had left for Canada.

"I see Jill has lost no time luring you into these nuclear shenanigans," Berrin said.

"*Si,*" his high whistling Mexican laugh, together with his volcanic black eyes underscored as *no problemo* any differences that time might have put between them.

"Beers?" from Stephanie.

Arturo turned, "*Ah, pero si, por cierto,*" identifying Stephanie as a true kindred spirit, his cheeks arching higher to bracket his beaked red nose. A blend of French and Castillano blood, irredeemably seductive.

Berrin didn't hesitate. "And a Corona for me, Stephanie, for old time's sake." He sat, jiggling the table, a tight enough squeeze with the planter behind him, but he was seated between Arturo and Jill — and across from stone-faced Barry.

"You're still abusing that gut too much, Berrin," Stephanie said, as she got up to get the beer.

Arturo shoved a slow punch into Berrin's shoulder. "My beautiful *señorita*, he was my Sancho Panza in Mexico. He's finally filling out the part."

A disconcerting remark, but Berrin had to admit that his relationship with Arturo had always felt a bit like that. Arturo evoked the political, drew you toward engagement. Witness Jill's fawning over him. Well, almost everyone; Barry was leaning back on his chair, quietly seething.

The opening banter broke off for a second when Stephanie returned and passed around the bottles. Berrin sensed it was time to recount his time with Arturo in Mexico, though he found himself looking mostly toward Stephanie as he skipped through the bare bones of the story. At the mention of Eileen's name, Arturo raised both arms: "Ah, Eileen. What is she up to now?"

"Well, by chance, she dropped in last night and stayed over. She lives upriver in the country."

"She might be back this evening," Stephanie said, very matter of fact, but the inference unavoidable.

"You mean the woman who was with you last night?" Jill asked.

"That's her," Stephanie smiled this time.

"That's great," Jill said with an air of complicity.

Barry remained mute, still rocking slightly in his chair.

"I think she's breaking up with her husband. So it's the couch for me again tonight." Berrin hoped this bit of info was enough to stop the inevitable speculation.

"*Bueno*, I'll be glad to meet her again. That mountaintop episode was rough on her. Poor kid got mixed up in the rancho's politics after Berrin left."

"I shouldn't have left her alone. Joan probably could have helped me." Blank looks, even from Arturo. "Joan was a nurse in the neighbouring rancho."

"Ah, Joan, I remember her. Berrin, you needed penicillin for your blood poisoning, not that devil." Whatever that meant. Berrin could remember one minor event at their CIASP apartment in Mexico City when Joan suggested that Arturo wash some dishes; he had shrugged his shoulders, taken another puff on his black Faro cigarette, pulled his agenda book from inside his vest pocket, and walked over to the phone.

Berrin felt somewhat anxious that Arturo might yet blow his cover story about his own troubles in Mexico. He had once mentioned at the supper table that he had been cut accidentally by another *peón* while chopping sugar cane, but then it turned out it was his foot that got infected from a minor blister.

"It was a stupid move on my part. It was after I left our rancho that Eileen got into trouble somehow. She told me she would stay in the next rancho with the other students there — Joan was one of them. But Eileen returned to our rancho and something happened, I never found out what exactly. She almost had a nervous breakdown already in Guadalajara, she got caught up in a demonstration there and some people were killed; that was tough on her."

Arturo interjected. "*Sí*, we hoped the mountain air and the ranchos would be enough."

"It might have been more than the trauma," Berrin mused, a thought. "Arturo. I remember visiting the museum in Mexico City with its exhibits of Aztec huts. But in the ranchos, we were as irrelevant as those artificial exhibits to real life. Maybe Eileen felt this more than the rest of us."

"*Bueno*, Berrin, none of us appreciated her stress. So fervent little missionaries, all of us. Illich put it best, we were all driven by a, he had it *exactamente: a deep sentimental attachment of a non-overtly sexual nature.*"

Arturo's delivery was exact. Berrin recognized the icy slant of each word slicing the air like a chopping knife, Illich's trademark delivery that had them inviting him to Guadalajara in the first place. It was his lecture as much as the volatile times that left most of the Canadians questioning their mission, and in a few years CIASP had disbanded itself. Yet Arturo seemed to be as active as ever.

Drinks arrived, and Arturo raised his in a toast. "All anyone ever needs is friends like you guys; *la lucha continua.*" And reaching over Tshabalala's head, he pulled it close to his. "*Si*, and now we are about to engage the entire African continent in our struggle."

Ripples of the African baritone resonated with the Mexican tenor, though Tshabalala seemed to have a momentary problem, his ivory eyes darting up to his toque, worried it seemed about Arturo knocking it off as his arm swept over his head. Stephanie's hoarse laugh sounded like a teasing warning. Then the secret struck Berrin: An afro, evidenced only by the bulge of the toque that drooped below his ears and over his forehead, a bulge that up till now he hadn't given much thought to, seeing it as the natural shape of the toque, its bright colour distracting the viewer's attention, orange against his skin. Why Tshabalala was afraid to show his afro was a mystery — no missionaries or head lice here.

The general mirth spread around the table. Jill had cut herself off from the camaraderie by reaching over and grabbing her essay from Berrin. She skimmed through it, and then circled a paragraph on the second page and drew an arrow to the top margin, where she wrote something, and handed it back to Berrin. He read,

> Check out their arrangement for these forts — like pearls strung across the countryside, peasants no more than grains of sand cemented by coercion, the cosmopolitan gems as elusive as ever.

Her meaning was as puzzling as was her composition, even after he followed her arrow down to the paragraph on fortified villages.

Tshabalala's reaction to Arturo's embrace had likely led to Jill's inspiration, his eyes darting up to his toque, orbs of such nacreous beauty that it was no surprise how Jill had fixed on her metaphor.

His thought went to the pearl, how wise it made an oyster look.

Jill took the essay back and gave it to Barry. "What do you think, Barry?"

Her actions were only too obvious and not fooling Barry — flirting with Arturo and pretending the contrary.

"A pearl, cosmopolitanism?" Barry snorted. "Maybe a clam shell would be more like it."

Berrin laughed, he had to hand it to Barry again, a much more apt metaphor.

Stephanie raised her glass, "Here's to your gem, Jill."

The revelry revived, and Jill's pearls were forgotten.

Berrin looked over at Tshabalala, who had remained a silent spectator throughout. With a semblance of a smile cutting through the chatter, Tshabalala was beckoning Stephanie to look over at another table tucked into the corner behind them. A man and a woman were sitting side by side, their chairs pushed back against the wall abutting the glass perimeter, and their table pulled in against themselves. The man was dressed head-to-toe in black, black overcoat and black suit; he might have been wearing an old fedora if he were intentionally trying to be theatrical. Berrin thought of the RCMP, and Barry's persistent worry about the suspicious cars parked outside their house. Jill had concurred; the telephones could also be tapped. She had made them all aware of the "Puzzle Palace" in their own national capital. Her first boyfriend worked there, *The Communications Security Establishment*, a truly post-modern marking of our civilization. However, this man's clothing was too soiled and tattered; the sleeves covered his thumbs, and his baggy legs stretched too gamely out from under the table. The woman, in a fake leopard skin coat, was stroking his head. An easy-going conversation, but from Berrin's angle of vision it was obvious that the fun was happening under the table, mostly hidden by their coats, where her other hand was gently priming him to a point of peak pleasure.

Berrin chuckled. The devils, his mother's word for it. The dark figure could have been straight out of her dreams. He also found himself beginning to sweat. A headache mushrooming.

He leaned back to massage his neck. He had skipped breakfast, another oversight to complement his whiskers. Under the table, Stephanie's leg was reaching across to kick a now widening grin off Tshabalala's face.

Jill had noticed the attention shifting to another table and turned as well, a quick glance, as was her style. "He looks like a cop."

Laughter, and Tshabalala's head made a slight swivel sideways. Stephanie raised her glass again, this time in a toast with Tshaba-lala.

"Here's to fission and fusion, gyrotons and pylons, and all other revolutions and uprisings."

Jill, baffled, gulped down the remainder of her beer.

Arturo didn't seem to care that he didn't understand. Here was his kind of sentiment, and he thrust his mug against the two meeting at the side of his head.

Barry raised his mug in a token gesture. Berrin met the gesture by clicking his beer mug against theirs. Though a sip helped, if he didn't eat immediately, a full-blown migraine was a certainty, and he'd be closeting himself in the darkness of his bedroom for the remainder of the day. He stood up, asking if anyone wanted to join him for some enchiladas.

Barry rose immediately, stepped around Stephanie, and kissed Jill on the cheek, a peck only, he had to get back to the bookstore, he said, with not a hint of a smile. He couldn't have eaten, either, Berrin realized. Jill interrupted her dialogue with Arturo to receive the kiss-off, and then as quickly turned back to delve deeper into the mysteries of the *problematique* she was entertaining with Arturo.

Tshabalala had his classes and Stephanie her shift at El Sol. They extended hearty handshakes with Arturo, they hoped to meet him later, then returned a perfunctory wave from Jill.

Stephanie whispered to Berrin as she passed, "Wish Eileen were here to party with us. But who knows, there might be space enough for her after all." A quick wink and she headed for the exit.

Berrin couldn't contain his smile . . . yes, some hope there, were Jill and Barry to part ways — and Jill wasn't averse to pushing it by inviting Arturo to stay over at the co-op. Arturo did attract this kind of attention.

Habit made Berrin turn to look down the aisle toward his booth. Dead space, not a customer in sight. The lampshade lady had left the building and a few booths still remained closed.

He then noticed a lone, middle-aged, unshaven man in a drab, open windbreaker reaching around the fishnet that covered a rack of batik silk blouses and scarves. He was nonchalantly stuffing scarves inside his shirt. Berrin hurried over. The man was drunk and humming to himself.

"Oh, I'm just trying them on."

"I think you should put them back and leave immediately."

"Okay, sure, mister," he slurred, handed over his booty, and then continued down the aisle to stop at the Chinese trinket stand ten staggered steps beyond. There, he proceeded to stuff fistfuls of miniature steamship pencil sharpeners into his pockets. The owner was in, but seated in the centre of his booth, apparently jotting down figures in a ledger, hidden behind his racks of paper umbrellas, rice-paper lampshades, beaded pouches, T-shirts silk-screened with cartoon characters, and any number of other imported paraphernalia. Berrin again directed the old crooner to empty his pockets, who finally awakened to the danger of being turned over to the cops and, without stopping, carried on toward the exit doors at the opposite end of the building.

Berrin turned back, but Arturo and Jill had disappeared as well. They must have wondered why he had left without saying goodbye.

Berrin paid for his enchiladas and returned to sit inside the row of ferns, his back to the cathedral behind him.

Why had he bothered, about the hobo, or even about what the gang might have thought about him? Arturo had again gladly sacrificed himself to the cause, more power to him.

The man in black had also left with his consort. He knew his priorities as well.

The man's appearance was more of a jolt than he cared to admit, back to worlds prior to puzzle palaces, to priorities as pressing as anything Arturo could resurrect.

The farm. He remembered. The man had reminded him of Alex's death.

Berrin stared past the empty tables to the frosted windows. Winter had been the worst for Alex, few visitors coming after hunting season. But was there any one season he ever enjoyed? April was the cruelest month, breeding more cattle out of the muddy earth. In the last few years, he'd taken forever to get himself out to the tractor. Then the haying season, and back to logging in the winter. It would be the hunting season he might have looked forward to the most. Alex didn't hunt, but the regulars always returned, and the stories began anew.

Until stories were no longer enough to counter the isolation. Alex's out, a massive heart attack.

He had heard enough from Claude Lacroix at Alex's funeral to draw his own conclusions. A lumberjack, Claude had stayed with Alex over that last winter, sleeping in the extra bedroom. He had described the lead-up to his heart attack, weak spells one afternoon while shovelling snow after that perennial last hurrah of winter at Easter. Alex insisted that all he needed was a good night's sleep. Claude warned him he might be having a heart attack, but he wouldn't listen.

The next morning, Alex had insisted he felt all right, that the only problem was the new snowfall. Common knowledge, he said, fresh snow always gives off a gas. Give it a day and it's all gone. And so he went out to shovel the drift from behind the truck and drove off to the village for the daily paper and mail.

And what Claude said next clinched the story. After returning from the village, Alex went down to the barn and shovelled manure out of the stalls — Hercules back to the stables.

But for his mother, a hero enough that Alex was the last of her family. How she had hoped against hope during those three final days in the hospital that somehow he'd pull through, never accepting the finality of his heart attack.

Then her dream, the night after the funeral. She was sitting on Alex's bed in his bungalow on the farm. A dark figure, so black, she had said, he sat beside her, leaning back against the wall, laughing. "Laughing," she said, her eyes large in alarm. "It was frightful, a horrible, maddening laugh. And then he said to me, 'I got him in the end, despite all your efforts.'" Then her hands snapped up like branches in a wind, "I grabbed him by the neck and he went limp. He just disappeared. I woke up feeling a whole lot better. You can give the devil his due, but he darn well better know his proper place when *my time* has come." Afterwards, she easily took full rein of the farm herself.

Or so she had tried. She needed a different ending to her story, one that he, Berrin, couldn't provide. It wouldn't be easy. He had known the farm since childhood, had grown up with it, knew it inside out, her point of view, Alex's, Martin's. Only Martin had escaped.

He could write his own script as well.

He could move forward, a simple, straightforward settling down, and he could shed the anger.

CHAPTER 23

As cold as ice, you're so cold

"THE FARM! THE FARM! Fuck the farm."

"I ought to clean out that mouth of yours with a bar of soap."

"Can't you see that after three generations it's nothing more than a pile of rocks, a delusion?" Berrin leaned back in his chair, swung his two legs up onto the corner of the kitchen table, and looked out the side window toward the deer pen. None of the fallow deer was in sight. Probably hiding in the ice house out of the sun, but his angle of view cut it off. He looked down at his novel.

His mother waited before answering, as if to get her second wind. She stood with her back to Berrin and stared out the window over the kitchen counter. The ice house was straight across the yard in front of her, but her mind was elsewhere. Her left hand still held the phone receiver she'd replaced on the wall mount. She let go of it to rub her ear, sore from pressing the phone against it. She had been calling the neighbours about a helicopter that had been crossing the farm, then she called Dad to get him to report it to whatever police department or patrol car he could find.

They had spotted it immediately upon entering the farm, or, rather immediately after their car topped the knoll at the northern entrance and the full valley below came into view. The helicopter was moving from right to left, crossing over the houses and barns in the middle section of the two lots that made up the homestead. It was trailing a long pipe at the end of a cable tied to its underbelly. "Something funny going on. It's not right . . . it's not right," she had shouted as he drove down the lane between the two front fields. By the time they drove up to the bungalow, the helicopter had disappeared over the bush behind the beaver meadow.

There was nothing that he could have done about it, or the farm, which was where their arguing took them. "Mother, there are better ways of getting screwed. You want me to end up like Alex?"

"Have you nothing good to say about any of your uncles? Always the profanity. The big city, what good has it done you? Sashaying around down there as if you owned the place."

"It's only because I've been in Ottawa all summer that I've been able to drive you and Dad up here." His anger was subsiding. He was already regretting his outburst.

"I should have come up with Dad," she replied, not quite a shout.

He dropped his legs and rose from the table and crossed behind her into the living room to sit in the swivel chair that had been Alex's favourite perch. Through the large picture window he could take in the old house and barns and all the back fields as far up as the rise at the lake. The other picture window beside him faced east, where the helicopter had disappeared over the low, level horizon. Holding his novel between his knees, he leaned into the windowpane and studied the grab-all garage that sat immediately across from the car. Its lower row of wallboards along the cement foundation was rotting away. He looked up toward the far ridge that marked the field leading to the lake. An abandoned log barn defined that slope, the logs at ground level also bulging out from too much rot. Too many jobs to do.

His mother spoke again. "So tell me, smarty-pants, why those lawyers and politicians want it so badly? They're all as crooked as blazes."

He looked back toward her to give her the eye, but she was

hidden behind the narrow partition at the end of the counter. "Mother, drop the helicopter. It's gone."

"But this is the second day it's been around. That's what Vera's just told me. It's been criss-crossing her farm all morning. Then it high-tails it as soon as we show up."

"The government's carrying out a mineral survey or something." His voice was softening. "Just don't bother about it."

"Easy for you to say. Wait until those uranium miners show up. You've heard about them."

"Mother, have a tea and relax."

"Alex would figure out what to do."

"And let loose a few bejesus blasts from his old Ross." The image improved his mood.

"And a tongue-lashing for that filthy tongue of yours, my boy. I'm going back to work." She rummaged through a drawer under the counter, then walked into the living room, crossing behind him. A quick glance told him enough. She was carrying binoculars, a pen, and a writing pad that she now placed on the television cabinet enthroned in the corner between the two picture windows.

"You could use that .22 calibre gun in the corner behind the kitchen door. It's easy enough to shoot."

"Guns, me arse." She rearranged the items once again, placing the pen on top of the pad, then taking it off and laying the binoculars flat on the pad and aligning the pen on the binoculars lengthwise between the two eyepieces. Reassured by this setup, she turned from the television and headed for her rocking chair that faced the other picture window. Her grip on the arm of the rocker as strong as ever, with the thick wrists of a long line of farmers. He looked at his own hands, too pale and too delicate.

She sank back hard against the wooden slats, her back to him, and took a deep breath. Her view took in the hayfield that stretched to the border of trees beyond the beaver meadow where the strand of hemlock stood guard above the swampy hollows, and where the helicopter likely would reappear.

"Look at that field, ripe and ready. I only hope Joey is mowing it again this year." The neighbour had the hay in exchange for paying the taxes, a good deal for everyone.

"Joey was Alex's best friend; he'd never let you down, Mom."

He turned back to his own view. The old homestead house across from the garage had always fascinated him, how it held up over a hundred years, and abandoned for the past thirty. A two-storeyed, board-and-batten log building, built from the original timber off the farm, now a museum of old furniture, a piano, and a pump organ. But it had been a great playground for children; the main hallway downstairs turned to total darkness when the end doors were shut, and they'd race about screaming to be scared as much as to scare. It was only in the summers that the house had come alive, when family and relatives came, cleaning it enough for their vacations, and helping Alex with the haying.

The early afternoon sun struck the window in the attic above the summer kitchen, the wavy glass like a pool of water between the slopes of the galvanized tin roof. Alex once told him when he was a kid how glass actually was a fluid, that it flowed like the waves on the lake coming to shore, and over the years leaving the glass thinner at the top and thicker at the bottom. He repeated Alex's punch line, "You know, Mother, it's time for a centennial celebration of the old house — we can call it *The Turning of the Panes*."

His mother hadn't heard, or was paying no heed to him. She was reaching into a large garbage bag full of wool that lay on the floor beside her rocker. She pulled out a handful and began picking the burrs and twigs out of the wiry mohair, difficult, given how long it had sat in the plastic bag, becoming tangled and matted and harsh to the touch. But he was glad she had found work that she could single-handedly pursue while resting at the same time; she might even get back to knitting. She then hesitated. She had spotted a cocoon buried in the wool. That definitely had to go. She worked quietly, glancing up every few minutes to check out her window.

It was her farm to defend, now. She always had a stronger heart than Alex. She jerked her head up, as if she'd heard the helicopter, then relaxed and began rocking, obviously brooding over the more immediate danger, the trailing pipe in the sky.

She spoke as if talking to herself. "At least you had girlfriends when you lived close to home."

She shook her head, as if to drive away any doubts about his coming to his senses, and returned to cleaning her mohair.

Movement in the yard caught the corner of his eye. A groundhog stood erect about ten feet away directly behind the garage. The old orange and white tabby crouched low on the grass below his window, its tail sweeping back and forth. The groundhog bounded forward, he could hear its angry whistle, but the cat easily dodged it and raced around to crouch again directly across from it.

He found himself rooting for the groundhog. Suddenly the two adversaries froze, cowering near the ground, and raced past each other, the cat disappearing under the windowsill and the groundhog ducking back into its hole at the corner of the garage.

The windows rattled and the house shook. In a bound, his mother grabbed her binoculars, pen, and pad and headed for the door. When she reached the front landing, the helicopter had already disappeared over the homestead house.

His mother seemed confused, taking one step down then turning and stepping back up. Given the angle of its flight, the helicopter must have doubled back to Johnny Miles's, the adjacent farm, abandoned now for at least two generations. No one left there to phone. She turned back again and took to the steps, her hand stretched out, touching the windowpane for balance, and continued toward the garage, disappeared behind it, then reemerged to tackle the grade toward the knoll. This ran up from the hay barn to where the ice house stood, or rather slanted forward, slowly sinking into the crest of the hill, like a faithful old ocean liner ploughing into another wave. From the higher ground, she'd likely gain a better view of the serial number, if that was what she was after. But then, there was the other option. The helicopter might have swept past the lake, only to follow the mountain backing it, and fly over the fields behind the barn.

As she approached the ice house, four fallow deer raced out. The largest, a buck, leapt through the air, bounced high into the chain-link fence, its legs punching through with a rattling clatter, rebounded, and raced off with the others around behind the ice house, its white tail high like a warning flag.

She stood shaking her head as if to say, Lucky you didn't break a leg. The deer pen at the ice house extended through a gate a half-acre farther down the slope, not the best. There was no argument that pushing the fence past the horse barn into the field would give the deer the few acres needed to reach the creek. But he had long ago concluded that the entire affair was wacky. If he got down to the brass tacks of this business venture, they'd be sure to be arguing again as soon as she returned inside.

He had decided to ignore the helicopter as he drove down the entrance lane; given her excited state, he knew it would compound her worries if he were to put forward any plausible explanation for its presence. But once inside the bungalow, she had deftly returned to the subject by bringing up the problem of fencing, and then the larger issue of the farm's future. There was no avoiding an argument.

"Berrin, I've been thinking about what you said."

"What did I say, Mother?"

"The last time we talked. Berrin, I don't want to fight like this, and it upsets your father, too. That's why he got up and went into the backroom the last time he came with us. But he likes it when you come up."

"What did I say, Mother?"

"Oh, you know. About the deer. There is a good bounce to them, you are right about that, but the fence only needs to be a foot or so higher. It'll be good for you to get out of your books for a change."

"It's not only the fence, it's also the upkeep. And it takes six thousand years to domesticate wild animals; fallow deer are only semi-domesticated. I've read up on it. They'll get out sooner or later, believe me, even if they're only half the size of wild deer. And they carry a lot of diseases."

"And there's no wild deer left in Europe because of people like me. You've said it all before. Nothing to do with all those wars they're hell-bent on waging over there. You have to be as blind as a bat not to see the real problems. The summer is in full bloom and the grass in the pen's no higher than the hairs on a pig's back. They need more space."

The four deer were now crowded together in the far corner of the small corral that surrounded the ice house, their satin tan bodies parallel to each other, and every head turned toward her, the buck with its full head of horns keeping to the rear. Venison, the best-tasting meat, likely her only thought about them.

She stood on the high ground overlooking the barnyard where it sloped down to the creek below the hay barn. She was looking over its roof up toward the lake. *No, Mother, no helicopter in sight, and not likely to return.*

Her gaze seemed to rest on the three pine trees at the horizon of the mountain beyond the lake. Perhaps Alex was close at hand, supporting her. The many scheming developers circulating throughout the countryside, eyeing the best buys, getting ready to pounce . . . they didn't intimidate her any more than the helicopters. She wouldn't be selling.

She turned to eye the floor inside the ice house, as if pondering how much it had risen with the cattle wandering in and out of it over the years, the overhead barely high enough for the deer. He remembered, he had to have been quite young, when Alex dug a block of ice out of the stack of sawdust and carried it to the icebox in the summer kitchen.

He looked back at the summer kitchen of the old house. A wedding ring still sat in its case on the gun rack under the stairs. A story never told.

His mother was now looking across the creek toward the opposite hill where Old Dolly stood alone among the few remaining Herefords. The folly of selling the other horse . . . Old Dolly must be thinking he's a cow by now.

A breeze fluttered her dress. *Mother, Alex would indeed be proud, you've kept some cows and brought back the chickens, geese, and ducks*, though he never saw a snapshot with geese or ducks or goats in it. And no pigs. She once told how a big sow had attacked her in the barn when she was a child, knocking the wind out of her.

She was looking at the old Gobbler beside the icehouse, its rusted seat naked against the clear sky. Then down at the old rake lying half-hidden in the long grass, left one evening after Alex had broken one too many forks on a rock; perhaps reconsidering her position.

She had the farm, she had her snaps, and probably had even drawn Alex back from the grave. She could raise a stink like a polecat.

"Alex at least is keeping an eye on me."

She had reached for the phone, and he had tried to get back to his novel. The neighbour was worried as well, but knew nothing about it. A second call: Dad didn't seem interested, and she had slammed the phone down onto its wall mount. "What's the use of getting angry? Like my mother once told me, it is best to ignore men when they ignore you. Berrin, you can't say it's not your home, you can't deny that. You know who your neighbours are. You've even forgotten your religion."

"Well, Mother, you can't be forgetting the child abuse in Williams Lake? At the very least, Martin must have —" but he stopped himself from finishing the sentence.

Her knees had buckled and she hung on the phone for support, looking down into the sink. "I won't hear of such dirt about your uncle. Please."

"I'm not accusing him, Mother, but at the very least he must have known."

"You're as blind as a bat," she was pleading. "It's our life. The farm — "

"The farm, the farm . . ." The cursing had burst out of him.

He now had to squint, the sunlight suddenly too bright as it poured in over his swivel chair. He pressed his lips together to clamp down on the memory of the argument.

The helicopter might be a concern, especially if government were involved. She didn't have the wherewithal to handle that. He would relish the challenge of taking on those lawyers.

She was standing as motionless as the wisps of cloud high above the mountains. Silence. Perhaps trying to catch the call of a loon carried on the breeze.

He thought to go out and warn her to come back inside — she'd die of sunstroke. But at that moment, a mini-twister crossed the yard in front of her, twirling up a funnel of dust that travelled down the hill toward the barn. A raven swooped down from the roof, as if born in the swirl of dust. It swerved past her head, startling her.

Perhaps she'd see it as another message from Alex, telling her to come inside. She turned and stepped back.

Better ravens than helicopters.

Her foot struck something and she tripped, stumbling sideways, dropping her binoculars and pad. A step behind her, the old stone boat; she kept her balance long enough to land on it.

He got up and raced to the kitchen door. From the back steps, he shouted over to her: Was she all right? She held up her arm and waved him off, as if to say: *Yeah, yeah, just leave me be.* She sat, head bent forward, probably catching her breath, and then she looked around. Even from the distance of thirty feet or so, he could also see the end of the whippletree sticking out of the ground near where she had stood, a relic likely from the days when the blocks of ice were drawn down from the lake by Dolly.

It would be some weeks later, after she had been released from the Civic Hospital, that he understood what had happened next. From the steps, he had watched her rise from the stone boat and head back, taking the shortcut behind the garage. She would not want him observing her, so he retreated inside and decided to wait in her rocker, which he turned around to be facing the kitchen. He had resolved to apologize and let the conversation proceed as it may; at least they would be on friendly terms again. He was about to get up to check again when the kitchen door cracked open. Once inside, she seemed to freeze, one hand still on the doorknob as she leaned on the counter for support. She was staring straight ahead as if she had spotted someone across the table, but from the living room he was unable to see down the hallway that led to the bedrooms in back. She took a step forward, uttered a few words almost in a whisper, incoherent, she was cold. Then she collapsed.

She told her side of the story as he sat in her dining room of their town house in Old Chelsea. She played solitaire as she talked, his dad remaining in the living room watching the news on their old cabinet television. She had cursed the whippletree, then cursed herself for swearing like him. Even being as rotten as it was, the wooden shaft had managed to trip her, the iron tip with its ring intact and as solid as new. Strange, she said softly, how it never rusts, coated in its layers of dust, like bones must get.

"My chest was hurt," then she frowned as if from the wonder of it, and she glanced up from her cards, hesitating, as if her own storytelling awoke some doubt, as if she were questioning herself. The fall hurt, she said. "The planks of that old stone boat are so well spaced and squared — Alex was very good with an axe, you know — I was able to get a grip on the planks and raise my hindquarters first, as wobbly as an old cow, but who cares when someone's my age. I had to hold myself together, but I made it back."

He remembered how she had crossed her arms on her chest as she headed for the bungalow.

"I wish someone would fix the stairs of that old porch." She stared straight over her cards at him when saying this. "The lowest step was rotten. But I held onto the railing and pushed with my other hand against the wall."

The sharp stones of the stucco had dug into her palm. He

remembered, as she lay unconscious on the kitchen floor, picking out two tiny green and white pebbles imbedded in her right palm.

"At the top of the steps, I had to stop to catch my breath. My heart was bursting, there was this numbness all through my body. Slowing up . . . I have to face it, I wouldn't be finishing everything.

"I looked around at the mountains. Do you remember standing there with me, Berrin, when you were a tiny tyke, and we'd shout out together across the fields and wait for the mountains to return our cries?"

She smiled and shuffled the few cards remaining in her hand. He felt he could again hear the cascading echoes of their shouts, their ricocheting against each other, merging, transforming, and yes, he remembered, they had only to listen closely enough, the sound of their voices first reflected off the side of the large hay barn, then the distant mountain added a second reverberating echo.

"I took a second breath, and then I knew: give you more time. Time transforms; you will come around. I saw pictures of butter-flies and whippoorwills. And then I felt Alex was nearby. The latch gave way. I almost collapsed against the counter. You must have been looking at me, weren't you? I didn't see you. But Alex was there, standing at the far side of the table. He's alive, I thought. I can't be staying here at the door. I wanted to walk up to him. He looked so grand, standing there, looking right through me. I had to get closer and hug him. My, what a grand smile he had, a real pleased look."

He had seen her manage the one step forward and put out her hand, and then, as she concluded her story, he heard her final outcry, "Oh, God, your hands are cold, they're as cold as ice, you're so cold!"

CHAPTER 24

Dance me a jig

THE RINGING OF THE TELEPHONE pulled him out of his recollections. It felt like pins pricking his brain, even from four booths away. Minds in sync, definitely his mother calling. Or maybe Alex from on high, to get in his side of the story. Berrin took the last sip of his Corona as he rose from the table and squeezed past the ferns, and in passing the slippers, he hit upon one possible solution for his mother. Orville, the craftsman with the sheepskin, might know how she could unload her bags of mohair, rotting away as they were in the old horse stable. Since her heart attack, she'd become less insistent about her plans. He had helped her sell the remaining animals, convincing her to leave the farm fallow for a while and just enjoy her weekend outings. Only the wild tabby remained. Developments that helped explain why he was beginning to enjoy the visits; he'd ignore her badgering and go for her stories.

The sixth ring, "Hello, hello?" No answer. The line was dead.

He raised his hand to his forehead, numb and cold. The enchiladas had helped; now for some fresh air and that book he's been brooding about for weeks. Business all but dead, and already into the afternoon. Within minutes, he returned, carrying a brown paper bag.

"What is the book?" The heavy French accent came from behind the watercolours. "The" sounded as "de." *Richard* was in.

He was looking up from his sketchpad, his manner of working through the day whenever his girlfriend wasn't around.

You get labelled by your habits — so much for trying to hide his wanton expenditure.

"Good morning, *Richard.*" He pronounced his name in French — Ree-shard — though almost everyone else in the building seemed to keep to the English. "I needed a good read. To drown out the traffic in here."

"Let me see the cover," *Richard* persisted, so he held it up. William Kennedy's *Quinn's Book.*

"The southern Irish, great storytellers. A bit pricey for a paperback, but I couldn't resist."

"You're in luck, Berrin. I saw it in hardback at Coles. A toonie or two."

"You're sure it was this one?"

"*Oui.* I looked at it because I remember you talking about the guy, and the cover's the same, that pencil drawing of the shore and the boats. I liked it."

"Well, if you're sure, I'll take it right back. I have something else to read anyhow." Somehow he had ended up keeping Jill's essay.

"Berrin, I had a good book yesterday. I can lend it to you. She's a Canadian writer. But very interesting. Experimental. She's a friend of a friend. You will enjoy it. It's interesting how she experiments wit' language."

"I'm giving up on that. Anything not straight up front is suspicious." And that word experiment, using it twice, *Richard* would normally have been interested only in the cover.

"But it is great writing, different."

"What I like right now is a solid story, a good read."

"It was also up for a Governor General's Award or something."

"Good for her."

"Berrin, I'd love to have your opinion on it. She's English and living in Montreal. I tell you, you will like it. I will bring it in next week."

"Fine. I'll return mine. Can't read now, anyhow. I got a headache.

Keep an eye on my booth, will you please?"

He should have gone to the music store in the first place, he remembered; he had intended to look for a copy of "Moonlight in Mayo."

The phone was ringing again when he returned. The heat inside the building was suffocating, reviving his headache.

"Hello." No answer again, but the line stayed open this time.

"Mother, are you there? Are you all right?"

"Of course I'm here, where else would I be? And why wouldn't I be all right?"

"I'm just asking. You sound upset."

"No. You know about that helicopter?"

"Yes, Mother."

"It was searching for marijuana. Can you believe that? I don't know why they're bothering us. I know they've found some of it up the Pontiac, but there're no hippies this side of the mountains."

"What about those running that store in Wakefield, where you wanted to trade your wool?"

"Such a sweet, hard-working young couple, they'd have no time for that nonsense. I can see a plant or two for the fun of it. Alex once tried growing a pot of it on his windowsill, but then nearly jumped out of his skin when a police car drove up one day. He chucked those plants mighty quick into the wood stove. It turned out they were after poachers."

"Looks like the stuff attracts company, at least."

"Winter will do that well enough, I'm afraid. Any young galoot on a skidoo will have a free rein of the place. That, and the wild deer. Joey said he saw twenty-nine of them in the front field the other day when he was checking things out. The place is becoming a zoo whether we want it or not."

Farms closer to Hull had been expropriated for a provincial zoo. She was again launching into the story, years ago and no zoo yet, how lawyers can take over your land at any time. He rested his elbow on the counter to wait it out.

Frost had formed on the window in front of him, screening out the street with a sweep of perfect ferns. The temperature had taken a surprising dive. He leaned out from his stool, reached across to the glass, and started tracing his fingernail along the clean outline of the leaves. The ice crystals melted where he touched them, and through the tiny rivulets that streaked down the glass, he saw a solitary shopper hurrying past, her head bent to a frigid wind.

He rotated his head several times to massage his neck muscles.

". . . my lawyer could have handled things differently. He didn't need to tell Dad that the farm belonged only to me. But we married out of Quebec, no changing that. You've seen him with money, likely to sell off any part he'd own. Too much bone in his head and never enough dough in his pockets."

"Yes, Mother, we men do love money too much."

"Women! Baloney." It took him a second to catch her take on the "we men." "You men never listen. Berrin, you could work out something with Dad. Just talk with him."

Above the frost line directly in front of him, he noticed a pigeon perched on a parking meter.

"Berrin, you could have a garden, a few chickens."

"There're enough pigeons in the market here for a feed, Mother." Plump and ready for winter, like himself.

"So much cockamamie, just too clever you are with your tongue, always trying to derail people with it."

He concentrated on the magic in the frost. "I'm sorry, Mother. Listen, someone could rent the bungalow for now, and we'd have money to fix up the old house. You know how people are these days, so many separating."

"Herb down the road dumped his wife for a young thing. She supported him when he went for retraining, then he up and leaves her for someone he meets in the class. My dates were like that, always after one thing, as if there were nothing else. Except your dad. He always respected me."

"The modern way, Mother."

"I remember one of my first dances with your dad. It wasn't a date, just a church picnic. We finished the dance and crossed over to where his parents were sitting there along the wall. His dad dropped his cane, and I bent to pick it up, and he brightens up, my, he had a sense of humour, and quick, that's what I liked about Grandpa. I handed him the cane, and he says with a laugh that got everyone in on the joke, 'Take me cane, Nelly, and dance me a jig.' Every eejit in the room split a gut laughing."

He wasn`t certain if she intentionally was telling an off-colour story. His hand had soaked up the cold of the window pane and he rubbed his neck with it. His mother had fallen silent, likely lost in her reverie.

"I'll pay you and Dad a visit soon."

"Promise?"

"Promise. Say hi to Dad."

"I knew you would change your mind."

CHAPTER 25

What number are you?

BERRIN PULLED THE SLIDING DOORS open to the sidewalk outside. He stood in the gap to take in the fresh breeze. The feel of snow in it, snapping the city awake, attention turning from brisk tasks to group outings, skaters on the canal, skiers to the hills, hockey loudness. The goalie in the gap, no score; if he only put his mind to it he'd be part of it. He heard a familiar giggle from across the street, while across the floor behind him, Stan shouted, I'm freezing, then the snickering — a head like a puffball that would explode with a swift kick. Berrin surprised himself by this burst of anger, then he realized his target was outside, the giggling, and he looked to see Eileen and Jeff crossing the intersection at the far end of the building.

Probably heading for the rear door, coming to visit. Eileen was leaning into Jeff, at such an angle that were he to take one step away she'd surely fall, if she didn't first slip on the frozen pavement. Her laughter still challenged, a playful test of their relationship, daring Jeff to let her fall. Berrin couldn't believe his eyes.

Jeff continued straight ahead, like a fence post, expressionless, any reciprocal smile frozen out by a firmly set jaw. How could she let herself be so easily fooled?

Before they reached the sidewalk, a woman pushing a baby stroller stopped and looked at the children's shoes in the window.

She motioned to enter and threaded the gap he vacated. As she jostled the stroller around the pottery stand to the shoes, he shut the doors. Perhaps they would not be visiting. No hale heartiness wanted.

The woman's inquiries were a welcome distraction. They're handmade, Madam, by a leatherworker out of town. The colour you want is over here. And they moved to the front near the aisle where more shoes were stored under the sheepskin display.

He was kneeling in front of the stroller, prying the child's foot into a blue and mauve Oxford, when he felt Eileen standing to his right. He looked up. Apologetic eyes, but she said hello nevertheless. Jeff repeated the greeting, first to him and then to the customer, feigning a great interest in all the activity. He nodded down for Berrin to finish off the sale and smiled to the woman holding the other shoe. A slim, black, imitation-leather zip-up pouch was tucked under his arm. He was dressed like a yuppie, a grey jacket, suede, a blue silk shirt, no tie, but open at the collar to reveal a suggestion of chest hair, matching charcoal-grey trousers and nubucks. You'd think it was summer. Eileen was wearing her overcoat, her collar buttoned up, but her neck bare.

They couldn't have been outside for long, probably sticking to the inside malls of the Rideau Centre until Jeff insisted on a better deal, like the Giant Tiger's bargain bins down the street.

Eileen moved toward the stained-glass jewellery and then turned to the competitor's booth in the middle aisle. Pan crossed the floor to serve her.

Berrin was writing up the bill for the shoes when his attention returned to them. Eileen was bent over the glass showcase, looking at the customized wristwatches, Jeff ramrod at her side, as if giving her all the time she needed.

When Berrin stooped behind the counter for a shoebox, Jeff crossed over and engaged his customer in conversation. Eileen remained fixed on the watches in the middle aisle, bowing down to examine the intricate artwork on their faces, the heels of her palms pressing against the top corners of the glass to support herself. Stan retrieved the key from the cash box at his booth and returned to open the case.

Jeff had somehow guessed the customer was German and began speaking in a bantering fashion as if they were old friends. A surprise he could speak a second language, but his speed in switching back to English showed up his fluency. The woman had shoulder-length, dark, straight hair, a slightly pale complexion, her black leather overcoat clinging to a slender body, muscular like that of a racing filly. Jeff's guess that she was German might have been his as well, Berrin realized, had he the interest.

The woman switched to English in turn, "But where did you pick up German?"

"A few lessons in university. I didn't continue, but I want to travel to Germany someday. I wish my German were as good as your English."

"I've been here a few years, but my ex-husband won't be leaving for another year. I want my son to be near his father." She laughed politely.

As she spoke, Jeff casually unzipped his pouch as if he were fidgeting and laid it spread open on the glass countertop beside the cash register. A writing kit in fake leather, with a notepad, miniature pen, envelopes, and a digital timepiece in a white plastic frame shaped like a loonie. And a lackadaisical Jeff glancing down toward it for whatever reason, but the woman showed no interest.

She spoke in German again.

Jeff laughed. "It's fascinating. German vows are somewhat pagan, aren't they? *As long as need and desire doth last.* I like how 'desire' is written in German, l-u-s-t."

"Given my experience, the word should be translated as lust."

Jeff shied away from the edge in her voice by again looking down at his kit.

"Why your interest in marriage rites? Planning to become a minister?" she asked.

"I'm an amateur." Jeff quickly glanced sideways at Berrin. "An investigative journalist, as it were. I collect stories about people. A hobby, it keeps my batteries charged." He had rattled this off without a stammer.

"I see, like collecting different marriage vows from around the world." Her lips now tightly drawn, almost a smile.

"Yes," and he looked over at Eileen who stood more erect now, more composed, attentive but still looking down at the watches. She turned as if anticipating Jeff's question.

"And Eileen, what number are you?"

Eileen's face turned white and her smile froze. Jeff didn't notice this transformation, so caught up by his incontinent wit that he immediately turned back to his real target.

Berrin offered his customer the distraction she needed. "Would you like anything else, Miss?"

She took her bag of shoes, gave Jeff a blank look, then offered Eileen what seemed a slight smile of condolence, and looked from Berrin to the doors. He hurried to slide them open again and she jiggled the stroller over the tracks to outside.

Jeff remained at the desk. He picked up his note kit, held it shut in his hand without zipping it up, and said, "Honey, we gotta go. Time's running out on the meter."

Eileen had returned to the watches, her voice sharp with an air of insistence. "Look at this one — she must be Aphrodite. And there's a unicorn."

Jeff stepped up behind her and gripped her elbow as if to tug her toward the door. She jerked it away. He then looked over her shoulder to give his cursory agreement on the watches. Stan, seeing only a prospective sale, pointed out that the watches were made by a woman in Montreal, that in fact all the crafts in his booth were Canadian.

Berrin returned to the high swivel chair behind the desk, to wait and watch.

Jeff was leading Eileen away. His saccharine jabber continued, about how beautiful all the things in the building were, that they must return sometime. Eileen looked through the plate glass exterior and pulled her collar up tight around her neck. Jeff stopped and turned back. He opened his note kit again and pointed to the white plastic timepiece, holding it over the counter so Berrin could have a better look.

"I bought it at the corner store. A dollar ninety-five. You gotta keep an eye out for any bargain, don't you, eh, Berrin?"

An ingratiating remark, or compensating for having ignored him till now? Or a barb aimed at Eileen?

His own nod, inadvertent and immediately regretted. They were about to pass through the doorway when he collected himself and called, holding a finger up, "One sec, Eileen," and ran to the adjacent booth. A pilfered silk scarf, a just reward for his earlier vigilance, and he wrapped it around her neck. Eileen kissed him lightly on the lips and hugged him goodbye. A muzzled Jeff turned and followed her outside.

He watched them cross the street. They walked side by side, both very upright.

Instead of elation, his mood took a dive. He locked his till and stepped outside and closed the glass doors behind him, his gesture with the gift probably as irrelevant in Eileen's life now as was Jeff's cruelty.

CHAPTER 26

I'm with you

IRRATIONAL HOW HE SUDDENLY needed to hear Stephanie's voice, a raw pitch that matched her wry smile, ready with a quick quip when needed. Eileen could use some of that defiance. Arturo was right: She would have fared better had she remained in Ottawa, around friends to support her.

The front windows of El Sol were still covered with pastel chalk paintings of grass and flowers and a child's beaming sun. His sternum constricted, at least it was a counterweight to his aching head. He tried to ignore them both as he entered the store, then thought, a health food store should have a cure. In his readings, he had come across a welcome bit of folklore that echoed his own condition, an eighteenth-century account of an Irish peasant who sought relief with a herbal lady who placed a glass over a lit candle on his chest to suck his pain away. His own chest pain then was real, if not altogether genetic, and definitely not some modern neurosis invented by Freud and his gang to delude mankind with, ever after.

Stephanie was not in sight. The cashier glanced at him and continued ringing up more items for a customer. Dry herbs hung along the windows. The scent relaxed him somewhat. Next came a pungent scent, mildly choking, and he spotted the burning stick of incense beside the cash register. Giving the space its proper sanctity. The New Age zeal, though likely much healthier than his own lost ideologies. But he *was* trying to adapt. He had been coming to the store for a few weeks already, growing familiar with the produce and trying to persuade himself that Stephanie might be right about his diet. He moved to the end of the counter, but his eyes were too sore to be reading the magazines. Deeper down the rows, now less unfamiliar in their layout. Incense decreasing.

Sampling the dried fruit was tolerated, and a bit of fructose was supposed to be better for hypoglycemia than sucrose. Some of the bulk bins were without covers — how quickly we revert; he hadn't minded the hordes of flies in the restaurant in Tepepan-tiango after surviving the rancho. He tried reading the backs of packages to decipher the contents and settled on the larger font of product names. Foreign, mostly. Ume-su-umebosh Vinegar, at least one familiar word there. Dulse, kombu — seaweed, the better to put you in touch with your instincts. Garbanzo, lima beans, lentils. Tofu, the ingredient his recipe called for.

He was standing by the dairy cooler in the back section of the store, trying to decide between the soft and the firm tofu, when he heard familiar voices, an edge in them catching his attention, and he looked up to see Stephanie standing beside a grocery cart half full with store stock. She was in profile, talking to someone in front of her, more feisty than usual, the person hidden by the half-wall that separated the store from the office and storage area.

He turned back to the tofu before she could notice him. Focus on the colours of the packaging, a more analyzable phenomenon. The firm tofu was blue and the soft was red. Stephanie's slicing voice made him look up. She had spotted him and sharpened her tone.

"Berrin, do you want to know what we're fighting about?"

"I wasn't actually listening."

"He thinks all feminists are lesbians."

Berrin moved away from the cooler to put a face to the other voice . . . Jacques, one of the store owners, standing at the door to his tiny office, his hand raised to his head. He was gripping his heavy tortoise-shell glasses between his fingers, then readjusted them on his nose. His eyes were watery and his baby face flushed redder than usual.

"This conversation has become very convoluted," Jacques said, his slight stutter suggesting annoyance.

Stephanie interrupted. "He can't handle the fact that I might be attracted to different people."

"I was making a joke." Jacques's red cheeks were now speckled with white spots, as if frostbitten. The dark frames of his glasses matched the colour of his short, curly hair, hair that together with his boyish chubbiness was groomed to champion a persona of New-Age innocence and sensitivity. Good that Stephanie was ruffling it.

"I suspect this is part of a larger conversation."

"He's been talking about sex all afternoon," Stephanie said as she returned to pulling bags of cereal from boxes and loading them into her cart.

"Sex is a favourite subject in the Market generally, isn't it?" A neutral enough stance, he thought, however much it lent some support to Jacques.

Stephanie's chin jutted out as she spoke; he had never seen her so upset. "His girlfriend was here earlier shopping out front and he whispered to me, 'Isn't she beautiful?' A nice remark, I thought, and I agreed; I said I found her attractive."

Jacques interrupted, "And I made a joke, I said, 'So you're a lesbian!'"

The white spots were now as red as the rest of his face.

Stephanie exploded again. "A lesbian! And what does that mean? So I said, 'What?' And you said, 'Oh, I mean you're a feminist.'" Stephanie scored her points by jabbing her index finger to a spot in front of her. Had Jacques been one step nearer, sternums would have been set to hurting for seven generations of his offspring, another piece of trivia he'd picked up at the magazine stand.

"Just no sense of humour," Jacques said as he shifted his gaze away from both of them to some shipping invoices on the green plastic clipboard that he held above his belly bulge. He then waved his fountain pen at her, smiling now. "She always takes me too seriously." His pen matched the colour of the clipboard.

Silence. Jacques and Stephanie had stalled in their battle. "Well, Stephanie, all feminists are lesbians, it's obvious. Like all true love is homosexual." She should have smiled. An artist had recently uttered this statement at a Toole Gallery vernissage while they stood in a circle of aficionados around him, this self-styled intellectual implying several layers of meanings without committing himself to any one of them, but once proclaimed, witticism became a truism. Ridiculous, little more than a revision of Freud's fear that all men were never man enough.

Stephanie hadn't picked up on his allusion. Her face was pale, with dark circles under her eyes. It might have been the fluorescent lighting; he hadn't noticed it earlier in the Market building.

"Right on!" Stephanie exclaimed, "I was thinking to myself, if I were a man, I would be attracted to her; but given the choices around here, I'd definitely be lesbian."

Something was awry. Even with Barry, she had been somewhat forgiving. He didn't bother to follow Jacques's next few utterances as he persisted to make light of her mood.

On her feet all afternoon should not be that strenuous. However, Berrin's blank-eyed bafflement did spur her on.

"I told him that no man really satisfied me until Tshabalala came into my life. And he can't handle that statement."

Gargoyles in the new world order. Perhaps Jacques harboured the same fear, being seen as another stock item, to be placed back on the shelf, a commodity to be exchanged for the next new brand.

Berrin looked from Stephanie to Jacques and back to her. This wasn't helping his headache. He juggled his two bricks of tofu from one hand to the other, pretending to compare their weights.

The dispute should then have exhausted itself, but Jacques

dropped both his hands to his sides, looked at Berrin as if to convince him he was joking — it must be in such moments that men become old buddies.

"We men must stick together." Humour, as lame as Jacques's persistence, and Stephanie's slight smile threatened to become a definite sneer. "I mean, I agree with you, Stephanie. But things become so adversarial, don't they?"

"It really has nothing to do with him, anyhow." Stephanie was tiring of it all, waving them off with her free hand as she turned back to her cart.

He raised the scout's salute in return, Good Luck. If he had more time, Berrin thought, he could put some surreal angles on the mixup. And then his mind went blank, at the point where the pun on cereal suggested itself to him. Stephanie was holding a bag of puffed kamut in her hand, the words written in the same block lettering that Jill had used on her protest signs.

"Well, Stephanie, I'll be *Mr. Kaput* if I don't hurry up. My night to make supper, remember." He turned away without asking if she liked tofu, as she forced a see-you-later smile.

A few minutes later, he spotted her down the aisle from him. She was replenishing the rice cakes.

"I'll have some of those, Stephanie. They look like giant-size communion hosts, don't they?"

Stephanie handed him the rice cakes. He tore open the cellophane packaging and bit into one of the cakes. The unavoidable crumbs fell to the floor.

"You can find a broom at the back of the store, sir, in Jacques's office."

The rice pellets stuck to the roof of his mouth, giving him an excusable pause before answering. "Maybe it's none of my business, Stephanie, but I'm surprised someone who's basically a bureaurat got to you like that."

"Like I said, I don't have a cat to kick around." She pulled some more rice cake packages out of the box and put them on the top shelf. Underneath were a number of finely crafted pewter bowls and kerosene lamps displayed on a glass shelf; her gaze fixed on them.

So, it was something else. "What are you doing for Thanksgiving weekend?"

"Tshabalala's folks are coming to town. I don't think they know about me."

"He's not mentioned you yet?"

"No, he hadn't, and he just did."

"Just now? I mean, he's told you this just after you left the market?"

"Yes. They're forever jet-setting around the world. We'll work it out somehow."

But that wasn't a look of happiness on her face. And she obviously didn't want to talk about it. She pulled her cart closer as she rested her other hand on the glass shelf. The shelf crashed. He reached out to grab her, his touch only glancing her other arm as it swung around to check her fall and landed on the wooden frame above.

His chest ripped open and his love rushed out to her.

She then was holding her fist in her other palm as she turned to sit on the bottom shelf, a wooden shelf.

The hole in his chest closed as quickly as it had opened.

Love? Or a shot of adrenalin, such was his immediate thought, but his chest had snapped shut as surely as a bear trap, giving him greater pause.

She spoke, exhausted, it seemed. "Sometimes I think I'm at the end of my rope."

She looked first up at him, then down at the floor as she continued. "I don't know how I keep on going."

"Did you cut yourself?"

"No. The end of the glass must've slid off the metal prong as I leaned on it. I keep telling Jacques this kind of shelving is criminal."

"You okay?"

"I'll be all right."

"Are you sure?"

"Really, finish your shopping. I need to rest a sec."

He stepped aside and she picked up the glass shelf and from her sitting position placed it into her cart. Luckily, it hadn't broken. She began slowly collecting the pewter pieces that lay at her feet. Everything had survived intact. No need to linger any longer.

After some wandering through the aisles, he settled on an additional purchase of brown rice. The label on the front of the plastic bin read, "Long Grain Organic," wording he could understand. He again crossed paths with Stephanie at the cash. Beyond giving him her regular smile, she concentrated on punching through his items. The bag of rice, the rice cakes, his box of tofu, the bottle of soy sauce.

"I can't remember to call it tahini or tamari," he said.

She ripped the receipt stub from the cash register.

"I hope that that's the end to the cheesy renovations around here," she said as he picked up his bag of groceries.

A final salutation, it wouldn't hurt. "Keep up the good fight."

"It wasn't a fight; there never is a fight."

"I see." But he didn't see. "I mean, I'm with you on it. I'm with you."

Her face remained blank as she turned to the next customer behind him.

CHAPTER 27

The bear meant no harm

BEST IF HE WERE GUILLOTINED. Should have grabbed a tofu burger instead of a cake of sawdust. Berrin headed down the hall to the kitchen, poured himself a glass of water, and sat at the table. He dribbled some into his palm and slapped it on his forehead. *I'm with you.* His comment had dogged him all the way back. No way did he have any "with" with Stephanie, totally cracked to think it. As dumbfounding as Eileen's appearance with Jeff.

It had to have been her idea to drop by, not knowing it was likely the last act in their drama. She had been laughing when leaning into Jeff while crossing the street, in open sight of his booth. Total trust. They were again reconciled, the scene she wanted him to witness. And Jeff's trip to Toronto, likely legit. Straightforward enough, or else he would not have returned sooner than expected. But as much a jerk as ever.

He pressed the wet heels of his palms against his eyeballs.

As much as he was blind. His dream last night his warning: getting involved with her would swamp him. A trap. Regardless of the flames and snakes, his attention should have been on the trap door, and the debris floating underneath.

His other mistake, retreating to his chair behind the counter after the German lady left, hoping for some detachment. Staring down from the heavens, the proverbial fly on the wall, a Zeus changing himself into a fly but landing on the fly sticker. So much for the fullness of the quaternity. Like Christ's descent into hell, add that to his triple personality and you get the real story, another journey through the four stages of life, and someone very square. *The Godfly and the Trap Door*; he could work it all into some kind of script, even include a recent dream that had him in the role of a Christ figure.

He massaged his forehead. Travelling to the four corners of the universe for a goddamn bit of love.

Need to sleep. A power nap. But no sooner was he under the covers than the doorbell rang. Jerome, surprise, which is how he greeted him, and he wove back down the hall, Jerome trailing after him. A perfume-like scent struck him, almost too pungent.

Best to make supper right away.

He pointed to the table to tell Jerome to sit while he poured himself another glass of cold water. The mirror on the cupboard door caught his rising vertigo. His eyes smarted with the brightness of one suffering from a fever. He returned to the table as Jerome began to talk, nasal, white noise, how he'd never visited and so was taking him up on his offer, then came the apology for being in such a foul mood on the phone.

"Francine wants us to remain friends. For the sake of the kids."

"Sounds like progress to me."

"Friends? The bitch wants it both ways." Jerome's mouth remained open, as if a good healthy yawn had been caught short by this nonsense.

Berrin remembered a game Eileen would play on him, sticking her finger into his mouth when he yawned, to tease him.

Jerome continued, "I'm beginning to think that real friendship exists only between men." Then he stopped and dropped his gaze to the floor.

A moment of silence, a blessing. What to add? He had already given Freud the boot.

"Do you mind if I smoke?" Jerome broke in again.

"Yes."

Jerome's face turned redder.

"Berrin, the new show's opening tonight. The media had a field day with last night's lead-up. Attendance can only go up. Know that puffy broadcaster, what's his name?"

Jerome was sitting at an angle, as if with a pain in his ass. Like a puffed-up teddy bear that someone stuffed into the chair and pressed firmly into place to ensure that it wouldn't topple over, his button-blank eyes never focusing.

"Always with the bloated opinions and never the straight news? And you're surprised?"

"Can't find out how he turned up. If he'd only read my curatorial statement, he —" Jerome's voice was rising.

How to turn down the volume? The cold surface of the glass against the forehead, some relief. He rolled it from one temple to the other.

Jerome, the self-styled temple oracle, the talking head, blank and bald and as red-faced as the prick of a dog.

Perhaps a bit unfair; he needed to refocus. Jerome was going through his own rough times.

He refilled his glass with fresh cold water and sat down again. Silica cold, if only his mind were as crystal clear. From upstairs, a printer was ripping up the air. Mariachi music. He angled his head to press the glass against the back of his neck. Some water happily spilled down his spine.

Jerome had stopped talking and was again staring at the floor in front of himself, his eyes sending out a supplicating message, unnerving.

Jerome then put a question, "So, I'll see you at the vernissage tonight? We've scheduled the artist talk as well. Hit them with everything up front."

The naked artist talk, why not. "I don't know, Jerome, I might. But this migraine has been getting worse all day, and I have to make supper. Maybe food will clear it up. I'll see."

He led Jerome to the door and found himself trailing the distinctive odour as he returned down the hall. Most likely perfume. Or else Jerome was handling too many of those exhibition pieces. A sharp pain spread from one eyeball to the other. Time to prepare a hearty meal.

The front door opened and Barry entered, loosening his tie as he came down the hall.

"What's for supper?"

"Curried vegetables and tofu." Berrin pulled a cookbook from the top the fridge. "I've decided to give Jill's regime a try. I think she's home."

Barry turned back and bounded up the stairs.

The grinning face of Sri Chinmoy stared up at him from the front cover. He had bought it on impulse, heedless of Jill's zeal for wholeness, thinking instead of Stephanie's concern for his health and not wanting to disappoint. It was Stephanie who had recommended the book, Jill's only cookbook being by Frances Lappé. Very tasteless recipes for a beginner like you, Berrin, and very out of date, Stephanie had cautioned. And now he saw that Sri Chinmoy looked too much like Jerome. He had already bought the ingredients, therefore best to plough ahead.

He was stirring the vegetables in the spitting oil when Barry's voice broke through the ceiling. *Arturo*, the one clear word. His stomach muscles knotted and his hand began to shake. The tension coming through the ceiling felt like someone was slashing his body with a razor.

The front door opened again. Stephanie entered and came straight down the hall, a hungry pace. She flung her coat over a chair, dumped her backpack on the counter, took a glass from the cupboard, and twisted the tap open.

"So, Berrin, what's for supper?"

"Curried tofu." His pronunciation left a slurred "t." His tongue felt numb and thick, as if it were swelling.

"I've been out looking for an apartment."

"Oh, did you?" A larger relapse. He'd have to go easy with the hard consonants.

"I need to get out of here. Maybe you should do the same."

"I like it here. I like you, Stephanie." The upstairs fracas had died down, no need to point out the exception. He curled his tongue against the roof of his mouth to keep it in check.

"Thank you, Berrin, but I can't stand it, myself."

He wanted to explain, at length, but his tongue continued to rebel. "I need to be near people."

When he lost Eileen the first time, he had moved up north. The Canadian way, what he called his "Far/ley" response. Then to the oil rigs off Newfoundland, alone again. He'd had enough of it.

"But close to whom?"

"Well, Stephanie, I think we're close. Like, right now."

Her mood had definitely more to do with Tshabalala and his parents, not the co-op.

"You'll never concede a point, will you? Berrin, you'd drive me nuts with your pig-headedness. But I'm out of here." She got up and refilled her glass.

Almost as petulant as she'd been in the store.

But she was right about his obstinacy. Eileen had called him shithead, though the topic then was children, not new lodgings. And to give Stephanie her due, she was right; he was actually hoping for a move as well, wasn't he? A slight nod then to acknowledge her point, which made his brain slam hard against the front of his cranium. She didn't seem to notice the bang inside his head nor his accord.

"Tshabalala's agreed about the apartment. Though he said he won't be moving in with me right away. We looked at ads and dropped into two places in Sandy Hill on my way home. This fat guy said his sister had left and I could have her room. His ad never mentioned he came with the place, so I told him to lose some of the midriff first. But he had a good sense of humour. He said the surgery would take six months of convalescence and by then I'd have found another place. The next apartment was ideal, but it's eight hundred a month. So I'd have to share it.'

"Maybe I could split with you. I'm going to freeze my butt off in that back room." His tongue felt considerably thicker, but he hadn't lisped till the "that."

"You mean it's your nuts you'll freeze off." She returned to her chair, no smile.

"Maybe they're lost already."

"Too bad, man, too bad. It's not worth it. I can't understand why men want to marry, these days. They'll get screwed every time because the wife gets half what he owns. And the woman loses her freedom. There's no way I want to fall into either pit. At least make it a contract from the outset."

"It's so calculating."

Perhaps Tshabalala had proposed, likely very conservative beneath that Rastafarian panache.

"And men don't calculate? Put the calculation up front, and somehow I think it'll disappear."

"Maybe." He wondered how Tshabalala held up under this fire. Change subjects. His head didn't need the debate.

"Are you drawing up contracts for your boarders?" His spatula spilled some onion on the stove, bright curry stains against the white enamel. "Stephanie, can you get the tofu for me, please? It's in the fridge."

She continued talking as she obliged. "My bottom line: no eunuchs and no one else with a home job. It's enough that the one person working in the apartment all day is me. I will need a room for my art, so my computer will stay in my bedroom. But another body in the house all day would be too much. Definitely nobody who's depressed. That's self-explanatory, don't you think?"

Eunuch, or depressed, both remarks stung. He took the box of tofu from her and grabbed a knife.

"Why work from your bedroom?" He hoped she wouldn't ask

about his clipped sentences. He tried punching through the top edge of the box.

"I agree. It's always a big temptation to lie down or trim toenails instead of banging out another measly underpaid contract. But the best ideas come from the bedroom, don't you agree?"

The humour was lost on him because at that moment the paring knife slipped and cut the side of his finger. Luckily only a nick. She reached out to the sink, pulled open a drawer, and handed him a bandage, then took over the box as he sucked his finger.

"So, you're looking for a roommate?" Pressing his tongue against his finger as he spoke provided double relief.

Stephanie was hacking at the box. "Roommate? Tenant. I've had enough of co-op relationships." She was avoiding his real question, about Tshabalala. She refocused. The knife's tip broke through the plasticized paper and water spilled onto the table. His brain would be the next to follow if even one more thought needled it.

"I'm not feeling well, Stephanie. I've got this terrible migraine." He got up slowly. The vegetables were sticking to the pan, and he moved it off the grill. Stephanie dumped the water from the box into the sink. He switched hands and continued stirring. She walked up behind him, massaged his neck for a moment, then took over the spatula.

"You better lie down. I won't wake you for supper; we'll save you a bit." She turned him back to his bedroom door and gently pushed him through.

He thanked her, his tongue so swollen now that he knew he was noticeably lisping.

The door closed behind him as he fell into bed and pulled the blankets tightly around his body. He rolled a few times to find the best position. How to relax? Tshabalala's face rose in his mind again, but no thoughts came with it. He lowered his head back over the end of the bed frame and pressed the base of his skull against the angle iron. The cold metal relaxed the nerves in his neck, two taut cords that hurt all the more as he forced them to curve around the bend of the metal. He rocked his head slowly from side to side to massage the pain away. When the metal no longer felt cool, he pulled the chair with the television closer and jammed his head between the wooden seat and the mattress, cool against both temples.

He was wrapped as if in a straitjacket. A prisoner, like the definition that was once applied with unexpected wit to his predicament by the army captain in Tepepantiango. You are a prisoner, therefore you are a criminal.

And lovers . . . trapped in a box.

If only he could have been as witty with Stephanie. Put him in an apartment and . . . a question. Easier with Jerome. Put anything in a gallery and it becomes art.

The Christian canon of creation: You are created, therefore you are a sinner. The essence of all religions.

His feelings of being a sinner and a criminal coalesced. He took a deep breath, and thankfully his body relaxed a bit.

He was a prisoner to his body. A prisoner to his headache, to the headaches of the world, like everyone caught up in events, in the world, in their bodies, the longings and desires, captive in a post-primitive global village, futile to try to escape, like smashing one's head against the wall.

He pushed his head lower down the wall to find a cooler spot in this liminal world. Stephanie and he were trapped in a hut. Barry was on guard. How to break free? He found himself picking up a large rock and throwing it at Barry's head. The rock split open. It was hollow inside, like the mountain itself. A volcano. An avalanche came crashing down and he was running down the mountain, hand in hand with Stephanie. Their feet dashed from side to side to escape the cascading rocks. Then they were laughing and their scampering was like dancing.

Below, they met a maenad-like, golden-haired girl running through a barren land with a dog gambolling alongside. She stopped and bit the head off the dog.

A large black bear began chasing them. They ran across fields and through a tunnel in a riverbank to escape. He sensed that the bear meant no harm, but only wanted to take them back to its cave in the mountain, keeping them forever in its furry embrace.

They sought refuge inside a cottage on the slope of a hill. They stood on top of an old, cast-iron cookstove in the kitchen and flung the round lids down at the approaching bear.

He awoke in a sweat. Eileen was sitting at the foot of his bed. His headache was less severe, a dull throbbing. Flakes of snow blew past the dark windowpane behind her. The room was colder. The snow would explain the bear, he said aloud to himself, incoherently. Then he sat up and swung his legs out of bed.

"I need to eat."

His words came out again in a slur.

"What time is it?"

"Midnight," she said. She was crying . . .

CHAPTER 28

Nothing is forever

HE HIT THE SWITCH of the kitchen light, but the white stamped tin ceiling magnified its wattage tenfold. He flicked it off.

"Sorry, Eileen. My eyes can't take it. I've got a bad migraine. The bit of sleep helped."

He turned to the small neon light over the electric range, hidden by the overhang, sufficient, but cold and flickering; too abruptly awakened in the middle of the night.

"I prefer the dim light as well," she said.

He could see that, full of fears and tears and trembling, huddled in her overcoat, still with the silk scarf . . . a good sign. He opened the fridge.

"I'm not hungry," she said, but he went ahead and heated up the ample bowl of leftovers he found. Stephanie hadn't used the tofu. The red box sat in the door; he had chosen red finally because of her hair. Thankfully, she must have run to the corner store for some chicken.

She accepted one of the beers he had bought the night before. She talked as he ate. Jeff said he was returning home with the kids. He had left them at some friends' nearby so he'd be free to do the town with her. But more to frolic. She stopped him on the fact that she didn't know these friends of his, and they argued about leaving the children with strangers. She couldn't bring herself to follow him home in the car, but instead wandered around the mall, then drove around town, had a coffee in a restaurant, then returned here.

"I'm living only on the outside. I don't feel anything. I know I am somewhere here, but I can't reach myself, not for a long time now." Her speech faltered, as her words struggled with her sobbing.

She was confused, but he realized that she wasn't taking Jeff to task on anything. "You're trying too hard to please him. Only kids need their mother." Like cubs their mama bear. Such lucidity under a Frigidaire's neon. "Everyone needs to take control of their lives. You as well, Eileen."

"Like most men, you mean."

"Like most men, my ass." He looked down at his food. "Sorry."

"Whatever. Whatever choices I have, I don't have the will to go on."

"Will is fundamentally the admission that one is alive." The irritation in his voice was diminished, but noticeable still. They were dancing through the avalanche.

"Will has been my leading the life I chose, what I thought we had chosen together, and raising my family. That's why I married Jeff; I was happy to love him. Love gives you strength — I learned that much in Mexico. You can't seem to understand that. It's not my fault that he's turned out to be such a jerk. I don't think I'll ever understand what men imagine love to be."

She wiped her eyes with the heel of her hand, her other hand clutching the beer to her side as she continued hugging herself.

He didn't want to see her in another downward spiral. Best to remember their younger days together. Will was no problem then. Once, they had walked through suburbia late at night and passed a house where the figurine of a black jockey was holding onto the reins of a stallion. She had kicked it over, exclaiming, "Don't they know that nothing is forever?"

"Remember our days together on our magazine?" he said. "And your hero then, Simone de Beauvoir, I think. Remember when she was learning to drive, she'd take to the countryside, drive for days, free, she said, to go anywhere she pleased? You liked that, but I wondered where would we be if everyone on earth had a car? But you were determined to break out, I remember that."

"Now that I've learned to drive, looks like the only option is to drive away. Disappear. Pathetic, isn't it?"

The bear barging through the front door, another version of the grim reaper, calling again. Wittgenstein's axiom, that a proposition must always keep a back door open. Padre Nómez, the same instincts. His mind was racing again. How to find that back door?

"There are alternatives. What about us the other night?"

She hesitated, took a sip of her beer and shivered. "You've always brought out the worst in me, Berrin." She set her beer on the table.

"You still want to stay with Jeff? I can't believe it!"

She shrugged. "I know I want you to come up. You can talk with him. Then I'll see what comes of it. It would do him good to talk with someone."

The stellar trooper, but what choice did he have? Exactly why she thought Jeff would talk with him was a mystery. He nodded his agreement nevertheless.

"There's a bus Saturday night. Returns Monday morning. And I have the long weekend off. But really, Eileen, I don't think it'll change much."

She unwound her scarf, pulled off her overcoat, and flung it over the chair beside her. She was stunning, even in the dead glare of the neon light. She was wearing a white jacket, silk or at least fine linen, with motifs of narrow black stripes in square patterns, its slightly padded shoulders and tailored cut leaving her looking slimmer. A black metallic tie pressed into the fold of her blouse. He pulled his chair closer to the table, as if to be closer to his plate. The tie was a delicately crafted mesh of tiny bevelled diamond shapes, obviously very expensive. She likely was wearing this outfit at the market, easily upstaging Jeff's style.

"You look wonderful."

She smiled, her eyes still wet. "And how can I afford this, you may ask?"

"Yes, exactly — seeing what you were wearing last night."

"Charles gave it to me this morning. You remember Charles. He's now manager of Holt Renfrew. I went to see him about a job — show Jeff I was serious." She flicked the lapels of her jacket, her eyes still glistening with tears. "A gift, Charles said, to our future partnership. Pressure tactics. I said I only *might* be looking for a job. I can play a game as well as he can. He was after me before I got married, to work in his store as a sales clerk."

"Looks like the offer has its benefits."

"I don't intend to marry the guy. He keeps his paws in his pockets, though he will sneak a look down the front of your blouse."

"I imagine Jeff was more than surprised."

"At first, yes." She shrugged.

Berrin could imagine the reconciliation, then Jeff's offer to go shopping, then his gift of a writing pad, a joke, a challenge back. And dropping in at the Market for a real gift. Then changing his mind . . . or, rather, losing it.

"Why don't you return and finish your degree? You should never have dropped it."

"I"m actually looking into that as well. Carleton University, social work. There must be a winter session."

"Now you're talking."

While he rinsed his dish and fork he suggested going with her. He had to register for some courses to continue living in the co-op. She wouldn't have to go out of her way because he could take the bus back to the Market. He was talking non-stop again, but no stopping himself. It looked like another cold night; he could put a sleeping bag on the bed as an extra blanket. She sipped her beer and replaced it on the table, still full. Thanks, the sleeping bag would be great. It was stashed in the far corner of the bedroom. He tucked the blankets in and quickly spread the sleeping bag over top. They hugged each other goodnight.

And the lone ranger returns to the sofa bed.

CHAPTER 29

Above the dark waters

HE LAY AWAKE, unable to sleep. Thoughts . . . too many thoughts. They came tumbling past him, large and fragmented and struggling to form themselves into clear propositions.

Will is leading the life I choose.

Her words.

They paraded across his mind, like the magnetic letters children stick to refrigerators, scrambled but with a fragile confidence.

No, she was more sure of herself than that.

Her family was about to break apart. A tangible loss.

He held his breath and listened. He was certain he could hear her breathing from the back room.

He rolled onto his back.

She might still come to stay with him.

Face the facts.

The essence of a fact is in what it might have been. A basic postmodern eye-opener.

Such as his dreams of late: being a burglar, entering a stranger's house, trying to steal what he didn't deserve. Yet she was letting Sir Charles feel totally at home.

The essence of a story is in what it doesn't say.

How to rewrite the story? In the beginning was the flesh.

He was circling like a tethered dog. Caught, he was caught. Lost in the interval of story lived and story needing to be relived, reaching for your double, suspended in the recess this doubling creates, and if not caught, then enclosed within a new beginning . . . he was getting closer to it now. He was travelling through a dark and flattened land toward some fortification, a walled medieval town in the distance. Ahead of him, a dark creature on the stone wall, raven-like at first, then, nearer, a woman with tall black wings that she clutched to both sides of her body. Her breasts excited him, full and open, her body poised like a perched bird, covered entirely with feathers except for her chest and head. But how to make love with such a creature? Fear, he feared the impossible, and she took flight, rose high past the stone walls and disappeared southward.

He found himself skimming down a river in a narrow dugout canoe, propelled as if by a will of its own. Stephanie was sitting behind him, and he pushed himself back, so close to her that her feet were pulled up against his hips. Four men in black overcoats raced downriver alongside them, their boat longer and faster than theirs, but he was certain he could overtake them. The river was now a swamp. They skirted islands, narrowly missing them and the numerous deadheads that projected above the dark waters.

Their hull glanced off the tip of one of the deadheads. The other boat passed them.

When next he saw the boat, it was stopped at one of the islands where the bird must have landed. The leader of the four, sinister in his black suit, seemed to be trying to catch the bird, to kill it. But the bird was now a large octopus-like creature, with four enormous tentacles waving in the air, the centre one standing upright and staring down at him with its one bird-like eye.

He grasped its neck to choke it.

Struggling.

Dive into the water to escape.

CHAPTER 30

Magic birds

AFTER WATCHING BERRIN disappear into the undergrowth across the Araña, Eileen retraced her steps up the trail, alone within herself. She hoped to meet the fruit lady again. She arrived at the log fence, but everything appeared locked up. No pigs or hens in the yard; even the honeybees were silent. Just as well. If she had stopped, she would surely want to stay the day, losing all the willpower it would take to make the long journey up the mountain and on over to Tepetlatla, the neighbouring rancho.

She continued up the mountain trail, repeating the old woman's words to herself like a mantra: *Tlasokamati, Tonaltih, Tlasokamati, Tonaltih.*

At the first fork in the path, she opted for the quicker route home, and in ten minutes she was out of the heavy undergrowth and again making an ascent under a scorching midday sun. The lumberjacks were gone, a relief, since she had been apprehensive about meeting the stump man again. Her forehead burned under her thin cotton scarf and her mounting thirst made her regret travelling so light, her small canteen clipped to her belt already empty. The path snaked up through fields of wilting cornstalks. Her thoughts drifted back over the week leading up to Berrin's departure. Shreds of her argument with him now seemed a confusion of scruples and desire. Pouncing on him about the fruit lady had been the right thing to do; she couldn't have let his *tonto* blunder pass. But it was her mistake letting him cross the Araña with barely a hug, without talking with him some more.

He would likely take his time returning. He said he would stay a week or so with Padre Nómez to recuperate, but he also had things to investigate, he said . . . the politics in the ranchos had to include the pueblos . . . important matters.

Her climb up the steep section of rocks steeled her resolve, then the path levelled off and the walking got easier. She would soon be reaching the cut-off to Cochitlahuantla, two roads diverging in a yellow wood. Berrin's desire clearly was for the one least travelled by. Natural, perhaps, to want it, but why live your life always regretting another not taken, sapping the energy from the one you're on? He clearly craved the politics, but politics for what?

She groped for the decision she had to make, for she had to decide. Then she saw the paths anew. They weren't leading onward but instead were converging upon her, carrying two selves long lost to each other but finally meeting up. She felt more resolute. She tried again to focus on Berrin and his recent actions, but this effort pulled her down. His image was fading . . . let it go, a spectre that needed to be free of her.

She reached the top of the mountain where the path split into the two familiar directions. She was happy with her decision; she would not be turning left to follow the ridge down to Tepetlatla. She didn't need the many arguments about their project, bringing water by pipe from the top of the mountain down into Tepetlatla. With a tap only in the centre of the rancho, the better-off families benefited the most, yet everyone was paying for the water pump and the weekly supply of gasoline, somehow still needed despite the system being gravity-fed. Then there was the friendly Frazer University giant who ate anything that came within range, the weekly supply of groceries from Tepepantiango lasting no longer than a few days. A roll of Black Diamond cheese had provided some respite. The next shipment of supplies was due in a day or so, when the resentment would unfailingly flare up as soon as he dove into the new box of oatmeal. If anything, by returning to Cochitlahuantla she would have more to eat, although her appetite had evaporated in her fatigue. She needed her own spot. She turned right.

The ridge spread out as she entered her rancho. One path dropped off to the right, where it skirted the lower side of the rancho. The other opened up into a wide lane that ran between the rows of huts to finally disappear over the ridge at the far end of the rancho. There on the highest point on the horizon sat the Catholic church with its whitewashed adobe walls and bell tower that dominated the view. Perhaps CIASP's project next summer could be a floor for the church. That would surely please everyone in the rancho, not to mention getting the children off the dirt floor, some comfort for their morning reading and arithmetic classes.

There was a small gathering of people at the first hut she approached. A man crouching on bent knees was cutting the hair of a boy seated on a low stool, his head sticking up through a white sheet wrapped around his shoulders. A stolid child no more than five or six stood in ramrod maturity behind them studying the shower of curls, his arms crossed on his chest, with an infant strapped to his back in a *rebozo*, a strand of her thick black hair curled over one of her eyes, giving her a solemn look. For a moment, Eileen wondered if the occasion might not again be a death in the family. Then the mother appeared at the door of her hut and said something that made everyone laugh and look up at Eileen as she closed in upon them. Eileen shook her head, she did not understand *Nahuatl* enough. More giggles and smiles greeted her perplexed look, and the youth being clipped slipped his hands from under the sheet, joined one thumb and forefinger together and moved them up and down over his other outstretched forefinger which he stretched out towards Eileen. Louder giggles and wider smiles.

"*No es necessario*," Eileen stammered. The children screeched louder.

"*Puedes quedar aqui este noche, señorita, con Porfirio*." The mother, still grinning, looked down toward the boy on the stool. He was familiar but definitely too young, perhaps Porfirio's brother. The lover she was being offered had to be the same young man who had been their porter — he lived at this end of the rancho. But he couldn't have been more than fourteen or fifteen himself.

"*No, no es necessario*," Eileen repeated, almost stuttering, and continued on, looking straight ahead and forcing herself to maintain her smile and poise, while trying to decipher the event. Were they mocking her? Not likely. It was obvious that Berrin hadn't returned with her and local custom demanded that she not be alone for the night.

But they must have known that Berrin wasn't her lover. She remembered how the children would crowd onto the basement windows at all hours of the day and evening. These foreigners were like a circus coming to town. There was probably nothing about their habits they didn't know. Perhaps they thought it strange that these Canadians lived in the same room but slept in separate cots, and so were offering her a better man.

Or the mother simply wanted to hitch her son up to a better future.

She decided to duck around the next hut and take the lower path until she reached the shelter of the school. No need to chance running the gauntlet of more offers. Her head throbbed, too much sun and not enough water. She stuck to the shade of the few trees against the mountain slope. Some lemons were within reach and she stopped to grab one. Tasteless, not yet ripe, but beautifully moist.

A woman screamed from within a hut behind her on the lower side of the path. The hut had to have been recently built, its freshly cut sap-yellow boards not yet darkened by smoke and weather. She recognized the hut as the one that the catechist had warned her about, where someone had threatened to kill the Canadians. A man emerged carrying a machete in one hand and in the other a Coca-Cola bottle half-full of a clear liquid that splashed over his pants. He walked as a rag doll might, his wandering eyes soon fixing on Eileen. She screamed and ran, stumbled, and took off again.

She was slumped over the front steps of the school verandah when a band of men emerged from behind the hut near where the haircutting had been in session, but now abandoned. They were pushing and pulling a man down the lane toward her, his hands tied behind his back, staggering, obviously quite inebriated. She then recognized him as the man who had just scared her. People emerged from their doorways and stood watching in silence. The man was swearing and spitting, but everyone else was silent, as if the ritual were as distasteful to them as it was necessary.

The group continued toward her as the lane spread out into the wide yard in front of her. This was the area in their rancho that normally served as a playground for children and the volleyball court on Sundays. The men passed in front of her but paid her no attention. They stopped at the one of the net posts, which now became the man's prison as they tied him to it with more ropes. Everyone then quickly dispersed, leaving the man to bake in the sun as he slid to the ground, his legs outstretched and kicking up dust. Soon the entire stretch of the main street was devoid of both people and animals.

From the safety of the verandah she watched the man, who never once noticed her presence and soon fell asleep, slumped forward in the sling of the ropes. No one had offered him a *sombrero*. She now saw he was the same diminutive *peón* with the melon-shaped *sombrero* she had spotted in the neighbouring rancho as he stood on the sidelines watching the children play volleyball. A volleyball court was surely his nemesis.

But at the town meeting, his dignity had shone from spitting into the official's face. She had assumed that he was from that rancho. Had she recognized him immediately without his sombrero, she might not have run, and maybe succeeded in getting him to talk.

If only someone for once would volunteer an explanation. Perhaps the cardinal rule he'd broken was hitting his wife. And if the neighbours had heard the wife's screams, they had heard hers as well. Yet it was she who was the guilty one, not the prisoner. She couldn't feel anything but guilt for being here, intruding. The crusading anger that she had felt in the *manifestación* in Guadalahara, which had propelled her here, was gone.

As if on cue, a much-fattened pig appeared from behind a hut, wandered across the lane, and approached her. It smelt of the earth, clean. Its back touched her leg, then pressed onto her ankle as it lowered itself onto the ground, yet its massive weight rested so gently against her foot that its hugeness felt immaterial, as light as the space it displaced. Her anguish likewise dissolved and she felt wholly present with the pig, the prisoner, the rancho. Tears welled in her eyes.

The drunken incident was a test of her readiness to reach out. Good that Berrin wasn't present, Berrin, CIASP, and all the talk about their many projects. No one ever asked: Was it fate that another child went hungry because the mother sold her last egg to Canadian students?

She looked back at the pillar. The man was still passed out. The street as silent and empty. Noon, siesta time — for good reason. She stood up and the pig squealed to protest her departure. A whisper for an apology, "Have to go inside." She was dizzy and thirsty.

Most of their provisions were stored on a rack that Berrin had built out of sugar cane stalks tied together with string. She had remained silent about his use of sugar cane, the ends cut at an angle, and she had difficulty approaching his contraption, even to look at it. She took an Aspirin and put the bottle back on the top shelf, then reached for the tin cup that Berrin had left hooked over the end of one of the spears and dipped it into the pail of water on the lower shelf. One sip would have to do, as the water felt like a flame hitting her stomach.

Berrin's paraphernalia was scattered around the rack. The central object was a CIASP plaque, in the shape of a large plate that displayed the emblem of two people reaching out to each other around a circle representing planet Earth. But never touching. A machete in mint condition hung in its tooled leather sheath, a sweatshirt flung beside it that he'd washed the night before but forgotten. His red headband swung from another spear, with its design of ecology circles linked like a dandelion chain that for some reason he never wore after he left Mexico City.

But it was she whose head was swirling now. Definitely sunstroke, and she headed for her cot.

She stretched out under the sleeping bag without undressing. She was home at last. The air coming off the cement wall and floor was cool and damp. The netting of the string mattress engulfed her like a hammock. The fire in her head subsided as her body welcomed the weight of the sleeping bag.

She pictured Berrin's seared, meringue-like tufts of hair. He had been feverish the previous evening and limped slightly, and in the morning she had invited him to snuggle up in her bed. As she glanced at his boxing shorts, she had to hide her surprise at his half awakened anticipation. He was still very hot and she bent down to check his heel and saw a red line running up the inside of his leg. He was telling her his dream. He was in a theatre with her. The movie was entertaining, and they were beginning to snuggle up side by side, when suddenly a body fell across their seats. A fat woman sitting behind them had fallen like a heavy shawl over their backs, and he woke up.

The fat lady has sung and the play was over. She should be laughing now, but remembering Berrin's dream revived her anger instead. She kicked off her sleeping bag.

She had reciprocated with her own dream. She had been

playing a strange musical instrument, what an orgasm felt like, she said, and Berrin had laughed.

"You find me funny?" she protested.

"No, no, I didn't mean to laugh. Tell me more. Please, really."

She demonstrated how she played her instrument in her dream. It consisted of a metal pipe with numerous rods and strings that she pulled and pushed between her hands.

"You look like a bodybuilder working out, but with more seductive biceps." He had looked at her outstretched arms and her clenched fists, and then at her breasts, as if he were seeing through her T-shirt. She continued spreading her arms slowly open and shut.

"When I was small, my mother showed me how to make a toy by looping a string through the holes of a button and spinning it by pulling on both ends of the string. She called them 'magic birds.' 'Tirez les bonnes ficelles.' That's what's on my mind. You know, like controlling a situation when . . . I mean, I've been pulling strings all my life but only at a distance. I'm finally after all this time remembering what it feels like. I'm taking control of myself."

"Maybe what you need control of is another kind of instrument," and he had kicked the sheet off himself.

He must have seen her disappointment spreading over her face, for he quickly pulled the sheet back over himself. If he did see her sadness, he didn't know how to respond. How cold the room had suddenly felt, as if a ghost had passed by. She had broken into a sweat, her body cleansing itself in a flush of nerves. And then the anger. She had pointed to his leg, "You have to get to Tepepantiango as soon as possible, before that blood poisoning spreads past that swollen lymph node in your crotch."

That had definitely shut him up.

Her throat was dry. More feverish, now, but she couldn't make the effort to climb out of her bed to get some water. So much for wanting control. Another illusion. Or was she searching for the wrong kind of control? For the wrong things to control? She turned on her side, pulled her knees up, and opened her eyes.

Someone passed outside and the pig now squealed non-stop. Even as the pig was driven across the yard back to its house, the squealing remained intolerable until it faded to a faint squeak in the distance.

Silence again, and her nausea spread from her head down her chest through her entire body, her misery complete. She opened her eyes and stared at the CIASP plaque hanging from the rack. The dim interior light of the room returned a moment of magic to it, magic that once was the rule of a simpler world.

Her vision blurred. The plaque grew smaller in circumference as it raced off into the distance.

A sour fluid flowed through her body. It swelled her limbs.

The rack supporting the plaque collapsed and faded into a horizontal stretch of blackness that separated into an upper and lower plane, opposing universes of matter and antimatter. The upper portion turned into a warm, soothing whiteness that blanketed the horizon before her; the bottom, a swirling abyss she struggled not to tumble into. She was rescued by the string that stretched across her vision, drawing a secure line between the two spheres that were contending for her being.

This bifurcated world then congealed into a black ball, a knot that raced back and forth across the taut string. She clung to the black dot, trying to control its movements left and right.

After some minutes, and for no apparent reason and quite independent of her will, the knot settled at the right end of the string and her body began to relax.

She closed her eyes and fell into a deep sleep.

CHAPTER 31

Morning frost

REUNION TIME, appraisal time. As he entered the kitchen, Berrin was happy to find Eileen sitting at the breakfast table, though dressed again in her Holt Renfrew garb. The entire co-op gang had gathered around, getting acquainted — minus Barry, who had skipped out first thing in the morning. Not to disturb them, he circled around to stand next to the fridge. Jill complained that no one had introduced her to Eileen properly the previous night, but then agreed that Jerome did monopolize the conversation. They traded views on the performance; the selections committee had wanted a break from the endless squabbles of the contending Ottawa art cliques, meaning, Stephanie said, that Jerome had his way by bringing in his Toronto friends; gets the curious out at least, Jill; which allowed for his own sober comment about another month of an exhibition empty of any significant number of visitors until the next wine and cheese ... why don't they try to attract more people in between, pitch to high school kids or something, which made Stephanie laugh, "Imagine the teacher's horror when her students are faced with that defecating contraption of a machine that's supposed to replicate the digestive system!" Eileen, who was picking at her egg with her fork, pushed it aside.

"Oops," Stephanie said, and everyone laughed, Jill's laughter a high screech like a bird.

Leaning back against the fridge, Berrin picked at pieces of tissue paper wedged in the corner of his pants pocket, his glance falling on the circle of legs under the table, then to his dream. Stymphalian Birds, a man-eating maiden with the legs of a bird — trouble enough even for a Hercules — and the multiple legs under the table, yes, the Hydra. Eileen's legs were crossed. Stephanie's . . . hers jerked up and down as she pumped the floor with the heel of her foot, otherwise she seemed totally relaxed. Jill's sat flat on the floor, she would be the Stymphalian woman; her legs pulled back toward her chair as she poured Stephanie and herself a coffee, then offered some to Eileen. Studiously attentive of Jill, he thought, but Eileen pointed to her glass of orange juice, still very full.

The drop in the conversation provided him the opening to tell Eileen of their meeting Arturo in the market, how Arturo had asked about her. This got only a nod from her. Why should he have expected otherwise? She never had much to do with him, never overtly friendly during their orientation period in Mexico City; and on the two more traumatic occasions — their trip to the *Barrancas del Cobre* and his rescue mission to Tepepantiango to retrieve her — she was struggling to make sense of the world, not Arturo. Berrin continued with the belated introductions. Eileen might be moving into town, she needed to get away from Jeff, for a while at least, her husband. Suddenly self-conscious, he stopped his jabbering, pushed himself away from the fridge, walked across to the far end of the counter, opened the door under it and dropped his tissue ball into the garbage pail, then turned back to his perch.

"Well, there you have it, I suppose," Eileen said, shrugging. She mused about her options, which essentially swung from reforming Jeff, to returning to work, or completing a university degree. No mention of Charles and Holt Renfrew. But that option was very evident, dressed again to kill. Even with a touch of mauve nail polish to complement the sleek look. No way was this student garb.

Jill commented, "Don't wait around for any man to reform."

"What did Oscar Wilde say — experience ends with hangings

and weddings?" Stephanie's deadpan delivery made everyone laugh.

"What about passion?" His exclamation surprised even himself.

"Give it up," Jill said, leaning forward to admonish him, her barrel chest pushing against her cup and spilling coffee on the table.

"You tell me about it, Berrin," Eileen sighed. "You witnessed my man's passion yesterday, front and centre in the market."

Stephanie crossed her legs and sat back, looking across at him. "Passion? It's like fear. I think you have to overcome it. Like the Buddhists do, displace it, set it aside, most of the time, at least."

A surprising statement coming from her, the red-headed fireball: contained, but definitely not to be set aside.

"You mean, deny it," he corrected her.

"No, rise above it, you move to a higher plane."

"Ignore it." Jill, now, catching on. "That's the word they use, isn't it? You must see it as an illusion."

"I've never really liked religions." Berrin, adopting a sober voice. "A monk's another dung beetle atop his dungheap, silly-looking at best."

"Not monks, Berrin, gurus," Stephanie grinned.

"I'm too confused right now." Eileen took a deep breath. "I don't know about denying it . . . that won't help me much. I'm going to have to worry about getting ahead."

Get ahead. Dead ahead. Deadheads. "Getting ahead. A daemon enough to wrestle to the ground — you have my sympathies," Berrin said.

"For sure, Berrin, it won't be easy, but change is in the works." Then Eileen sat up, as if refreshed. "I had a great dream last night. There was this magnificent tropical parrot, bright aquamarine blues, oranges, and reds, but mostly blue. It was perched near the ceiling. I opened the window and let it escape. And then my mother appears. I'm so happy for her — she's finally going out on a date with a new man."

"Aarrrlllllrrrrright!" Jill said.

Her father had been dead for some years, so the dream wasn't that surprising, Berrin concluded. "Puppy love returns."

Stephanie pounced. "Nonsense, Berrin. Not the second time around. We're talking about a mature woman, here."

"Well, maybe. But, then again, blue in dreams points to the intellect. So, Eileen, the dream is telling you you need to finish your studies."

Stephanie couldn't miss a tease. "Here, Berrin, have some Vitamin C. Builds up your immunity to ideas." She unscrewed the bottle cap, dumped two tablets into her palm, and offered him them.

He grinned, "Too much to swallow."

She downed them herself, and took a gulp of her coffee.

Eileen spoke up again. "Berrin, it's not some notion I'm talking about, whatever theory you're building up now. My dear headmeister, you're forever buried in your books." She stretched her arm toward the doorway to his bedroom. An exaggerated comic gesture, from a touch of anger? He couldn't say. Books and burlap were all she could be seeing from her angle of vision. "Berrin, at least the burlap is a sensuous touch. Blue burlap. Hey, that's where my blue parrot comes from."

"Correction. That's a deep Irish moss green." The inside walls had been covered with thin hardboard, which, when he first arrived, had been painted a depressing mustard yellow. Stapling on the burlap was much easier than repainting. "I wanted to make the room feel a little larger. And the texture reminds me of Mexico."

"Like a hair shirt, you mean. The life of the ascetic," Stephanie said. "At least put some plants in there for a real live green."

He conceded and smiled. "I'm atoning for all the sins we've inflicted on the world."

"I'm afraid only victims atone," Stephanie shot him her wry smile, "like the scrawny, exiled, underfed Third World, and you don't fit that bill, Berrin."

"At least the room's small, sets a limit on how much debris you can accumulate."

"Your problem is that you've been hiding away as long as I can remember," Eileen said.

Though she held the teasing smile on her face, Berrin felt the needle sticking in. "Not so quick, Eileen. Maybe you've been doing much the same."

Jill spoke up. "You know, prisoners in Nazi concentration camps told of how they grew to need their walls and barred windows and began to even like their guards; it seemed their memories of freedom faded as fast as the trees and grass until only mud remained. Just like marriage, I'd say."

Fortified camps, her metaphor for everything, Berrin thought.

Eileen sighed. "Marriage isn't the total wasteland you're making it out to be. There is some green in it, even if you have to plant most of it yourself."

"That's only too true, Eileen," Stephanie said.

Berrin felt the urge to move and he again walked across the room to the garbage can. "I'll have to start cultivating my father's green thumb."

Eileen raised her glass. "Berrin, have a seat. We'll toast the sunshine."

The others took this as a cue and got up to leave. Stephanie told Eileen she could stay as long as she wished. "And don't feel shy. I'm sure Berrin loves the couch."

"It's much warmer than my room," he replied.

As they disappeared down the hall, his spirits sank. He had been pacing the floor for a reason. Something was askew. Her *haute couture* jacket and tie.

"Sorry about last night, Berrin. I'm still a wreck and out of it. I like your friends. Maybe I should be considering something like this. And the children would have more people around, different father figures for a change." She stopped for a second, looked down toward her plate.

He spoke, to state the obvious. "It's been a while since we shared so much as a drink." He passed his glass across to her for a fill-up.

"Berrin, you must remember that time we were visiting the rancho where the young child was dying, and the whole family carried on with their work? Everyone was related. A Nahua lady was grinding corn on her *metate* . . . she was as tall as the mother. I remember, they were sisters. She offered us some water, but we were too scared of it and opted for the piping hot coffee instead. Her brother returned with a load of firewood and stood at the door. The scene is burned in my mind. At the time, I resented all that activity. It seemed to deny the tragedy of their child, but they were getting on with life. I was very frustrated about the child dying, but I was also feeling good about something. I felt at home with them."

"Yes, I remember the hut."

"Berrin, you know, it's all right here."

He smiled and looked down at her untouched breakfast.

"That's great. Can I get you something else to eat?"

"The juice will do." She took another sip. "Remember afterwards in Cochitlahuantla when you ruined our only two eggs?"

"No."

"You took it upon yourself to prepare breakfast and broke the first one into the saucepan, and it was rotten. You shook our second and last egg next to your ear and to prove to me it was also bad you took it outside and broke it over a puddle. It turned out to be a good egg. The logical end to your reasoning. A perfectly good egg floating in the muddy water, but there it was: an instant transformation, a perfectly bad egg."

"I do remember."

"I was so angry with you. It was that last morning that you left for Tepepantiango."

He didn't want to think about that morning. If anything, he wanted to know what had followed.

"You never told me much of your story after I left. It took you over a month to recuperate at the Civic Hospital, remember? When I'd visit you at first, it seemed like I was the enemy. You blamed me for a lot."

"I really could only blame you for those eggs."

"Well, maybe, but everything changed afterwards, whatever did happen. Then one day you snapped out of it. We were friends again. Which was great, except you never talked about Mexico again. You never told me what happened."

"Well, you never told me what happened to you when you cracked your own egg."

"I was shot at and sliced with a bullet."

"That everyone can see."

"Not much more to speak of, just politics, as you would say."

"Well, Berrin, Mexico was only part of my problem."

"I feel like I'm now in my mother's position . . . it's almost funny. She wondered why Mexico had changed me so much, but I couldn't explain anything."

He took a sip of his juice, to give himself a moment. "Remember our magazine, *The Left Bank?* Everyone called it a hare-brained scheme."

"They were right."

"But you agreed to work with me on it. Then you just as suddenly took off with Jeff."

"Well, blame it on life, Berrin. I wanted to be happy."

"I can see that now. And I'm very glad you're back. Maybe I don't want us to be as bad together as the world in general, or as most couples are, like Jill and Barry, for instance. You missed him this morning, but you saw him last night in the gallery office. He was the one leaning against the wall across from Jill."

"The guy with that moustache."

"Yes, I mentioned him last night, the deconstructionist. Except, now it's Jill who's deconstructing their relationship. You should see them carry on."

He took another sip, then swirled the remaining juice around in the glass and looked up, one of those vacuous moments that can make you smile. He smiled.

She nodded, but relaxed.

"After I left you at the Araña, I returned to Cochitlahuantla and sat a while on the verandah. This pig lumbered across the yard and lay down beside me. All sense of difference between us disappeared, our bodies dissolved into this one being. It's difficult to explain the feeling, like two species becoming one. Sounds corny, but I had been waiting for that feeling all my life, and there it was. It hit me hard."

"I heard from Arturo how they found you and brought you back."

"But nothing much happened. I remember having this terrible sunstroke, and I did some crazy things, I suppose, but I knew I had to keep the feeling alive somehow. That's what I remember. I recovered when I made that resolution again in the hospital. Despite the drugs. And you did help, too, Berrin."

She reached across the table and gripped his hand, then patted it. "Maybe you're the one who needs an Aspirin or two. How's your big egghead this morning? You didn't seem to be in much better shape than me last night. Sorry it was all about me then; I couldn't help it."

"You're going through a lot." He automatically rubbed his eyes. "They are still sore a bit. Like two marbles in my skull."

"Just don't go to work today."

"Better if I eat breakfast. I forgot to yesterday; that was one of my problems."

The main problem, her story of the pig, left out more than it told — but then, you have to concede, stories generally didn't capture visions very well. Nor could he hit upon the right question to put to her about it.

He got up and opened the fridge. Sausages quickly dismissed. He reached for the eggs but decided against them as well. Bread and cheese. And he'd borrow some of Barry's bacon.

"The Market seems like an interesting place to work. Lots of time for reading, I bet. And great material for stories, right?"

"You remember Ivan Illich, the guest speaker in Guadalajara

who admonished us about our missionary zeal? Arturo quoted him yesterday. And I happened to hear him recently on the CBC *Ideas* series, still going strong. He claims he can tell when anything is written on the computer, as opposed to longhand. Myself, I still stick to longhand for my first drafts, then rewrite on the computer. But the writing is dragging. I've started a language project. I'm calling it 'One World Language and Peace.'"

Eileen perked up; she seemed genuinely interested. Berrin opted for more background. "I was thinking about our time in Mexico. Remember those mimeographed sheets we were handed describing Paulo Freire's literacy project?"

"His highfalutin' theories. It took us the whole month just to begin understanding the people in the rancho. Forget about community development."

"His strategy did work in Brazil. That's why the military kicked him out. His approach is so simple, identifying key words to get people reading; like Portuguese, you need only fifteen words."

"Wait. Berrin, I thought you were through with saving the world."

"I was always charged up by ideas, more than the action part, I guess. I'm talking about how literacy is challenging. I think I've invented a kind of new international alphabet. It goes beyond key words or learning the phonics for each language. I remember how bad it was for us with Nahuatl."

His bacon done, he sliced some bread and sat at the table. Eileen stood up and carried her cup and plate to the sink.

"Don't bother, Eileen; I'll wash everything later."

"I'll do them while you eat. My room and board, eh?" She opened the door below the sink, found the garbage pail, and dumped her egg.

Her leg stuck out as she bent over. The slit of her skirt slid above her knee; a black skirt that matched her metallic tie, in fine wool.

She glanced back at him. Eyeing her was not the message he wanted to give.

"Well, Eileen, everybody's communicating with everybody around the world at lightning speed, and in English. But there are over six thousand languages in the world, over fifty alone in Europe."

"What about Esperanto?"

"Even that's split off into five or more streams. There were people as far back as Descartes who've thought about it. I'm talking about a neutral language, easily learned no matter what your language. I believe I've come up with an answer in a new alphabet, based on a few simple strokes — I guess in a way like Freire did with a few key words."

He took out a pen and grabbed the newspaper lying on the table.

"You've seen digital dials on alarm clocks, how the numbers change by lighting up different bars." He drew a vertical line. "The number one is formed by two vertical bars." Eileen looked over. Then he added a cross bar, "There's the seven." Then he dropped another line off the seven, reaching half way down. "Now in my new alphabet that's the letter *i*. Simple as falling off a log. A vertical bar gives you the *d*," he sounded it as the phoneme, "but two bars linked with a dash, see, almost like an *n*, that gives you the *a*."

Eileen had at this point crossed over to the fridge, glancing at his paper as she passed.

"Why not make that an *n*, like it looks?"

"In English it does, but we're after a universal application. You'll have to see the whole thing when it's finished, which won't take me much longer. I've already made another discovery. See any resemblance to Celtic art? Look at those key patterns the letters form. It's easy to make them interlace, like knot-work. Also looks like Aztec patterns, doesn't it?"

"You're right, Berrin. I loved those blouses the women wore in the rancho with their beautiful stitching." She opened the fridge door and began rattling through the bins.

He raised his voice. "I can see this is reverting to some universal pattern for a language; it perhaps goes back to that needlework. I wouldn't be surprised that key patterns rose out of men watching women at needlework, or basket-making or braiding their hair. Men simply abstracted the patterns they saw in the plaiting and weave. I've read this might be the origin of religion — I mean the abstraction behind it — when they projected the forms onto the skies, which led to astrology and mathematics.

"There you are, Berrin, proof the Irish live in their heads too much."

"Well, they pushed the spiral into interlacing patterns, then onto circular knot-work designs, the continuous unbroken line followed, that's the symbol for eternity. The loop, you know, for the fish, it's a Greek symbol for 'Jesus Christ, Saviour.' A salmon is the Celtic symbol for all knowledge past and future. You see it in the Book of Kells. The links go on and on."

"Loopy, anything to get out of making baskets themselves. It's all quite heady. I have to hand that to you, no changing that, and I wouldn't want to."

"You don't have to change me. Just say you find it interesting or not."

She stood up straight, holding the fridge door open. "It's interesting. Honest. But where does it all lead?"

"Well, I guess for me now it comes down to my universal language. I figure that each language can come up with its own dictionary in about sixteen weeks, and anyone can learn it in a matter of months."

"Great plan. I love you for that. Right now, all I need is a beet."

"A beet?"

"As in vegetable, please." She tried the top bin.

"I'll have a look-see." He opened the door under the counter and pulled out a tray from underneath. There were two left.

"Who would have thought? The smallest one will do. Thanks. So, tell me more."

"They're Stephanie's. She doesn't like how they sweat in the fridge. It's cool under there, with no insulation in these old houses. Anyhow, if you're asking about what plans I have, I don't know. Hell, maybe the United Nations might strike up a committee on it. Wouldn't that be something?"

"Yep." Eileen sliced off the end of the beet and walked over to the sink. Looking into the mirror on the cupboard door, she dabbed the cut side of the beet onto her cheeks, then rubbed the deep iron-red dye into her skin with the tips of her fingers.

Enough then with the language and world peace. "When did you become a nature girl, Eileen?"

"That's the only good trick I picked up in the country."

Her skirt pulled up again as she stretched to get closer to the mirror. She was searching, trying everything, anything, even if it had once been taboo for her.

And the probable reason for making love with him.

Her face and neck were a soft gold, the window shade transforming the silver frost of morning into the light of sunset, her skin smooth.

He was like a caveman approaching a fire.

She rubbed her cheek hard to even out the colour.

"Eileen, I need to know about the other night. What did it mean?"

"You mean, me sleeping with you?"

"Yes."

"I guess I was lonely. I told you that. And cold." She continued working in the dye, only slowing up slightly.

"But the way you made love with me."

"Things led up to it. I don't think I intended to at the outset, you must know that."

"It doesn't add up."

"Drop the math, Berrin. You got lucky, and I felt like it, finally."

"You seemed ticked off." Odd how kissing can be more intimate than intercourse.

She turned to face him. "I don't think I was angry. If anything, I think I came to a conclusion, that you have to go after things yourself, and accept the give and take."

"You kept turning aside when I tried to kiss you."

"Sorry." She turned back to the mirror.

"You were all cuddly, then you shifted gears."

"It wasn't any fault of yours. Maybe there was some revenge in it — I'm sorry for that. I didn't mean it. You've always been good to me." Her voice softened.

"I know I'm out of practice."

"It's not a matter of practice, Berrin. Anyways, I wanted to be close to you. And I didn't say anything to Jeff, if that's worrying you." She hesitated. "And now you'll be dreaming less of me, seeing that it's not all that it's cracked up to be."

"What about our friendship?" His lips quivered and he turned in his chair to look directly at her.

"Berrin, I've just finished saying it. We are good friends."

"But?"

"*But* your first love is your writing and your books and your ideas. Look how excited you are about this language thing."

"What's wrong with that?"

"Nothing. There's absolutely nothing wrong with it. I wish I got as excited."

"You once did."

"Then if anyone is mired in the mud, it's me." She looked at him for a moment, and he felt his touch of anger melting. She turned back to the mirror. "Berrin, I think it's time I started my day."

It felt like she had thrown a pail of cold water on his head. And, surprisingly, it felt good.

Yes, she had made her mistakes, he his, and they had both got stuck, each in their own way in their own rut. It was time to move forward, for both of them . . . at least time to move past this conversation.

"With that outfit, you'll need some lipstick."

"Nothing beats this, even good for the lips." She rubbed the beet across her lips, then rubbed them a few more times with her finger, evening out the redness.

CHAPTER 32

A Zen master's punch

THE CAR WOULDN'T START. A Volvo, twenty years old or more, but in decent condition, safe, the kind of car he would have wanted for Eileen. The ignition was dead. He lifted the hood and twisted the battery cables. Nothing. He found a screwdriver in the back seat and shorted the bendix switch, something he remembered his father doing. It clicked with an arcing spark. Finally, the starter caught, the motor slowly rolled over but wouldn't start. Eileen stepped out of the house. He twisted the battery caps off, a difficult task, given how his fingers were stubby and slightly swollen. Two cells were very low. Eileen worried about tap water; it was clearly written on the battery: only distilled water. They compromised on the bottled water from the fridge.

His belly pushed against the fender as he bent to pour the water, keeping him slightly off balance. Water spilled beside the hole, running off the sides of the battery, catching in the ridges, picking up a bit of dirt and grease, which joined the stream of clean water hitting the cell directly.

If she noticed, she kept quiet.

They were heading to Carleton University, following Colonel By Drive, paralleling the Rideau Canal. Drained for the winter already. Berrin mentioned the upcoming winter festival on this, the longest rink in the world. Eileen smiled at the idea, she would like the skating and pulling a toboggan full of her children. It could be the exercise he needed, he agreed, if skates didn't cramp his feet so much. Yes, soon the multicoloured toques and multicultural scarves would be trailing after kids on sleds, skaters in pairs, and single-minded speedsters weaving through the crowds along the middle strip of ice.

She passed a slower car, the winding road leaving few lengthy, straight stretches. She drove swiftly, almost recklessly. Luckily, there weren't many cars and not many connecting side streets. The comfort of the car also diminished the sense of danger, but her speed disturbed him, and she was needlessly rough in shifting gears.

He needed to shift his thinking.

"I like your outfit." But her attire remained as perplexing as her driving, though he was happy about his scarf; it draped down the front of her overcoat, which she had left loose as well. He fixed his attention on her tie. The sunlight pouring in through the windshield made its black enamelling glitter as if wet.

"The clothes do make a change. Like your shaving. You feel younger, don't you, Berrin?"

"Suit and tie, smooth skin. More feminized, more androgynous, that's a current buzzword. If I became bisexual, I'd be at the head of the cultural revolution."

She smiled and looked out at her side mirror, then back to the canal.

He admired her resolve, envied it even. It wasn't easy returning to university. But that wasn't a choice for him, not full-time, at any rate.

"Hey, look at that sign. Pig's Island!" Eileen shouted happily . . . a small island in the bend of the canal near the wall, and a tree branching toward it parallel to where the water would have been touching it before the canal was drained. The branch then turned upward at the wall, full with its foliage, a surviving lone cedar.

Eileen looked up at the clear sky. "And such a beautiful day. Just like that day in Cochitlahuantla, that pig and I, we were together on the mountaintop surrounded by the huts, the dust, the parched trees — and the sky was this topaz blue. That's the feeling you don't want to lose."

The tree, with its dip to kiss the water, happiness, hope. He smiled. Not the time to pursue the matter of the pig.

"How is your mother faring?"

"Solid as a rock, better than anyone would have expected, though not as great as in my dream, if that's what you mean. She needs a farm like your mother's to keep her busy."

She swung out to pass a cycler weaving along the road.

It stupefied him. "Why can't she take the bicycle path? She's going to get herself killed."

His parents . . . he was at a loss what to say about them.

"You know the joke, octogenarian couple seeking divorce, counsellor asks them, 'Why now? Why did you wait so long?' and the wife answers, 'Oh, we had to wait until our children died.'"

Whatever his point, Eileen's follow through was seamless. "I could never think of my mother living alone. My dad, yes, but not my mother. I guess that's the crux of the problem, isn't it? We women never see ourselves without a man around."

"I think my mother was married to her brother as much as to my dad, perhaps because he kept the homestead going. She runs it now, or tries to. I convinced her to rent the land out to a neighbour."

"I remember her. I'm sure she keeps her say in it, right?"

"Headstrong, it runs in the family, I guess. Mother doesn't make it easy. She fights any real change. Even with her brother dead now, she keeps his name in the local phone book, as if he were still around."

"Hard letting go."

"It can't go on for long. I was toying with the idea myself. It would be hard though, by yourself. That's what drove my uncle mad."

"Family farms, Berrin, they're a rough row to hoe, how the tractors and animals always take over, and it's never enough."

"Never enough?"

Her head remained tilted to the curve of the steering wheel, no response, as if her mind were elsewhere.

He looked across at the landscape whizzing by, the stretch of lawn that in the spring would again display its rows of tulips, the bicycle path weaving along the guard rail, the ribbon of water not yet frozen by the first cold spell, the Experimental Farm on the opposite side, where willow trees glided by in synchronized slow motion, with the arboretum on the horizon above them, a motionless line of pure demarcation.

A cramp gripped his stomach, a burning sensation, then came the image of Jerome and the bear in his dream, like a jump cut in a film sequence.

"Why can't we ever say NO straight out?" He pounded the door. "That's it! I get it now." Then he felt it again, his tongue, as if pricked by a dentist's needle. I don't want anything to do with you.

He'd seen the need in Jerome's eyes, yet ignored it, denied it.

"Berrin? You all right?"

"I dreamed I split open my head last night."

"I was hoping that migraine wasn't as bad as it looked."

"You're right, but I was thinking of another headache — Jerome. One of the gallery's inner circle you met, that plump teddy bear with the fishbowl. He visited me last night before supper. He seemed to be up to something, I felt there was a strategy behind his visit. At first I thought it had to do with his wife, who's just left him, what Stephanie was telling you. But he didn't talk much about her. I thought he was wearing perfume, or maybe he simply farted when he came in the door."

"Did you know that to give perfume that animal piquancy, they add a minute dash of fecal material into the mix?" She brought her thumb and forefinger together in front of her face to emphasize this finer point.

"You're kidding. Shit is everywhere, isn't it? What confused me was that while he was coming on to me, I didn't really let myself see what he was doing. I even had a dream about it afterwards, about a bear, a mother bear who wanted to take us back to its cave, and, I guess, mother us, and smother us to death."

She laughed. "I must say, I didn't like the once-over he gave me. I don't see why homosexuals are any less screwed up than men in general about their mothers, and wreaking some sort of revenge on every other woman who comes their way."

"If Jerome has turned, I wonder what set him off. Maybe something that Francine did or didn't do? His ex, now. Maybe she wanted him to get a real job. I don't know about the mother stuff; you also have to factor in the father. But who cares? I think I've had my fill of theories."

"And there I thought I was doing great for once."

"Your theory's as good as any."

"If it only told me something about love. It always astonished me how Greek philosophers, all men, of course, made Eros out to be a male god. Maybe that kind of intimacy is possible only when sexual difference no longer complicates things."

"What amazes me is how naïve I can be. I was unconsciously trying to avoid the possibility that Jerome was queer, and at the same time I couldn't tell him straight out that I wasn't. The fact is I didn't pick up on it. I could only see his egomania."

And then there's the tongue swelling. That would have to wait for another time, if ever.

"Well, Berrin, I met this guy at Charles's the other day. One of his salesmen. I was attracted, Charles could see it, so he told me the guy was irredeemably queer. If not for that, I might have spared you."

"So, that was it? . . . You *were* wanting to!"

"Exactly. I can understand the part of wanting it straight out. I'm speaking as a full-bodied woman. But what a waste. It may be congenital for those guys, but for most men I think it's totally genital. They want an endless orgy, the just-fuck society, a real endless banging time of it, and they'll get it anywhere without having to worry about the implications."

She obviously had missed the double take in his response — that he had been right about her wanting to make love with him; but he hadn't considered the possibility of any calculation on her part. She had also missed his detection of her fib. Or did she care? But then again, possibly not a lie at all, only a slip-up, about being at Charles's *the other day*, which made it the day *before* they had slept together, a day before her note about going to see him about a job. She would have been returning to see him a second time. Maybe a third. Impossible. In the fraction of the second that fell in the middle of his response, he opted for the only other explanation — that she simply had switched days by mistake.

They had stopped at the barrier at the university's parking lot. She paid the attendant and headed for an empty spot behind the booth.

"I'll walk you to the library," Berrin said.

She pointed to the campus map beside the sidewalk, "The quad. I think that's where I need to go."

"It's in the central square. It's been years since I've seen it." He wasn't ready for the recurrence of the lisp and the slight slurring in his voice.

She was in no particular hurry, the change of speed a welcome relief. The various buildings and landmarks recalled different stories from their college days together.

A nudge. He had wandered too close to her.

They climbed stairs and then stopped, a momentary rest. They were standing on the promenade surrounding the square, directly across from the Dunton Tower, the "Arts Tower," in their day. Some kids were skateboarding off to their left, next to the library, supreme in their attempts at flipping their boards with their feet. Banana-boards, the original name for them; definitely more appropriate.

Eileen was admiring the youth as well. "I hope I'll be able to land on my feet half as well as they do."

She leaned over and kissed him on the cheek. "See you on the weekend?"

"You can count on it, Eileen. Come to think of it, I've never been up your way."

"Your track record has been atrocious."

She hesitated before continuing. "Phone me." She wrote the number on a business card that she pulled from her overcoat pocket and kissed him again. "Thanks for all your help, Berrin. It was more than I expected."

"It's been great."

She was already gliding down the steps to cross the park.

He flipped the card. Charles Wedderburn, Manager, Holt Renfrew & Associates.

As he looked up, Eileen was kicking aside a soft drink can, sending it out of sight under a pine tree with other plastic cups and bits of newspaper. She stuck to the path, swinging behind the tree momentarily, bounded up the steps on the opposite promenade, turned sideways through the large glass doors, and disappeared into the Tower. She hadn't looked back.

A universe apart. He felt himself beginning to sink again into a black hole. A matter of perspective. Maybe take heart from the newer cosmology, that a black hole could be a gateway between two entirely separate universes, a long, trumpet-like depression in the fabric of space-time, the depression, a necessary transition, a breakthrough, as his psych 101 had postulated. If only.

He sat on a bench and copied the phone number onto the back of a library notice and threw the card into the wastebasket beside him.

He found himself seated across from a sculpture, a column of metal about twice the human scale. A suggestion of a head and open torso of a youth rose out of a cylindrical column of steel. Slim and hard like the German woman in the Market. What was surely meant to evoke vulnerability and ripeness now sat weather-beaten in a coating of rust and bird droppings.

He shivered. An anxiety attack. And a cold, damp bench.

The morning shadows streaked across the park in front of him. The park was a square the size of a small city block, brown and green in the autumn air, bordered by the cement and glass and bricks of the university buildings. The landscaper must have been thinking of a Japanese rock garden. Its walkways of gravel zigzagged through mounds of sparse grass, random placements of boulders, and a mixture of evergreen and deciduous trees now bare, likely designed to lead the stroller through a garden of serene contemplation.

It was a Zen master's punch to the jaw that he needed now.

The first time he was on this campus was for Gunner Myrdale's talk on his monumental three-volume study, *Asian Drama*. So political, then, so eager to grasp the many issues in international development. Myrdale had concluded his speech by lamenting the number of weekends with his family he had to give up, a remark that had earned considerable admiration from him at the time. He couldn't have imagined an alternate scenario, such as the one made by a recent critic of Bertrand Russell, another hero of his at the time — how Russell got intensely involved in social issues whenever his marital life became too problematic. This observation had driven him recently to reread Russell's autobiography; but he should have anticipated that nowhere in all three volumes would Russell have mentioned anything about his mistresses.

Irrelevant, now. Forget the issues. Forget the politics. Forget the parallels between Russell and Myrdale. So much more solitary confinement atop a one-dimensional mountain in whiteout.

Eileen was now registering for her courses, somewhere within that tower rising above the square, the tallest building on campus, a blunt, humourless obelisk, obscene in its stolid height. He shook his head slowly, not conscious of its movement, only of a sour taste rising in his mouth, and then the realization that he couldn't ever again bring himself to fit into those towers, those Halcyon days, forever deluded in their disconnectedness.

To shake off those memories, he looked up again, hoping to determine which floor she was on, perhaps spot the window where she might at this moment be looking down at him.

His fingers gripped the bench, feeling the dew on the under-side of the wood slats with the same suspended consciousness as when he sometimes read aloud from billboards along the roadside.

In his confusion, he looked around, as if someone at that moment were about to step forward and speak, say something he needed to hear. The sculpture again caught his attention. He leaned forward to read the plaque at its base, to identify something about it, perhaps a fortuitous message. *Head and Torso*, as minimal as the sculpture. Barry's voice took hold of his thoughts: It's to leave you to free-associate with it, a pillar of Hermes protecting a newborn Dionysus, or inspired by a girlfriend and soon-to-be wife. He could easily picture the girlfriend, likely with the German woman's build, tall and slender, her short, dark hair lost in the smooth orb of the head, though a ring of metal around it could easily have captured the woman's locks curling slightly out behind her ears and neck, its strands stuck together and highlighting her narrow face and pointed noise, no suggestion of that either. A broadaxe driven into the featureless sphere would be the post-modern touch it needed to put some relief in her face.

Defeat: That was the message of the sculpture. Innocence bared then erased. Minimalism, the logical reprieve from today's pandemonium. From minimalism in art to neutron bombs to minimal collateral damage, the bare facts of a wasted world, still denying the complicity, everyone aiming at keeping the story as simple as possible.

He thought of Stephanie's paintings. She had achieved some sensuality in the texture of the strokes and thick ridges of oil — even in how she had painted each wall of her bedroom a different colour.

Eileen once told him that she sometimes had to change clothes over and over again in the morning until she came up with the right outfit to match her mood for the day. It would have driven him crazy, he had told her. He wished he could have a rerun at that conversation.

At one with a woman. He hoped it was not too late.

At one. Atone.

It would be another day before he could see Eileen again. Some action was required. Call in on Jerome, and expel at least that daemon.

CHAPTER 33

Goldfish in a bowl

HE MOUNTED THE STAIRS slowly. At the third landing, he heard Jerome's voice through the ventilation slats above the door. Obviously in the bath, and humming a Wagner melody at the top of his lungs. He knocked. The singing stopped. He knocked again. Water splashed.

"It'll take a minute." Jerome's voice cracked, likely from the combined strain of yelling and lifting himself out of the tub. On the phone, Jerome had warned he'd be in the bath, after having the kids all morning: "It's always like that, fun but exerting. But Francine has probably filled you in on all that, hasn't she?"

The door swung open. A bald head, a towel thrown over his shoulder.

The head spoke up. "Well, I never expected to meet you on my own turf." Jerome took the towel and began rubbing it over the stubble of his newly shaved skull. He hesitated, as if considering whether or not to step back and invite him in. He finished tucking his shirt in, white cotton against black trousers, chic if it hadn't been so wrinkled. They stood face to face, as if in a standoff.

"The minimal look, I see. Moving on, are you?"

"And you, Berrin? Returning to investigative journalism?"

Without waiting for an answer, Jerome stepped back into the

room. Yellow string criss-crossed the one-room apartment, looping in and around the few objects it could find to form a large,
intricate lattice.

"See, it's like the cat's cradles my father used to make. The trick
is to step through them and not touch one." Jerome offered up his
space with a sweep of his arm, as if inviting Berrin to the challenge.

"Looks like fun."

"It was, except for the pain of dealing with Francine."

Jerome stepped over the slack string attached to the door
handle and walked to his fold-up bed that lay under the window.
He stooped to untie the string from the rusted angle iron of the
leg.

"So, am I to assume that Francine did not send you to snoop
around?"

"Look, there's no way I'm taking sides in this. If anyone's
concerned, it's Stephanie."

"Another lady on the make and can't take the time to understand. The kids had fun, though, the two of them crawling over
and under the string." He looked up at Berrin. "Segmented space.
Difficult to get through, isn't it?"

Berrin shifted his weight, he felt his jaw clinch. "Why not take
a knife and cut a path through?"

"An impatient bugger, aren't you? The trademark of a committed investigator."

"It was a cultural rag, not reporting. So you can drop that line."

Jerome crossed the room to a chair against the wall, unhooked
the string from its back, crossed in front of Berrin to the doorknob
again, then returned to an end table that sat at the head of his
bed. He unhooked the string from the white porcelain knob of the
drawer. "I got this table in payment for some work I'd done for a
carpenter. You know what Francine's response was: A table! How's
that going to feed two children?"

He stood back and gazed at his installation. On top of the end
table sat the glass fishbowl from his office, filled to its brim with

water. The goldfish was gone. Behind the bowl, a sheet of silver paper stood upright against the wall. The water magnified a black dot drawn at the centre of the paper. Target-on. And around the bowl, three hammer heads, spray-painted but naked without their handles. Jerome must have placed them with much deliberation, a red and a yellow one on opposite sides of the bowl, and a blue one lying on the margin of wood in front. A precise constellation. An oval native mask carved in wood hung on the wall over the table.

"What's with the dot and fishbowl?" Berrin asked and stepped forward for a better view.

"It's something I created out of stuff I found here, apart from the fishbowl, that is. It was obviously junk to the former owners, but they're interesting artifacts."

"Looks like a shrine. Or maybe a new art form?"

"Is that what she had to say?"

"What?"

"You can tell Francine I'll be tearing down this installation tomorrow."

His mood switches were disturbing. Jerome returned to rolling up the string. At the centre of the floor, it looped under two broken halves of a breadboard and stretched back to the end table, where he stopped again in front of his installation.

A sparse room . . . Berrin hadn't expected this. Apart from his desk in his office, which usually was bare, there was nothing else about Jerome that hinted at this bent. Nor at this conversation, though he hadn't ever had much of an exchange with Jerome. Perhaps the flowery student placement had turned him down.

"I see you don't need much furniture." Berrin tried to be as offhand as possible. Other than Jerome's neatly made single bed and his end table, the only other furnishings were in the kitchen area at the far end of the room, a table and two chairs sitting across from the counter. And a cold stretch of Varathaned hardwood flooring; no carpets anywhere. For a room that a few hours earlier had supported two sprightly children, it was spotless.

"It's surprising. I mean, your room. You lead a lean life, Jerome."

"Time to turn over a new leaf, pull myself together. Everyone's downsizing these days." He laughed, but remained stock-still, facing the end table.

Berrin looked back toward the kitchen area. The small, round table, an inexpensive type with two flaps, was painted yellow. One chair was blue, the other red. Like the hammer heads, they were newly coated in bright acrylic.

"The gods laugh, and the goddesses stare."

"What's that?" and he turned to find Jerome now squatting in front of the fish bowl.

"Have you ever seen a picture of the Venus of Laussel?" Berrin asked.

"I've seen one."

"The woman with the horn?"

"Like the Venuses of Willendorf and Lespugue. I've been interested in this stuff for quite a while."

"Glad you're with me, then. Paleolithic primal mothers, the source of all our dreams and fantasies. Can't you see that swollen womb and the belly button?" Jerome bracketed the bowl between his two upturned palms and outstretched thumbs, as he would do to frame a camera shot. "I didn't see it when I first put the paper behind there. Imagine that! A real pretty lady sitting right there on top of my little table and I hadn't seen her till now."

"You've turned off women altogether, then. No wonder the gods are laughing."

Jerome hesitated, took his towel from his shoulder and tossed it over the bowl, then pointed to the kitchen table. "Have a seat." He opened the end-table drawer and placed the ball of string inside. His knuckles curled against the top as he remained slumped over, as if waiting for a moment of vertigo to pass. "I don't expect you to understand. Or anyone, for that matter."

Best to let the topic drop, Berrin thought, and instead of sitting, he moved to the counter. The counter was totally bare of any utensils, containers, cups, or anything you'd expect in a kitchen. A single sink, its aluminum shiny, with a hot plate near the far wall, no fridge. A pint of milk sat in the windowsill above the sink, sufficiently cold, probably, now that winter was settling in. He leaned against the counter to look outside. A steady stream of cars passed at eye level beyond the backyard. They flowed past at an angle, like a giant toy racing track that was tilted toward the window, surprisingly silent, as the Queensway took a turn around this end of town.

He turned to see Jerome move toward the kitchen area, walking with a slight sideways twist of his own, as if he were simultaneously contemplating turning back. He moved with short, shrinking steps, like a lobster, and stopped at the end of the counter, where he picked up the phone. He bent down, pulled the cord out of its jack in the wall, passed Berrin, and dropped it into the garbage pail in the corner. He stood looking down into it, twirling his finger beside his skull as if a curl remained.

"Stuck in a small, round, black hole." Almost a whisper, as if Jerome were speaking to himself.

"*In and out of the Garbage Pail.* Remember that old book by Frederick Perls on Gestalt psychology?"

"Great idea, Berrin. From now on, I'm doing mail art — see how she likes that." He reached down, retrieved the phone, wrapped the cord methodically around it, and placed it back on the counter. "Put it in a brown paper bag, address it with a large red marker, and mail it off to her." One would have expected him to laugh but he again pointed to the table.

"Be my guest, please."

Berrin pulled a chair out. It scraped along the floor, the sound amplified by the emptiness of the room.

Then with an aristocratic English lilt, Jerome exclaimed. "You've chosen the blue chair, old love!" His sense of humour, possibly.

"*What* do you think of that?"

"Reason over passion." Jerome chuckled.

"Seems to be a theme, these days."

"I painted stuff to give the room some life."

Having Jerome positioned at the counter, above him, unnerved Berrin. He looked around the room. "Why don't you add some plants?"

"No, not that kind of stuff. I mean, it needed a sense of theatre."

"Your room looks more like an abandoned gallery."

"If you'd been by last week, everything would have been purple. When Francine phoned, I had to make a change . . . you know, for the kids. Red, blue, yellow. Primary colours."

"You certainly are on the fast track to fundamentals." Berrin looked back at the phone on the counter, then up at Jerome. As if from a flush of self-doubt, Jerome brushed his hand over his scalp to stroke the phantom hair.

"The hammer head appearance, wouldn't you say? It brings me back to my younger days, with my buddies on the hockey team. I really can understand those *Field and Stream* guys. Then again, you might say I've appropriated the 'butch look.'"

Jerome stepped forward and sat on the red chair across from him.

In response, Berrin positioned his elbows on the table and pressed his palms together in front of his chin, fingers pointed upward, touching his chin. "Jerome, you have me totally confused."

"That's very appropriate. I should have given you a prie-dieu to kneel on." Delivered with a smirk.

"Perhaps." And appropriate. Jerome had touched a sensitive point. Still the altar boy, pious like a chubby church mouse. He repositioned his hands under the table and absentmindedly started playing with the hinge that held up the table lap, pulling on the spring.

Jerome continued, "Francine sat on that chair this morning, still with that hurting look in her eyes, like when she knelt at the end of the couch and looked up at me with those dark Québecois eyes and pleading, I'm a beggar for love."

"That must have been humiliating for her."

"Who was humiliated when she took off out of my life, 'to find work,' she said?"

The table flap snapped down in front of Berrin, snapping whatever comeback he had in defence of Francine. He left it hanging down.

"How's it going for you at the gallery?"

"I'm quitting."

"You *are* full of surprises. I thought you were enjoying shaking things up."

"I definitely did that. Got the picture hangers very upset."

"The board won't be happy with your decision to quit."

"Not Francine. She pretends to like art, even Stephanie's, but you don't see her hanging around the gallery much for any exhibitions. The hand-to-mouth existence of an artist's life isn't for her. She doesn't see how lucky she had it with me. A part-time job, and half the week I work at home, around the kids. Fathers are too absent from their children."

"Things change, don't they?"

"At first it was only a room of her own — she was oh so innocent about it — still, her things cluttered my space. Then she'd appear out of the blue to get some clothes. Finally, it was she who'd disappear altogether. If I'd ask, 'Where to?' she'd say, 'None of your business,' just to rile me."

"You should give her more time, Jerome. You should give yourself more time."

"I give her everything I have. In fact, she can have that end table."

"You're making absolutely no sense."

"Everything comes down to food. I'm getting rid of everything."

"There might be more to it than that. I mean, I've been told that I've been running away all my life as well."

"Women still want the finery, lots of pretty things around them. You have to strip it bare." Jerome sank back and cupped his hands on his lap. His vacant stare had crept back.

"The world is definitely hell-bent on denuding itself," Berrin said.

"Women still want to be pursued, don't they? Well, no more for me. It comes down to having nothing, pursuing nothing, consuming nothing."

"Regrets?"

"Regrets! I can't work like I used to. I can't settle down. But I'm beginning to adapt."

"Adapt? Jerome, you're falling apart! I see you're even losing weight, which might be a good thing." He chuckled, without effect.

"When you're hungry, anger has nothing to feed upon."

Berrin leaned back on his chair, looking away. He pondered the empty counter again, then looked into the living room area, and noticed a bread knife was placed between the two halves of the broken breadboard lying on the floor. It was a homestead model, where the serrated blade ran alongside a shaft of wood that extended into a handle. A relic? A memory?

"What's that supposed to mean?"

"A common enough sight."

"I never get this deconstructionist stuff."

"Everything has its spot. If you use it for anything else — " Jerome's voice quivered. His arms hung loosely at his sides, but he remained rigidly upright, staring past Berrin — as if he'd regressed into a catatonic state that could easily be his normal condition when alone.

Berrin turned to see what he might be looking at. An iron frying pan hung on a nail over the sink. A black dot on a white wall.

What to say? He returned to fidgeting with the table leaf, moving it back and forth, then leaned back into his chair to let it pass his belly, and the spring snapped back into its holding spot.

"Jerome, with the shape you're in, you know this won't be the best place for your children. I'm sure Francine would come around if you tried talking with her again. Show her you're serious about making a go of it again."

Jerome rubbed his scalp. "You ever see a tiger change its stripes?"

"You're at the end of your rope. Why don't you come have supper with us?" He stood up.

"I'm crawling straight toward that bed."

"It's not my night to cook, it's Stephanie's." No reaction. "Perhaps if you talked with her."

"Why would I talk with Stephanie? All that flaming red hair." He laughed and then stopped.

"I don't know what to say, Jerome."

"Francine has her mind set. And it seems she's gotten through to everyone else."

"It can't be as bad as you think. I'll stop by again."

"Don't bother."

"I'll let myself out."

"Suit yourself."

CHAPTER 34

The prodigal son

TELEPHONE LINES undulated at a steady level with the window of the bus. Speeding off, the same feeling as when he'd fled up north, leaving everything behind. But this time it was positive. The countryside dipped and rose in the twilight, almost playful. He folded the newspaper into the pouch in front of him. Off with the light above. With his eyes closed, the clickity-clack of the wheels hitting the cracks in the pavement sounded like a train. He leaned into the aisle to see the road ahead. A panel of blackness in the windshield.

The Laurentians were on the right. Only a margin of darkness, as if the bottom strip of the deep mauve sky had been ripped away. His uncle's farm — his mother's now — would lie about an hour's drive north beyond the skyline, the same land here with the same people there. The return of the prodigal son.

Reverting. The feeling set like a lump in his stomach. His homeland, as unalterable a fact as if he were indigenous . . . he definitely had been fighting it in different ways all his life. Perhaps it was the sparseness of the land, the frugality, the closed-in horizons. Rarely were there moments of exuberance, like that touch of bountifulness in the tins of Spam that Alex invariably twisted open for dinner after Sunday mass.

Perhaps it should be Jerome and not him making this trip;

Jerome's bent toward the patriarch a better fit, though he was now acting like the dethroned king and unhinged in the process. His visit with him did have the touch of the sanctimonious, Jerome was right about that. But it wasn't only Jerome's relationship with Francine that took him to visit, it was the uncertainty. So Jerome was not gay — his many protestations did eliminate that possibility. Francine was right to break away. And Jerome: tempting to say he simply needed to let loose; such in any case would be the advice he'd find in this neck of the woods.

His visit with Jerome also removed any doubts about seeing Eileen. He wouldn't be dabbling in the deeds of a do-gooder this time.

At that moment, the bus passed a Jehovah's Witness Kingdom Hall, its sign lighting up the roadside. The bright orange lettering curved in a shape of lips, like a clown's mouth laughing.

As if back in a busload of CIASPers heading to Mexico, when after a rest stop in one of the central U.S. states he found himself having to take the front seat opposite the bus driver, which gave the best view of the road ahead. Everyone exchanged seats after a stop, except for those who were asleep in hammocks they'd strung between luggage racks or at times curled up in the racks themselves, the three-day-and-night, non-stop trip necessitating any number of creative ways for some shut-eye. The CIASPer who sat beside him was a new face who had boarded the bus soon after they crossed the border into Detroit. The man began talking right off about his America, pointing to the highway and exclaiming, "You know, there are over thirty million miles of highway in the States, more than any other country in the world." Rosy, full-shaped lips, that was what was astonishing. Then for some reason the man-child switched to talking about religion; perhaps he was from the part of the country they were passing through, or perhaps it was the effect of the desert-like countryside stretching to the horizon in front of them. Religion often came up in conversations because of CIASP's missionary roots. He began speaking about fundamentalists in the area, Christians who, in the climax to their church services, sought redemption by handling rattlesnakes, a handler lifting one to the heavens as it dangled between both hands, then sinking into a trance, speaking in tongues, and quite often getting bitten and dying days afterwards. Both ways, bitten or not, you reached salvation, his self-anointed friend laughed as he concluded, as proud of his story as he'd been of the highway stats.

With any luck, the opiates in this Pontiac county, while less venomous, might be as bewitching. Such as those notices in the health food store, advertising the services of shamans, invariably urbanites who during the week held down jobs of the high-tech ilk. Reiki sessions and solstice circles and sweat lodges: he was ripe for these rites. Then off with Eileen under the naked stars to share a cup of Kombucha, a veritable snake-oil remedy perfectly suited to these more hiemal climes.

But the gateway to the underbelly of life had to be simpler. He'd been avoiding the obvious for too long.

Like how he had cut off the remainder of his sidekick's story to punch a pothole into his world view of macadamized supremacy: "Aren't you exchanging a country for a desert? I understand your highways have dried up the water table by ten percent or more. And you want more of that?"

That mania for statistics, never very suited for nourishing friendships, even if they did give a measure of a country's spiritual state. And Eileen? What were his odds? Definitely time to ignore the numbers.

The bus took a curve that opened upon an expanse of farmland below, and as they dropped into a flat stretch, he caught a glimpse of the Ottawa River beyond the far fields where the line of trees broke off. The band of silver in the dusk took a turn away from them. He would likely not be seeing the river again.

Nor the covered bridges, red against the green of the fields and the blue waters. Especially the postcard six-spanner a bit farther north near Calumet Island. However, covered bridges seemed a more common feature on the other side of the mountains toward the farm. More Scottish and Protestant in this region, more Catholic and Irish up the Gatineau River. How different would their stories be? Something to look into.

A woman beside him was curled up to the window, like a bird hiding itself away. In her mid-twenties, he guessed, slender, silent, and keeping to herself from the first moment he sat down beside her. A uniform under a light jacket, probably a nurse off work, rushing off without a sweater, but it highlighted her lines. Blue canvas running shoes to match, needed for being on your feet all day. Her belly quivered at intervals. Then he noticed that she was quietly crying.

He wondered about her story, how it set against the beauty of the land, the magic that should set everything right, even throwing in a miracle when needed.

Which it did at times, another positive for moving back, with its Willie McCaffreys. As a youngster he had heard of Willie's miracles, his uncle good for those stories, saying that the miracles came from Willie's natural way with animals, aided by his bottle of the timeless Elliman's Universal Embrocation and a generous application of Sloan's horse liniment. That, and his knack of appearing out of the blue when needed, a story on Willie could be his first on the region. Like the pre-war accident at the Farrellton bridge, when a crew of local farmers was hired to repair the bridge, he could easily write it up, send it off to the local paper, if it didn't make him stick out too much, doubtless offending some sensibilities, the many contending clans; he never did care enough for that form of local entertainment. But a ballad of the region already had Orvil Daly bragging how the $8.50 daily pay on the bridge job kept him in beer for a year. The barroom minstrels could use another such tale; he knew enough of it already that it would almost write itself.

The fast current of the river had piled up logs against a middle pier, and the entire bridge was in danger of collapsing. To clear the logs and do repairs, the crew had strung a cable to the next pier and

was using a small scow pulled by a large winch on shore to transport men and tools and materials to the pier. In a few moments
of neglect, the cable was left to hang too close to the fast-flowing
water, and a flow of logs caught on it and started piling up. The
bridge began to creak and groan. Either the bridge or the winch
was going to give, but the men in the scow at the pier were in the
greatest danger.

His uncle's account of the story had Lamarche, the foreman,
acting first — perhaps Eileen would know more details, since
this all happened near her village. From the shore, Lamarche had
worked the winch, starting up the engine to tighten the cable, then
cutting it for slack. Some logs were dislodged, then more floated in.
A second and third try failed to dislodge any more.

The two farmers from the scow had jumped into the river.
Kelly and Monnette? He'd have to get their names right. They
would have known the river well enough, having also worked the
rafts upriver above the Paugin Dam, collecting deadheads to add
to their income.

The deadheads in his dream, he should have known.

They made their way hand over hand along the cable toward
the pile of snared logs. Kelly climbed onto the logs while Monnette
stayed in the water and pulled himself around to the upstream side,
where he began kicking away the ones that were not too jammed.

Lamarche started the engine again and the cable went taut.
Then it snapped, catching Kelly in the arm as he bent to grab an end
of a log. He was whipped into the river and disappeared instantly.

The miracle, Willie McCaffrey appearing on the shore. But
everyone was so caught up in the panic that no one had actually
seen him ease down the steep embankment. Willie was spotted
only after Kelly resurfaced, a few yards upstream from Willie
near where Lamarche was standing and was able to wade into the
water and grab him. Kelly was unconscious, his right arm limp and
dangling at the elbow, but a quick one-two pounding to his chest
brought back a sputtering breath and he would live.

A wonder, everyone agreed, how Kelly resurfaced so quickly, so near shore, and upriver from where he had shot under. A miracle, Foreman Lamarche said, but Willie only remarked at the wonder of those underwater currents.

There would be other stories. He was returning.

A few seats in front of him, two teenagers were making out. To be envied, these times, even in this river-born, faith-bound region that sported the highest incidence of teenage pregnancy in all of Quebec. One had to admire the kids' progress. First sitting sideways across their seats, then slumping to the floor. Where could they find the room? Soon back on their seats, and throughout determinedly serious in gluing their mouths together, the bus driver never once glancing into his rear-view mirror, the darkness their best friend, though it didn't dim their eagerness in showcasing their passion. Everyone else as deliberate in looking straight ahead, even the middle-aged Chinese couple in front of him.

A robust enough life beyond the urban landscape, he could fit in. He settled back into his seat.

Humming came from across the aisle, one seat back, where an obese woman criss-crossed her fingers through the circle of an overhead light. She was reading Braille in a large scribbler of brown sheets. The spot of light somehow belonged.

He looked back toward his window. The non-consoled nurse had fallen asleep.

It was too dark now to see out any window. The blind woman's humming broke into a soft song, slightly louder than a whisper, but with the resonance of an aria. He would soon be at Eileen's.

The bus's headlights provided momentary assurance as he stepped onto gravel and into a cool moonless night. A full moon would have been more appropriate after the incongruous romance of the bus ride.

The Chinese couple hadn't gotten off the bus with him . . . not the people, then, who had started up a ginseng farm across the road from Eileen's — she had mentioned it in his phone call for better directions. Given the darkness, he'd not likely in any case see the field of shades that protected the ginseng from direct sunlight. The cool night air held currents of warmth. Indian summer coming on, boding well for the weekend.

Supposedly only a half-mile to her house by this side road; dark, she said, but safe enough. First some woods, then open fields — and, though admitting it to himself didn't help, back to his childhood fears of the night. Wolves in the wild, wolves at the door, the three little pigs had reason to cower. No rational argument on his part allayed his instinctive fear. His could be the first statistic of a wolf killing a human; that is, if any evidence remained this time. He finally crossed railroad tracks, a side line that Eileen had said led to an abandoned iron mine, a welcome touch of civilization that abated his dogged urge to run. The road there crossed a secondary highway . . . pavement. He should soon be reaching her driveway. He remembered to turn left onto the next side road, the original asphalt. So many roads and so few houses. Weeds sprouted between the cracks in the pavement.

He spotted Eileen's house on the left, two storeys, but small. He envisioned rooms with cramped spaces and low ceilings. White aluminum siding picked up the little light that fell from the vault of stars. A dim light shone from the front roadside window; likely the kitchen. The location was isolated and choking in dampness, hidden in a cluster of tall pines and canting birch.

Off to the side of the house, a rhomboid of light cut across the gravel driveway that ended at what looked like garage doors. He approached quietly. The picture window opened up to the living room, where Eileen, in profile, was seated at a small table to the left, facing the wall. A doorway beyond her led into the kitchen, where a bare bulb shone from the ceiling, the light slanting across her table. He was certain she couldn't see him, the angle of the light leaving him in the shadows. The table was cluttered, as if she had dumped a box of objects gathered in a bout of cleaning. She wore black leotards and a long, loose, cotton top. She bent over the table, intent, too intent to be simply idling away her time waiting up for him. No one else about.

As if playing a Ouija board, she was moving some of the items around on the tabletop. Her movements were slow, yet she seemed annoyed, her face pale and drawn.

Aligning and arranging, assigning meaning, seeking solutions. She studied each object with the intentness of a medium.

A box of baby powder — love, its cover half white, half black. The nail clipper, shaped like a boat — perhaps fate. And the two bottles of perfume? She held them in each hand, the oval one — romance, the flat one — hopefully not her future. Balancing them on her palms, then letting them swing between the grip of her fingertips, perhaps pondering how to join them together. She aligned them side by side and added a pencil.

Her breast fell free, she adjusted her blouse, and her hand returned to its task.

He pulled away from the window, his boots almost silent on the frost-hard gravel, leaves decaying and crumpled twigs, wanting warmth inside. He turned back to the front of the house, mounted the two cement steps, and knocked. A spotlight flicked on over-head, and she appeared in the doorway.

They hugged and she kissed him lightly on the cheek. Her lips felt feverish.

"Don't bother with your boots."

"No, I insist."

He needed the interval.

She stepped back to wait.

"The kids are asleep. Jeff is in town, likely with the girlfriend."

Another moment of silence. Her eyes were red.

She led him past the kitchen on the left, the staircase to the upstairs on the right, down the short hallway into the living room, which they crossed to sit on the couch. She pulled her knees up under her chin and leaned against the arm. He sat near the opposite end. Across from them, the large, night-filled picture window.

The slight chill he had trailed in from outside had sunk its teeth into both of them. "Did Jeff know I was coming?" he asked.

She looked at the floor.

"I don't like you seeing me like this. I promised myself I wouldn't cry again."

A tremor in her voice.

"Tomorrow I'll show you around, introduce you to the neighbours. Maybe we can go horseback riding."

"I'm not interested in seeing anyone else."

She pulled a smile. "I need to get out of the house. Jeff will be back by then with the car. I don't like driving the van."

She looked somewhat toward him, but kept her gaze to the floor. Her blouse had a pattern of wild roses, as if a hand-me-down from her mother.

"Sorry to see you so down in wifedoom, Eileen."

She didn't smile. Instead, she stretched her legs out, moving them in and out like scissors, then dropped them back to the floor.

Delicate ankles, more slender than ever before.

He lifted his left foot and stretched and crossed ankles with her.

"There, the *cross of life*, the Ankh. That's what the ancient Egyptians called it, the union of male and female. Numbers two and six, if you're into numerology, and if you multiply them together, I think you get close to the number of years we've known each other."

"I suppose so."

He withdrew his foot. The seconds stretched out. He hadn't struck the right chord. She stood up.

"Let's watch some television together. I'm tired of talking and thinking and analyzing . . . games, more mind games. Who needs them? I'll make a cup of coffee."

"Make it tea, then. I'll have enough trouble sleeping as it is."

"Channel 8, that's enough numerology for me."

She stood for a moment looking at the screen, then returned to the sofa, as if she hadn't mentioned the coffee.

"This is a great film. I don't know why I like it so much. It's so American and the guy is too perfect. But it still draws me in."

And talking like Jeff now.

The film was familiar to him, and he remembered it more the longer it played. Black and white, still camera shots, Americana, a relic from the fifties or earlier, about a crusading young teacher, another white knight, not having to face a languid lover but instead having to cope with a listless group of black teenagers slumped around tables in a shack that served as a schoolroom. Another missionary world separated from civilization by a river, a universal story, replete with that "deep sentimental attachment."

He relaxed and lowered himself into the couch, and his head struck Venetian blinds behind him. A small window behind the couch, the white frame yellowed and smudged. Eileen reached over and pushed the blinds in against the glass. All the while she avoided looking at him.

A spring was pushing itself into the small of his back. He shifted his weight into the arm of the couch, his gaze now falling midway between Eileen and the pane of darkness in front.

"Why are we watching television?" He tried not to sound strident.

"Better than talking about Egyptian feet and numerology." She kept her eyes on the television.

"Eileen, I'm here because I like you very much."

"I wanted you to come and talk with Jeff, remember."

"Let's talk about him, then."

"I'm too upset."

"About us, then."

"About us?"

"It's as good a time as any, don't you think?"

"Berrin, you want me to start digging up stuff, then I will. There was a time — you know when — when we might have worked through stuff, but you were off being the hero in Tepepantiango."

"That's a bit unfair."

"Afterwards as well. You could have talked with me in the hospital. You were too scared or something. I wasn't the virtuous, high-minded woman any longer. I don't know any woman who wants that. You wanted to be nice and visit me."

She looked back at him.

"You want a confession, Berrin. All right. I spent the night in Ottawa with Charles. I didn't return here right after Carleton."

He gripped the underside of the cushions, holding himself down.

"Charming." He shifted his position, turning away slightly. Off to his right, the table of clutter, forgotten.

"Actually, he tries to be."

"You really are amazing, Eileen."

"I wouldn't say that."

"But what about attraction? I mean, there doesn't seem to be much of that in the mix."

"You're still not getting it."

"What is it? Is he married?"

"Was. His wife just died of cancer. He's in mourning."

"That's sad." She's sleeping around, the conclusion stared him in the face.

Classical music. The teacher was standing behind the students as they stared at a Beethoven record spinning on an old portable wind-up turntable at the front of the classroom, all quite listless. The teacher tickled one of the students on the back of the neck, then moved to another, trying to elicit a response from them.

"What is really going on in that head of yours, Eileen?"

"Maybe I'm still after revenge. I'm forcing myself to make a change."

"You're floating, Eileen. Who is it that you want to be with, anyhow?"

"You've always respected me that way; let me love as I wanted."

"Nice guys always come last. And how nice is Charles?"

"I didn't make love with him."

"Poor Charles."

"Knock it off, all right?"

"What is it exactly that you learn to love?" The question had slipped out, incoherent.

"What? That's a strange question."

She got up and turned off the television.

She walked over to a closet and opened the door. A linen closet. To even think of breaking off for the night made him angry. She started speaking, her back to him, half hidden where she stood at the entrance to the hallway, her voice coming to him as if in a letter from far away.

"I had an aunt Bertha who died of TB in 1929, at the Civic. I can't tell you how many times while lying in the hospital I thought of her all those years ago, perhaps in the same bed as I was in. She had a vision of St. Thérèse of Lisieux, "the Little Flower," she called her. The Little Flower appeared at the foot of her hospital bed like a glowing light, then she saw that her bed was covered by a mantle of white material with red roses all over it — real roses, that's what she wrote in her diary. She asked the Little Flower to cure her, and the roses formed three words in the shape of a cross: resignation, surrender." She stopped, as if to think.

"And the third?" But he knew the answer already.

"Love. It formed the upper portion of the cross. She believed the Lady would cure her on an exact day, the twenty-seventh of April — no more numerology, please, Berrin. And when that day passed, she had nothing left; nothing except her suffering. It was the only act of love left her, the only thing she could offer the world. I got better when I realized that about her, that that was what my vision in Mexico was about. It's all about loving, I mean giving love, you have to let your love flow out. It's not my fault that my husband won't love me back."

No, it's not your fault. But these words remain buried in his eagerness to know more. The right questions failed to come . . . his mind was crashing . . . and absentmindedly he said aloud, "The year of the great crash."

Frowning, Eileen turned to hand him the towels. He was still on the couch.

"Sorry." He stood up, as if in slow motion.

"I've never been able to tell that story before."

"No, I hadn't heard you tell it. So tell me what happened in Cochitlahuantla."

"If I did, I'd get that kind of flippin' response you've just given me. A kook."

"You're definitely not a kook."

"Let's talk again in the morning, all right?"

"It's just that whatever happened, that's what has always come between us."

"Maybe it's how the cards are stacked."

"You sound like my mother again."

"The details won't help, Berrin. Like all that planning you'd put into the community development projects."

"You've got a point, there."

"I'm sorry, Berrin. Maybe you're right to be like that, like with your language project. Maybe it will work, I don't know. Maybe it's how you want to be the shining light. I'm fed up with the bright ideas."

He bowed his head, contrite. Her comments did hurt, but he realized they could as easily be directed at Jeff. Jeff was the target.

"You can sleep in the children's room, next to mine. Tomorrow's another day."

The staircase entered one of the two rooms upstairs. She unrolled a futon that was stashed in a corner, and stood facing him.

"You know, it's really not your fault." Her eyes were teared up.

The door that separated their two rooms closed behind her.

CHAPTER 35

A pure spirit

FIRST LIGHT, silver-blue crystals of dawn floating on the surface of her eyes, leaves dew-bright green, a fine-grained, sandy earth, tan, cool . . . feet bare and legs clammy in the damp air draping her. Consciousness returning. A cloudless morning, an infinite stretch of blue above the curl of mountains, the line of the horizon swinging back to the rise where the church stood, bringing her back to herself. She was awakening and standing above him. She had no recollection of rising from her cot or coming outside or walking across the yard toward him. He was asleep, the ropes still holding him against the post, loosely; he hadn't tried to break free. His clothing was threadbare, immaterial against the long, cool night, goose-bumps down his arms to where his hands huddled between his thighs for the little warmth there. She saw his entire history in the few facts she remembered about him, facts that should have left him blameless for his few misdemeanours the day before.

His slumped figure evoked a profound compassion within her. She needed his pardon for her intrusion. A hard worker who did his best for his family, he didn't deserve this punishment. He was beautiful and good. She felt that if she were to stretch out her hand his goodness would rise into it and flow up through her body, dispelling all that had deluded her until now. She stood apart, separate, disconnected. How to break free from her cage? A storm had raged within her over the days leading up to Berrin's departure, much of it wrapped in denials and excuses. Planning, projects, preaching hygiene, empty formulae that only left them more irrelevant, leaving everyone to resent if not hate them.

Everything was talked about, everything but the need to love. Her thirst had been this longing, a love born of weakness and frailty but now released to give her strength. The stronger she felt, the more her soul burned with love for this man at the stake. Love would bridge their worlds. This was the meaning of her vision in the night, a realization that was not so much a memory as a sense of delight that engulfed her body.

She reached down and touched him.

Good brings forth goodness. She felt released. *You are free to do with me as you want . . .* a thought that shrouded her as a mute but irrepressible passion.

The man opened his eyes, not stirring for a moment, as if trying to remember where he was, why he was sitting on the ground. He shook his head and cupped it between his hands. Then he noticed her two bare white feet at his side and looked up. She spoke, trying to tell him that she could untie him, but with a quick squirm and twist he was free of the ropes and stumbling across the yard toward the huts where the path led down the slope.

She ran after him and was able to grab his arm as he turned into the bushes below the last hut where the turn of the path would take him home. He turned on her, his face a glower of revulsion, causing her to shriek. But he stepped back again and she lunged to hold him and caught the hemp string that held his trousers. In a fury he grabbed at the open collar of her shirt, no more than the ripping and an orange flash at the fringe of her mind. She jumped back. But he didn't attack her further. Instead he started pulling at the cloth and tearing it to shreds.

Her sin only then became apparent in his revulsion and anger. She was the prisoner, of privilege and power, she could see that now, her apparel as unsightly to him as her ignorance was now her shame. Her clothing was his suffering. His suffering had furnished the grounds for her happiness. How to free herself from all of this? Shed her power? If he could see her as she was. Suffering made garments irrelevant. She should be happy with any kind of garment, with his, with nothing.

In a fury of moves she pulled off the remainder of her shirt, her trousers, her undergarments. She was naked in a matter of seconds, and her clothing lay in a ring around her feet.

She stood still as she faced him. His lips quivered.

If she couldn't be helpful, she would be as helpless as possible. Her nakedness, her aloneness, her helplessness was what would bring forth love. How right it felt. She looked down her body. Her clothes were not hers anyhow, stolen from him and his family and his people, nothing more than spoils in the plunder of so-called trade and aid. She was returning them to their rightful owner.

But before she could utter a word, he turned and scrambled off again, his arms and legs flailing in all directions as if he were again trying to hit the volleyball across the net.

Very much like the black ball that she had tried to control in the night. They both needed a game where the ball was tied to a string, sad somehow, then comical, then her spirits dropped again and she started down the mountain more and more removed and meditative.

How long she wandered didn't matter because her conviction grew that she had been heading down the path of willfulness for too, too long. She squatted under a bush, unable to decide which way to turn. An iguana scurried up to her and stopped. A medi-aeval creature, its limbs in mail and a stoic head with a ridge of fleshy spikes stretching down to the rings on its tail. It lay flat on its stomach facing her, its fish-like head and iguana smile turned up to her. She reached down to touch it, then grabbed at its tail as it turned to escape, leaving its tail dangling in her grasp. A rash deed, but forgiven, as it would grow back. She started up the path that the reptile had taken. Without her clothes it was much easier to walk, then to run. An unutterable sweetness of self-sacrifice filled her as she raced upward. The image of the iguana blended into the spirit of the man at the stake as the mountain lifted her higher, pulling her more and more out of herself. She felt a peace that surpassed all contemplation. A pure spirit. Oneness.

CHAPTER 36

That's how a man was built

BERRIN AWOKE TO a noise, darkness still, and a muffled exchange as Jeff climbed into bed in the adjacent room. Silence returned. A purling, hummingbird-like breathing drifted from the far side of the room where the children slept. He wanted to sink back into his dream, to remember it all come morning. Being awakened by Jeff in the middle of it would help. He wanted to return to Eileen . . . they were lying on a mattress on the floor, and he was snuggling up to the curve of her spine. The floor was on an uneasy incline, as if something were pushing upward from the earth below, from another world, cold like frost. They were talking, as intimate as he had ever wanted, catching up on their stories, their former hopes and desires, their unlived histories.

Her hand brushed him where he was pressing up against her. He was searching for her. Next, they were sitting at a table, talking, about her marriage, about his life's twists and turns. Somehow they were maintaining their balance, despite the angle of the floor.

She'd placed a large brown envelope in front of him, unsealed. But he understood that he had permission to pull out only certain sheets, and only one at a time. They told of her life, so much so that he wanted to rip open the envelope, pull out any sheet at will, throw them wide open, lay them flat on the table. He needed to act this way, he told himself, that's how he was, that's how a man was built.

An older woman entered the room and walked past him as if he weren't there, past the table where he was grabbing another sheet at random. She was interested only in Eileen, who was preparing a meal at the stove. She told Eileen to move on, that getting kicked in the teeth was a good lesson for her. Then a voice boomed out as if from nowhere. It came from above and at the back of his head, loud, like a thunderclap: "You will never be her husband."

CHAPTER 37

Quicksand

HE AWOKE TO a rattling overhead. Black stovepipes emerged from the top of the brick chimney off to the side of his head, stretched across the ceiling, and fell to the floor at his feet. The noise came from the point where the pipes met the bricks. Eileen opened her bedroom door and dashed across the room, grabbed a chair and stepped up to break open the pipes. A small black bird flew out, circled the room and bashed against the window across the room. Soot fell like black snow. The bird then circled back and disappeared through the door into her bedroom. Eileen chased after it.

He caught a glimpse of her body as the morning light from her room struck her T-shirt. She was thinner than he remembered. Some glass broke. She returned and stood in the doorway. The sun shone through her yellow full-length cotton skirt that obviously served as her nightgown. The inverted "V" silhouette of her legs floated on the pattern of roses. "She wasn't hurt," Eileen said through a spreading smile. "She kept on flying up into the trees. Imagine that. The little thing didn't even touch the glass."

The strength of the bird breaking the windowpane. For the second it took him to notice the broom handle still in her clenched fist, he thought that that was how the bird had escaped.

"Does that happen often, a bird getting stuck in the chimney like that?"

"Too often. Jeff says he's going to cap it with a screen, but never does." She looked refreshed by the excitement.

"Maybe I could fix it later. The window that is. There are limits to my heroism."

"Don't you dare. See you at breakfast."

"I'll be right down."

She smiled and turned back into her room. He heard Jeff pulling off his blankets, and muttering, "What the hell's all the commotion?"

"You'd sleep through an earthquake," Eileen answered loudly and her legs re-emerged into his line of vision as she hurried down the stairs.

From the living room below, cartoons on television.

Eileen was cooking eggs and motioned for him to sit down, her smile gone. The kitchen floor was a chessboard of faded black and white linoleum tiles, a few broken at the corners. He felt like a pawn, and likely to be knocked off in the upcoming chess game. The children sat at the far end of the table, across from Jeff, who looked up from a computer manual to greet him with an ingratiating, "Good morning, Berrin," and returned to flipping through the pages. The king, pivotal, but the weakest of players. Eileen poured the coffee and kept busy. Jeff seemed to be looking up something as he glanced back at Berrin. Eileen kept to the eggs; she hadn't said good morning yet.

Her mood had clearly reversed; he regretted waiting until Jeff was up before coming down himself. He sat at the table across from Jeff and sipped his coffee. He considered getting up and washing the dishes piled in the sink, but dropped that idea. The iron frying pan rattled on an element as Eileen flipped the eggs with her spatula. An antique wood stove, but with electrical elements, some convenience. The rest of the kitchen was taken up by the table that was pushed back between the refrigerator and the counter. Everything cramped and unforgiving. He could see no alternative to this arrangement, as the table wouldn't fit well in the living room, either. The window looked out onto the crossroads that was partially hidden behind a row of tall, overhanging maple trees.

The children had stopped eating, the presence of a stranger obviously stifling their usual morning antics. He hadn't thought of himself as a stranger. The girl was older than he had imagined, at least three, but still in diapers. She was kneeling on her chair to eat and looked up at him from across the far corner of the table. Catching his eye, she turned shy and returned to the serious job of eating her granola that was soaked in water. He would have expected milk with the granola, and a dim memory of his own childhood returned: The first time his mother had used instant powdered milk, its metallic whiteness telling him that something was wrong, since he never before had seen such suds in his porridge.

The boy was squeezed in his high chair in the corner at the end of the table. He tugged with one hand at the strap that secured him while his other hand gripped the blue plastic handle of his spoon, outstretched and waving in the air, his eye fixing on Berrin for the time necessary to register Berrin's total irrelevance to his needs, and then he, too, turned to his own dish, mashed bananas.

He definitely didn't belong here. He looked toward the ceiling, as one would in prayer, searching for an answer, trying to pierce through the gaps in time. Spiderwebs had accumulated in the corner above. Why hadn't he come to visit when the children were born? Eileen had insisted on home births and had asked him to come for her first child, for support. At the time he could not understand; she had Jeff, she had made her bed.

"What's your name?" Berrin asked. The curly head was bowed to its bowl and trying to fish a raisin from the quicksand of cereal.

"Kim." Her tummy pressed against the edge of the table, bare between the Pampers and a T-shirt stained with granola and apple juice dribbles. She followed his gaze to her stomach and then looked back at him. She stared at his scar, stood up on her chair and looked back at her belly, then traced her stubby fingers along the red line left by the tabletop. Her other hand hovered at her side, grasping at some essence that was visible to her only. She then froze and stared down at a point somewhere between him and her belly, her white tufts of hair like burst pods of milkweed, her mouth open as if to hold a robin's egg.

"Kim, sit down before you fall down," Jeff shouted and then turned back to Berrin. Suddenly very animated, Jeff began talking, as if preprogrammed, about his plans for a community newspaper using computer technology and the emerging Internet for dissemination, his hand outstretched and jerking back and forth to punctuate the points he was making. Impeccable in his dark suit and holding his book like a preacher his Bible, a virtual non-stop delivery, while Eileen served the eggs and poured another round of coffee.

"Berrin, you could say it's my latest kick-at-the-can, a crusade against pet peeves. But it's more than jumping on a bandwagon. I see it opening up so many opportunities. I've even made contact with a local liberal."

Eileen sat at the end of the table and to make some room for her plate of toast and cup of tea she moved the butter dish to the centre. A round, hand-thrown piece, a buttery smooth speckled glaze, with a flash of the wood ash hitting the knob on the lid, a welcome touch of warmth in the room.

"Why don't you tell him the whole story, Jeff?"

Berrin turned back to Kim as she climbed down from her chair, crawled under the table, and emerged to run off into the living room.

"This porky politician," Eileen continued, paying no attention to Kim, "took to inviting us to his place for supper — he's got this winterized cottage down by the river. He figures we're hippies, into free love and all. Our casual clothes I guess . . . we're young and from the city . . . who knows! On our second visit, after we finish eating, he begins talking about love and the need for this area to open up to new styles and soon he's saying he wouldn't even mind if we all took off our duds and sat around the table naked."

"He didn't actually say that and he doesn't talk like that. He said he was more open than most around here, that he could understand nudist camps and people sitting around naked. He probably imagined more, I admit, testing the waters. Likely a lonely man."

"A dirty old man who thinks he can get whatever he wants. Just like he doles out the party's pork barrel of government grants."

"He has connections. That's good news for me," Jeff said, turning to Berrin. "I'll be driving him around this afternoon. He wants to introduce me to some friends."

Me, me, and me, the sum of his calculations. And why hadn't Eileen caught him up on this? Then came a tug on his sleeve and he looked down to find Kim holding up a board with an assortment of blocks on it. He turned to place the board on his knees and began helping her pile her blocks. He lost the drift of their bickering for a moment. Jeff was miming playing the violin in response to something Eileen was saying, who countered with: "For sure. You do know how to jump whenever someone snaps a finger."

Berrin balanced one of the smaller blocks on the tip of his upturned fingers and snapped his fingers over it, making it disappear, his middle finger flicking it so that it shot up his sleeve past his cuff that he had surreptitiously unbuttoned beforehand. Kim stared in silence, then broke into crying and ran into her mother's arms. She then fixed him with a set of scrolled eyebrows.

"You twicked me. You are a bad man. You twicked me," she said, and continued to cry.

He laughed. His surprise was unmatched by either Eileen's or Jeff's reaction, taking her outburst in stride. And how could he explain his trickery to a three-year-old? The explanation that rushed into his mind instantly, that it was good to learn early in life to second-guess reality.

Eileen wiped the tears from Kim's cheeks and told her to run upstairs, she'd be up right away to help her dress. Kim ran past him without looking up. Jeff reached for his book and the baby banged his red plastic cup against his tray. Berrin placed the board and blocks on the water heater across from him.

Jeff began speaking in automatic again. "These manuals tax my patience and my energy system at times. About my newspaper, Berrin, maybe you know someone who's looking for a column. Here's my new business card." Jeff pulled a deck from his shirt pocket and handed him one.

Eileen sipped her tea and stared at the table in front of her. The inside of her pottery mug was heavily stained.

He recalled Jeff's manner with the German woman in the Market. No charming manners, now; more his real self. But remaining Eileen's fix nevertheless. He'd seen enough.

"Thanks, Jeff." Only half finished his eggs, but the urge to escape was irrepressible. He stood up as he reached for Jeff's card. "If you guys don't mind, I'll take a little stretch outside. Thanks for the breakfast, Eileen, I'm sorry I can't finish it. Guess I'm not used to such hearty meals so early in the day. I'll be back in a jiffy."

Eileen opened her mouth to speak, perhaps to warn him about a migraine, but Jeff cut her off, he could visit the ginseng farm next door but they were away, he could also follow the road back down past the mink farm, with the long barns; he had passed it in the dark. There was a beaver pond in the dip of the woods just beyond it. He might see one.

Standing on the concrete landing, he breathed in the foliage-fresh, manure-scented breeze and relaxed. A warm spell was on. He should have asked Eileen to come along for the walk. He unzipped his windbreaker and felt for his notepad in his pocket, an impulse to write, more a hope. As he touched it, he remembered, "You will never be her husband."

He'd invite Eileen for a walk, regardless of what Jeff might think, and he turned back to reach for the door handle.

A sound coming from beside the house stopped him. A growl. He stepped lightly down the cement steps and peeked around the corner. A cat was curled on the gravel in the sun next to the wall. It didn't notice him. One paw curled in mid-air, then swiped at its tail, a grey tail that came to a point so narrow that it looked like a rat's tail, twitching. Its eyes were frozen on the constant twitch. Suddenly, with a final warning snarl the head snapped at the tail, nipped it twice and froze again to renew its stalking of itself.

Berrin turned and crossed the lawn.

An obscenity, the single row of small, mesh-covered windows low along the length of the barn. How many captive minks could there be inside those cells? Four to six to a window? Each awaiting its meal of minced meat from carcasses of cows that had been struck by lightning or mired in creeks and drowned . . . he understood, all part of a cycle — a bit of trivia that Eileen had passed on to him, like her tidbit about perfume, disgusting as well, however much the mink farmer played a useful role in the great chain of being.

Understandable that she could never bring herself to visit the farmer's wife. The white house, across the laneway from the barn, was as large as his uncle's farmhouse, and needing a paint job as well. His mother regretted that Alex hadn't renovated the old house instead of building a bungalow. A bungalow didn't fit the land, she was right about that. Bungalow, the Hindi word for summer house.

Farmhouses now harboured only the secluded and abandoned. The barn was in better shape than the house.

He looked away from the mink farm to the field across the road. A healthy stretch of corn left unharvested for some reason. The stalks rattled in the light breeze. Demeter's daughters. He pictured a black horse galloping through the rows of brittle golden husks, earth cousins to the dying sun. Kim's gaze, the trust that her silken hair marshalled. He shouldn't have tricked her.

The ridge of trees at the far end of the field would likely be leading down to the creek and the beaver dam. Other cornfields and other embankments . . . he'd seen enough of them.

CHAPTER 38

Behold, the man . . . shoot the man

THE RIDE IN THE PICKUP to the outskirts of Tepepantiango had not been the most difficult part, the head-shot almost therapeutic.

Not so for Profirio. From altar boy to porter to possible rebel in less than a month. Perhaps Berrin's presence had saved Porfirio from being tortured, given the captain's expansive mood of clemency. Profirio had been arrested for snitching the photo that incriminated the army. They get shot who also stand and witness.

His own act of heroism? Best to view it from the public realm . . . Berrin the brazen lad, not telling the captain where the photo was or who had given it to him. Some satisfaction at least in seeing the look of disdain in his face. The army likely knew the details even before his arrest.

The captain at the army garrison had his own sense of decency when it came to foreigners. Tall and slim and cinematically gallant in a starched, green uniform, only his demeanour presented the threat of torture. The captain rose and walked around his desk to confront Berrin as soon as he was marched into the room, his arms gripped firmly by the two soldiers, one on each side of him. He stood face to face with the captain, whose face was flushed, the emotions ambiguous until he spoke. "An American who can't leave us alone? You are all alike. Meddling. Forcing us into corners we don't like. If it's dirty work you want to see, you will see it, *bastante, mi amigo.*" As he continued barking out his denunciations like curses, his forefinger repeatedly shot out and stabbed Berrin's chest — which unfortunately easily rivalled the captain's.

Nevertheless, Berrin had stumbled backwards, surprised at the degree of pain one slender digit could produce in his sternum. He fell into a chair behind him. Then came the cliché movie scene, with the predictably bare bulb above and a small, wooden table between him and his executioner. It felt removed, unreal . . . it didn't fit.

The captain opened a binder lying on the desk. Berrin grabbed the moment to glance around. The room was like a bunker, damp and arbitrary and smelling of urine. The cement walls were a washed-out green, the paint peeling in mangy patches. Off to his right through a door, the corner of a bed frame stained with what could easily be mistaken for rust. He was in a predicament; as his dad would say, you don't get out of this life alive. If he wasn't to be tortured with electric probes, he might be thrown into a wet strait- jacket and left to compress on those bare springs, images recalled from an Amnesty International report, and he suddenly felt light- headed. He pictured himself lying in his straitjacket, truly mad, his fear of being tortured raising goose bumps down his arms. How intense pain could get, he couldn't imagine . . . wouldn't . . . and he found himself disassociating from the thought.

The captain looked up from his document, viewing Berrin for a moment, stonefaced. "You are a prisoner, therefore you are guilty. And if not guilty, you are at least insane, for you obviously don't appreciate reality in this country. We can't be wasting valuable resources on insane asylums for deranged foreigners, *es claro, no?*" He said this in an almost perfunctory manner, in an easy English, its impeccable logic adorned by his soft Castilian accent.

Berrin stared at the captain. Some sarcasm, tempting, *You are* El Capitán, *therefore you are the* Omniscient One. But discretion told him to try and weather this out in silence.

"You know there are laws against foreign agitators conspiring against the state. Article Thirty-Two of the Criminal Code. You can expect nothing less than capital punishment."

Berrin looked upward, to give himself another moment. On the wall behind the captain, an incongruous image of Christ with his exposed heart wrapped in thorns. Obviously a strategic set-up. The slogan was clear and easy to translate: "Reveal all and be redeemed."

"*Capitán*, the existence of a statute doesn't make me a criminal."

"The people you associate with do."

Images of Porfirio and Padre Nómez flashed through his mind. "Then I guess half the inhabitants of the ranchos are criminals, those who don't like cheese, or who can't afford water pumps or cattle."

"Who do you think you are?"

"I am a Canadian."

"No!" the captain shouted back. "A gringo, a gringo who doesn't know when he has crossed the line, and you have done that, *cabron*. A photo for the media — *muy loco*."

A sinking feeling overwhelmed Berrin. This captain had total control over him. He saw how they had stripped the teacher and hung her upside-down, slicing her in half like a carcass of beef. The image of bloodied corpses next flooded his mind, stacks of bodies in Tlatleloclo square in Mexico City, photos of them in an old, yellowing edition of *El Sol del Hidalgo* that Padre Nómez had stored on a shelf in the sacristy. The newspaper featured the massacre of students and civilians, bodies in business suits and daily dress, some randomly piled four deep in a stairwell. Reality was returning to mock him, not the Olympics this time, but politics, still the politics of mining, of oil, politics of drugs, politics of politics — or, more apt, the politics of cows — it was all the same in the end. And the world said nothing.

"We will be searching you, you know that. But you hand over the photo voluntarily, and you and Porfirio can go free. That's the smart thing to do. You see, we can be very civilized."

It all came down to this, such a simple gesture. And all the mastery that the righteousness of their development projects had bestowed upon him, his sense of mission and worth, his world of truth and knowledge now appeared for what they were, a hoax.

The captain barked an order. "Give me that photo, pronto."

He reached up for the photo in his pocket, then his hand continued on up to scratch his head.

The captain saw his movement, and motioned to the guard, who reached around and tore open his jacket, finding nothing. The guard then pulled him upright and searched his jean pockets, then pushed him back into the chair.

Berrin smiled. He knew it mirrored a Humphrey Bogart smile. But it took only a second for him to recognize his emotion. Shame. He could have betrayed everyone, but it was his body that remembered the photo wasn't in his pocket any longer. His shame was self-inflicted, without redemption, he had no one to appeal to, not even himself.

Berrin looked away, his focus now freezing on the floor. The violence of the room, its sadism and perversion, almost a welcome remission from his simple-mindedness. He was no longer in the world in any case, a world apart that was quite content with his arrest, as commonplace an annoyance as a bump along the road, his arrest a jest. He started to laugh.

The captain let his binder fall to the desk, and he laughed as well.

His soul felt cleansed by his brief moment of absurdity. It was as if Christ himself was mocking him, when the captain gave the final order:

Behold, the man.

Shoot the man.

CHAPTER 39

Put a man and a woman together

ONLY AFTER DINNER did Berrin get a chance to be alone with Eileen. His flashback in the cornfield had sobered him. He had continued down the road, nature itself a blank slate, welcomed to that extent, and turned back before reaching the beaver dam. Never once had he dared to compare his trauma with hers. He had come to view his near-death experience as very much a stroke of good luck, the shot to the head little more than that knock on his noggin his mother had called for. And he had survived. To talk of it in any other way would be to glamourize it, much like soldiers from a war refuse to talk of it, each for their own reasons. Perhaps why Eileen had refused as well. The bare truth: they had survived. And leaving the field of action felt like betraying their ideals, the shame no less for being a survivor, a shame equal to those who had stood by.

With Jeff off chauffeuring, Eileen moved their chairs onto the gravel and away from the shade of the house to catch the sun — a few yards across from where the cat had curled in upon itself. Though the autumnal air was warm, the kids were bundled in coats and caps and left to play at the end of the driveway beside the garage, the baby in a crib under a crabapple tree, and Kim keeping her distance from Berrin, pushing a weather-beaten baby carriage around the trunk and punching it into the crib on every other turn.

"Kim, honey, stop running into Jessie like that!" Eileen said in a raised voice.

Sibling rivalry might have been at play, but play was the predominant game here, for Jessie was laughing each time the netted walls came bulging in towards his face. Eileen's nerves didn't need the aggravation.

"Your children are beautiful."

"Tell that to Jeff."

Enough said on that, so he looked back at the children. Kim was now running around the trunk of the tree, trying to make herself dizzy, her hand scraping the bark as she turned.

"I guess more than loving him, I wanted to lose myself, bury myself in him. It was more than wanting security. We could build something together. Maybe I liked his scheming nature more than yours, Berrin, I don't know. I've been throwing my love away for nothing."

Jeff's schemes appealed because they tried to beat the world at its own game. But how to change the topic? To Mexico? Likely not the time. He spoke instead of the cat, how it kept biting its tail. She looked over at the children while he spoke.

Kim had returned to her earlier game with the carriage.

"Kim, I told you to stop running into Jessie like that. Now put that carriage away." Eileen pulled her knees up on the edge of her chair and hugged them.

"It was outside on the roof yesterday, right below our bedroom window. It's getting worse."

And then as if the floodgates had opened, she gave way to a rush of words and tears.

"I hate that grey cat. I moved here because Jeff wanted to. Cheap mortgage, he said, and he could easily set up shop in the garage. After a few days here, some Jehovah's Witnesses dropped by, very English accents, Why, we're new in the area, too, they said —" Eileen's voice in imitation of a squirrel-like chatter, " — neighbours down the road. And then they told some highfalutin story about their cat. They returned the next day, to drop it off, they said, had its distemper shots and all, and thanks for taking it off their hands, though I don't remember ever having offered. Kim liked it right away, and when she reached up to take it, it peed on the woman's dress and jumped away. It only came back when it was starving and ran off right after eating. Kim couldn't play with it. It got so scrawny. Worms, Jeff said. As if then it was *my* job."

He wanted to stop her flood of words.

"Worms make me think of fishing."

"People like Jeff, people without backbone."

Eileen dropped one leg to the ground and looked up at him.

"You remember that job I had at the university? I got it after you shut down your magazine and took off up north. It was better working with you, Berrin. Much more pleasant than banging away at those damn DOS codes. I just love manuals."

He had closed down their magazine not because he loved the north but because she had stopped showing up at the office. She had dropped out of sight with Jeff.

"I couldn't keep it going without you, Eileen. I knew nothing about the entertainment side of things."

She looked away and started to shake.

"And he expects me to be interested in his scumbag politics and his damn newspaper."

The bathroom was located in the old summer kitchen attached to the rear of the house. He had to stoop to avoid the light bulb, as the ceiling was even lower than in the main part of the house. The toilet was stuck in the far outside corner beside a small window. He stopped to admire the large iron bathtub with its rusted lion claw feet, its well of white enamel corralling the afternoon light from the window. Thistles and nettles peeked above the sill. Mindless for the moment, from his seat he looked out past the row of thick trunks of maple trees to the road beyond. A hunchbacked man in overalls and a baseball cap came into view, pushing a wheelbarrow that he had with obvious pride painted red and upgraded with a set of automobile lights on the front rack. An orange squeeze horn was bolted to the rack on his right; a bicycle mirror stuck out on a long arm to his left. His staggered steps led forward with unimpeded progress, in a direction that likely was taking him home. Berrin continued staring, transfixed, but not wanting to feel anything in particular about the man, who eventually disappeared down the road behind the branches and weeds.

No hurry either for him to move from his secluded throne. An overall lumbering afternoon, as if back in the days of powdered milk and water.

"You will never be her husband." A traditional marriage — was that what he had always wanted? His fears pointed to the flip side. Grasping at straws . . . or nettles, a more appropriate metaphor. He tried to raise the window, but the frame was stuck in a lifetime of grime and cobwebs, and he settled back onto his seat. Arranged marriages; love *can* be born out of the ceremony of words. In all likelihood, Eileen would have refused any proposal from him, although he never came close to one, because she had stifled her tears by getting up to pull the kids apart again, Kim trying to climb into the crib by stepping onto Jessie's head, which was again bowed forward into the netting. Eileen decided to put them to bed for their afternoon nap, Jessie crying only when she lifted him out of the playpen.

He had waited outside for her when Jeff turned into the driveway and reported that his politician had to delay the meeting till the following weekend. Jeff invited him to see his office, and stepped behind the plum and birch trees that bordered the driveway across from the house. He kept his printer and computer in a shed that sat back behind the trees, a one-room cabin that he had winterized for his office.

And a future storage depot for another scheme.

Berrin looked around the bathroom again. The wall across from the bathtub supported shelves of junk smeared in grease and cobwebs, a box full of large bolts, a set of discarded disk brakes, a jar of nuts and screws. Jeff might have better expended his energy renovating this room and partitioning off the bathroom area. The walls curved outward. The floor was set directly on the ground, the walls rotting away at ground level.

The whistling of the water filling the toilet tank gave way to a similar but more piercing sound from inside the living room. He took a few seconds to recognize the growling, long low groans that rose to a high pitch and then snapped with a snarl into silence, broken again by more low growling.

Then Eileen shouted, "The laundry! The laundry!" By the sound of her feet, he pictured her running in from the kitchen. Jeff shouting back, less loudly, almost conciliatory, "The kids let it in." But the kids were upstairs, sleeping.

He belted up as he hurried across the floor, almost on tiptoe, and eased up the two steps that led from the bathroom to the living room door. Eileen screamed, "Can't you smell it? And now it's on the laundry and the couch," as he stretched to look through the lace curtains in the high window of the door. The cat was lying on one end of the couch next to a pile of clothes. Jeff was seated at the other end, leafing through a newspaper.

She started to cry. "You belong together: the smell, the couch, this shack," she stammered. "And you," the words pounding to escape her skull, it seemed. "Look at the leg — you'll never fix this couch, or the bathroom, nothing. We're all becoming savages."

She turned on the cat and gave it a sharp swipe as it raced across the linoleum. "I hate feeding it, and I don't want it around. You won't even buy a bit of medicine. You don't give a damn."

"I need to show Berrin something. Why don't you do something in your spare time, for God sakes? You have plenty of it here."

"I should never have left Ottawa!" she shouted, leaning into Jeff's face.

"But you've never been happy anywhere: Masham, too small and mangy, like your cat . . . or Ottawa, what was it you said? Too arty? Nothing ever satisfies you, no one, nowhere, not me, not anyone. How many men did you say there were before me?"

That's it, Jeff, shift the blame. Her fists clenched against her temples as she continued staring at him.

Her gasping voice turned to a gagging as she clutched her stomach and slumped to the floor. Her fist hammered into her stomach, she expelled a groan, unrecognizable at first, a squall of hollow sounds like No's unfolding in the air, the pitch then rising to a winged scream.

She lay curled in a ball on the floor. Jeff stood up, walked around her, took his coat off the hook in the hallway, and quietly left. The pain would have been less had he at least slammed the door.

Berrin pushed on the bathroom door, but it was stuck. The noise of his kick must have broken through to her, because she was attempting to stand when he entered.

He looked around for the kids. Of course, they were upstairs.

For an instant he wondered why he thought first of the kids, as her weight pulled at his grip, her body dead in his arms. They sat side by side on the couch for the next few minutes without talking, and then in a slack voice she apologized. She needed to rest; and she disappeared up the stairs.

Berrin sat at the kitchen table while the kids played in the living room with crayons and a colouring book. Kim was still shy around him and stayed close to Jessie. Jeff hadn't returned, but Berrin still hadn't seen much of Eileen. She had brought them downstairs and set them to play, then returned upstairs. He tried to write, to focus on his memories of Mexico, something to connect with Eileen.

Eileen made her appearance again at suppertime. She exchanged nothing more than idle chat with him and the children as they ate, then returned upstairs to put them to bed, apologizing for being so out of sorts, but she had to be alone some more.

He remained at the kitchen table, but he realized whatever he wrote was redundant and recycled, and he didn't see any progress. He turned to some old issues of the *Pontiac Bulletin* that were stacked under the stove's hot water reservoir. An advertisement for a hardware store caught his attention: "A Solid House Makes for a Happy Home."

Again the slogans, like what the captain had posted in his torture chamber. He remembered photos of Nazi internment camps and the motivational signs that could be seen on the walls of the work area, "Work shall set you free," common-sense values that get repeated worldwide whenever the saviours gain control.

The captain had retained a civilized veneer, sticking to the statutes and demanding that he comply, and for a few bravado minutes he had spoken out in defiance.

He flipped the page in anger. The prim *capitán* behind the table under a lamp, insisting that he comply, that compliance more than the photo would be what redeemed him. Compliance again the winning ticket.

Civilization, a well-curried word, the ultimate self-evident truth.

At this point, the quiet and empty space around him felt too oppressive, and he, too, retreated upstairs.

Sometime in the night, Eileen entered his bedroom. He was alone in the room, since the kids had remained with her, snuggled and secure beside her in bed. As she pulled back the blankets, she whispered, "Just hug me." He was glad she had come; his feelings were revived . . . he couldn't put a name to them . . . he was simply relieved she was there. Still, hugging her was clumsy, given his size. She relaxed into his arms and held him in turn, her body stretched out alongside his. He was nude, and fully erect, but this didn't seem to catch her notice. How to comfort her? His hand roamed up and down her back, rubbing it, then wanting to do more, and he found himself stroking her thighs, and upward under her skirt. He nudged closer, pressing tight against her body, and to his surprise he entered her. Only slightly, he realized, and without intending to; and then he ejaculated immediately.

She lay without moving. Then she sat up, swung her legs out of the bed, rose, and walked out of the room.

The next morning, Jeff still hadn't returned. There was the van, though. Eileen offered to drive him the four miles to the bus station in the nearby village. He could catch the bus where it stopped at the railroad beyond the mink farm, but he accepted the ride for the time together it would give them. They hadn't talked much through breakfast and the silence was unbearable. Not a word either at the dip in the road where the busy beavers worked away. Rolls of baled hay streaked past them, stretching out in converging lines from both sides of the road, gigantic mutant versions of the shredded wheat they had had for breakfast. He tried to focus on the imponderables ahead. How to move forward? Should he speak first? Apologize? Was a worry about pregnancy keeping her quiet? How to go deeper?

Even the sunshine was hushed. He knew that he should trust his instincts and remain as mute, but he couldn't support the silence.

"About last night —"

"What's there to say? Put a man and a woman together, and what can you expect?"

CHAPTER 40

Beginning the dance

SEATED ALONE IN A PUB, Berrin numbered himself as one of the regulars with their tabulated banter that added up to endless, meaningless clatter. A long sheet of paper, the length of the bar, stretched above it to present the noonday specials. He studied it like a patient on his deathbed, as if in a morphine high and trying to make sense of the angles and forms of the room hovering above him. A computer printout with individual letters made up of innumerable X's repeating themselves. The Generation X supreme.

He caught the barmaid's eye. She surprised him by sporting a close-cropped head of stubble.

Another hammerhead? "I'm curious. Why did the curls have to go?"

Not the least hint of a smile . . . not that he wasn't a regular.

"No matter, you're probably right; frizzy hair does suggest empty-headedness to most men."

He got the definite sneer now. Perhaps timely for her, anguish has no age. She returned with his beer, handed him the tab, took his money, then continued on to the next table.

"Hey, you know you don't touch a woman," from a group of guzzlers at the table nearest the bar, the uproar of voices catching his attention. But he wasn't the target, the speaker reminding him of his uncle, the jutting jaw, the determination in the high brow. The man was telling of rising from his table with four buddies, "Without a word, we led the prick out to the back parking lot and kicked in a few of his ribs. A bit of his own medicine."

"I hear that's what homeopathy is all about," the second joked.

Another, "He didn't even have the sense to keep it to himself."

No wish to keep to himself, either. Thanksgiving weekend for the celebrating celibate . . . Berrin, the brawny lad, ailing with a band of lost lushes in the Lafayette, going to seed in the neediest of watering holes. He reconsidered: Perhaps return to the bus station and take the first Voyageur back up the Pontiac; appeal for forgiveness.

The reality? From the voyageur to the voyeur, that was the sober truth of it. And back to the pub, playing his game of detachment, wanting for people around, everyone putting a pot to their bellies, going to pot together, listing, listening, not so much for an answer from themselves as settling into the genial stories that inevitably were let loose as those magic amber lanterns twisted open.

Am beer.

Sip, sip, slip, slip.

Three red-faced men of unrecognizable ages sat at the table next to his and soon an array of emptied draft glasses spread out in front of them as well. He didn't have to strain to overhear as their boasts simply bounded past him as so much game fleeing past a hunter's gunsight. His attention sharpened when their talk turned to home issues.

"That Hindi guy one floor up was usin his washin machine again and drainin it into his kitchen sink directly above me and the soapy water was bubblin up and overflowin my sink directly below. I had to plug it to keep out the stench, and the dirty water then began pourin out of the tap."

"You should have plugged him."

Another, wearing a cap, "Didn't you tell the superintendent?"

"He said I shouldn'ta plugged my sink. What about the

regulations about usin' only the washin' machines in the basement? I said. No such regulation. They're all in cahoots."

"They're the ones that wear those turbans, covers their entire heads, that's what makes them holier than Jews, I guess, but give 'em a chance and they're as superior as the rest of 'em." This observation was made by the baby-faced one, as he leaned forward to bury another empty glass among those in the centre of the table, his smile shaping itself like a car spring, his Beetle face settling around it.

Social realism. Perhaps pay more attention to that. Forget the dreams. Ground yourself with the simple chatter, the people's epic. But their talk now swung to Ski-Doos and the best trails for the upcoming winter. Nothing more of note there.

Reconsider your situation. Your one-world language project was a laughable scheme, a demented idea, just as Eileen had probably thought it was. He remembered the CIASP meetings that took place in The Oasis, the student union building; it still stood around the corner from his co-op. He would meet his friends there every Wednesday to plan the summer projects in Mexico. A Scientology fanatic would often be seen sitting on the floor in the lounge busily writing letters on a coffee table, convinced that the prime minister would grant him the special audience he needed to demonstrate the surety and sanity of his world-wide governance design. The Lone Ranger rides again, Nietzsche's niche for every dreamer. Or Yeats's take, don the mask, impersonate yourself if you are to move the crowd. Bleak at best.

Maybe his forte would be children's stories. Use his afflicted dreams in a proper way. He had enough of them, especially of bears. Children liked bears. And the touch of the child biting the head off a dog would go over well. He could populate the story with the other animals that inhabited his nightscape. Like the crocodile and fish and dog that sat with a bear on his couch one recent morning, talking, and finally telling him directly what they signified, a key discovery that he treasured for a wide-eyed moment in the middle of the night but promptly forgotten upon reawakening in the morning. He could only remember the wash of colours on the wall behind them, bright blue, reds, yellows, greens, amoebic shapes flowing into each other. Children could likely unravel such things easily enough.

But even these speculations exhausted him, a needless weight on his mind. And who was he kidding? Writing, another escape. Creation, the bane of original sin.

Definitely sobering up with the drinking. He stared past the row of empty tables to the far window. Drizzle, mixed with snow, so early in the year. He thought of his uncle Alex and his chest tightened. Another martyr who lived life to the fullest.

He felt his own pulse, that irregular skipping that had been with him all his life, starting in his childhood and on through high school with his yearly bouts of rheumatic fever. Thankfully, it had never been his obsession . . . nor Alex's, for that matter.

He looked around the room. Two new drinkers near the bar. The regulars do keep the loneliness at bay, until the last butt is out.

The ruling facts — he hadn't intended to enter her, at least not then; his ejaculation had surprised him as much as it had her. But his ark was sunk.

Like Alex's. He recalled parts of the second found letter from Colleen to Alex, the only testament of his follow-up trip to Ireland — and ample evidence for his mother that Alex was a fool to have pursued the woman. She had found it under the newspaper lining of the top shelf of Alex's bedroom closet.

How infuriating it was, she had said, that Colleen could have treated him so callously.

He had pried his mother for some details, as she stayed at the window, a rainy day at the farm. "You must have been curious."

"Best to let sleeping dogs lie."

Alex's choice as well, with his occasional allusion to the trip dropped into conversations at random. He had stayed longer than planned to learn a few new tunes on the fiddle, which he played for years afterwards in the pub or at house parties, until the enthusiasm petered out. Her name would slip out as if unnoticed, Colleen had to remain to take care of her own mother. One had to conclude, given the second letter, that Alex's trip had amounted to another proverbial once-in-a-lifetime missed opportunity.

. . . Your returning was a surprise, after such a long absence. You have to admit you hadn't communicated much in the interim, so what was I to think. But then we did deserve a good visit. And then you surprised me again by your offer and the turn you took. It was so unexpected. I was not angry though, don't think that, just thunderstruck, and I remain totally perplexed, perhaps angry at myself for having thought differently. How time does change our lot in life.

I hope you don't think it stupid of me writing you like this, but I felt I had to say it. Your presumption hurt, and my feelings for you are again so confused. I can't say much more.

I'm sorry it turned out this way. I was happy to return your prayer book in person. May it protect and guide you in a life long lived.

Colleen

He could see himself sitting here with Alex, together till the last of the suds, dancing around the facts.

"Alex, listen. I did try to talk with Eileen. I literally pushed for an answer. That may have been my mistake."

"Answers are never enough."

"I thought of returning, making a reappearance, the double-take to get it right. If we just took another day. All could be forgiven in time. Believe anew, chant it enough, and it can become reality. You did that, didn't you?'

"*I did. She had written soon after my first visit. If I couldn't make it back soon, she'd pay, she said; she'd saved up — she had that job in the government, you know, with her sister.*"

"*You returned with the ring, didn't you? I saw it sitting on the gun rack in the summer kitchen, under your grandfather's old Enfield. You'd think she'd been happy about that.*"

"*My second coming, it did surprise her. But I'd waited too long. I should have written more. She was an impulsive woman. You need to write your Eileen.*"

"*So you didn't give her the ring? Maybe you just mistook her surprise at your appearance.*"

"*I was foolish. I got angry. She wanted to put things off. She said I should understand; but I had a mother to care for just like her, and she had a sister, I said. She didn't want to lose her job — it was like that because of the war; if she got married, she'd have to give up her job. Her job over me? I shouldn't have accused her. She shut down.*"

"*But, Alex, you had another chance.*"

The third chance: Colleen's return visit years afterwards, after her own mother had died, and staying two weeks or so in town, seeing the sights, then returning with him to the farm.

And then the farewell party. He had hung around the bungalow most of the day, wanting to find out as much as possible about this Colleen and what she meant to Alex. They were flustered about something, keeping so polite and formal with each other. And everyone else too protective. There had to have been clues, but he was too young to see them.

He had stood beside the stove in the kitchen throughout the evening, keeping a bit away from the crowd that encircled Colleen in the living room. Alex was seated beside the kitchen table, he had taken out his fiddle, The fiddle will make it a ceilidh yet, he said. He practised a few double-stops and adjusted the strings, half-listening to Gerald Laroche, who was leaning against the counter and regaling him with another of his innumerable stories.

Then Alex getting visibly upset. He was trying to get the tune right, ignoring Gerald's blarney. But Gerald had a tongue on him as long as the bow that Alex was bouncing across the fiddle next to his ear, and much more interested in his story than Alex's feelings, his story having something to do with Alex and Colleen, as he would glance over at her at particular points in the telling.

The impish tone in Gerald's voice told how he liked to string out a good yarn, a talent that probably got him through the war safe and sane. "I've joined a Bible group. We meet once a week. I must confess, half the reason I'm attending is the sandwiches the ladies make. Little round ones, you know, with a different pâté in each one." He indicated the size of the sandwiches by forming a circle with his thumb and forefinger, then pointing to the circle repeatedly. Alex had put his fiddle down, but Gerald talked on. He acted as if he had never once weathered Alex's temper, a very risky statistic.

His own rising anxiety at the time must have deafened him somewhat, for he remembered hearing only a sequence of disjointed words from Gerald, "eight ladies," "my wife," "referee," as Alex turned to face the kitchen door and drop-kicked his fiddle against it.

What words had Alex spoken before that final break? Likely the same words he himself might have spoken to Eileen, trying to get it right. Perhaps if he had listened more to her concerns. Or she might have been waiting for something else from him, certain signals, the subtlety of an eyebrow raised, sharing a scone and clicking mugs of tea together, some laughter. Perhaps he had banked on the security in the expanse of fields, the surrender demanded by the circle of enveloping forest, the fantasy in the swoop of a flight of barn swallows — instead of a moment simply holding hands.

And then he remembered a final moment between Coleen and Alex. She had crossed from the living room into the kitchen and laid her hand on the slope of Alex's back as he sat looking up out the kitchen window, as if he were only checking on the oncoming northwestern stream of clouds. He held back his tears, and they moved together into the living room, stopping at the south-facing picture window and looking out. Everyone else moved back, sipping their teas and beers, and keeping to a distracting talk of their own. Colleen's voice was soft at the best of times, and Alex didn't speak.

He remembered the final moment now. He had stuck to his spot by the stove, close enough to pick up key words that for him didn't amount to much at the time. But her last two now stood out — the moment when Alex turned and walked away.

"Never enough."

Eileen's words as well, as they drove along the driveway. Even Padre Nómez's prophecy: never enough people.

So fleeting is your possible moment of redemption. His mind began racing again, searching for something, a solution, an option, he needn't give up on redemption. His mother would be happy with this touch of religion revived, and he laughed — the steadfast Irish don't cry. He blinked, then rubbed his eyes. A blink, the moment of redemption, can't last any longer than the flash of darkness that comes with a blink.

Berrin was busy shutting, then blinking his eyes, to test this thought, to distract himself, when a woman approached his table. She didn't introduce herself as she draped her raincoat over the chair across from him. She was almost seated when he looked up, seeing first the green plastic that backlit the woman.

His mind blinked. Had his touch of religion done the trick? He sat up straighter in his chair, and forced himself to smile; like some recent research suggested, an act of smiling can bring on the respective emotions.

His mind then jumped to a set of comparisons. Not as solid in the chest, and shorter than Eileen, jet-black hair, casual dress, jeans and a loose, open denim jacket, tight tan sweater. His assessment halted on the small silver cherub brooch above her left breast, perhaps a childhood trinket. Too young. And not his type. But, then, he shouldn't ignore an angel.

And what was his type? he asked himself.

"Are you alone?" she asked.

"I don't remember."

She smiled. Dimpled cheeks and a pointed nose. But a wide mouth, he did like large mouths.

"I'm waiting for a friend. Game for a beer in the meantime?" she asked, resting one hand on the table and drumming her fingers. The other remained at her side. No purse. Three silver bangles jangled from her wrist against the table edge, and an equal number of rings. Likely seeking some redemption herself, and needing the luck in the event that the cherub's life lacked the afterglow. One ring was made of entwined strands of silver, another an amoebic shape of amber in a solder setting, the third a mood ring or opal, he couldn't tell the difference, but the colour was favourable: red. All were clearly handcrafted.

"Can't argue with that," he answered. "I like your mood ring."

"Ruby. If it were a mood ring it would be blue."

Soon they were engaged in casual conversation. He couldn't bring himself to tell his tale of Alex, too close to home, too soon. So he talked of listening to the jabbering around him, one of the few real pleasures in life, he said, and he told the story of the flooded apartment.

She listened, interested, it seemed, then asked him what he did: a writer, she bet.

"As good a guess as any . . . a prospector, an inventor, worked on oil rigs, a dreamer, you name it, screwed my life up totally." He shrugged, almost a wince.

"I like dreamers."

"Thanks. I'm thinking seriously of pursuing the writing part, starting with my daft dreams. Ever dream of animals?"

She stared, silent, as if deciding about him.

"What kind of animal would you say I am?" he persisted.

"Crocodile, fish, dog, or bear?"

"Crocodile makes me think of lizards, but that's not you. Lizards, you know, are one of the reptilian races that make up the Illuminati."

"Time for everyone to lighten up."

"Lizards are the hidden hand behind corporate globalization; perhaps they are threatening to take over your dreams as well."

"That might be true if only those corporate heads weren't so slimy. What I need are far simpler inventions, sorry."

The Star Chamber stuff, from admonitions to munitions, a familiar path, this version of hers, adding up yet again to more politics, however colourfully you dress it up. Politics and weather, the Canadian way. Incongruous, though, for a gypsy fortune teller, which he now pegged her for. What next? Crop-circle makers, the Interdimensional Sasquatch, Goat Eaters. He could mention that one time in Mexico City when his urban hosts kidnapped a goat from the side of the highway and roasted it on an open pit in a corner of their backyard in order to feed the late-night revellutionaries. But, now that he thought about it, even they had claimed it was Freemasons who ruled Mexico, from political parties all the way down to unions — and lawn parties.

"Actually, a girlfriend and I have invented a new religion. 'Da'ism.' It's going to succeed Daoism." She laughed. "It links the fun and the mental in life, body, and soul."

It took a second, then he laughed in turn. "Maybe the world does need a new fundamentalism."

"People are so caught up in timetables they have no time for anything. You know Lao Tzu's thought — the eleventh poem in *The Way of Life*," and she rattled off the poem without faltering.

A bit nervous; probably a student doing field research.

"Isn't that beautiful?" Then she repeated her favourite line, *The hub of the wheel is nothing without the hole in the hub*. "The absence is all — sheer poetry, don't you think?"

Her antics were loonier than his own. Whoever she was, her

presence was filling out that peculiar emptiness that defined all hotel bars, an undeniable downside to sitting in them. He'd play as well. "Art is balance, like this honeyed ale in times of need."

"My girlfriend says it's more about losing yourself. We are all one and the same in wanting to do that, don't you think?" She sat back, appearing inquisitive.

A follow-up failed him. She seemed to be alone. Maybe needing a fix. One way or the other, it didn't seem to matter if he agreed or not.

"Maybe the poem is simply about usefulness." He spoke in a monotone to render himself as dull as possible. "As it's turning out, my usefulness is in being all the things I'm not." Definitely getting maudlin, if not drunk.

A standoff. A second round was his best rejoinder. She virtually chugalugged hers and gamely toasted him a second time with her empty bottle, exclaiming, "Fully empty."

He was warming up. "No. You are only missed when you're gone, and then you have nowhere to go." He downed the last of his own and tapped his gut with the empty bottle; he couldn't have dreamed of striking a more lugubrious note, for he was concluding that the conversation had already gone beyond its natural end.

"Well, I'm ready to go," she said.

A coming together in some manner, or a simple coupling against the night?

He swished his bottle around in a circle in front of her, with a slight smile. *The dregs, his life, best to avoid it, lady.* And he thought of one of Stephanie's friends, an artist who tried to hold the void in moulds. Using cups, pails, anything hollow, he'd cast latex-like jelly forms from "found objects"—old plastic shower curtains, plastic shopping bags, soap containers, objects that never fully melted, condoms, even that green plastic raincoat of hers. Moulds probably meant to be as amber clear as his mother's gooseberry jelly persistently resulted in objects glutinous and turd-like, never achieving anything near the purity of the primordial plasma.

He jerked awake from his reverie when a small black spider raced from under the table and abruptly stopped near his empty bottle. Instinctively he raised his bottle but a hand grabbed his wrist. "Leave it," she said. "Afraid of a little spider?" And she pulled him upward with her laughter.

He wound up at her apartment in no time. He had decided not to doubt his presence here with her, nor to question the absence of her friend. Nor his good fortune, though he could as easily have allowed himself to loathe it. But he had not chosen it, his sodden brain told himself, never mind that he wasn't that aroused. She didn't seem to mind his absence in turn, nor his excessive corporal presence, and she came down on him. "Needed to make it once," she said, and he must have smiled, and surely smiled as the release came.

She then threw back her head and gargled.

In a second he was standing beside the bed and jamming his feet into his trouser legs. He shot a twenty-dollar bill down at her. Her smile collapsed as her face turned as white as a nun's and he left without giving or seeking an explanation.

Disgust? Or was it simply the phoniness? His reasoning powers fell away. A sense of foolishness spread over his entire performance, all the way back to when she sat down at his table in the bar. His disgust probably stretched back to his adolescence. He remembered the first time trying out a condom and then pulling it off. It seemed like the end of his penis would come with it, like an earthworm breaks when you stretch it too thinly.

It was definitely the gargling, even if she was pulling another prank. He picked up a bottle from the gutter and flung it into the darkness of the alley beside him. The crisp shattering of glass, an antidote . . . he continued down the sidewalk, enjoying the hardness of the concrete beneath his feet.

It had been a definite high with her. . . he had let go, if only for Alex's sake, one for the Gipper. But no home run for him, just slammed down, back to earth, a hard landing. The gargling. Like a slit throat.

No sense in wishing he hadn't acted like an idiot again or returning and asking forgiveness. He needed to get some perspective, memory screened as much as it framed events. So he hopped a bus and within an hour was inside his parents' living room, the nearest form of time travel he could think of.

CHAPTER 41

The carousel of fantasies

AS WITH MOST VISITS to his parents, his mother was in the kitchen and his father was watching television in the living room.

"Ladies and gentlemen, Sergeant Slasher has thrown Rambo Man over the ropes."

A crucial time in the wrestling match that was not to be interrupted, and his father gave him only a cursory hello. His mother shouted from the kitchen, "Say hello to your dad, then come and see me."

A tag-team wrestling match.

His father sucked in a deep breath and held it.

"Rambo Man has landed on Miss Suzzi. Sergeant Slasher has thrown him back into the ring, and obviously Rambo Man doesn't know his girl is flat out on the floor. She was standing at ringside below the ropes. She must be unconscious. She's not moving."

His father leaned forward on the edge of the couch, his belly cradled in his lap.

"Wait. His partner, the Mighty Khan, has jumped down to help her."

"You can't say that's all faked." A grin spread wrinkles across his father's stubbly face, and his bushy eyebrows lifted, drawing more wrinkles across his forehead. He wore an old set of glasses, pockmarked from years of welding sparks.

"He's listening to her heartbeat. Now he's picking up Miss Suzzi and carrying her down the ramp."

His father's laughing brought on a fit of coughing, the hoarseness coming from deep within his chest, a cough born in his younger years as a diamond drill operator in the Sudbury nickel mines. He shot a glance at Berrin.

"Mighty Khan is finally earning his millions."

"The Mighty Khan is laying Miss Suzzi on a table in the infirmary. Wait, that's no doctor. Rambo Man has rushed in and has grabbed Mighty Khan by the hair. He's furious. He's punching Mighty Khan in the face. He'll murder him."

"The Mighty Khan is really no match." His laugher squeezed out from between clenched jaws. He had forgotten that Mighty Khan and Rambo Man were tag-team partners in the match.

Best to visit Mother. Not finding her in the kitchen, he continued into the dining room. She was sitting at the table playing solitaire. He caught the end of a song she was singing to herself.

And when you see the enemy
You shoot him in the rear,
Singing oh boy oh joy
Where do we go from here.

Singing to herself while playing cards was a recent activity; he hadn't known her to sing. In fact he couldn't recall even a radio in the house when young, or maybe the radio was such a poor one it was seldom on. Music was never a part of his upbringing, though it must have been for her, given the organ and piano still sitting abandoned in the homestead house on the farm.

His mother looked up from her cards. "Well, hello, stranger."

"Hi, Mother. So, it's solitaire time again for you."

"I like playing cards and doing crosswords. It leaves my mind free to what's going on around." She nodded her head in the direction of the living room where Dad still watched the television, why she had to stay alert. Their townhouse mirrored the farm's bungalow, with the dining and living rooms forming an L-shaped space, open. His dad's heavy breathing from around the corner was audible over the din of the television.

"Did you hear of the mayor's recent plan, he's trying to rezone the land, move it out of agriculture and then up the taxes."

"Mother, maybe we could try something different. Like a co-op. Run the farm as a co-op, it could bring in more people."

"You've been into too much of the drink, I see. It's clouding your brain."

"Just winding up a Thanksgiving weekend. I'm fine."

"Well, the mayor's got a jump on your co-op idea. He's pushing to rezone the valley for a zoo, seems like the one closer to town isn't a go. Well, they may think I'm only an old woman, but as Alex used to say, I can fight like a bobcat."

"I'm sure you'll put the kibosh to those plans."

But she was again leading up to the plain and simple question for her: "When are you moving up to the farm?"

He escaped answering this time because the television was turned off, and she promptly sent him back to continue his visit with his dad while she prepared supper.

His father was reading his newspaper. Berrin returned to the easy chair across from his father, who had sunk back into the chesterfield, its carpet-like cushions so puffy that he looked like a corpse already in his coffin. His father pulled off his glasses and stared at the floor, perhaps still thinking about the wrestling match because he asked, "Been able to drag the missus to the altar yet?"

No answer necessary. The obligatory parental reprimand.

He looked up and asked Berrin to turn the television on again. Time for the news. "Use the zapper." He turned back to his paper and continued talking in his wheezing whisper, he needed to clear out, travel to P.E.I., get some of that red soil under his fingernails for once in his life. Was he interested in taking him fishing in the Atlantic?

"I never went fishing, Dad."

He passed Berrin the travel section of the paper and returned to the television. His dad had never travelled much, not that he hadn't wanted to. One old photo in Mom's photo album had him and his wife-to-be standing beside his '34 Sport Roadster, a second-hand prize that he had wrecked a few days after the photo was taken, when he hit a slippery curve, backed up a bank and flopped over. His only comment: "Too expensive to keep up anyways. And way too fast for those winding roads up the Gatineau."

Easy to imagine the sense of escape as he scooted down the highway, the thrill from the asphalt speeding along inches below the undercarriage, wiping out all anxieties about his upcoming marriage.

"I've got to get away from the loonies around here."

"Dad, the only fish I ever saw was the odd whale off the oil rigs." He tried to sound empathetic.

"How can she run the farm? Explain that to me."

"We all need a break from the farm." He turned back to watch the news.

Berrin wondered for a moment if his mother could possibly hear them from the kitchen. Not likely, the television being so loud. His father's many potted plants lined both sills of the picture windows, the green thumb, a carryover from his love of the bush. At times, he'd wander aimlessly around the house, exuding a need for a good hug, much like the plants in need of watering. But Mother's cure for his moping was to ignore it, or bring the hornet's nest down over his ears, blast the politicians and lawyers who were swindling them out of the farm, demand he do something, anything. The question still hung in the air: Who understood whom less?

His mother shouted from the kitchen, "Berrin, your meal is ready." His dad continued staring at the television.

He sat down to a full plate of pork chops, potatoes, and canned peas, and his mother returned to her game of solitaire. She slowly shuffled the eight or so cards remaining in her hand and counted three out and laid them face up on the table, then took the top one and methodically ran it down each row in front of her.

How to avoid more inconsequential talk of the farm? "Mother, I was remembering the old roadster Dad once owned." He hoped she had looked at the coffee table book on cars that he had given his dad for his birthday.

Her eyes brightened, she had taken the bait. "I remember the first car we owned, a second-hand thing Dad found somewhere. It might have been a Model T, I can't remember. In fact, we had a silly argument over it. Dad said he never owned a Model T. It had a big square rad up front, and the tires stuck out like a grasshopper's legs. We were driving back to the farm and we hardly had any gas left, so he drove backwards up the hill at the entrance. Poor Pa, he couldn't see why we were driving into the farm backwards, but he had a good laugh about it. When Dad explained that the gas tank was behind the back seat, and gravity fed the motor, he laughed all the more. The younger generation and their inventions and all, he said. But your dad loved cars and fixing them. Everyone had to have a car, it felt grand, it was freedom. That's why he finally left the mines and built his own garage."

"Like computers are for us, I suppose. But with cars you actually get away."

"Your dad was so different then. Sure, we had our share of hard knocks; 'twas a toss-up at times figurin' how he'd turn, a toiler or a tinker, there'd be nothing in between, but I never doubted him. Somehow we'd straighten things out and get goin' again. And it would be his fault, he always took the blame. We got along so well. It's the cancer, I think. It's changed him so much."

She spoke in a voice so low that she might have been talking to herself, never taking her eyes off her cards.

"Your dad once offered to take you hunting, you were eight or nine at the time, but I could see in your eyes you didn't want to go. I came to your rescue by sitting you on a chair and had you stretch out your arms and I looped a skein of wool around them and sat in the rocking chair in front of you and began to wind it into a ball. Your dad said nothing and left. My mother explained it to me when my own dad had to go out with the year-end hunting party. She said that I was not to fret, that men had to get out and spill their own blood. They were built like that, she said."

"That was one smart mother, Mother."

He could almost remember his outstretched arms growing heavier and heavier, and how they dipped slowly as she reached out to jerk the yarn over his wrist when it got snagged.

She continued her game of solitaire.

"Do you miss those times?"

She looked up over her glasses, puzzled.

"Was your life in the convent much better?"

She looked down at her cards. To soften his questions, he told of his meeting the two hooded women a few days earlier. Probably nuns, he added. He talked about visiting a church and how he liked the play of light and shadows within it. "It made me wonder about your time at the Dominican convent, what it might have been like for you."

Her eye flickered, as if for an instant she was remembering being a novice. But it was obvious she was having nothing to do with his great hunger for stories; "It's been a long time since you've been to church, young man."

"I used to go, Mother, but then came that preparatory seminary at St. Pius. That's what really smartened me up, remember. We were all becoming axe murderers."

She shook her head, frowning. Obviously not remembering the nightmare that had driven him from the seminary.

"If you stopped thinking so much and prayed some more, you'd get your faith back. Maybe you'll see that you never lost it." She reshuffled the few cards remaining in her hand. Then a smile. "You know, I've heard Alex in the house as well."

"He's followed you here?"

"No, we were up at the farm on the weekend."

"Dad was driving?"

"No need to fret, Berrin. He's all right in the daytime. I was lying on the couch in the living room when a rattling in the kitchen woke me up, like Alex would make when he had his tea. I can still see his cup and saucer on the yellow oilcloth, his big hand fingering the handle like he would do when lost in his thinking. Your dad heard it, too. He shouted at me from the back bedroom where he was taking a nap, and I shouted back, No, it wasn't me making the racket. Then there he comes dashing down the hall, but he found neither hide nor hair of anything."

A mouse snooping around. But he conceded one possibility, if faith could conjure up Alex's ghost for him, he might begin to believe again.

"I felt him as close as the last time I saw him seated at the kitchen table, when I asked him what was on his mind. The New Land, he said; he was going to finish his father's work and clear it all the way down to the swamp. It was the best stretch of land around."

She began stringing out another row of cards for a new game, having won. She was happy — she had him thinking of the farm again.

"You win so often, Mother. I can't even tell how you cheat."

Her protest burst from her still rosy lips. "I never cheat." Tears gathered on her eyelids. "I think of my mother when I play solitaire. She'd play a lot as well."

"I'm only teasing." He patted her hand, its skin cold and dry.

He began picking up his dishes.

"Oh, don't you dare. Go back and talk to your dad, he needs some company."

Evening setting in, but he took to the easy chair again. His father was still fixed on the television. The greenhouse within highlighted the onset of autumn outside, with barely a leaf left on the poplar and birch that bordered the lawn. The sumac still held their orange-green leaves, their clusters of deep crimson berries starkly erotic.

"It was quite a wind, wasn't it?"

His father looked out, possibly thinking of the upcoming hunting season. "Our neighbour once hired me and my brother Johnny to fork windrows into stacks. This twister dropped down from the near ridge and crossed the field between the rows straight at us, and we went scurrying for a tree. The haystacks were scattered everywhere across the field, but most of them landed on top of the trees around the field. Diotte was so angry with us for throwing away his hay like that we never did get paid. So we headed for the nickel mines up north."

Berrin remembered an old Falconbridge Annual Report from years ago, it must still be somewhere in the house, which had captured his dad in a square-set stope leaning on a jackleg at the rock face, his moustache and face smeared with grease and dust, rendering him a well-tanned Clarke Gable double.

"There was that picture of you on the jackhammer."

"I wasn't at that for long. I soon moved on to handling the dynamite. You had to have a feel for the rock, how hard it was, how soft, this told you how deep to drill into the drift. If you got it wrong you could get a blowout, and the blast shoots out the end of the hole instead of lifting the rock. Joe O'Rourke, we nicknamed him Jackleg, he killed himself by being too cocky about it."

"When I worked up north, in Val–d'Or, the mines were all closed down. I tried walking the bush like you used to do; like you say, you never can tell what you'll find."

"I see. Copper Cliff is closed down now, as well. Falconbridge's still open, you might try that. We were lucky, turned out I knew the foreman."

"Maybe a new start is what I need. What did your brother work at?"

"Oh, Johnny soon found better work with the railroad. From fireman to engineer in no time. A smarter man than me."

"I doubt if VIA is hiring nowadays. Dad, what about that vein you found on the farm — wasn't it dolomite?" His dad had come across the outcropping of rock somewhere behind the west ridge of the farm.

"Mostly moonstone is all there was, but enough to bring in a bulldozer and blast some of the rocks to smithereens, make a lot of noise, and then offer shares."

"I was never enough of a schemer."

"I knew two shysters, they got their windfall grubstake near Strathcona Mill. They then bought up a good many of the penny stocks themselves, moved a lot of stones around for the hype, then sold after a few weeks when the price rocketed to fifteen cents — a good amount in those days — and hightailed it back to Toronto." His father fell asleep during his pause, wondering perhaps how much in today's currency his friend the foreman might have lost on the scam.

Such different stories his parents told. His mother, the more enigmatic, seldom talking about herself. It was his father who held onto dreams.

His mother had retreated to her bedroom. He left.

Back at the bus stop, back in the dark, but nothing like a visit to the home hearth to properly bring you down to earth.

Odd, then, how home was never enough.

Not even a bus shelter this far out in the country. And no lights. Pitiless as Yeats was when the darkness dropped, and yes, the best lack all conviction when faced with the slow-moving shadows. He played with the poem to distract himself.

And somewhere in the fields of this night,
A shape with a wolf body headed for a man.

His fears remained, which should nix any move into the country. Like his mother said: You don't drop your religion at will.

The Big Bad Wolf, an image he couldn't shake. Perhaps fairy tales had it right, dressing him up in the clothes of a grandmother. She could fight like a polecat — and be even as stubborn when it came to his own plans. Eileen saying the same thing, headstrong.

Every life's the story of pursuit and pretense, whoever that writer was, until the carrousel of fantasies stop. His dreams had definitely stopped stock-still, and he was the reeling one. Stopped, dropped, drooping, free falling. His mother's tally of his follies rang through his head . . . a fat-headed dolt, a *shoneen* in a spin, a simpleton, a nincompoop.

He pictured the St. Sebastian holy card with the children dancing their carrousel, circling hand in hand despite the nightmare of apostolic emissaries surrounding them. Quite a spell since he felt that kind of freewheeling joy, not since his own escape from the seminary — and there was no denying it, in the end he truly ups and blows it.

The Lafayette lady had gargled; he should have welcomed that spark in her. And again losing his head.

CHAPTER 42

Desire adrift

Standing on the porch, he listened for movement inside. Quiet. He gripped the doorknob and took a deep breath. Cold and damp and arbitrary: the air, the doorknob, his body.

And back to student housing, ironic, given what he first wanted from university, and pushing everything else aside. Finnbar, the one whose head he had chopped off. The fair-headed lad of promise had also left the seminary to marry. He had let Finnbar drop out of his life, so afraid at the time of another quagmire, wasting one's life driving a taxi. Prophetic, since a car in a dream can be your body.

To bed straightaway. He needed to be alone. He entered as quietly as possible. But once inside, he was alone. He had an urge to cry out, awaken everyone, anything to avoid the void.

Head upstairs. Take a bath, his body needed something. Deathly quiet. Too early actually for anyone to be in bed, no lights from under the doors in the hallway. He turned on the tap water in the bathtub, stripped, and stepped in. No sooner in the tub than he found himself rising. He rose on his knees, the leggy Lafayette lady there with him, and together they came. He adjusted the taps so that the water poured out as hot as he could bear. He flipped the drain stop on, and sank back exhausted. The water crept along the length of his body, past his neck, cradling his head. Steam massaged his face, a sensation that complemented the relief his body took from the buoyant heat — and completing the flush of the orgasm.

He lay without moving, half submerged, half floating. His toes curled around the taps and slowly worked them shut. The water drew a red line where his legs angled out of the water. Jerome popped into his mind. Cooked lobsters both, he thought.

And then he saw the fallopian shape, in the way his feet spread outwards from the tap, and the red line, a scarlet cord tethering his ankles.

He pulled his feet apart and wriggled his toes. He then smiled in the simple wonder of the stream of thoughts his mind poured out — their true meaning would come to him in time — and he lifted his feet above the taps and began to sing.

You can truly rise now,
Rise above the waters.

He felt exhilaration. His voice sang out in the alto-tenor of a boy, and without any inflection he chanted the verse as if in a trance:

You can rise and go now,
Rise above the muddy waters.
Up, up above the clouds and thunder,
You are flying high now.

The edge in his voice gave the pitch to the water where the waves slapped silent into the white enamel walls. He started over, "Yes, you are above it now," the waves rippling past his feet and flowing on toward a shore that stretched beyond the boundaries of the bathroom toward an open sea beyond. "Follow your flight south —"

"Berrin, can you pipe down a bit? I'm having enough trouble getting to sleep." Stephanie.

He jerked his feet back under the water. "Sorry, Stephanie. I got carried away," shouting his apology, and as he climbed out of the tub he heard her door open and steps heading down the stairs.

She greeted him as he joined her. She was seated at the table, drinking tea. That direct look, unnerving him.

"You look bushed, Berrin. Not such a hot weekend, I'd say."

"I'd rather forget it all."

He took a beer from the fridge. It was cold but the alcohol would help him sleep. He awaited Stephanie's reminder, how he'd be waking much too early when his sugar levels dropped and his dreams turned to food.

"And why are you angry with her?"

She had decided to push for answers.

"Watch it, or I'll knock your block off as well."

"Now, now. I'd say that that would be somewhat politically incorrect."

"Time *that* changed as well." He popped the bottle top a few times by quickly flicking his thumb in and out of the top. She maintained her impenetrable inscrutability.

And he realized the popping sounded like gunshots. "Sorry. This entire mind/body thing, I never did get it right."

"Too bad life is such a pale reflection of dreams. It's a bitch, ain't it?"

"I'm not that bad a guy, am I?" Grovelling now, but what had he to lose? "I also visited my parents."

"Home to mammy. That is one option, I suppose." Her voice dropped off and she took a sip of her tea.

"She's a good talker, but never about herself. She's a good argument for the church ordaining women."

"Blame the mother. Berrin, you're finally coming into your own as the typical male."

"Wrong. If I blamed anyone, it would be my father. Dads are too absent from our lives. That's what Jerome told me the other day."

"Daddies are more important, aren't they?"

"You can't have it both ways, Stephanie."

"I do keep making that mistake."

"I think you were mistaken about Jerome as well. I don't think he's gay."

"He's been bi for so long it's a wonder he didn't attack you as well. But, if you remember, I never did say that was his problem."

"Eileen says homosexuals hate their mothers and take it out on all women thereafter. He does seem to fit that bill."

"Show me any man, gay or other, who can enjoy a woman, at least for very long. Perhaps Eileen is right about the revenge stuff. But I think it's a twisted form of penis envy that comes into play, not a castration complex; call it castration envy. I'm talking about all that pressure on a man to make it, to carry the world on his shoulders, be a better patriarch. I'd want to run away as well."

"Possibly." He rubbed his neck. "But why become the thing you hate? It's totally screwy. As for Jerome, he's simply nuts. You should see his place, barren as a desert. He's also taken back the fishbowl, but the goldfish is gone. I suppose you need to be a bit touched to be an artist."

"Doing less with less all the time." She hesitated a moment. "Well, Berrin, this sucker has found herself an apartment."

"That's great, Stephanie. Or maybe it's not so great. I'd prefer you stayed here. Then again, maybe I'm looking to move out as well, if I can afford it. How can you, for that matter?"

"Berrin, you can't always be putting the cart before the horse."

She sipped her tea, slowly, as if not caring where the conversation went.

"So, then, why do you look so down?"

"Just registering the condition of a twenty-three-year-old single woman, something my mother has always warned me about. No money, no man, a beautiful sunny finality to a Thanksgiving weekend and a perfectly empty room; an all-around big chump."

"You're kidding. A Thanksgiving breakup?"

"Tshabalala's finishing his degree this semester and has received *The Word* from his folks. His dallying days are over. The return of the native son. You think you've got problems with your parents? His have chosen a bride for him back home."

"That's outrageous."

"Man, could that guy make love. That's what's so outrageous."

"You sure he's leaving?"

"I've got it right, all right. Unfortunately, that's the story. And that big black face of his couldn't hide his shame. Let alone his bald head. Oh yes, he even took that trimming."

"Cut off his afro!"

"My Samson castrates himself. Don't men always end up doing that?"

She sighed and grabbed a chunk of her hair in each hand and pulled on it, hard.

"Whenever there's a big change in my life, I go for a new cut too — or else change residences."

Her hands fell into her lap. No tears.

"So what are you going to do? Quit your studies?"

"I'd quit them in a minute if it would make any difference. I don't know what dreams your parents enrolled you in; mine was university with a MRS degree that's beginning to look a bit mildewed."

"I don't understand."

"You know, liberal arts, but I took the studies part seriously. And what I chose was even more impractical, a fine arts degree. I'd even settle right now for a man snoring away at my side as I plough through another Margaret Atwood."

"Maybe it's your choice of men."

"It's their choice of religion. He wanted me to convert."

"I thought he was Christian."

"Maybe my shade of Christianity is the issue. But it's not the kind of love I envisioned. Next thing, I'd be singing at Sunday choir and wearing a broad-brimmed hat with a veil to hide my face — my white face."

"Decapitated again."

"Why do we always end up cutting out what's good for us?"

"Didn't the Buddha tell his followers to kill him if they met him on the road?"

"There you go again, changing the subject."

"Sorry, Stephanie . . . this woman I met at the Lafayette. She sat at my table, a total surprise. Turned out she was into far Eastern religions, and wearing this cherub pin on her sweater. It all kind of threw me off."

"Her guardian angel. It's like bringing a dog into your house, everyone wants unconditional love. In high demand these days, and I must say, I'm beginning to need some of it myself."

Stephanie fell silent a moment. So much for the happy puppy scampering along.

She continued. "Even my parents are beginning to be seriously kind to me. 'Don't worry, dear, I'm sure you'll find a decent paying job if you keep trying; we have faith in you.' At least they've stopped wondering about my sexual orientation."

"Looks like they should have wondered about the religious orientation of your boyfriends."

"I should move into the country. Break out into song, Maarrrrching to Preeetooooriaaaaaa."

"Signing up on the side of the Empire?"

"Anywhere away from this infernal city. Some place I can afford, with a river and a garden."

"A river and a shanty."

"Yes, sunk back into the bank . . . dote on the flowers and contemplate the flow of time ever-present."

"That was my dad's lament all his life, not to have built that cabin in the bush."

She fingered her cup. He added, "So, you'll still take a man with you?"

"If you're asking about the cabin, it's solitary abandonment. As for the apartment, men or women, gays or lesbians, hetero or bi,

I'll take anybody."

"Seems there's fewer and fewer of those straight straight guys." To be her roommate, a perfect illusion, but bursting now as quickly as a kid's soap bubble. "I'm sorry it's come to this, Stephanie."

"So, Berrin, what are my options?"

He didn't answer, but turned his chair to an angle and shrugged: "Vent?"

And she vented, and he leaned back, balancing on two legs, precarious, like one of her television sets on its conveyor belt, rising and tumbling over. Objects, random and arbitrary, solid physical objects reasserting themselves with a catatonic insistence on their presence, repeated enough that they begin to assume a meaning and significance, somehow becoming personal, and if not a lover, you at least acquire an audience.

". . . till the ends of the earth." Stephanie stopped. He couldn't tell if she had noticed his tuning out for a moment.

"You might have to sit back and contemplate the scenery for a while."

"You know what the turning point was?"

"Not his parents?"

"The other night, that show at the Toole."

"The blood and cum stuff. It doesn't surprise me."

"He was dumfounded. He agreed with Barry, but he didn't speak up until Barry had left; he couldn't figure it out either, he said — the performance was disgusting, like the name of the upcoming show. I got too smart for my own good. I said it probably meant Enlightenment for some folks here. Why would anyone want to be associated with it, he said. He was furious with me. I then dropped the joking, said that Jerome as likely scheduled it to show up my work, and all of the art in Ottawa, for that matter. That won him back a bit."

"The noise was the worst. Make it so loud that it becomes so goddamn important, somehow."

"We returned to his apartment afterwards to mellow out. I was sitting with him on his couch, being warm and close, though he wasn't saying much. He asked about my portfolio, I had picked it up as I was leaving the gallery. We flipped through the photos. He hadn't somehow seen my paintings, and I guess I never did mention them."

"He hadn't been to your room?"

"Not yet; and now, not ever. We were sitting there, he wasn't saying a word, so I moved to kiss him, and he pulled back and said, 'This isn't working. I can't go on with it.' Then he got up and walked into his bedroom and closed his door. He hadn't even asked me to leave, so what was I to do? I was totally lost. I shouted at his door, What was it that wasn't working? Me? Our argument? But he didn't come out of his room. After five minutes, I walked out myself. I couldn't believe it."

"But things seemed all right at the Market."

"It's been a roller coaster. He apologized next day, said he shouldn't have let his anger about the performance spoil everything. But it wasn't the performance. He shut down after I showed my portfolio. Maybe it was my paintings. Or maybe my photos, who knows? There were a few photos of me in high school when I first took to art. I was a pudgy kid."

"Maybe he saw he didn't fit in — with that history, I mean, with your background . . . I don't know, with the entire country."

"Or that I didn't, with his. I shouldn't have let it drop, he was hiding something. But I told myself, it's our first real fight. It's normal. But he wasn't the same all weekend."

"It's hard to tell sometimes."

"It's all laid out now as clear as his bald head. He had to make a decision, he said, and I guess he did . . . final, *finito*, caput."

"I really never would have expected it."

"When I was sitting on his couch with him, my instincts told me to kiss him, that something was wrong. In my gut I knew something had changed. And I really didn't know why. So I tried to kiss him."

"A kiss. If it's any consolation —" Berrin couldn't finish the sentence.

Instead, he reached for the bottle of Vitamin C that had become a fixture in the middle of the table: 2000-mg tablets, from the essence of orange and mango, chewable like candy, the label said; how she had downed them whole, flicking out her tongue, as confident as a lizard catching a fly.

"Two each morning and evening."

"Funny."

"I didn't mean to make a joke. I was reading the label in auto mode. I don't know what to say, Stephanie. You still have to take care of yourself. You're so pale."

With one last swig of tea, she turned to the sink and washed her mug. She glanced back at him via the mirror.

"Stephanie, I wish I could help you."

"I wish you could. Like knocking some sense into that thick skull of his. But that's not to be, is it?"

"Sorry. If there's anything I can do . . ."

"Thanks anyway, Berrin," and she turned and disappeared down the hallway.

He crossed his arms behind his neck and again leaned far back on his chair. Teetering.

Perhaps you have to go all the way, push it beyond the limits. He looked down, as if from a great height. Need only complete the conceptual piece, a looping film of oneself falling backwards onto the floor, repeatedly smashing the back of your head open, uncapping the pain again and again.

Old houses had hardwood floors that mattered.

CHAPTER 43

At the brink of oblivion

HE WAS SITTING with a man on the couch in the living room, a stranger. His father was in the kitchen standing beside the stove. Through the window, he saw a disc descend from the heavens. The spaceship flew through the open window and bounced from wall to wall until it entered the living room, trying to hit them. His father entered, and the disc swept back out the kitchen window and crossed the sky in a large arc. His father took off his hat and flung it through the window toward the flying saucer high in the air, capping it. Upon contact, the disc exploded like an atomic bomb.

His imminent doom awakened him. The air was freezing. Snow was creeping in under the door; Eileen hadn't closed it tightly. The first real snowfall of the season; hopefully it would melt by morning; he wasn't ready for winter yet. He pulled the door tight and selected a book, *Snake Poems: An Aztec Invocation*, from the shelf next to it. The Haiku quality of the poems might be the medicine he needed, and then he retrieved *Celtic Art*, which was still sitting atop the pile of books on his desk. He remembered he had another book of poems by Alarcón, *From the Bellybutton of the Moon and Other Summer Poems*, and took that from the shelf as well. Time to get back to work.

He poured his coffee, set two slices of bread to toast, sat at the table, and picked up the *Snake Poems*. Two of this author's books had been translated into Gaelic, an inspiration. He remembered a photo from a Celtic history taken of a line of Mayo peasants wrapped in their shawls, some hunched on the sidewalk outside a shop, some scurrying with their wicker baskets back into the shop to escape the camera's eye. Maybe the Mayan descended from the Mayon.

A moment's chuckle. Then he pictured the universality of marching troops and burning huts and brightly dyed shawls pulled over terrorized eyes.

The snake on the cover — it could easily be formed from his new alphabet; he'd have to come up with a name for it. But the title *From the Bellybutton of the Moon* tugged his attention and he opened it at random. "*Whenever I say 'Mexico'/I hear my grandma telling me/about the Aztecs and the city they built/on an island in the middle of a lake.*"

He looked back at the title, *the Bellybutton*. The spot that definitely defined you, your island in the middle of the milky way, the shack out back, and his mind drifted back to his dream. Nuclear explosions, he had a rash of those dreams years ago after Eileen had driven off into the country.

He grew drowsy, a vertigo dragging him down into a liminal swirl of intimations that rendered the space around him incandescent. How to fix on the feeling bearing down on him? No questioning or worrying about circumstance or intentions. He sensed a presence. How to move closer? So fleeting that it was about to vanish, and he knew it would if he didn't act. Put the books down, they had set up the connections, but pointless now, no more than a pattern on the table. And the pen? The pen that you laid beside the bottle of vitamin C tablets, it becomes part of the play. But not the vitamin C. Keep the dance going, it was still possible with Eileen, only a minimum of elements needed, juggle the possibilities, keep the balance so that the hope is held suspended, unsuspected, capped at the brink of oblivion.

No matter that Stephanie was not inviting you to share her apartment — you were still friends, a dance in itself. You also felt the dance when you left the bar with a total stranger, heading back to her apartment, in the easy banter and back-and-forth teasing as a few cars sped by and you crossed the street and felt the winter in the twilight while you stood together on the opposite sidewalk. It's early, she says, her apartment's just a few blocks away, his empty bed not much farther in the other direction. Turning and circling each other, she skips along with you. The daaaa/nce replaces hoo/oom/e, she sings. And you swing through the entrance doors and circle each other as you descend down her long hallway.

Hold onto all the images, your empty bed, the wet pavement, her open raincoat flapping green against bare legs, the sweep through the doorway into her apartment, her laughter piercing you, too deeply, then the surprise release within your chest, like the elastic core of a golf ball exploding at the cut of a knife.

He coughed. Smoke engulfed him at table level. Waves of it floated down from the ceiling. He jumped up and twisted open the side flaps of the toaster, both slices of bread now smoking chunks of char that he dumped into the sink and doused with tap water. The smoke filled the corridor, but somehow no one upstairs had awakened. After a half hour of waving a newspaper side to side through all the rooms, he had closed the windows and doors again and was back in his room wrapped snugly in his cocoon of blankets.

Extinction, he had had an intimation of it.

CHAPTER 44

Fix the images

TUESDAY MORNING. Not many customers. If this kept up for long, he'd be out of a job. But that was not an important consideration, he now realized, an echo of his father's nose-to-the-grinding-stone life. Turn on the lights, count the float, check the stock, dust — swing into action. With feather duster in hand, he swept the pottery bowls with a flourish, dusted the leaded glass and rattled through the rack of earrings, not caring if he broke anything. It was fun, and he was acting on impulse . . . Yeats's lament, that had he acted upon impulse rather than reason, he would have created a finer world. That was the resolution he had awakened with in the morning. Act on impulse.

He looked out through the plate glass to the grey pavement, bare except for wisps of powdery snow that blew across it. The winter had slid in firmly during the night. Long strips of ice glistened on the pavement, oil-black like the backs of humpback whales, at that point where they plunged back into the depths, what his father would have savoured.

Across the building, Stan was opening his booth, first switching on a light above his table display of stones, then to the one inside the corner cabinet. He sat behind his collection and turned to stare out the plate glass wall. His light-blond head nodding slightly.

Marge, a silversmith, stood at her booth beside his, separated by a small walkway. Bent over her chest-high counter, she was busy cutting an article from a newspaper. Berrin crossed the floor, almost floating as he walked.

Marge was working on her scrapbook of humorous and quirky stories collected from newspapers. She kept only newspaper stories. He had given her the odd clipping as well, like the photo that presented the Toronto CN Tower rising out of the partially opened Skydome in the foreground, ensuring the photographer a page across from the Sunshine Girl. Marge handed him her new entry without speaking.

The same genre this time, an article about a man arrested for indecent exposure in a car, caught by a policeman while he went zigzagging down King Edward Street, driving while his girlfriend sat on his trouserless lap.

Marge repeated the punch line as he was reading it. "Not guilty, the judge said, he was adequately clothed. Adequately clothed? Man, I'd say he was."

Berrin laughed as she took the article back and applied glue to the backside.

"How's tricks, Berrin?"

She had caught him off guard. "Nothing much," he said. "Do you know if anyone might be looking for extra help around here?"

"Not happy with your sheepskin, Berrin?" Stan giggled from his corner across from them, his humour as obvious as ever, but this time as likely a product of the toke he held pinched between his fingertips.

Marge provided the retort.

"Up all night, were you, Stan? As much as you can be up while boozing all night." Her dimples darted back to Berrin.

Stan held up his contorted paw, smiled, eyes squinting, savouring the sweet smell of the marijuana.

"I have a friend from out of town who's looking for a job," Berrin announced.

"A girlfriend?" Stan asked.

"She stayed with me last week."

Marge tapped him on his arm. "When are we going to meet her?"

Stan looked over the rim of his eyeglasses, arched an eyebrow, and added, "I'd never bring a girlfriend around here if I were you. Never mix business and pleasure; the business will gobble it up every time."

"He's fantasizing again, Berrin. He sees himself as our resident Big Bad Wolf. Bring her around."

"She's at loose ends about what to do. Isn't there always some-one off south for a week or two this time of year?"

"You could ask Lisa. She's visiting her folks in Sweden, but she'll be back for the Christmas rush."

"I'll ask her."

Lisa wasn't in. His mood dropped as he returned to his booth. He found Saturday's *Globe & Mail* folded under the till and tried the book reviews. The nerves at the back of his neck were taut. Maybe go outside, walk a bit, buy a smoked meat sandwich. He passed the Mexican fast-food stand, pushed open the doors and looked down the street.

The strip of black ice. Eileen's tie.

When he returned, he found a book lying on his counter. He turned it over: *Heroine*, the title written like graffiti over a collage of photo cut-outs and computer-generated brush strokes, the same pastel colours that branded the cartons of soy milk Jill liked to buy.

He glanced at the blurbs on the back cover, then flipped it over again to read the author's name: Gail Scott.

He looked over at Richard to give him a thank-you nod. Stan was also looking at him — and also grinning.

Pranks were a plus for working in the market. He set it back on the counter.

Seeing this, Richard walked over.

"Berrin, you're terrible. She's a good writer. She comes from Toronto originally."

Berrin flicked through the pages. "And —"

"Well, lesbian. But that shouldn't —"

"So that's what you think — risqué stuff for the straight guy." Berrin turned aside and reached for his newspaper. He stifled his impulse to pick up the book again, to see how good a writer she might be.

Snow dusted the brickwork of the sidewalk outside and piled atop a fruit crate left lying against the glass door. He propped himself against the counter to settle his nerves. The dyke comment? It felt like a setback. And Stan's taunting did upset him, however much he pretended otherwise. He breathed in deeply, his chest heaving with the intake of air.

Then a voice spoke as if from the back of his head: *Eileen, I want to love you.*

His legs weakened, almost buckling.

He reached for the stool behind himself, his elbow landing on the countertop, stabilizing him. He tried repeating the sentence that had come out of nowhere, *Eileen, I love you.* No, not quite. It was the voice. Its clarity. Its singular impulse, clear like a vision.

He grabbed a pen and a sheet of paper; he needed to focus. But nothing came, a tombstone silence. He turned his gaze toward the street. Winter's bite gnawed at the windowpane. *Stone-cold panic, nothing less*, he thought.

He pulled himself up and breathed in deeply. Take the time to relax, he told himself. He leaned into his words.

My hand in yours.

He had formed his words in the perfect calligraphy he'd seen in Colleen's letters. He looked up again. Winter crisp through plate glass.

my hand in yours, snow on a box
its airy weight pressing

He reread his words; he'd have to ignore the style, however deriva-
tive, it wasn't a matter of liking or disliking it . . . remember, keep
with the impulse, whatever it was.

my hand in yours, snow on a box
its airy weight wanting
to split through the slick patina
of painted nails and tanned panels

He felt the energy, diffused perhaps, he knew it would get
better. He didn't reread his poem; it was enough that the words
had poured forth.

Lisa did want a worker, for the two months leading up to December.

His forefinger punched out the numbers on the telephone, got
the last digit wrong, and he focused for the second run-through.
Only the answering machine, Jeff's voice, which he forced himself
to ignore.

"I'm sorry, Eileen. My behaviour was inexcusable. It was unin-
tentional. We could start over. What can I say? Maybe with a bit of
time. Eileen, there's a job available in the Market, short term, but it
would get you resettled. Stephanie is moving out of the co-op. You
can have her room, I've checked with the group. You also forgot
your sweater on my armchair. Give me a call. Please, Eileen."

Jeff could also be the one hearing the message. No way to
retrieve it. He was committed. Again he cursed the contraption.
If someone had answered, either one, he would have been happier.

There was a brief rush of customers in the early afternoon. He
sold in quick succession two pairs of sheepskin mitts and a pottery

casserole, the sales some welcome action.

He decided to leave early and was counting the money in the till when he spotted Al pushing through the doors beside the thatched hut. Al had likely spotted him from the street. Needing someone to talk to, someone sympathetic. He had seen Al at a distance earlier in the day, likely moved into the area, staying at the local mission. And always walking with his steady gait, never soliciting as the homeless did or stopping at garbage bins. He moved straight ahead with a sense of purpose. And he now was aiming for his booth.

Al bent over the desk, keeping his gaze directed down at the counter between them.

"I went back to that lawyer I had up in Bourlamaque. After all the money I was duped into investing as start-up . . . you wouldn't know about that. He was even wining and dining me in Montreal, pretending to be talking to someone on the phone when I saw him in his office."

To appear indifferent, Berrin made an elaborate show of finishing his cash and locking the drawer. Al kept his eyes on the counter, paying no attention to the money.

"He was my first lawyer. But I didn't say a word, let him talk on and on, let him dig his own grave."

"Smart, Al."

"They'll stick it to you like an earwig; the only thing's moving is its whiskers. My engine's gone; no motor, no money."

The telephone rang.

"You got my message? Just a sec, Eileen. I have someone here."

He stood, and Al stepped away, half raising his arm while turning around.

He waited the few seconds it took Al to walk out of earshot.

"Toronto? You know anyone there? . . . Charlie? . . . Where? . . . But why go to B.C.? . . . Sure, I understand . . . I do need you, Eileen . . . I'm really sorry to hear that. I can't understand it, or maybe I can. But don't you think? I mean, Lisa here, she sells batik clothing, she's off to Europe for a month and needs someone to tend her booth . . .

No? . . . Well, afternoon tea at the Empress is attractive."

A moment of silence, his senses had taken flight. The conversation would end too soon, but he needed some time to let her words sink in.

"Berrin, I'm leaving for T.O. . . . I'm meeting Charlie . . . We're heading west . . . Vancouver Island . . . He's offered me that job again . . . Let's not get sarcastic, Berrin. You're jumping to conclusions again. He really needs me. I'm leaving with the kids. Jeff won't even notice we're gone . . . No, Berrin . . . I have to get out of here, can't you see that?"

A void replaced the silence.

"Berrin, are you still there?"

"Yes, Eileen. I'm still here."

"Berrin. I now have to think of the children. And they are a handful. Try waiting for a bus and keeping an eye on them and also on a pile of suitcases at the same time."

He had no answer.

"Berrin, you were right about Jeff, and me. I never really loved him deeply. You saw that from the get-go. I was too determined. I'd keep falling in love with the next guy. Look, I even fell in love with that pig in Cochitlahuantla."

Silence.

"Berrin, you mustn't think bad of me."

"I don't, Eileen."

"The bus is loading up. I have to go. I will send you my address, and do write me, you always write great letters."

"Yes, I was —"

"I will truly miss you, Berrin. And please don't worry about your last visit, it was all right in the end."

"I'm not so sure."

"Things work themselves out somehow, don't they? I have to rush, now. Take care, Berrin, I'm sorry. Goodbye, Berrin. And do write. You need to write. Goodbye for now, 'bye."

"Eileen, don't be sorry, there's time now —" but she had already hung up.

He lowered the phone back onto the receiver. The sweater, he could have mentioned the sweater. "You need to write," her final declaration. Blindsided. Blind.

His arms seemed to drain of blood, the veins shrinking, his body shrivelling. An icy numbness spread through his body. Where could all that blood go? The thought held his grief momentarily at bay. She had hung up. There was nothing to get a handle on, nothing to touch, nothing to say. His veins on the back of his hands looked flat and parched.

As he turned to sit again, he caught his reflection in the wall mirror. A quick glance. But enough to see the defeat in his eyes, his pallid cheeks puffed out as he exhaled, an empty shell like an immense cavern. There he sat, a Neanderthal, cowering like a child, unable to distinguish between the shadows and the reality outside, trying to fix the images.

He glanced back at the window. A flash of fear. Someone seemed to have passed by.

His legs quivered. He shut his eyes and exhaled again.

A bolt of electricity discharged at the base of his back, shot up his spine, and exploded like a rifle shot inside his skull.

He opened his eyes. The objects around him were transformed, their colours brilliant, like pebbles become when washed by waves breaking on a beach.

He focused on a pottery platter set upright in the booth in front of him. Deep blues on its rim merged into chrome greens. A spray of white clay across the platter curled into flakes tinted in apple-blossom and melted back one upon the other to leave innumerable ridges of iron-blues and browns along the fissures of cobalt. The zircon-tan centre, a cratered and parched earth from which veins of blue flowed out toward a sea of turquoise, a universe that might have existed at the moment when the gods had first parted the earth, the waters, and the heavens.

He looked away from the platter ... whatever object he viewed revealed another universe to him.

He walked out of the building.

CHAPTER 45

Skimming across the surface

HE EMERGED into an emerald city of silver-blue brilliance. Every building and inch of ground was covered in plate glass, so that the sky and buildings and earth merged to form a mercurial firmament suffused with light itself. And in the distance a sound of waves rushing to shore. He headed toward the water and encountered a wall of policemen, horses, women, children, cars, taxis. He plunged through the chaos, stumbling forward, trying not to fall. Voices called beside him, inside him. Fall into line, hold the line, toe the line, stop the bosses, grab the harness, step into harness. He crossed the field of mirrors toward a gap between a stone building and a cloud-filled glass tower, keeping the sound of the cascading waters ahead of him.

He was running now. The terrain became muddy, the land desolate, the air oppressive, like a lumber camp from the settler days. The edge of the field dropped off and plunged into a void.

A young woman ran up beside him when he stopped at the fence overlooking the escarpment. Trees stretched out from the embankment. She jumped the fence and hopped from tree to tree downward and followed a jut of land where it came to a point at the ridge below him. Poised on the ledge, she looked out into the empty space that reflected the sky. She seemed then to trip and fall out of sight and re-emerged, skimming effortlessly across the surface of the river with each foot riding on a log. Surrounding her were globes of light, supporting her, guiding her as she raced toward the far shore. From the opposite bank she shouted back: "Trust in the light. The light will come with trust."

CHAPTER 46

Keepers of the Light

HE NEVER RETURNED to work in the Market building. When asked why, he would say it was never a healthy place to begin with. He passed most of his days pushing his grocery cart. He accepted Stephanie's help in finding a room for himself. Occasionally, he walked along the outside of the glass walls. His friends treated him well; he was thankful for that. They would question him about his new occupation, suggest a second-hand store or garage sale where he might find more treasures, wish him well. They never asked what had happened that day months before when he walked out of the building without closing his booth or putting on his coat. Jill explained what luck it was that she was standing on the sidewalk slightly away from the main group of protesters and had spotted him and watched as he crossed the street and staggered through the construction site, crossed the park, and headed for the fence at the far side. She obviously hoped her parsed narrative would make him understand more clearly the sequence of events that led him to the brink. She had caught up with him and grabbed his leg, he was almost over the railing she said, and then had shouted, "Are you trying to kill yourself? Three people have already died falling from these cliffs."

"Yes!" he shouted, "Yes, yes." But not in answer to her. He was still looking at the light from across the river when the grab of her hand on his ankle pulled him back. The dread in her voice cut through his vision. "No," his reaction to his tethered ankle, still wanting to reach the light. Then more awake, "No. I see a light. The light."

Jill was convinced that his initial response was the honest one, at least the only rational one, she said, if that were possible. *I see the light . . .* he was joking, he always tried to get out of a tight spot with a pun or a joke, and now he was trying to achieve the same end over a longer term.

Suicide? No, not now. He must admit that he might have been thinking about it, perhaps right up to the edge of the cliff; he couldn't remember. But the pain had completely disappeared at that point. Thoughts of endings can accompany orphaned longings, he saw that now, yes, when feelings cannot bridge the gaps in our lives.

If we could know where or how these gaps were born. Maybe it's congenital. He remembered reading some studies about suicides that suggested that people who hanged themselves often had umbilical cords wrapped around their necks at birth. That would mean that suicides who kill themselves with a bullet to the brain once felt the force of forceps on their temples, or those who slash their wrists are recalling the light piercing the slit of the Caesarian section. Our endings must begin in such breaches, where impulses go awry and intentions cannot untangle the knots that snare our lives, in times foregone, in times wanting, in times never begun.

When his handwriting was clear and straight, he knew he was unravelling the casuistry behind this truth. These were the times when the workings of time and space were so in sync that he was reaching out and touching another dimension.

The evidence is there if you want to see.

He caught himself speaking this last sentence aloud as he crossed the street. But it needed to be said. The end of the day and his cart was half full. Average when you're hunting for the rare finds.

If someone had asked him, he would have explained that while he enjoyed the hunt, the evidence *was* in the very air. Even this morning it was suspended in the pungency of this first day of spring, drifting across the fence from where he spotted his neighbour stepping out after breakfast onto her backyard patio to greet a man carrying a toolbox. A single mother since the birth of her son now about twelve, she seldom had visitors, at least male ones, and so the thought of her years of celibacy was what surely gave the appearance of a handyman that air of restrained urgency that inevitably marks such propitious moments. The carpenter had come to repair her patio steps.

"I could as easily have been that man myself," Berrin said to himself, and he stood more erect as he approached the street corner, yes, like him, straight and upright in a defining midlife moment, a seasoned worker, his boots apart and well anchored to the ground.

The carpenter slid the board under the railing and sat on the deck at the top of the steps and took out his pencil. She pulled back the sliding doors and hesitated, perhaps because of his receding hairline. He bent down and looked along the board from that inverted perspective, then picked a square from his toolbox and laid it across the board. He looked up at her, his bright eyes telling her that he amounted to more than a handyman about to cut a board cleanly on his first try, and she walked forward and reached down to grasp the board at the opposite end. He laid the square next to her fingertips where the grains of the wood continued up the veins of her hand, hesitated, then drew a line where he had set the ruler. The spread of time, a fact of time. She stood up, then planted her foot on the board as he gripped the circular saw and made his cut and reached over for the next board. She took her broom and began to sweep the sawdust off her deck floor, preservative-green planks . . . she laughed lightly, no words spoken. The breeze a whisper. The tulips in the pot beside them a witness as well.

The curb stopped Berrin's cart with a jolt and he jostled it up and over the edge. A bottle rattled against the grating of the shopping cart, the Acqua della Madonna water bottle, the glass dark ultramarine like squid's ink, propelled in a flash against the side of the basket. A dog raced up from the far side of the sidewalk, nipped at his heel, and ran back to its master, who in the dying light looked like a pile of rags thrown against the brick siding of the storefront. A startled or mad dog? A boot to the head would have made no difference. Action, reaction, an unconscious, unforgiving battle. A beggar as well in the battle for a handout if he were to let himself sink so low.

Suddenly in front of him, a child leaning away from her mother's grasp pulled free, then stumbled forward as its tiny feet tripped over the pavement as if trying to catch up to its gleeful laughter, a surprising counterpoint to the alarm in the mother's scramble to grasp the tail of his coat and rein it back before her child fell headlong into the street.

Yes, children are as contrary as trees, leaning sideways out of the landscape, blown by a fatal wind that parents never foresee, reaching beyond the limits and making for happiness . . . he should have known this all along.

He continued on down the sidewalk. His awakened senses caught the drift of perfume coming from the bus shelter next to the street. His neighbour returning from work. Like the fragrance of the lilac trees along her fence, how they had shimmered in the breeze. Then the rasping saw through wood overtaken by the roar of a lawnmower one yard farther away. You might rightly argue, immortality can be detected in that practised delicacy of domesticity, movements below the mediocre; that something in everything that can take you so very far away, if only you let yourself see it.

You can find the light everywhere, in people or in so-called inanimate things, which were definitely easier to catch hold of. He grinned.

Telling his friends about the light was fruitless; he soon gave up on that. They always looked down and away from him toward his grocery cart, pretending not to see it, not appreciating how his act of choosing was as important as the objects he chose during his day's travels. He wondered at their evident confusion.

Some things were easy to explain. Walking was good exercise, his friends could see he was losing weight. They also agreed that this simple physical change could give anyone a different take on life. They advised him to remain open to all the possibilities, though he really was not seeking their range of choices. He needed only the clarity. The world was different now and he was at peace with everything, so long as he could collect the purest objects, the brightest moments, store them in his room, study them, and write about them.

Recently he tried explaining one last time, to Richard, thinking he would understand, since he was a painter and dealt with light all the time. But to no avail. Richard only chose the colours that best took the light. Yes, Richard suggested, maybe he was one of a new class of people, one of the "Keepers of the Light," he called him, much like those Celtic monks had been, walled up inside their monasteries throughout the Dark Ages. Berrin agreed that it was even possible that he, too, could have lived inside those walls, if dreams were evidence of previous lives. If so, there was a rhythm to life and death.

A bank of television sets in a store window halted his progress. The glare streamed out into the indigo dew of the diminishing twilight. He remembered his mother once trying to explain the light after her brother Martin had died. He had angered her by his response when she spoke of the flash off the television at the time of his death, six years before Alex's death, so far away at the mission house in British Columbia. The bright light had startled her as she lay on the couch, like Alex had done with the cup and saucer, letting her know he was still around. The light had beamed itself straight from the tube into the living room. It had to have been at the moment of Martin's death, she said, with no kinfolk around to comfort him. She knew this because she had phoned the hospital in William's Lake immediately after the light had vanished and learned that Martin had died fifteen minutes earlier. Being the smart aleck then, it was a wonder, he had said to her, how it took Martin's ghost a full fifteen minutes to cross the continent; suspicious — what could have made Martin hesitate?

Thankfully, he had moved beyond that mindset. She had been right about the light all along, and he nodded as he turned away from the television sets.

No question that the light could be confusing. The previous evening, on his way home, he had again spotted the red-draped figures he had seen entering the church in Sandy Hill. Perhaps they were nuns in their modern dress. If they had looked at his cart, they could have been transformed by the light, what it reflected back to them; but instead, it was death, death, and more death that shrouded them.

He stopped and retraced his journey a few steps back, to the spot before he got angry. He had much to learn, he told himself. Clearly, heaven remained the realm of false hope and might-have-beens, a proper match for the folly of this world. That was the only message that awaited the nuns inside those stone walls. But, as his mother would say, no sense in getting into a tether about it. He smiled again. Anger only darkened your spirits. You needed instead to let out the light.

And it was clear that few if any of his friends understood him, which shouldn't be worrying him, though it did. When they got to read his chronicle, they would begin to see. He felt he had done well enough with this one. Eileen's letters had helped, however brief they were, but they kept coming regularly. He smiled again; he was surprised that she had continued to write. The bit she wrote about her time in the rancho was sketchy, but enough . . . enough for him to see.

Now to send the chronicle off to her, something substantial in return. Only a few words more, for even yet he hadn't delved deeply enough. He stood in his spot, not moving, neither forward nor backward. That pit at the base of his sternum remained; a mystery.

He hadn't paid much attention to that moment with Stephanie in El Sol, how his chest at a simple touch split open, but as quickly his ribs snapped shut. Another realm, perhaps the other side of fear, a parallel universe.

He bent over the handlebar of his grocery cart. The Acqua della Madonna water bottle, its long and narrow neck rising above its bulbous bottom. That teardrop shape defined most of the objects he had collected; he hadn't noticed that before. Perhaps he should have been paying less attention to the light and more to the shapes and what they held.

His chronicle wasn't enough. He stood upright, not moving for another moment, but not taking a step backward, either. He could continue collecting the chosen objects, continue to marvel at the light that shone from within and reflect along with them. But more than that, he could now move to see into the dark matter behind those shapes.

He took a step forward, liking the feel of the pavement under his feet. He did need to remain grounded. Perhaps he should get himself a dog, have it walk with him daily. *The Diary of a Cursed Man*, an ageless history there, he'd let the dog tell it. He remembered his struggle over where to start his chronicle, how to see the trajectory, and now discovering that the story lay elsewhere. So, it will take a dog to tell the tale, and perhaps a pig as well. He laughed into the night. The dog and pig as best friends, the new deities . . . he could do worse.

KEVIN MORRIS has drawn his inspiration for this story from his international development experiences in Mexico, his work in artist-run centres across Canada, and his Irish roots in rural Canada—as well as from his varied careers as a potter, teacher, youth worker, and community developer for youth centres across Canada. He has been previously published in *The Antigonish Review*.

TO ORDER MORE COPIES:

GENERAL STORE PUBLISHING HOUSE INC.

499 O'Brien Road, Renfrew, Ontario, Canada K7V 3Z3
Tel 1.800.465.6072 • Fax 1.613.432.7184
www.gsph.com